SWEET'S FOLLY

SWEET'S FOLLY

A Novel by

Fiona Hill

Published by Berkley Publishing Corporation

*Distributed by G. P. Putnam's Sons,
New York*

PRINTED IN THE UNITED STATES OF AMERICA

To Stephanie

SWEET'S FOLLY

Chapter I

Nothing daunted by Honoria's silence, Mr. Claude Kemp, Esquire, cleared his throat briefly and renewed his addresses. "I flatter myself," he said, "that in desiring you to become my wife, I act in a manner which is not quite wholly selfish. I am acquainted with your predilection for music, your fondness of books, and your taste for society: as mistress of Colworth Park, whatever you fancy in the way of these more, ah, cultivated pleasures will be at your disposal. And as I share your interests in such pursuits, I make bold to imagine that many happy hours might be passed between us indulging in them." Mr. Kemp paused here to smile, an expression he accomplished (Honoria had sometimes noticed) using the muscles round his mouth only, his eyes and cheeks appearing to have nothing to do with it. She glanced up at him, as if to see what more he might have to say. What she saw was the face of a very handsome gentleman of some thirty-two or -three years, his blue eyes fixed attentively on her own. Mr. Kemp was a large man, squarely and solidly built; his countenance was square as well, and topped by a thick mass of blond, gleaming hair. His ice-blue eyes were the most arresting element in his regular features, but there was something to be said too for the decided nose, the well-moulded lips, and the firm set of the jaw. His complexion was ruddy, his hands broad and even; altogether, he presented the appearance of an extremely healthy, somewhat refined country gentleman, which was precisely what he was. Honoria was too familiar with his broad shoulders and sturdy physique to pay them more than passing notice, but they might have raised a sigh in many another maiden. All she remarked now were the iciness of his eyes and the smugness in the set of his mouth; to her, these were clearly legible signs that Mr. Kemp had yet more to say, and would not be satisfied until he had said it. Her hypothesis was confirmed when, after a few moments, he continued.

"Miss Newcombe, I make no doubt that this, ah, parlour and indeed this whole house are—to you—familiar and well-loved; however, I cannot but think that you must sometimes long for more, ah, spacious and well-appointed surroundings, which would suit your own attractiveness much more satisfactorily. Nor do I doubt your affection for your aunts, or indeed theirs for you, yet I am persuaded you must sometimes tire a little of their society; it is only natural in a young lady, you know. And while I am very fond of Pittering Village, and consider it quite charming in its, ah, antiquated way, it yet seems likely to me that you must sometimes long to leave its bounds, if only for a while." Here Mr. Kemp paused again, this time because a cat— one of several dozen who nestled in every nook and cranny of the small parlour—had seen fit to deposit himself in his lap. Mr. Kemp lifted him up and tossed him to the floor rather rudely. For the first time since the start of their interview, Honoria smiled a little.

She raised her hand to her mouth as if to conceal this slight discourtesy, but the attempt was wasted. When Miss Honoria Newcombe smiled, no matter how slightly, it spread throughout all her features, and lit up her countenance quite delightfully. It was a delightful countenance, anyway, fashioned in the most delicate and agreeable manner imaginable: two sweet brown eyes gazed softly from under dark lashes and brows; her small, up-tilting nose and full, curved lips were set in a sea of rose-and-cream coloured, velvety skin. Her brown hair, drawn back in simple and becoming fashion, glinted richly, and her white neck flowed smoothly into a pair of graceful sloping shoulders. Her figure too appeared fragile, though delicately rounded, and she moved with an ease and suppleness that perhaps belied the strenuous activity of which she was capable. The only fault to be found in her appearance, if fault it may be called, was the tendency of her features to shrink away from any direct regard, to withdraw inward with an expression that was neither pensive nor reserved but in fact distinctly self-effacing. Distinctly, that is, to the careful observer; most of the inhabitants of Pittering Village and its environs merely took her to be a quiet girl, unassuming by nature, never guessing the odd fancies and deep sentiments enclosed within her. Mr. Claude Kemp, alas for him, was a member of this school of thought: the timid rejection that his advances had thus far encountered seemed to him no more than a show of maidenly modesty, easily overrided (he thought) by a little calm talk or, failing that, a touch of cajolery. Had he been able to perceive Honoria's emotions at that moment, he might have been consid-

erably shocked. As it was, he merely discarded the offending cat and
went on in smooth, assured, rather voluble tones.

"My dear Miss Newcombe, to my certain knowledge you have
never been farther from home than to Tunbridge Wells. You are
aware I reside half the year in London: all its amusements will be at
your disposal. Indeed, our honeymoon alone will take us abroad, and
after that there will be as much travel as you care to undertake—Italy,
Germany, Greece. I have been to these places, Miss Newcombe, and
long only to reveal their glories to you. And, of course, we shall stop
half the year in Pittering, so that you may be close to your good
aunts."

As he said these words, Honoria might have been observed to bite
the rosy edge of her bottom lip with her tiny, even teeth. It was the
gesture of one who finds herself confronted with temptation. Mr.
Kemp did not observe it, or he would surely have pressed his advantage home. Instead, he returned to the drift of his earlier remarks and
closed thus: "Miss Newcombe, I am at a loss to express how deeply I
desire your hand. The happiness I experience merely in gazing on you
makes it difficult to contemplate, let alone to expound upon, the joy
that might be ours were we to marry. Your youth, your beauty, your
refinement all inspire in me a love most deep and enduring; if you can
in any measure return my regard, I beg most humbly you will consider my offer, and return your response in the affirmative."

Mr. Kemp had spoken with eloquence but without precision. Mr.
Claude Kemp, Esquire, had never in his life done anything humbly,
least of all begged. So certain was he, in fact, of his success, that he
was now engaged in thinking where to kiss her when she answered
yes. And though Honoria did not guess this last, she perceived the rest
of the case shrewdly enough, and had less trouble than she might
have in rousing herself to disappoint his hopes. A flame of resentment
leapt within her at his calm presumption, and though it did not reach
her tongue, a firmness of conviction—of which Mr. Kemp could have
no notion—underlay her words.

"Your offer is most flattering," she began, gazing steadily not at him
but at Mistress Muffin, a large tabby who had recently become a
mamma, "and I am sorry indeed to be obliged to disappoint you."
And as she spoke, she did become sorry. So sweet was her nature, she
could not for long believe that others might be less sincere in their
speeches than was she. Though still aware that Claude had addressed
her with presumption, almost with insolence, she had forgot already
the injury to her pride, and was now wholly concerned with the inevitable hurt to his. "You must not believe that I am not fully sensible of

the compliment paid me, dear sir, nor that if there were any hope of my accepting you, I should hesitate to say so. Unfortunately"—and the misery she herself would have felt in his place impelled her now to take up his hand and stroke it gently—"most unfortunately, sir, I am not able to accede in your wishes. Were there any possibility of my feeling otherwise," she repeated, "I assure you I should say so. However—" She could find no way to soften the blow, so her words trailed off into silence.

Surprise shook Mr. Kemp's soul with a violence that was truly painful. He was as startled as if she had declared Pittering Village the equal of London, or her aunts' humble dwelling a palace—and this despite the fact that he had twice before offered for her, and twice before been refused. It might have been expected that his surprise would grow less with each occasion, but on the contrary. His confidence, perversely, had increased with successive rebuffs, so that on this evening he had made quite, quite sure of winning her consent. Instead, her refusal had been stated yet more clearly. It was extremely confusing, and so startling that he spoke (for once) before he had time to think. "Miss Newcombe," he said, a strong note of authority in his voice, "I am sure you cannot have thought this out reasonably. Setting aside all consideration of who, exactly, I am, or what your advantages as my wife might be, do you not think it your duty to remove yourself from your aunts' poor household with all due speed? Miss Newcombe, while I am certain they are fond of you, they are evidently forced to practise the most painful economies already. Do you mean to continue with them all your life?" He gestured widely at the ill-lit, shabby parlour in which they sat, and which was, moreover, shared with them by upwards of a score of felines. "These cats, Miss Newcombe, which your aunts take in through charity—these cats are dumb beasts, as are their neighbours next door." Through the wall could be heard the aimless yapping and whimpers of a large number of canines. "They cannot know the burden they place on the Misses Deverell's paltry competence . . . But you, my dear ma'am! You!"

Honoria was taken aback, not only by the sharpness but also by the content of this reproach. It had never occurred to her that she might be a burden on her aunts; on the contrary, she had always viewed herself in the light of an assistance. It was true that they were poor, but were they that poor? The little house in Bench Street, where she had lived since she was orphaned at the age of two, was cramped indeed— what house would not be that had forty animals within it?—yet it had gone on through the years just the same. Aunt Mercy had continued to lay a nourishing, if not varied, table; Aunt Prudence had never yet hesitated when a stray cat came to her, or a wounded dog appeared; if they practised severe economies, nothing ever had been said of it to Honor, and she cringed at the thought of having been too callous, possibly, to have noticed.

Mr. Kemp was waiting for an answer. In a frightened voice, with words less fluent than before, she replied, "I am sorry, sir, most sorry, to confess that I never considered my circumstances in that light. If my aunts are hard pressed, they have not yet said as much to me." She recovered herself a little and added, "In any case, Mr. Kemp, if I am a—a burden to them, it is a domestic matter to be discussed among ourselves, and one with which I beg you will not concern yourself."

She had meant exactly what she said, but Mr. Kemp took these last words for a snub, and rose directly. "I think our interview is at an end," he said and bowed. "Pray convey my thanks to your aunts for their, ah, hospitality tonight." And so saying, he picked his way rather ungracefully among the many cats, and let himself out of the room. Honoria was left alone with the menagerie, to ponder her new status as a burden.

She could not quite believe it, yet it might very well be true: her mother had died in childbirth, leaving no fortune; her father, killed in a riding accident soon after, was of course a baronet, yet he died penniless as well, and no provision had been made except that her aunts assume guardianship of the child. She had taken her lessons with them, at home, because they all preferred it, she had always thought, but now it seemed that perhaps it had been because they lacked the money for an academy. The Misses Deverell's charity to animals was well known through the neighbourhood—in fact, they were thought to be more than a little queer about it—but Honoria had never deemed herself an object of their kindness. They were kind, of course, but from love, not pity. And yet . . . she would have to ask them, that was all, she concluded—and then shrank. To ask straight out would be too awkward. She would have to observe them, and then see if her presence truly worsened their circumstances more than it aided them.

Consequently, when, at the end of half an hour, her Aunt Prudence peeked into the parlour, Honoria invited her in and reminded herself to listen closely to everything that was said.

"Is young Kemp gone, then?" asked Aunt Prudence, poking her head through the door somewhat farther.

"Yes, quite gone."

"O, I am so glad," she said, bending to scoop up an armful of cats. "La!" she continued, kissing one on the nose; "you've had quite an evening, haven't you, Divinity, listening to grown-up conversation all night? You must be quite fagged. I know I should be." She struggled to hold up the hem of her old-fashioned skirts as she made her way among her purring pets to an ancient Confidante. She set Divinity down on one end, then picked up several kittens and seated herself on the warm cushion where they had been.

"Do you dislike Mr. Kemp?" asked Honor, curious to know why her aunt was glad at his departure.

"O no, not at all, my dear. I am sure he is a very pleasant young man, as young men go—which is not, in general, very well," she added somewhat obscurely. "I only missed my little kitties, didn't I now, Désirée?" She kissed this animal on top of her head. "Well, and if he is truly gone, I suppose Mercy may come in as well, don't you think?"

"Certainly, Aunt Prudence."

"Mercy!" she called, in a shrill, cracked voice. "Mercy? Do come in; the gentleman has gone away."

A moment later a second lace-befrilled head appeared in the doorway and peered in hesitantly. Mercy Deverell was four years her sister's junior, which meant that she was sixty-four years of age. Being the younger, she was used to being quite cosseted by her sister, and when she hovered at the door Prudence urged her on with a soothing "It's quite safe, my dear; do come in."

"I only—I did not wish to intrude," said Mercy, a tiny smile lighting her withered countenance. As with many elderly people, her face had come to reflect, through the years, more the experiences she had had in life, and less the features she had inherited. Therefore, though there was yet a distinguishable likeness between the sisters, Mercy's face was somewhat softer than Prudence's, and not nearly so intimidating. Of the two, Prudence had always been the leader, and this habit of command had caused her cheeks to sink a little into rather harsh lines, at the same time increasing the tendency of her nose to jut out into something like a beak. Mercy's traits were milder, and told of a more sheltered existence; indeed, hers had been a life of following, and she would not have known what to do at all had it not been for her elder sister.

"You do not in the least intrude, my pet," Prudence now assured her. "Honoria promises me that Mr. Kemp has quite gone away, so there is nothing here to frighten you."

"I am so glad," said Mercy, unwittingly parroting her sister's words. "Not but what he is a very agreeable gentleman," she hastened to add, turning to Miss Newcombe, "but I do think gentlemen are so alarming, don't you? All that vigour and heartiness; they are quite apt to startle one, I think." Her sweet voice, soft as the fur on the feline she was holding, went on in this vein for a minute or two, for Mercy could be quite a chatter-box, and more than compensated in this way for her taciturn sibling.

"Yes," agreed Honor kindly when Mercy had done talking, "it is true that gentlemen—in our age, at least—do tend to be bolder than ladies." She sighed almost imperceptibly.

"Men are beasts," Prudence pronounced suddenly, and shut her lips with a snap.

Mercy addressed her niece as if her sister had not spoke. "And did Mr. Kemp offer for you again?" she inquired, her faded brown eyes alight with solicitous interest.

"Yes, he did," said Honor slowly.

"Well, I suppose that was very kind of him," Mercy observed. "And what did you say, my dear?"

"I said—I told him no," she replied.

"Same as before," Prudence pointed out accurately.

"Just the same!" exclaimed Mercy, as if struck. "I hope he was not very angry with you," she continued anxiously.

"O no, I do not—that is, he was disappointed, of course, but I do not believe . . ." Since she knew that Mr. Kemp had indeed been angry, she said no more.

"A very attractive young man," murmured Mercy.

"Good specimen," declared Prudence, echoing her sister in her way.

Honoria's forehead puckered a bit. "You didn't—did you hope perhaps I might accept him?"

"Hope you might—?" Mercy repeated blankly. "Do you mean—?" She stopped, evidently puzzled.

"She's looking for an opinion," her sister explained. "Did we have an opinion?"

"An opinion of whether Honoria ought to marry? How odd! Why should we have an opinion, Prue? Should we?" she asked, sincerely bewildered.

"We might or we might not," said the elder. "It's nothing for you to worry about, dearest. If you have no opinion, you may simply say so. Honoria won't mind, will you, Honoria?"

"No, not in the least," asserted the lady applied to, accustomed to such discussions and inquiries. "I shan't mind at all, Aunt Mercy."

"O, I am so relieved!" said she. An instant later, she added, "But did we have an opinion at all, dear Prue? My memory is not what it once was, you know."

"No, dearest; I don't believe we did."

Mercy was much comforted, and smiled tranquilly. "I hoped you would say so, dear Prue, for I made sure I could not recall one. I shall tell Honoria as much, shall I?"

"Yes, of course, dear; do."

"Honoria, your Aunt Prudence and I have formed no opinion at all whether you should marry Mr. Kemp or not. We do not care one way or the other," she elaborated, pleased to be able to inform her niece of so much. "I think you might say we were indifferent on the point. Mightn't you, Prudence?"

"Certainly," the elder corroborated briefly.

"There, you see?" Mercy went on placidly. "This entire investigation has been to no end whatever." And, satisfied that she had reached a judicious conclusion, she bent her head to the cat in her lap and nuzzled its soft cheek against her own.

Honoria, fairly reassured that Claude Kemp's assessment of her as a burden to her guardians was mistaken, mused for a few minutes longer. For a while no sound was heard in the little parlour except the ticking of the grandmother clock (which never told the correct time—unless, as Mercy once pointed out, one cared particularly to know the time in Moscow) and the purring of the cats. Then Honor rose and trimmed the lamps, excusing herself for a moment while she went to fetch a book—a book that had recently arrived from a shop in Tunbridge Wells, and that concerned itself largely with the travels of a certain Mrs. Penstoke in the regions of the Nile. Reading books on foreign lands was Honoria's chief passion or at least her most intimate delight, for she was very fond of music, but everyone knew that. In her heart she cherished a secret longing to make journeys herself, to visit exotic places, and to explore the wonderful monuments to be found abroad. It was this desire that had made her sigh when Mr. Kemp chanced to mention travel; had he expatiated longer on the subject, she might have been greatly tempted to accept him merely in order to be able to see the Continent. Fortunately, he had not divined this. Honoria spoke to no one of this wish to venture forth from Pittering Village except now and then to one of the cats, not even to Emily Blackwood. Emily was her bosom bow, and though they kept no secrets from one another, Honoria said nothing about this, for the simple reason that she could not think how to tell anyone without conveying the impression that she wished to leave Pittering Village. And that was *not* true, that was most certainly not true; Honor had no complaint to make against Fate, and if her aunts had seen fit to dwell all their lives in Pittering, why then it was a beautiful village, and most positively the very place she should have chosen to live in herself. To that she would gladly have sworn, and she never doubted it . . . but to go away! To be abroad and see new things all the time! Even to see London would be more than she expected—or had reason to expect, she reminded herself severely, and redoubled her determination never to say anything to anyone, not even to Emily.

Reading books about distant places was the only indulgence she permitted herself, and she went off to fetch this particular volume with a feeling of agreeable anticipation. Her aunts merely nodded when she excused herself from the parlour, but as she returned down the narrow corridor she heard their voices murmuring in conversation. Ordinarily she would simply have reentered, with no thought for what they might have been discussing, nor fear that they might wish to be private. Mr. Kemp's impassioned discourse, however, on their impoverished circumstances caused her on this occasion to do something she had never done before, and which was against her nature utterly. Hoping the ragged carpet would deaden the noise of her footsteps, she slowed a little as she approached the parlour door and stood in silence outside it. Ears straining, she listened to her aunts and what she heard, though it was indistinct, altered the course of her life considerably.

"It simply is not enough," Aunt Prudence was saying firmly. "It isn't enough at all, and it never will be."

"Not if we scrimp just a little more?" Mercy suggested in timid tones. "Just a little? I could easily do without my gifts this year, dear, truly I could."

Honoria's lips parted slightly as she heard this, an involuntary action that signified a startled disbelief. Christmastide was approaching, and it was an open secret that Aunt Mercy was to receive a new tea set—a set of no great value, indeed, but one she had had her eye on all year, and which would replace the cracked and faded set now in use. She had dropped hints about it for weeks during October, and Honoria knew she now anticipated its arrival with the most delicious sensations imaginable.

"Now, Mercy, you are kind to give it up," Prudence replied, "but I should not for anything allow you to do so. Besides," she added, sighing audibly, "it would make no difference, really. I'm sorry dearest; I know you thought it would help."

"Yes, I did hope it would," came the answer. Deep in her heart, Mercy was terribly relieved to know she need not make such a sacrifice. "Well, then, what if we let a room to a boarder? Surely that—"

"Boarders! Impossible. Anyway, the extra money would hardly be sufficient."

"Dear Prue, it does cost a great deal then, doesn't it?" said Mercy, in tones of wonder. "I had no idea!"

In the corridor, Honoria silently seconded these words, a sinking feeling invading her chest.

"What if we turned off Mary?" Mercy continued, referring to the one servant employed by the Deverells. "We could get a boy to carry the wood, and that sort of thing, and I shouldn't mind cooking at all, really I shouldn't," she insisted pleadingly.

"My dear Mercy, I'm afraid you really have no notion what sort of expense we are up against," Prudence said, almost despairingly. "Even if we got rid . . ." and then her voice sank so low that Honor could no longer hear it, try though she would. When it rose again it was on a note of feeble resolution, and Honor only caught the final phrases: ". . . with Kemp. Yes, with Kemp to help us we could surely do it, but I see no other way. Rather a pity, after all, about Honoria, but . . . You know Proctor Kemp simply dotes on his son; I've always said it was shameful. But what's done is done. I don't expect he'll ask again. Tonight made three times—or was it four?"

"I think . . . O, yes, I think it was three," said Mercy, trying to be helpful. "Of course, it may have been four," she amended, wanting to be just.

"Well, three or four, it makes no matter." There followed a number of remarks that Honor could not catch, not only because they were spoke softly, but also because her mind was racing so quickly she could hardly listen. Mercy's sweet tones were clearer.

"Prudence, you do know best, of course, and I've no doubt this is a silly question—but did you ask him? Perhaps it will do just to ask him! He may be well-disposed enough towards us to do it. Goodness knows it is his duty as squire to concern himself with the needy . . . and as magistrate too, in all conscience."

Honor could almost see her Aunt Prue smiling indulgently as she answered, "Mercy, you have such faith in the goodness of men. I don't know where you get it, my dear, but in Squire Kemp it is misplaced. In fact, I did once hint at the topic with him, but it was clear he did not wish to understand me. And I've known Proctor Kemp since before you were born, my love, and when his mind is set heaven and earth can't move him." She paused for a while and sighed again. "No, my dear, the most obstinate man alive, I'm sure. I think Claude's inherited it," she added. "Perhaps it's as well Honoria didn't marry him, after all."

"If you say so," Mercy returned dispiritedly. "Prue, I know I am not much of a thinker, but I will try to puzzle this out, I promise. Who knows? Perhaps I shall come up with something."

Prudence, though she thought this extremely unlikely, patted her sister's hand and thanked her very much. At this juncture Honoria felt she must enter, or her aunts would wonder what kept her. Her cheeks were flushed and her breathing a little quick still, but her aunts were both near-sighted and she trusted they would not see the traces of tears on her cheeks.

They were tears of remorse, of keen self-reproach, and of pity. *Claude had been right, O, so very right!* She thought again and again. Apparently, the Deverells were indeed in dire straits; it seemed, in fact, that they even thought of applying to Squire Kemp for aid! Honoria could not bear it. How distressed they must be—and how blind she had been! Her young heart ached with a host of unhappy sensations, and as the evening passed she was obliged to rally her spirits repeatedly so that she would not burst out into tears. Nothing must be said until she had thought things out alone, nothing decided until she spoke to Emily. Evidently, her aunts did not wish her to know what grave difficulties beset them; if it was their desire that she be ignorant, then ignorant was what she would appear. On this she was resolved already, and the brave front they presented to her touched her all the more because she could say nothing to them about it.

After what seemed like ages, Aunt Prudence arose and announced that it was Mercy's bed-time. She sent her younger sister up the stairs and went off herself to the little kitchen, to see about Mercy's hot milk. Honoria rose too and declared her intention to go up to bed, and she kissed both her guardians good night. She always kissed them good night, but tonight she did so with a tenderness and gratitude unknown to her before. The change in her manner was in fact so pronounced that Mercy noticed it, and whispered to Prudence (after Honor had gone, of course) that something appeared to be troubling the dear child. "Perhaps she is sorry about Claude, after all," she added.

"O no, I don't think so," Prudence responded. "Your imagination, dear; no doubt this business of the hospital has set your nerves on edge."

"That may be so," Mercy assented. "It is so dismaying, to think of all these sweet dogs and cats with no home to go to after we've passed away!"

"Yes, it is," said Prudence, her tone almost grim. "But we have set our minds to it, after all, and if Kemp won't help us establish one, then we shall simply be obliged to found it privately. We will find a way, I promise you, dearest. We always have." She patted her sister gently on the arm and then nudged her again towards the staircase. "Now, on up to bed," she said briskly. "I shall be there with your milk in the twinkling of an eye."

Chapter II

Miss Honoria Newcombe, arriving afoot at Sweet's Folly, was immediately recognized and admitted by the butler, who bid her good morning and continued, "Shall I send for Miss Emily, ma'am?"

"If you please, Jepston," Honor agreed, allowing him to remove her cloak and advancing some way into the marble-paved entrance hall. Sweet's Folly, the residence of Dr. Charles and Mrs. Corinna Blackwood, and their children Alexander and Emily, was so called on account of a Mr. Archibald Sweet, who had once owned the property. Mr. Sweet had thought to convert what was then a pleasant country home into a palatial estate, and had engaged architects and labourers to that end. Stone foundations had already been laid when Mr. Sweet's son suddenly disclosed to him a sheaf of gambling debts amounting to a staggering sum; the workers were immediately turned off, and when Dr. Charles Blackwood bought the house from Sweet, the new walls had risen no farther than six inches from the ground. And there, to this day, they had remained, for though Dr. Blackwood might have liked to own a true manor, his conservatism in matters of finance restrained him. Yet, he did very well, indeed, being the most respected and best-loved physician in the parish, and having moreover increased his fortune considerably by means of shrewd and timely investments on 'Change. His chief goal was to make of his son a gentleman, for Dr. Blackwood had been the son of a green-grocer, and had scraped his way up into gentility with the most strenuous efforts; he was determined that his son should surpass himself in this wise, and should live the life of a true gentleman—which is to say, should not be obliged to work.

This ambition on his father's part suited the son quite well. Alexander was an intelligent young man of a serious turn of mind. His overriding passion appeared to be geometry, to which study he had devoted his years at Cambridge and his days now at Sweet's Folly. The usual activities of a country gentleman—riding, hunting, and fishing—did not seem to appeal to him: he spent all his afternoons shut up in his study, poring over formulae and diagrams, and seeking Absolute Truths. Though Dr. Blackwood teased his son for his remarkably sedentary way of life, he was yet secretly pleased with him, and felt that such arcane pursuits were exactly what befitted a young man in his position. Furthermore, Alexander was preparing a scholarly monograph—something to do with the intersection of planes—and this concrete evidence of his offspring's ability evoked a sensation of satisfaction in his father's breast that was not very different from pride.

About his daughter Emily's creations he was less certain. Emily, at the age of eighteen, had already begun to exhibit a dedication to art that was clearly more intense than the amateur's fancy. In fact, her only recreation (other than a little riding) was her painting and drawing. Moreover, her devotion to this work was equalled by—perhaps even excelled by—her facility for it. At fourteen she had produced portraits of her parents, her brother, and herself that were so undeniably just that the four of them had been hung prominently in the drawing-room. And these were not mere sketches; they were finished oils. At the time, Dr. Blackwood had been simply delighted with Emily's talent; now he was a little alarmed. A clever girl's happy success with her brush was one thing; a young woman who asked for nothing but paints and canvas at Christmas was quite another. Had she no fondness for gowns, and ribbons, and bonnets? he demanded of her mother. Had she no interest in meeting, and perhaps marrying, a young gentleman? Did she never inquire of her mother what new way she might dress her hair, or drape her shawl?

She didn't. Poor Mrs. Blackwood could reply nothing to her husband's irritable questions but No. No, Emily never showed the least bent for fashion; she had twice begged to be excused from dancing parties in the neighbourhood; it was all Mrs. Blackwood could do to persuade her to dress her hair at all. There was simply no way to pretend matters stood otherwise: Miss Emily cared as much for her art as her brother did for his geometry, and she showed no signs of changing.

Mrs. Blackwood frequently cursed the day she had engaged a drawing instructor for her daughter. However, she did so mildly and in her mind only, for Emily's paintings were the most beautiful things she had ever seen, and she should not have liked to part with one of them. Besides, Emily was the dearest and sweetest of girls, and pretty enough to present an acceptable appearance without the fussing and primping other young ladies insisted upon; and at least, if she showed no partiality for any of the young men in the neighbourhood, she did have a decided and very wholesome partiality for Honoria New-combe's company, which was more than one could say for Alexander. Alexander appeared to have no interests whatever in society, and though he was certainly courteous and perhaps fond of his family, he had not a single friend of either sex. This was a great shame, for Mrs. Blackwood thought, quite wisely, that a young man ought to have friends, and surely that a young man as attractive as Alexander might very well have a *tendre* for some young lady as well. But Alexander, to her despair, showed as little predilection for fashion and frivolity as his sister, and could not be moved to change his ways.

All the Blackwood family were fond of Honoria. The fact that she was, for all the shabby gentility of her present surroundings, the daughter of a baronet weighed somewhat with Dr. Blackwood; his wife was pleased with her quiet, unaffected manners, and her kindness for Emily; Alexander . . . well, at least Alexander always remembered to bow when he met her, which was what he did not remember with any number of other persons; and Emily, of course, was her dearest friend. On the occasion of this particular visit, no one was downstairs but Jepston, and so no one saw Honoria when she came in. Jepston, however, took her cloak and begged her kindly to wait in the drawing-room while he went to fetch Miss Blackwood. Honor, glad to sit down after her walk—for Sweet's Folly was at some distance from Pittering Village—proceeded in the direction he indicated and seated herself comfortably in the familiar room. Waiting for her friend, she looked, as she always did, at the wonderful portraits that hung near the mantel, and the skill with which they had been accomplished distracted her a little from the painful, unhappy thoughts that had absorbed her since the previous evening. The Blackwoods were a handsome family in general, all very regularly featured with clear, clean lines and strong constitutions. All were of middle height, fair and wide-browed, with rather broad shoulders and slender waists. Of course, the elder Blackwoods had greyed by the time the portraits were taken, and age pulled a little at Corinna Blackwood's cheeks, but both were handsome still and glowed with a healthiness that spoke well for the doctor's skill in his art. What was remarkable in the pictures was not so much that they retraced each family member's traits precisely, but that in their expressions and their attitudes, Emily had exactly captured the essence of the character of each.

Her mother was shown with embroidery in her hands, a very domestic pose, seated in a cosy red armchair; her eyes, which met the viewer's, radiated kindliness and warmth, and behind these pleasant qualities a subtle kind of weariness, almost a sadness, which indeed was discernible in her to anyone who knew Mrs. Blackwood well. The doctor's eyes, on the other hand, had a singular piercing quality: shrewd, observant, and powerfully concentrated. His shoulders were set forward a little, not at all as if stooped, but rather as if to indicate how determinedly he had fought his way through the world, and that he still continued to do so. This quality of fixed resolve was reflected in each of his children's pictures, too, but neither set of their blue eyes returned the viewer's gaze. Instead they looked away, Alexander's in a manner that signified mental absorption, Emily's with a rather more dreamy quality. Yet, even with that hint of reverie, it was evident that she had inherited her father's capacity for single-minded pursuit of a goal, and when she greeted Honoria—as she did now, interrupting her friend's perusal of these artworks—she did so in a clear, strong voice and with a plain, direct address.

"What a pity you walked over today!" she said. "I was meaning to come to you, and should have had an easier time of it on High-Stepper." She sat by Honor and took her cold hands in warm ones, chafing the frost out of them.

"It was not so difficult," said Honor. "It is hardly even winter yet, and I rather enjoyed the exertion." Her pretty cheeks glowed like apples, as if to bear witness to this.

"Honor dear, say you will sit for me some time again; I should like so much to do a sketch of you in charcoal. Will you?"

Miss Newcombe agreed, but it was evident she was distracted. "Is anything the matter?" Emily resumed. "You seem quite distant."

"No—it is . . . may we go to your sitting-room to talk, please? I must speak with you, dearest, and I should hate to be interrupted."

Miss Blackwood, though curious to know what troubled her friend, delayed her questions prudently until they had reached the shelter of her own snug parlour upstairs. "What is it?" she then said. "You know you may tell me."

"O, Em, it is all so dreadful, I don't know where to begin," Honoria almost wailed. She gazed sadly at her friend for a moment and then went on, trying to smile, "I suppose I might begin by telling you there is a smudge on your cheek—just there, all the way to your chin," she said, indicating it.

Emily borrowed Honor's handkerchief (she never had one about her) and rubbed off the offending mark. "There. Is it all better now?" she asked, and smiled.

"O my dear, I know you cannot know this, but it is not an amusing matter at all," Miss Newcombe replied. Slowly but with great accuracy, she poured out the whole story of last night—how Mr. Kemp had offered for her, and she had refused; how she guessed her aunts to be in hopeless straits; how brave they were about it and how desperately she desired to help them.

"Are you quite sure?" Emily asked, when she had done. "It is not possible you misunderstood what you overheard, is it? A great deal of mischief can be done when one eavesdrops, and not only to the persons one listens to."

Honor shook her head firmly. "I could die of shame," she said. "And when Aunt Prudence said, 'Even if we got rid—' I am almost absolutely certain she finished with my name! I must be a terrible burden to them."

"Is it not possible she meant to refer to the dogs and cats?" Emily suggested sensibly.

"Out of the question," said Honor; "because the next thing she was saying was about Squire Kemp, and Claude's offers, and so it must have been me she was thinking of!"

"But don't you think your aunts would give up the animals before they'd think of parting with you?"

Honoria shook her head miserably. "They are almost no expense, I know. Mr. Morley, the butcher, gives us all his scraps for nothing and the neighbours do too, and there is always more than enough; I know, because I feed them. It is I, Emily, I who has been the expense! I with my books and my dresses, the fire that is always lit in my room even when I do not want it, and of course they must light fires for themselves then to keep me from knowing that they do it only for me. Emily, I have been a beast, a wretched, selfish creature, and I will not let it go on any longer!" She spoke this last with marked resolution.

"What can you do?" Emily asked doubtfully.

"Well, I have been thinking and I believe—Emily dear, don't laugh, please—but do you think I could become a governess?"

But Emily laughed in spite of her request. "My dear, what on earth would you teach? Why you've had no proper training yourself. I mean, I know you can read and play and so forth, but no parent would entrust a child to a girl who had had no formal training at all."

"Not even a very young child, who only needed to know a very little?" Honoria returned dubiously.

"I am afraid not," came the gentle reply. "Besides, you are quite young, and your birth makes such a position almost unthinkable, anyway."

"I am seventeen," Honoria said with dignity, "and I needn't tell them about my birth—"

"I'm sorry," Emily repeated, shaking her head firmly. "But don't despair, my dearest; I have a thought—" She broke off and sat silent for some moments, frowning with concentration. "Yes, I shall tell you," she went on decisively. "I hadn't meant to, but this is—this requires it, I think. Honor, I have been keeping a secret even from you. Don't be angry; I felt I must, for it was too important."

Honoria waited breathlessly.

"Honor, do you recall I told you once of an annual competition sponsored by an academy of painting in London?"

"Yes, I believe so—"

"Well, this year I entered it," she said flatly.

"Did you!" Honoria fairly gasped. Recovering herself in an instant she added, "I am certain you'll win."

"Yes, I hope so," Miss Blackwood replied, with neither false modesty nor undue pride. "Of course, you see it had to be a secret for my father is—well, you know his feelings regarding my interest in painting."

Honor nodded; this was a familiar problem, much discussed between them.

"And then I could not use a picture they had seen, or they should miss it."

"No, of course not," the younger girl agreed.

"And so it had to be done in secret and concealed, and sending it off was no easy matter either."

"But what picture was it?" Honoria asked, fascinated with this news.

Miss Blackwood replied now with a shyness, almost an embarrassment, that was very unlike her. "It was of you," she confessed in a whisper. "That's why I asked you to sit for me again: I should like to do another to keep for myself."

"But you only did sketches of me!" Honor objected. "I saw them myself—in fact, I have some at home."

"I painted it from the sketches," Emily admitted, again with an air almost of shame.

"O, Emily! I think you were abominable not to tell me," Honoria cried, without conviction, "but how perfectly wonderful and clever of you. O, I am certain, certain, certain you will win," she repeated.

"Well, here is why I mention it," the elder went on in tones more usual with her. "If I do win—and I shall know before April—if I do win, I shall give you the prize money and"—her cheeks went crimson at this—"see if they will not pay me the tuition money as well. One wins an education, you see; they pay a sort of scholarship to the academy."

Miss Newcombe sat in wide-eyed silence for some time. At last she answered: "Emily, you were meaning to go to London and study, were you not?"

"I—well, my father would never permit it, of course, so—I shouldn't say exactly, 'I was meaning'—that is," she paused in some confusion.

"O, but you were, you were," Honor asserted, almost angrily. "Why, you perfect—you perfect idiot of a friend! Emily," she cried. "As if I should ever destroy your plans in such a way. Emily!"

And all of a sudden, the two young women were embracing each other and weeping plentifully on one another's shoulder, Honoria, because the magnanimity of her friend had touched her deeply; Emily, because her chagrin at having her sacrifice refused was exceeded only by her relief. In any case, there was Honor's new plight still to be considered, and they shed many tears (and were much comforted by it) before the discussion continued. At length, however, Miss Newcombe dried her friend's eyes with the charcoal-smudged handkerchief, and dabbed at her own. "I did think," she said slowly, while both women took deep breaths to calm themselves again, "I did think of one other plan, which may perhaps succeed."

Miss Blackwood was all attention.

"I am resolved—if we can think of nothing better—to accept the first offer of marriage I receive. No matter who it is." She spoke these words with an unwilling pathos that was almost noble.

"Honor! What if it is Claude again?"

"No matter. I will marry him."

"You mustn't. O, you must not," the older girl objected strongly. "No, you simply must not. Sooner take my prize money, Honor. Really, much sooner." No hint of her former embarrassment now lingered in her voice, only energy and strong good sense. "If I win, it is still excessively unlikely that I shall contrive to attend, and the prize money itself is of no use to me. Even if I *could* go," she continued, "I shall still have a long and happy life without it. But for you to marry a man you could not love—and for money—O, a lifetime of unhappiness, Honor! Really, do not speak so."

"My dear, you talk as if Claude were some sort of wild animal," the other objected, with a little smile. "He has faults, of course, but at base he is—" she hesitated.

"Base," Emily interrupted, with the baldest cynicism. "You know and I know he is impossible to love—conceited, cocksure, always pressing in where he is not wanted. I do not like him at all, Honoria, I never have. There is something sinister about him. I have always said so."

"Well, please not to say so any longer," said Honoria, on a note somewhere between anger and a pitiful pleading. "I may be obliged to become his wife."

"There is a better scheme somewhere, I am sure of it," Emily muttered. "There must be a much better scheme. Let me ring for some tea and we shall think of it. But as for marrying Claude—out of the question. I should never speak to either of you again."

With this slightly exaggerated prophecy, Emily pulled the bell-cord and terminated their discussion for some while. They talked of minor matters and then lapsed awhile into silence, sipping their tea thoughtfully and hardly tasting their cakes. When at last they returned to the matter at hand, it was Miss Blackwood who spoke, and she did so in the slow and measured manner of one who presents a project of whose wisdom she is unsure.

"My brother," she said, looking out of the window onto the frosty landscape, "has always been fond of you, I think. How would you like to marry him, Honoria? Now, think of it carefully and tell me the truth. It won't do to have you making sacrifices where none is needed."

"Alexander?" her friend responded, in a tone that made it clear the thought had never crossed her mind. "But, Emily, if he is fond of me it is certainly not—that is, we have been acquainted so long! It is difficult to think of him—not but what he is very kind, of course—but it is difficult to think of him as—" Her voice faded and she sat thinking quietly. "I should be very glad to marry him," she resumed at last, "were he ever to offer for me."

"You are positive?" Miss Blackwood asked.

A moment passed. "Quite positive," she said, without smiling.

"Then he will offer for you."

"My dear Emily, don't you think such a promise will prove—a trifle difficult to ensure?"

"I see no reason why," said the older girl.

"But—well, setting aside Alexander himself, there are your father's feelings to consider—"

"My father will be delighted," Miss Blackwood broke in. "I have long been aware he encourages your visits partly in hopes that you might indeed become Alex's wife."

Miss Newcombe was surprised, and could not conceal a small smile of pleasure. "Does he know I am without a dowry?" she inquired.

"I am sure he guesses as much. It is not money that interests him here; he can provide that. It is your position that attracts him, Honor. Very frankly, he might perhaps have preferred to see my brother marry a woman with both rank and resources, but Alex has been rather backward socially—"

"To say the least of it," Honoria agreed.

"—and I expect my father will be very glad to see him wed you."

Honoria took in this information and mused over it awhile. "That is all very well," she said at last, "but it still leaves Alexander to be dealt with. Are you quite certain he will be—amenable?"

Emily took her friend's hand again, and spoke gently. "Honor, of all things I should like least to offend you; you understand that. But we must be sensible and honest with one another. I think I know my brother better than anyone else in the world knows him, and so you may depend pretty much on my opinion. Alexander is a very good sort of man, very kind-hearted and well-meaning, and glad to help anyone in need. He is intelligent, perhaps brilliant, in his field. Emotionally, however—promise you will never repeat these words—"

"I promise."

"Emotionally, my dear, Alexander is a child. Except for his love of mathematics, my brother is entirely unacquainted with any passion. I do not mean to say he is unfeeling, only that his feelings have never come to him with any force or intensity." She sighed a little. "I seem to have inherited all the sentiment in the family. But Alex—to Alex, concepts such as loyalty, or courage, or love, or desire, are—are just that: merely concepts. He talks to whoever addresses him, eats what is set in front of him, wears what his valet lays out for him, sleeps when he is tucked into bed. If we set you in front of him, Honor, and tell him to marry you, and make it simple for him to do so, he will marry you, my dear, and it would be far from the worst thing for him. That is why you must decide now, my dear, before he comes to ask you. If you hesitate when he offers it will only confuse him, and make it difficult to get him to ask again."

Miss Newcombe heard this at first with disbelief, but as Emily continued she became increasingly persuaded. The older girl spoke with a kind of unwilling conviction, as if these were truths she had once refused to accept, but had had to resign herself to. By the end of the little speech she had been quite convinced of the possibility of Alex's offering for her; now other considerations presented themselves.

"If what you say is true," she answered, "—if Alexander is such a child as all that, then is it not wrong, perhaps, to manipulate him so?

He will find himself married to me before he knows what has happened. Suppose he learns to regret it?"

Miss Blackwood merely smiled. "I see you do not know Alex so well as I do. Honor, imagine to yourself, if you can, a young lady of birth and connection being told to marry my brother. I am speaking of a stranger, who has never met him yet. Imagine her dismay! She is presented with a young man who can hardly look her in the eye, who shrugs as he makes his proposal, who declares his love for her in a few phrases obviously prepared for him by someone else, and only memorized by him, who forgets to kiss her hand when she accepts. Imagine her inevitable distress! He is attractive enough, but untidy; he says what he is supposed to say, but in so absent a manner as to make it all meaningless—my dear! You at least have a partiality for him, and know his good points. At least he has learned to recognize you! Besides," she continued, in calmer accents, "if Alex could be made to understand your position, I know he would be only too happy to help. It is utterly indifferent to him whom he marries, if he marries at all. He would consent to it as you or I might consent to walk east, though we had thought vaguely of walking west. Now what is it?" she asked, as Honoria appeared to have some further objection.

"I think that—if you are so certain he will comply, I wish you will indeed explain things to him. Could you? Could you make the circumstances clear, and show him how he can help?"

"My dear, I understand your scruples, but I assure you it is not necessary—"

"If you understand my scruples, then say you will try, at least. I should feel dreadful if I thought I had—entrapped him, as it were. Will you try to tell him?"

Miss Blackwood smiled again. "I will try," she promised, squeezing her friend's hand. "And only think how nice! We shall be sisters!"

"That will be pleasant," Honor agreed sincerely, "though I am sure I have always loved you as a sister." After a few more remarks of this kind were exchanged, Honor rose to return to the house in Bench Street. "Emily, don't be hurt, please," she said as the two girls descended the staircase, "but I still feel I must accept whatever offer comes first. If Claude Kemp comes to see me again, I shall say yes."

Miss Blackwood was about to reply angrily, but Honor forestalled her.

"I must, dear. But you needn't worry overmuch. I believe he means to stop with friends in Wiltshire during the holidays, and then to go back to London again, so he will be gone from the neighbourhood presently, and won't return for a while. Besides, I refused him so clearly, even he is not likely to speak again."

"You underestimate him," said Emily, in the rather grim tone she reserved for discussions of Claude Kemp. Jepston was summoned; he restored Miss Newcombe's cloak to her and arranged to have John Coachman drive her back to Pittering Village. The two women embraced and parted. Emily went directly to her brother.

Colworth Park, which was situated off the same road Miss Newcombe now travelled, but several miles farther along, was at this moment the scene of a different parting. Mr. Claude Kemp, Esquire, having grown suddenly weary of his ancestral home and the society of his venerable father, was about to leave for Wiltshire, where his town friends—a rather foolhardy set of well-heeled bucks—were to gather during Christmastide at the home of one of their number. Young Kemp had been meaning to join them at a somewhat later date, but he had changed his plans unexpectedly on the previous evening and now entered his father's study to bid him good-by.

"Refused you again, did she?" the baronet snapped unpleasantly. Sir Proctor Kemp, Bart., was the most powerful man of his district, and had been for some forty-odd years. At sixty-nine he had a full head of white hair, an alarmingly bushy mustache, and a craggy face rutted with deep, severe lines. His body had grown somewhat frail and emaciated, but he still stood a good six feet, and was yet the most fearfully respected man in the area surrounding Pittering. Politically, no one with hopes of advancement dared to cross him; personally, though he was disliked generally, he was on all occasions deferred to. His son was the only man who stood up to him at all, and he only out of conceit, not courage.

"She'll change her mind," Claude muttered now. "I give her until next week. By the time the holidays have passed, she'll be furious with herself, and only hoping I'll ask again."

"Pretty certain of yourself, for a man turned down three times," his father observed, amused. In his heart (such as it was) he shared his son's opinion, however, and could not understand what made the chit so obstinate. Not that he particularly favoured the match—it was far from brilliant—but Claude had not asked his opinion, anyway, and it was acceptable.

"Why should I be uncertain?" the son demanded. "She will have nothing else to think of in this rural wasteland; she is as safe here from other suitors as if she dwelt on the moon. And another Christmas spent in the poverty of her aunts' home is hardly likely to make her more sanguine about her prospects. Are you familiar with that household, sir? It is shabby beyond belief."

"I've seen it," the baronet returned gruffly, with a sharp intonation that almost surprised his son. "In fact, Prudence Deverell came a-begging favours of me not a month ago—something about a hospital of some sort, for animals or some such nonsense."

"Yes, they are both quite mad about their pets."

"Seemed so. Hospital . . . humph! Wanted me to found it, or get funds from the city coffers—some rubbish. Offered to call it the Proctor Kemp Animal Shelter, in my honour. I can tell you, I wasn't persuaded!"

"No, of course not, sir," Claude agreed. "Interesting, though . . . wonder if Miss Newcombe shares her guardians' aspirations."

The old man snorted. "The day a Kemp has to bribe a lady to marry him—" he started, and stopped ominously.

"Yes, exactly, sir." Claude Kemp shook his father's hand briefly and bowed. "Until next time," he said formally. "Enjoy your Christmas, sir."

"Hah!" exploded Sir Proctor. He said "Hah!" to himself several times even after Claude had gone, largely because he had no intention of enjoying his Christmas, and well Claude knew it. Lady Elizabeth Kemp had died on Christmas Eve, twenty-seven years before; since then the squire had passed every Christmas season mourning her, in strict, irascible solitude. Claude was more prudent than heartless in making a habit of deserting his father at this time of year. Sir Proctor said "Hah!" once more for good measure, and settled back uneasily in his chair. After a moment he rang for a servant; one appeared immediately. "Stir up these coals, damn it, can't you?" he flung at the unfortunate footman, indicating the hearth where only one log blazed. "Damned fools," he muttered angrily, while the footman stooped to his labour. "I'm surrounded by a lot of damned fools! Hah!"

Chapter III

Miss Honoria Newcombe and Mr. Alexander Blackwood were joined in the most holy bonds of matrimony on the third of January, in the Year of Our Lord 1817, after due posting of the banns, by the Reverend Mr. Thomas Lester. The wedding party was small, consisting only of the happy couple and their immediate family; the bride wore blue and white. No honeymoon was planned by the new Mr. and Mrs. Blackwood, nor had they a home of their own in which to start their life together. They would reside temporarily with the parents of the bridegroom at Sweet's Folly, and to that residence they went directly following the ceremony. There a number of guests arrived, to celebrate the happy occasion with feasting and dancing, and to felicitate the newlyweds on this most solemn and joyful event in their young lives.

It was all extremely embarrassing for Honor, who felt that everyone must know this was a marriage of convenience, and little more. Alexander was affable, but distracted as always: the rector had been obliged to ask him twice to repeat the vows. Her aunts had insisted on bringing several of Honoria's favourite cats into the little church where the ceremony took place, and one of them had escaped and run up to the altar at just the wrong moment. Her aunts had been disappointingly serene when presented, several weeks before, with the news that Honor had agreed to become Mrs. Blackwood.

"Will you indeed, dear?" Aunt Prudence had said mildly. "Then you mean to disappoint Mr. Kemp, after all?"

"She refused him repeatedly," Mercy reminded her sister gently. "Don't you recall? Three or four times, I believe, was the number."

"Yes, of course she did," Prudence returned, smiling.

"And it did not signify to us one way or the other, do you remember?" Mercy pursued. "We had no opinion of it, I am certain."

"Quite so." She turned to Honor again. "Well then! Alexander Blackwood. I'm sure he'll make quite an adequate husband for you, if a husband is what you want."

"But—" Honor began, her brow wrinkling a little, and stopped. She had been about to ask whether her aunts were not happy to know she would cease to be a burden to them, but realized suddenly that of course they would make no sign of it if they were; she was not supposed even to know of their pecuniary difficulties. "Yes," she amended quickly, "I am sure Alexander will be a very pleasant husband."

"I like him," Mercy confided suddenly. "I always have liked him better than Claude. That Claude has such broad terrible shoulders; broad shoulders are a certain indication of a flawed character. Alexander is so much more narrow; I like him for it very much."

"Are broad shoulders really so significant?" Honoria asked wonderingly.

"O yes, my dear! Don't you recall the width of Mr. Morley's shoulders? Mr. Morley, the butcher, I mean."

"Indeed, I do," said her niece; "but I have always considered Mr. Morley to be quite a kind man. He does give us rather a lot of scraps, does he not?"

Aunt Mercy sighed and shook her head, smiling tenderly. "Poor Honoria," she said. "Prue, I think she is even more innocent than I! Certainly Mr. Morley gives us scraps, but he does not do so out of kindness, Honoria! He does so from guilt—to atone for being such a thoroughly nasty man to begin with. How could a butcher be a kind man, Honoria? Where have your wits gone begging? Of course, he is a terrible man, a cruel and bloodthirsty man, there was never a doubt of that in my mind."

"He is excessively polite to me," the girl said timidly.

"Of course, naturally! To keep from being brutal, don't you see? Not that he can help it, you know; it is a character flaw, as I say. His nature is to be coarse and unkind. That is the nature of all men. They can't help it, can they, Prue?"

"No, they cannot. Men are beasts."

The ticking of the clock was all that was heard in the parlour for a few moments. Then Aunt Prudence resumed, saying, "So Alexander Blackwood is to be your husband. How very agreeable that will be for you!"

It had been a disappointing reception of her sacrifice, to say the least. And Honoria had become terrified the night before the wedding.

She had looked about the little bed-chamber, which had been hers since she could recall, and the most doleful thoughts had come into her mind. This was the last night she would ever sleep there, the last night she would be Miss Newcombe, the very very last night. These reflections induced her to cry at first, which was not too awful, but quite soon her regret had turned somehow into fear, and that had been wretched! She had almost wanted to run away, and had grown quite hysterical in a very short time. Only the most diligent efforts to govern her feelings saved her from utter panic, but she had at last fallen asleep, consoling herself with the thought that at least she would have a pianoforte always near: her aunts did not own one, and hitherto she had always walked over to Sweet's Folly when she wished to play. There would be no more "walking over to Sweet's Folly" now. Now she would live there herself, with Dr. and Mrs. Blackwood, and Emily, and—and her husband. She slept that night, but not well, and the rings under her eyes were quite noticeable the next day, even through her wedding veil.

Dr. Blackwood would have liked a large wedding, to show that his son was a gentleman of consequence, but there had been no time for that. However, he had contrived to invite most of the neighbourhood to Sweet's Folly afterwards, and a late supper was arranged for the most select of the guests. After even these had gone, the Blackwood family kissed the bride and groom once more and disappeared discreetly. For the first time since he had come to Bench Street to offer for her, Alexander and Honor were left alone together. They sat in the drawing-room, where the family portraits hung; a small suite of rooms on the second story had been prepared for them, and Honor was tired, but she did not know how or whether to excuse herself now from her husband. It was all so awkward, so abominably awkward! Alexander said nothing, though he yawned (imperfectly concealing the fact) several times.

"It was a pleasant ceremony," Honor observed at last.

"Yes, very pleasant," he agreed.

"And the evening was agreeable, too. Your father has been very generous."

"O, quite generous," Alex replied. "He is quite generous, I think."

Honor felt almost ready to cry, so exhausted and lost did she feel. "A most liberal gentleman," she repeated at last.

"Most liberal," he echoed.

"Alexander—"

He turned to look at her, having previously been absorbed in examining the geometric design in the Turkey carpet that lay on the drawing-room floor. He was slight, of course—almost frail, in fact, for he took very little exercise—but if one did not regard his legs (they were hopelessly spindly) he was quite an attractive young man. In repose, his features strongly suggested his sister's, a circumstance that comforted his new wife somewhat. When he smiled, which was rarely, his countenance became almost charming: his smile was crooked, ingenuous really, and very appealing. Emily Blackwood had not been graced with this particular smile; it was Alex's own. His fair curls had been dressed with a good deal more care than usual for the wedding, and as his green eyes gazed now at his wife, she felt with surprise that he was actually quite a bit more handsome than she had supposed. Unfortunately, that did nothing to alleviate the awkwardness of the moment, and though Alexander turned his attention towards her, he said nothing.

"It has been a long day," she stated, rather lamely.

"Has it? But it is midwinter," he objected mildly. "Surely it must have been a short day, don't you think?"

"I meant—"

"O, I know what you meant!" he interrupted suddenly. His crooked grin broke out. "You meant it had seemed like a long day, that the day had been so full of different things, it had appeared to go on a long time. You were speaking metaphorically, were you not? How foolish of me!" Alexander was no simpleton, but he really had not understood at first what she meant. Such absurd difficulties in communicating were typical of him: he simply had not had much practise in conversation. "I am awfully sorry," he said now. "You are quite correct, of course. It has been a long day."

"And I am tired, Alexander," she dared at last to say.

"So am I, indeed." He paused. "O, but then you must go to sleep, Miss Newcombe. Shall I have Jepston show you to your room?"

"Alexander, I am not Miss Newcombe any longer," she pointed out. "I am Mrs. Blackwood. And I know the way to my chamber, thank you."

"Do you? But of course you do. We discussed it all last week, at dinner. Your chamber is to be next to mine—my new one, that is. I—" he broke off suddenly. "O dear! Did I call you Miss Newcombe?" he cried, truly shocked. "What a cake I make of myself! Mrs. Blackwood, naturally. Can you ever forgive me?"

He looked so dismayed and vexed with himself that Honoria forgot to be hurt. "Please, Alexander. Let us agree on some few things," she said patiently. "I shall call you Alex, or Alexander; and you may call me Honor, or Honoria. It is usual between husband and wife, and that is what we are now, though I know it surprises us both."

"It is rather a jolt, is it not?"

"Yes, it is." Realizing that she must make all the decisions between them, for a while at least, she continued, "I should like to go up to bed now, Alex."

"I pray you will not let me keep you!" he replied sincerely. "I myself must go to my study for an hour or two; we have been so busy today, I have had no chance even to glance at my work yet. Or, should you like me to escort you up the stairs first? It is late; perhaps you are frightened."

She was tempted for a moment to accept his aid, but soon saw the uselessness of it. "No, thank you very much. I shall do by myself very well." She stood, and went towards the door.

Alexander rose too, looking distracted again.

"Good night," Honor said quietly, turning towards him.

"Mrs. Blackwood—Honor," he said suddenly, in a tight, curious voice. "Honor—"

He went towards her, until he stood only a pace away. He seemed very tall to her at that moment, and his features drew together as if in intense concentration. With an abrupt, agile motion that startled both of them, he bent to her and kissed her full on the mouth. It was the first time he had done so. "Good night," he said, in the same curious voice, standing straight again. As he appeared to have no more to say, there was nothing for Honor to do but murmur good night once more and proceed up to bed alone. Hours later, as she sat in the great, canopied bed, nursing the end of a candle, she heard her husband enter his room and quietly shut the door.

In the little house in Bench Street, Honoria's absence was felt that evening and duly noted, but conversation turned only briefly upon it. "It was a pretty wedding," Mercy remarked.

"As weddings go," said Prudence, with a sceptical sniff.

"Do you recall Patience's wedding?" continued Mercy, referring to the third Deverell sister, who had been Honoria's mother.

"Patience? O yes! Though I never did understand why she married that Newcombe. She was perfectly welcome to stop on with us, I am sure. I always said no good would come of it, and I was absolutely correct, of course."

"I should say you were!" Mercy agreed, nodding energetically. "Why, it was the death of her!"

"Yes, and no wonder."

"Though, indeed, we should never have had Honoria, if it hadn't been for Newcombe."

"We haven't got Honor now," Prudence observed.

"No, in fact we haven't!" said her sister, much struck. She stopped for a moment to disentangle Calico from a ball of yarn she was knitting into a shawl. "That is not a toy for you," she said, almost severely; "it is a toy for me."

"Calico is fretful because her baby has been taken from her," said Prudence. Amber, the kitten to whom she referred, had been given to Honoria as a wedding gift.

"Still, I am glad we gave him to her," Mercy replied. "Patience would have wanted it that way."

"You are right," Prudence said, though Patience could not possibly have wanted any such thing, since she had never been acquainted with either Calico or her offspring.

"Marriage is a very sad affair, after all," Mercy sighed.

Prudence sniffed again, to signify agreement.

"However, we must not allow it to weigh on our spirits," she said briskly, after several minutes had ticked past. "We have a mission to accomplish, dear—or had you forgot?"

"The animal hospital? I should hope not! I have been thinking of it every day for weeks, and every night, too. Unfortunately," she added, "I have not thought of anything helpful."

"Never mind, dear; I have."

"Have you indeed, Prue? I made sure you would! The very thing—how clever you are. What is it?"

"Well . . . you may find this just the least bit unsettling at first, but bear in mind this is a terribly important mission, and the most desperate actions may be called for."

"I am prepared," her sister returned solemnly. A little thrill rushed down her spine at the hint of impending heroics.

"We are agreed, I think, that without Squire Kemp's assistance, our aim may never be accomplished. Is that not so?"

"Precisely so."

"Further, we know that Kemp is presently of no mind to help us. We know that because I asked him, and he said so."

"Yes, yes, go on!" To Mercy, her sister's remarks seemed the exciting fruits of the most rigorous logic.

"Therefore, we must find a way to change his feelings towards us."

"Prudence!" the other breathed admiringly.

"Now, how are we to do that?" her elder sister enquired rhetorically.

"O dear, Prue, is that all you've been able to think of?" Mercy almost wailed. "I am sure I don't know!"

"Wait, wait a moment," Prudence interrupted, holding up a frail hand. "I do have a scheme, but you must be willing to make some—some sacrifices."

"Anything at all, my dear."

"Good, then. In order to change Kemp's feelings, we must appeal to him on the most fundamental and primitive level. Mr. Kemp is not a subtle man. We know he is impervious to the demands of justice. We must go deeper than that," Prue repeated, drawing a deep breath, "and that is why *you* must make him fall in love with you."

"Make him—!"

"I cautioned you this was a bold scheme, Mercy."

"Yes, but—how should I—? Dare I? Dare I, Prue?"

"For Tiger, and Muffin, and Fido, and Lady, and all their heirs, assigns, et cetera? I should think you will dare, Mercy! I should think you shall!"

Mercy was still quite aghast. "It does not sound proper at all, Prudence. You know you have always had no idea of propriety, dearest, no idea at all. I'm afraid this—well, this fairly smacks of scandal, Prudence love. I really do not think—" She shook her head disapprovingly.

"Mercy, we agreed on desperate measures. Now, I tell you, I have thought about it thoroughly, and there is nothing else for it. What is your honour or dignity, compared to the welfare of our small friends?" Small friends was the term they always used to refer to their pets.

"Well . . . but, my dear, if I make him fall in love with me, then I shall be obliged to marry him."

"Not at all. After he has founded the hospital, you may break his heart."

"Prudence, how unkind—" she said unhappily.

"Don't be silly. Breaking a man's heart is in no wise the same as breaking a woman's. They don't feel things the way we do. It will probably spur him on to do something noble afterwards, like enlist in the army, or improve his land. Men are always doing noble things when their hearts are broke. This is no time to become missish, Mercy. I should do it myself, but you are much prettier than I, and know more of coquetry. I never could coquet."

"It's been years since I have!" Mercy pointed out.

"I have considered that, too. We shall have a few practise sessions here: you will attempt to flirt with me, and I will pretend I am Squire Kemp."

Mercy still felt rather uncertain of the wisdom of this plan, and even more so of her ability to carry it off, but her faith in her sister's logic was overwhelming. If Prudence said it was necessary, then it positively must be necessary. "You *could* do it," was all she said. "You are just as pretty as I, I'm sure."

"No, I really could not. Besides, once you begin visiting him and so forth, you will need a chaperon, and it is only logical that I should be the chaperon and you the lover, for I am older."

"Four years," Mercy murmured weakly.

"Older all the same," she countered. "Well, are we decided? Will you do it? Or, will all our small friends be obliged to suffer for your scruples?"

Prudence was really rather a bully, but that truth had never once occurred to her sister. She saw in her only an inspired leader, beneficent and brave, and impossible to doubt for long. "I shall," she said finally. In a more resolved tone, she repeated, "I will."

And from that day forth, the house in Bench Street bristled with preparation. All Mercy's gowns had to be altered, to make them more becoming: lace was added, ribbons looped more fully, necklines lowered, and sleeves shortened ever so slightly. A number of afternoons were devoted to discovering a more fetching coiffure for her long, silvered hair, and Prudence put her on a strict régime of rich foods, to plumpen her up. Every evening a full hour was passed in coquetry lessons, during which Mercy struggled valiantly to smile, simper, and tease as she had in her youth. Frequently she grew faint-hearted, and was once on the point of crying out that such behaviour was ridiculous in a woman of her years, but she realized that this protestation would be sure to hurt Prudence, who was, after all, even older than she. At the end of a fortnight Prudence gave her a final review, a full evening during which Mercy played the role of coquette to the hilt, and pronounced her ready to go into battle. The next step was to discover some means of throwing Kemp and Mercy together, preferably in a romantic setting. After some contemplation of this problem, Prudence (as always) arrived at a plan.

It was known throughout the neighbourhood that at three o'clock daily, just before his dinner, no matter what the season or the weather, Squire Kemp mounted his horse and rode round the perimeter of Colworth Park. The dimensions of this park were such that part of his round took him right along the road that led to Pittering. It was decided that on a certain day, at exactly quarter past three, Miss Mercy Deverell would be found at the edge of this very road, in a situation of the utmost pathos and distress.

"You will have been walking," Prudence dictated, "and will have sprained your ankle most severely. Unable to proceed, yet at a loss for what else to do, you will have sat down to consider. When Kemp appears, you will be in the process of examining your ankle, which you will declare to be very bruised, and moaning O! O! O! in excessively audible tones. Can you do that?"

"I suppose," Mercy said dubiously.

"Try it."

Mercy sat upon the ancient Confidante and held her ankle in her hands. "O! My ankle! O! O!" she wailed. A horde of mewing cats instantly rushed to her aid, and a mongrel in the dining parlour began baying.

"A convincing performance, obviously," Prudence approved, when some time had been spent reassuring the animals of their mistress's comfortable health. "When you do it in the road, however, I wish you will remove your boot."

"Prudence!"

"Remove it, and rub your ankle," she continued firmly. "You have a very neat foot."

"Yes, but really, dear—"

"For our small friends," the elder stressed.

"O," said Mercy in a small, humbled voice. "Indeed."

The accident was scheduled for Wednesday of that week, which was two days off. "I really think we might make it Thursday," Mercy said timidly, when given this news.

"Why is that, dear?"

"Thursday is—it is so much more likely a day for accidents," Mercy replied. "I have always felt that if I were to have an accident, I should like it to fall on a Thursday."

"My dear sister, if I did not know you better I should say you were frightened."

"O no, Prue, it is not that, but—Wednesday, as you say. It will be Wednesday," she agreed. Of course, she was in fact as frightened as could be, but it would not do to worry Prue with that.

The young Blackwoods, meantime, were busy with schemes of their own—or rather, with schemes suggested and contrived for them by Dr. Charles Blackwood, who saw (though he might have preferred not to) that the business of being a husband held not the least interest for his son. He had been expecting Alexander to approach him with a request for money to set up his own household, but no such request had ever come. At about this time, consequently, he sent for the young man and broached the subject himself.

"Neither your mother nor myself wishes, of course, to see less of you or Honoria," he explained, in the flat, slightly pompous tones customary in him, "but we understand that a young couple requires more privacy than your apartments here in Sweet's Folly afford. What you need, Alex, is your own establishment, so that you can learn to know one another properly."

He paused. Alex said yes.

"I've been scouting about a little in the neighbourhood, and it seems Stonebur Cottage is available for lease now. Stonebur's business obliges him to stop in Tunbridge Wells all year round these days, and of course Mrs. Stonebur is with him."

Again he paused. Alex said of course.

"So what do you think, son, eh?" he asked heartily. "Stonebur is not far from here at all—walking distance, indeed; and it's a snug little place. Not suitable for ever, naturally, but at least until you start a family. Eh? Tell me how it strikes you."

"I beg your pardon, sir?"

"I say, tell me how it strikes you. You and Honor living in Stonebur Cottage for a bit. What do you think?"

"I think—won't the Stoneburs be terribly inconvenienced, Father? It's an awfully small place."

"But I tell you they've put it up for lease; they don't live there any more," said the doctor, with more weariness than annoyance. The whole family had grown used to repeating things for Alexander's benefit: he had always been absent-minded.

"O! Well, in that case I'm sure it would be more than large enough for just two people. Mr. and Mrs. Stonebur lived there for years together, didn't they?"

"Yes, yes, they did. So shall I go ahead and lease it for you?"

"Indeed, if you like, Father," Alexander said amiably, "though I don't know that you need put yourself to the trouble. I am very comfortable in my rooms here, and I shouldn't think Honoria had any complaint. She never does; at least, she has not said anything to me—that I remember," he added, for he himself knew how absent-minded he was.

"Alexander," his father began, in a voice rather sterner than before, "you really must try to concern yourself more with being a husband to your wife. The two of you never seem to be together now any more than you were before you married. Except at night, that is—though I don't—er—" Despite his medical training, Dr. Blackwood shied from discussing such a topic with his son. "I don't understand it," he went on after a mighty "Harrumph." "Why did you marry the girl in the first place?"

"Because she—" Alexander began, and then checked himself suddenly. His father did not know that he had been asked to offer for her, and he had promised (though he knew not why it was necessary) not to tell him. "I like her," he said, rather feebly.

"So do I like her, too. And since you like her, you'll be glad to establish yourself at Stonebur's, eh?"

"O yes, glad to. Did I not say so?" Alexander inquired innocently. "I'm sure I meant to."

"Yes, yes . . . well then, it's settled. You tell Honoria, and your mother and I will begin seeing about furnishings, and servants and so forth."

"I tell her—?"

"Yes, boy, yes!"

Alexander agreed to do so, though he hardly understood why, and the interview between father and son was concluded. Honoria received the information with mingled emotions.

"Naturally, it will be pleasant to be mistress of one's own household," she told her friend Emily later, "and yet I can't but think the prospect makes Alexander uncomfortable."

"Well, my dear," Emily replied, "he will be obliged to reconcile himself to being married sooner or later. Hold still an instant," she added. She was engaged in painting Honoria again, this time an oil that would hang next to the other family portraits in the drawing-room. Mrs. Blackwood had felt it would be appropriate, and had asked her daughter to execute it. "You may speak now," she said, after a moment.

"It seems unfair to hurry him, though," Honor pointed out. "It was not his idea to be married in the first place, remember."

"But he is married, and as I told you before, it will do him no harm to learn a bit more about humankind. Frankly, I find his treatment of you most disconcerting as it is; he really could do much better, if he applied himself a little."

"He's very kind to me."

"When he remembers you at all," his sister said severely.

"Well . . ." She felt it improper to censure her husband, but it was undeniable. "I suppose so. But one can't expect Alex to behave—like any other—that is—"

"To behave like a gentleman, you mean. Why not? Honor, please stop hedging with me. I know you are trying to play the good wife, but it is too exasperating under the circumstances. You have not been candid with me since you were married, and that does no one any good."

As she often did, Emily had perceived the truth precisely. Honor considered her words for a moment and was obliged to agree.

"Very well, then," she said. "But one cannot expect him to behave like a gentleman because he is—he is not a gentleman. He is—he is a geometrician, that's what he is."

"But he is a man, too."

Honor did not appear to be persuaded.

"Isn't he?" Emily asked, setting her brush down for a moment. "Honor, he does—well, he is interested in—he kisses you and that sort of thing, does not he?"

Though she knew it was best to be frank, it was difficult for Honoria to answer this question. She coloured a little and spoke in a very low voice. "He—not precisely."

"Precisely, then—?" Emily pursued relentlessly.

"Precisely, he—well, he kissed me precisely once," she confessed. "I mean, except for on the hand or cheek, as he would kiss anyone."

"Honor!"

"Well, what on earth could one expect of him?" she demanded. "We knew this was no love-match! It does not trouble me," she went on proudly. "I know it means nothing—that is, I know it is not a slight, or some such thing."

"Yes, but really!" said Emily, whose passionate nature would have made such circumstances intolerable for herself. "O, something must be done about this. I wonder if I ought to speak to Father?"

Honor cried in horror, "O, do not! Please, I beg you will say nothing to anyone. This is in strictest confidence between us, Emily—pray!"

"Well—yes, if you insist. But we cannot let things go on so. Perhaps when you are alone in Stonebur Cottage—"

"But that is just what I am afraid of," Honor explained. "It will make it so clear that we ought to—it will be dreadfully embarrassing—"

"I wish I had made you accept my prize money," Emily said bitterly. "I am absolutely ashamed of my brother."

"I wish you will not be. I am really very fond of him," Honoria insisted. "He is always gentle with me; I know he means no harm. I am sure he would even like to be a good husband, if he knew . . ." Her voice trailed off into silence.

"I think you must seduce him," Emily said flatly.

"But perhaps he does not care for me! In that way, I mean. I am no great beauty, you know, and only think—!"

"I *am* thinking, Honor, which is more than I can say for you. Shouldn't you like to have babies?"

"Well, some time, perhaps. Not directly, but—Emily, shall I tell you what I really should like, more than anything?"

"Please," she said cordially.

"What I should really like most of all"—she drew a deep breath—"is to travel a little. At least to go to London!" she said, with a strong rush of emotion, for this secret had never been confided before, and it was a great pleasure to say it at last.

"Should you?" Emily replied, apparently not the least bit overset, though Honor had expected she would be. "Then, why do not you suggest it to Alex? You ought to have a honeymoon, anyway—perhaps while the cottage is being prepared."

"But it would take him away from his work," Honor sighed. "He would not like it."

"We are not consulting his wishes just now, but yours."

"Surely his wishes have something to do with it, however."

"Something—Honor, my dear, we must simply change his wishes, that is all. Or, could you not beg him to take you away? He will never refuse you, if he sees you truly desire it, and I am certain he will enjoy it once you are abroad."

Honoria shook her head stubbornly. "I will not take advantage of him in such a way. If he is to remain partial to me, I must certainly not demand that he do things that seem unpleasant to him. I have thought this out before."

Unwillingly, Emily deferred to her new sister's wishes. "Very well, then—but we are by no means defeated. Now, you be quiet for a bit while I paint your chin, and I will think. I promise you, dearest, we will find a way to make Alexander appreciate you, cherish you, and wish to be alone with you—and especially, a way to induce him to take you abroad. I promise absolutely!"

Chapter IV

Wednesday dawned drizzly and overcast. "Just the perfect sort of day," Prudence remarked bracingly, "to slip and turn one's ankle."

"If you really think so," her sister murmured doubtfully, "though I hardly see what is romantic in muddied skirts and boots."

"You needn't muddy your skirts," Prudence objected.

"I must if I am to sit down and nurse my ankle," Mercy returned. Her tone was a trifle peevish: she was unused to heroic sacrifices, and did not find them as much to her liking as she had expected. The two old ladies were engaged in taking breakfast together, which they did as always in the tiny breakfast room at the back of the house in Bench Street. "Might I have another cup of tea, please?" she continued, in the same irritable tone. "This toast is terribly dry."

Prudence obliged her sister and set about trying to soothe her by summoning up vivid images of the snugness of the future animal haven, and the gratitude of certain small friends to their valiant benefactress. Unhappily, Mercy proved inconsolable, and persisted in whining and hinting darkly at all manner of disaster throughout the morning. She passed well over an hour whispering wounded confidences to her favourite dog, a mongrel named Ragamuffin, and only consented to leave Bench Street that afternoon with the deepest expressions of misgiving. "He won't like it," she pouted, setting a tiny foot into the carriage that was to convey the ladies down the road towards Colworth Park. The carriage had been borrowed from Mrs. Fielding, who often provided such small services to her eccentric neighbours. "He is too old," Mercy continued plaintively, "and so am I."

"Our small friends," Prudence reminded her for the hundredth time that week.

"Yes, yes, our small friends. Well, drive on, Mr. Coachman," she returned, and the carriage, with a small lurch, began to move. Half an hour later they had arrived at a thicket some three hundred yards from the gates of Colworth, and Prudence gave the command to stop.

"Mercy dear," she said, kissing her sister, "you know what to do. You must make all shifts to stop as long as you may with Squire Kemp, and never falter. You are advance guard in our campaign, remember."

"Yes, indeed." Mercy's humour had changed from resentment to wretchedness as the fatal hour approached. "Prue," she wailed suddenly, her eyes filling with tears, "are you certain you wish me to do this?"

"Poor Mercy," her sister said, patting her hand. "But yes, I am afraid so." The sisters exchanged a few further phrases, relating to how much Mercy should be missed in Bench Street, and how noble her actions were, until at last there was nothing more to say and the younger Miss Deverell was set down on the road. The sight of her trudging off sadly towards Colworth brought tears even to Prudence's eyes, and she was loth to turn round and go home. Still, it would not do for Kemp to see the carriage, so turn round she did. Mercy, meanwhile, plodded through the thickening mud, reflecting moodily that it would not be difficult to turn one's ankle today at all.

"I shan't look pretty!" she sniffed to herself as a fat raindrop slid from her bonnet-brim to her nose, and continued sliding. "No one could, in all this wet. Squire Kemp must be a fool to ride out in this weather, and a greater fool to believe I've any business being here." A small rock, shiny with rain and mire, appeared in the road before her. Pettishly, she kicked it out of the way, and proceeded to kick every other stone she could find, so that she weaved her way from side to side along the road quite erratically. With each little kick she gave a small, rebellious "Humph," feeling very put upon and sorry for herself, to the point where she positively enjoyed getting as muddy as possible, and almost hoped she would take a chill besides. When a considerable shower began to fall, she welcomed it. "Prudence should have guessed I could not do this," she thought, booting a pebble neatly to the roadside. "I told her to make it Thursday; I begged her! She will be well served if I come home in a fever," she reflected, and this prospect so satisfied her that, perceiving rather a large rock lodged in the mud, she raised her foot with extraordinary energy and kicked it for all she was worth.

"Humph!" she cried aloud, and then, "O dear, O dear! O my foot foot foot!" she screeched with real dismay, for the large rock had refused to budge, and rather than knocking it out of the way, Mercy herself had been knocked quite over, and had toppled down into the mire. Not only had she turned her ankle most genuinely, she had also bruised her toes considerably, and there was something wrong with her hip. She noticed this as she struggled to rise, and her agitation increased when she began to walk again. "O dear!" she wailed piteously, limping with real difficulty to the roadside. She seated herself unceremoniously on a log and pleaded aloud—quite uselessly, she knew—for Prudence to come and rescue her. All this morning's resentment was forgot, and all her instructions, too. She crouched mournfully on the fallen log, and the very last thing on her mind was whether she constituted a picturesque sight. Her predicament was very real, indeed.

Fortunately, she had walked far enough by the time she fell to be almost where she belonged; that is, far enough to be found in the course of Squire Kemp's ride. Though she did not know it, it was now five minutes past three o'clock, and she had not long to wait before the squire would arrive. In due course he did come; she heard his horse's muffled *clomp-clomp* on the soggy ground, and moaned most convincingly, "Help! Help!"

Proctor Kemp could not fail to hear these piercing cries, and he located their source within moments. Riding through a break in the hedge, he caught sight of a frail old woman, evidently soaked to the bone, clutching at her ankle and whimpering frightfully. Now, this was not the sort of scene to evoke kindliness in the old man, but he did have a sense of justice in spite of what Prudence said, and he soon dismounted and waded up to her. "What's this? What's this?" he demanded sternly. "Who have we here? What is it?"

Mercy turned her face up miserably to his. The look in her sweet, mild eyes was so imploring, so hopeful, that it moved even Proctor Kemp's heart. "Mercy Deverell, sir," she said barely audibly, "and I do hope you will help me."

"Hey, what's that? Help! I'll help; of course, I shall," he muttered, and extended an arm to support her while she rose. "Now you just jump up on Charger here; that is, I'll lift you up," he grumbled. He continued to make similar remarks in a low mutter incessantly, from the moment he found her to the time they reached the manor's door, she riding uncomfortably and he making his way even more uncomfortably afoot. "Boothby!" he bellowed, when they had entered. "Boothby! Lot of scoundrels. Hah! Booth-beeeee!"

Boothby, the butler, appeared at last and confronted the scene in the front hall with astonished eyes. What he saw was his master of forty years, panting and wet through, with an elderly lady similarly circumstanced in his arms. Mercy, upon dismounting from Charger, had discovered her ankle to be too swollen to walk upon, and had had to be carried inside. The poor butler—taken utterly aback, for his master never returned from his ride before four, let alone with a lady in his arms—simply stared.

"Boothby, you brigand," Kemp roared savagely, "take this lady from me and get her to a fire. Can't you see she's injured? Call Mrs. Cafferleigh, won't you?" he continued, referring to the housekeeper. "Send for Dr. Blackwood!"

It was still some moments before the hapless Boothby took in the situation well enough to help, but in time he did bear Miss Deverell to a bedroom, handed her into Mrs. Cafferleigh's care, and sent the coach round for the physician. Squire Kemp meanwhile retired to his own bed-chamber, where he put himself into the care of his valet and abused that worthy roundly at the same time. He still had no notion why Mercy Deverell should be sitting about moaning on his land, but he did know he was far too old to run about rescuing damsels in distress, and the incident had vexed him considerably. Besides, he was drenched with the rain, and his new top-boots were ruined.

Dr. Blackwood arrived in due time to examine the patient. Squire Kemp had given orders to the effect that tea was to be sent up to her, and whatever else she wanted, but he had refrained from visiting his unexpected guest himself. Dr. Blackwood, always jovial when acting professionally, found his patient (who was also his new connexion by the marriage of his son) in tolerably good spirits, sipping an infusion quite calmly and questioning the housekeeper as to the origin of the tea-caddy. Her clothing had been removed and replaced by a dress-ing-gown belonging to Mrs. Cafferleigh herself, and she was tucked up in a wide, soft bed with a fire blazing brightly within the grate. Compared to her recent circumstances, she was now quite at ease, cheered by her pleasant surroundings and distracted by the hospitable chatter of the housekeeper. When Dr. Blackwood entered she had al-most forgot her ankle, and her silvered hair was nearly dry.

"My dear Miss Deverell," he exclaimed jokingly, "if you wished to see me, you needn't have gone to such lengths! You are always wel-come at Sweet's Folly. Had a bit of a spill, haven't you now?"

"Yes, a bit," she agreed, timid as always with the bluff physician, as she was, in fact, with any gentleman, and most ladies.

"Well, now, we must have a look at it, mustn't we?"

"Don't go!" she called out suddenly to the housekeeper, who was retreating discreetly. "Please," she added.

"No, indeed, Mrs. Cafferleigh must stay and assist me," the doctor agreed. He knew the Cafferleighs well, having treated all their brood when they were afflicted with the measles some two years before.

Mrs. Cafferleigh stayed accordingly, and the examination passed off without complication. Dr. Blackwood's diagnosis contained no surprises: Miss Mercy had sprained her ankle, jolted her hip out of line a bit, and bruised herself generally. He bandaged her efficiently, to ensure as much comfort as possible, and prescribed draughts that would soothe her nerves and lessen the pain. Of course, she was not to be moved, unless it was strictly necessary, and he imparted this information later to the squire, who listened to him while sipping at some sherry, forgetting to offer the doctor a glass. "Hah!" he commented, staring out a window at the bleak landscape beyond. The rain had lightened, but it continued to mizzle, and the day was very grey. "Hah!"

"I don't suppose her stopping here will inconvenience you much?" the doctor suggested, eying the sherry enviously.

"No, no," he muttered. "No. How long will she stop on, eh? That's what I want to know."

The physician shrugged slightly. "A se'ennight, perhaps. I shall come by and see how she goes on in a day or two. Nothing to worry about, but we must give her time to heal."

"Yes, yes, time," the other agreed impatiently. The prospect of having a female guest visiting Colworth Park did not please him. In fact, it doubly displeased him, for his son was expected back from London any day now, and it seemed to him Claude was visitor enough. "Mercy Deverell, did you say it was?"

"Yes, Mercy."

"And her sister—Prudence. How is it Prudence was not with her? I thought they always went about together."

The doctor shrugged again. "Something about a surprise for her . . . went towards Markhamton to get it . . . thought the rain would hold off till evening . . . I don't know, precisely. Anyway, you might send for Prudence; Mercy will be wanting her things from home, and perhaps a companion. Though, if you like, I'll send Honoria to fetch her; she'll be glad to take care of her aunt, I know. I think you are acquainted with my daughter-in-law Honoria—? She is the Misses Deverell's niece, on her mother's side."

"Yes, yes, I know . . . however they like to arrange it themselves," said the old man, thinking of Claude. That young gentleman had not yet learned of Honoria's marriage, and would doubtless be displeased. Perhaps he should try to keep the girl out of Colworth Park, lest

Claude be forced to deal with her more than he liked. But then . . . what was the difference, anyway? A pack of females was about to descend on Colworth, and there was no doing anything about it. Young or old, it made no matter. Nodding his head, he dismissed the doctor rather rudely, and sat down before the drawing-room fire to brood on his new misfortune. What he had done to deserve such nonsense was more than he could guess, and he sent for a footman to take away the sherry and scolded him roundly for nothing at all. As the innocent servant shut the doors behind him, he heard his master's unmistakable "Hah!" and knew that some trouble was afoot.

Miss Prudence Deverell received word of her sister's misfortune with astonishing calmness; at least so Honoria thought, for it was she who delivered the news. Dr. Blackwood had returned to Sweet's Folly and suggested to his daughter-in-law that she take a carriage into Pittering. There she was to visit her Aunt Prudence and inform her of what had occurred. Further, Dr. Blackwood had given Honor leave to wait in Bench Street while Prudence collected Mercy's necessaries, and to drive her (if she liked) to Colworth Park. Honoria herself had been terribly alarmed at the story of Mercy's accident, but Prudence seemed hardly to care at all; in fact, she seemed quite pleased.

"Good, good," she said, nodding slowly at her niece.

"I beg your pardon, Aunt?"

"I say, it is well—that is, I am glad you have come to tell me." It seemed to Prudence that no end would be served by admitting Honoria to the scheme. The less anyone knew, the less could go wrong. "Wait a moment and I shall fetch her things," she continued. As the old lady turned to mount the stairs, Honor could almost have sworn she muttered to herself, "Better than I expected—" but that was too ridiculous. She returned almost immediately, a small valise in her hand. Honor hastened to relieve her of her burden, but wondered at the same time how she had contrived to pack Mercy's things so quickly.

"Honoria, it is very well you have come," Prudence said. "I wish you will take this to your aunt for me . . . I cannot leave Bench Street, you know: it is almost time for supper, and since you have left us, feeding our small friends has become my task."

"But surely Mary could do so—?"

"No, no," Prudence snapped impatiently. "It would quite overset them. Mary is practically a stranger."

Honor was about to object that in a house so tiny as the Deverells' no one could possibly be a stranger to the animals, least of all the servant Mary, whom Honor knew to spend a good deal of her time with the dogs. Knowing the futility of arguing with Aunt Prudence, however, Honor kept her peace and acquiesced with a shrug of her shoulders. "I should be glad to stay here myself," she offered.

"No, no!" Prudence repeated, this time even more irritably. "It is better to leave her alone, believe me. That is—there are elements in this circumstance that you do not understand, Honoria. You run along with her valise, and tell her I shall come to call tomorrow."

The young bride was quite at a loss to comprehend her aunt, but as this was not unusual she soon dismissed the matter from her mind and simply submitted to her desires. "Tell her I shall be there tomorrow," Prudence reiterated, as Honor's carriage prepared to depart.

"I shall," she promised. The coachman gathered his reins, and within a short time the horses were picking their way diligently back towards Sweet's Folly. There Honoria made a brief stop, during which she informed her new family that she was on her way to Colworth alone, and might stop there the night herself if Mercy wished it. Actually, she informed Dr. Blackwood of this; Alexander was absorbed in his geometry, and only nodded distractedly when told of his wife's plans. Taking a few of her own things, in case she should be obliged to stay till morning, Honor again set off in the carriage. By the time she rolled up the gravelled drive at Colworth it was dusk. Boothby met her at the door, handed the valises to a footman, and directed him to show her up to Mercy's chamber.

"Honor!" cried Mercy, as if dismayed. "Where is Prudence?"

Honoria explained that her elder aunt had felt it necessary to stop in Bench Street.

"O, but she does not understand! She thinks it is all a sham! O dear . . ."

Again, Honor was baffled. "I am sure my aunt does not think you are shamming," she began soothingly.

"But yes, she does. Honoria, the things I have been through this day . . . O dear!" she ended on a wail.

Honor expressed her willingness to stop at Colworth if Mercy desired it. "As you like," her aunt returned fretfully.

"Of course, if it is all the same to you, it might be best not to inconvenience Squire Kemp overmuch." Honoria had private reasons for desiring to spend as little time as possible at Colworth Park: she did not know if Claude was at home, but if he were she felt it as well to avoid him.

But Mercy had had a sudden change of heart. "No, do not leave," she exclaimed vigorously. "I beg you will not. I don't care to be left alone here; I do not at all, no matter what Prudence thinks best. Do not leave," she repeated.

"Certainly I shall not, if you wish it," Honor returned. Really, both her aunts were too odd! Her marriage seemed to have made them queerer than ever, and she had noticed in Bench Street that not a single thing had changed. If her departure from the little house had been a relief to their budget, there had certainly been no improvements made to show it. The worn carpets and faded curtains were just as she had left them, and her Aunt Prudence had been wearing the same grey gown she had so often worn at home, the one with discreet patches at both elbows. And yet, as she helped Mrs. Cafferleigh to unpack Mercy's things, she remarked that new ribbons had been added to her green morning gown. It was all very odd.

The remainder of the evening passed away without difficulty: Squire Kemp still declined to visit his guests, but supper was sent up to them, and a brief message that Mrs. Blackwood was welcome to stay. Mrs. Cafferleigh installed her in the chamber next Mercy's, and Honoria, having heard nothing of Claude, concluded that he was yet from home. In this she was only partially correct. Claude was indeed out when she first arrived, but at about eleven o'clock that night his coach rolled through the Park gates, and in the morning all her worst fears were to be realized. Squire Kemp kept country hours, so that by the time of Claude's arrival, everybody was abed except a few servants. Claude, seeing no reason to disturb his elderly parent's rest, went straight to bed himself, so that it was not until morning that his presence was made known to the squire. By this time it was too late to inform him quietly of Honoria's having married Alexander, for Mrs. Cafferleigh had a place laid for Honor at the breakfast table and the two young people met one another there while the squire took chocolate in bed. It would have been difficult to say which of the two was the more surprised; certainly Honoria was the more dismayed. In a few words, she explained her aunt's recent misfortune, and her presence at Colworth Park.

"A pity about your aunt," Mr. Kemp returned, "but I am very glad to see you all the same, Miss Newcombe."

Honor hesitated for a moment. "But I am no longer Miss Newcombe. I am Mrs. Blackwood."

"I beg your pardon?"

"I say," she repeated, less timidly this time, "I am Mrs. Blackwood."

"But how is that possible?" Claude frowned.

"I am married to Alexander Blackwood," she said, repressing an involuntary smile at Claude's confoundment. "Had you not heard?"

"No, I had not heard," he answered, in a very unpleasant tone. "This is—that was rather sudden, was it not?"

"I have known Alexander all my life," she pointed out.

"So have you known me." His handsome features clearly showed his anger: he had come back to Colworth with the intention of offering for Honoria again, certain that by this time she would have changed her mind at last. "Do you mean you married that snivelling fool when you might have had me?" he burst out suddenly. "What on earth were you thinking of? Surely he cannot make you happy!"

Honoria cast a nervous sidelong glance at the waiting footman, who ought certainly not to be present during such a scene. "But he does— that is, I have been quite comfortable with him, thank you. We go on very well."

"Go on very well!" Claude repeated, with a snort that was extremely reminiscent of his father's.

"Mr. Kemp," Honoria said, staring hard at the footman.

"Yes, what? Oh," he replied, following her glance. "Bancroft, that will be all, thank you." He added a curt, decisive nod, and the footman scurried out of the breakfast room. For a while he said nothing more, merely chewing moodily and deliberately on a buttered muffin, and surveying Honoria with a keen, unembarrassed gaze. She was wearing a morning dress of embroidered clear lawn, with a pattern of rosettes repeated along the neck and hem. The delicate, gossamer-like stuff enhanced the clarity of her creamy complexion in a way she knew to be very becoming; she now regretted, however, that it flattered her so well. Claude's continual gaze was quite rude, she felt, and caused her such discomfort that she at last blushed under it. "Now, tell me again why you married him instead of me," he said finally, in somewhat calmer tones.

Honoria was about to explain, but it suddenly occurred to her that her first duty was to herself and her husband, and she revised her reply accordingly. "I do not consider that an appropriate topic of conversation," she said evenly. It cost her much to answer so coldly: it was against her nature to deny anyone anything, but she felt she really had no choice.

"My congratulations," Claude returned, with a slight, mocking bow of his head. "I see you are become quite a matron already."

"I am not become any such thing," she retorted, somewhat stung. "That is, I am still just what I used to be, only now I am married."

"If you are still just what you used to be," he answered, "Alexander must be a very queer husband, indeed."

Caught off guard by the extreme impertinence of this observation— and, worse yet, knowing it to be true—Honoria coloured again to the roots of her hair. "I am sure I do not follow you, sir," she said coldly, certain that he would not dare explain.

"I am sure you do," he responded smoothly, and fell again into a moody silence.

"I must go and tend to my aunt," Honoria said shortly, rising from the table. "I beg you will excuse me."

Suddenly, Claude smiled, and addressed her in the softest of accents. "It is I who must beg for your forgiveness," he murmured. "Pardon me, Mrs. Blackwood, for having spoke so unkindly before. It was abominable of me—perhaps even unpardonable."

Quick, as always, to forget unpleasantness, Honoria gladly relented. "Not at all unpardonable," she smiled back warmly. "On the contrary, it is quite natural. This news caught you unaware; you have had no time to adjust."

Claude rose and stood before her, his head a little bowed. "You are all goodness, madam," he said quietly. His blond hair gleamed dully in the grey morning light. "Please—if I may ask one more favour of you—will you allow me to kiss your hand? Then I shall be assured I am forgiven."

Ashamed almost of her previous coldness, Honoria assented wholeheartedly. Mr. Kemp, holding her hand as if it were a precious and fragile object, set his lips to it. Then he stood and hastened to the door, opening it for her with another tiny bow. She passed through it, catching his glance once more and smiling sweetly.

Her Aunt Mercy had passed the night quite comfortably, according to her own report, and was now in very little pain. Honoria discovered her sitting up against the pillows and writing a note on some letterpaper she had begged from Mrs. Cafferleigh. It was for Prudence, she told her niece, and she wished it to be sent immediately.

"Of course," Honoria said. "I am sure Squire Kemp will be happy to oblige you."

"I'll hand it round to a footman at once," Mrs. Cafferleigh offered, taking the sealed note from Miss Deverell. She opened the chamber door to accomplish this commission, and found Jenny, one of the underservants, just on the point of entering.

"The doctor is here," she said to the housekeeper. "Shall I send him up?"

"Yes, of course, do." Mrs. Cafferleigh bustled out of the room, pushing Jenny along ahead of her. Dr. Blackwood appeared some moments later, full of cheerful solicitude for his patient.

"Feeling better, are you?" he asked Mercy. "Slept the night, I trust? And you, my dear Honoria, I've a letter for you somewhere about

me . . ." He patted various pockets, searching for the missive, and
found it at last tucked away in his case. "Here it is, then," he said, handing it to her. "From Alex," he added with a wink. "Misses you, no
doubt."

Honoria doubted very much if her husband had missed her, but she
took the letter and thanked Dr. Blackwood for his pains.

"Nothing at all, nothing at all," he replied jovially, and turned to examine the invalid. Honoria, meantime, perused the letter.

To her surprise, it was in Alexander's own hand: she knew it was
because several geometrical figures had been sketched in the margin,
drawn, she guessed, while he had been thinking how to frame his sen-
tences. Formerly, all Alex's notes to her had been written by his valet,
for none of them had contained anything too private to be known to
him, and Alexander found writing a hard task. As she read further,
however, she realized—with a little disappointment—that Emily must
have instructed her brother to pen this note: it was too unlike Alex to
think of it himself. It read thus:

> My dear Honoria,
>   I hope you have spent an easy night at Colworth, and trust
> Squire Kemp's hospitality left you in want of nothing. I under-
> stand you must wish to be near your aunt, but hope you will not
> be long absent from Sweet's Folly all the same. Emily and my
> parents miss you, as I do.
>   My father informs me that certain decisions must be made soon
> regarding the furnishing of Stonebur Cottage. As I do not feel
> competent to make such choices alone, I should be most glad if
> you were to come home for a few hours at least, so we can go
> over the plans together. (At this point the letter was interrupted
> by a diagram of a triangle with a circle inside it.) Kindly convey
> my condolences to your aunt.
>
>   Respectfully,
>   Your obedient, etc.
>   A. Blackwood
> P.S. Emily desires me to inform you she cannot proceed with your
> portrait until you sit for her again.

Honoria read the letter twice, and closed it with a sigh. It might
have been written by almost anybody to almost anybody, except for
the line about missing her, and Emily, she felt sure, had dictated those
words exactly. She reflected how humiliating it would be if Claude

Kemp could see how formally her husband addressed her, and was very glad he could not. Dr. Blackwood interrupted her thoughts.

"Will you come home with me, Honoria?" he was saying. "Miss Mercy is mending very nicely today."

Honoria glanced at her aunt, who pouted fretfully. "Perhaps I shall stop until Aunt Prudence arrives, shall I? Did you ask her to come in your note?"

Mercy smiled gratefully at this correct interpretation of her pout. "Yes, indeed, I did ask her to come, and I do wish you will stay until she does."

"Of course, I shall. I think my father-in-law understands?"

Dr. Blackwood agreed heartily, but with a little frown that belied his words. His son, he felt, paid little enough attention to his bride as it was; if her absence were prolonged, he was likely to forget her altogether. "Indeed," he said, adding, "once Miss Prudence has arrived, however, I hope you will return to Sweet's Folly and let her stop the night here with her sister. Then you may come and visit your aunt with me each day, as long as she remains here."

So matters were settled for the moment, and Dr. Blackwood took his leave soon after, satisfied as to the welfare of his patient. A little time later, the messenger who had carried Mercy's letter into Pittering Village returned with word from Prudence, assuring everyone of her imminent arrival at Colworth. She did not, however, come until well past two, and that meant the morning had somehow to be whiled away between niece and aunt. For a time, Honor read aloud from a novel Mrs. Cafferleigh had fetched from the baronet's library. This passed the time well, but the hours hung heavily nonetheless. Mercy was anxious to see Prudence, and Honor had begun to wonder if, after all, Alex had written his letter by himself. She was eager to speak with Emily about it, and the idea so interested her that she frequently lost her place on the page, and repeated whole paragraphs at a time. At last Prudence's arrival interrupted them; her voice, floating up the stairs, brought a teary smile to Mercy's lips, and a grateful one to Honor's.

"Not been up to see her since the accident?" she was saying sharply. "The rascal!" This epithet was evidently meant for their host, who, fortunately, could not hear it, since he was at the moment closeted in his study with his son. "Just like a man, however," she continued, addressing (they soon discovered) the sympathetic Mrs. Cafferleigh. "Mercy!" she cried, bursting into the bed-chamber; "O my dear, I am so very sorry!" She flung her arms round her younger sister's neck, and comforted her at length.

Prudence, it was learned, had brought quite a trunk full of things from Bench Street. She intended to stay day and night by her sister's side, having entrusted the care of the animals to Mary.

"But I thought—" Honor began to object, and checked herself.

"Mary will do well enough on her own," Prudence said. "Now you run along home, Honoria. You will only be in the way if you stay."

Young Mrs. Blackwood was a trifle injured by this prediction, but she said nothing of it. "If you are quite certain—"

"Yes, child, yes! Now, run along like a sensible girl, and you'll see poor Mercy tomorrow."

Honoria obeyed, kissing her aunts before departing.

"Fido is downstairs," Prudence told Mercy as Honor left. "Honoria, when you go down, be sure to tell the butler what Fido likes to eat. And tell them to send his basket up to this room, so he can keep Mercy company tonight. I could not leave him in Bench Street," she explained, turning to Mercy.

"I am glad you did not! Dear, sweet Fido!"

Honoria smiled in spite of the sharpness of her aunt's instructions; she was wondering what Squire Kemp would have to say to the intrusion of Fido into his home. The "dear, sweet" animal to whom Mercy referred was an enormous mongrel, a mix (apparently) of German shepherd and golden retriever; the basket that Prudence desired brought up was at least three feet in diameter. Besides being large, Fido was high-spirited and excessively excitable. Though fond of the dog herself, Honoria suspected Squire Kemp would not care for him at all. Content to be on her way home, however, she held her peace and, finding the butler in the entrance hall, instructed him as Prudence requested.

"And do you think—" she added rather timidly, "might Sir Proctor be willing to lend me a carriage to go home in? I hate to trouble him, but—"

Mr. Boothby interrupted her. "The young master has informed me of his intention to drive you home. If you don't mind waiting a moment, I'll have him sent for."

Honoria became agitated immediately. "O no, I beg you will not worry him with it. Please, it is very kind of him, but I had rather not put him to the trouble." The prospect of a drive to Sweet's Folly with no other companion than Claude Kemp did not appeal to her at all, despite his apology that morning.

"Mr. Kemp was very particular about it," Boothby replied. "I know he will be angry with me if I fail to tell him you are going."

"But, Mr. Kemp—" she began, in a failing voice. "I do not—that is, if he was so particular," she sighed despairingly, "I suppose you must."

"Thank you, madam; very good, madam," Boothby bowed, much relieved. Young Kemp was never a gentle master, but when his orders were neglected, he was the very devil to deal with. Mr. Boothby directed a footman to seek out Mr. Kemp, and stood smiling gratefully at Mrs. Blackwood. She, for her part, attempted to smile back, but her anxiety was so great that she could not. Though she had utterly forgiven him his ill-conduct at the breakfast table, she was shrewd enough to know that Mr. Claude Kemp's humours never lasted long. How he would behave to her during the solitary drive to Sweet's Folly preoccupied her entirely, and caused a tiny vertical wrinkle to appear between her brows. Claude's arrival, in a smart blue Garrick with several capes, did nothing to allay her fears, and it was with the deepest apprehension that she allowed herself to be handed into the high perch-phaeton he drove, while Claude himself climbed in on the other side.

Chapter V

Prudence Deverell was extremely vexed. "We have won our way into the citadel," she informed her sister, "but the enemy does not show himself. This will never answer."

Mercy, afraid that she might somehow be blamed for Squire Kemp's having kept away from her, replied fretfully, "I hope it is nothing to do with me, dear Prue. I am sure I endeavoured to look as picturesque as possible yesterday, only it was difficult with my injuries . . ."

"There, there," the elder lady said soothingly; "only a beast with a heart of stone could fail to find you charming. Unfortunately, that is precisely what we have to deal with." She lapsed into a thoughtful silence while toying with the vegetables in her soup. To her great chagrin, she had not been invited down to dine with the squire, but rather had found her dinner sent up to her along with Mercy's.

"Pray, tell Sir Proctor I had rather dine with him, and beg him not to put his kitchen to the trouble of sending my dinner up," she had told Mrs. Cafferleigh, when that good woman had apprised her that the meal would soon be served.

"The master is certain you will prefer to dine with Miss Mercy," Mrs. Cafferleigh responded implacably, as she had been instructed to. "He anticipated your goodness, and begs you not to worry."

There had been nothing for Prudence to do but accept defeat (for the moment) and dine in Mercy's bed-chamber. "Drink up all your soup," she now told her sister, rather distractedly. "You will need your strength."

"Shall I, Prue?" Mercy inquired, with interest. "Whatever for, my dear?"

But Prudence did not tell her until both ladies had finished their repast and the trays had been taken away. "Do you recall the lesson I gave you in how to play chess?" she asked then.

"I recall it very well," Mercy asserted. "It was extremely unpleasant."

"Yes, but do you remember how to play, Mercy dear?"

"I remember . . . a queen can go any way at all, is that not so? And a king only one step at a time."

"Exactly. And bishops diagonally—"

"And knights one one way and two the other!" Mercy interrupted triumphantly.

"Two one way and one the other," Prudence corrected from habit.

"O," said Mercy, cowed, yet quite reasonably confused. "Indeed."

Miss Deverell went over each of the other pieces, making her sister repeat their names and abilities.

"But what for?" Mercy cried at last. "It is so very wearisome."

"I have a notion you'll be playing chess this evening," she answered cryptically. "Now, be patient, and you will be rewarded. Mrs. Cafferleigh?" she went on, poking her head outside the chamber door at the sound of heavy footsteps.

"Yes, Miss Prudence?"

"Mrs. Cafferleigh, I had a dog with me when I arrived, named Fido. Kindly desire a footman to fetch him to me."

Mrs. Cafferleigh looked sceptical but agreed. "My master doesn't care for animals in the house," she cautioned.

"Never mind, he'll care for this one," Prudence replied impatiently. "Please to have him sent up."

Mrs. Cafferleigh, looking a trifle anxious, hurried away on her errand.

"Am I to play chess with Fido?" Mercy asked wonderingly. "I really don't think he is fond of such games . . ."

"Mercy dear, you are such a goose. Of course you won't play with Fido. You will play with Proctor Kemp," she ended decisively.

"Shall I, dear Prue? But how?"

"Wait and see," the elder responded, nodding wisely.

"One more thing, Prudence," Mercy continued, after a few moments had passed in silence. "Do you wish me to win or to lose?"

Prudence stared, astonished that even her sister—goose though she was—could be silly enough to suppose she might win her very first chess game, and against an accomplished player at that. "You just do your best," she said, "and do not trouble about winning or losing."

"But it would be terribly awkward if I were to beat the squire," Mercy insisted.

"I do not think that is likely to occur," Prudence said. "Chess demands a great deal of thought and strategy—and practice, of course. You just put up as hard a fight as you can."

"If you say so, my dear," Mercy agreed meekly, but the possibility that she might win continued to trouble her so deeply that she altogether forgot to wonder how Prudence planned to get hold of the squire in the first place, not to mention for what purpose Fido was needed. Prudence for her part continued to smile and nod silently, and when Fido was brought (on a stout leash) she held a long, quiet conference with him, from which Mercy was excluded.

Honoria, meantime, had quite forgot her aunts' affairs, and was assiduously tending to her own. To her relief, Claude Kemp showed no tendency to hurry the horses—for she knew he was reckoned to be an excellent whip, and had feared he might decide to impress her by springing them. On the contrary, however, he drove very slowly, indeed, and devoted the chief of his attention not to the reins but to her.

"That is a new pelisse you are wearing, is not it?" he observed, evidently admiring the neat garment of brown sarcenet she had donned for the drive home. "It is very pretty."

"Thank you, sir," she said, unconsciously touching the embroidery that adorned its bodice. "It was a part of my trousseau . . . Mrs. Blackwood had it carried out for me. Mrs. Blackwood, my mother-in-law," she added nervously.

"I hope it is warm enough," he pursued, having made a faintly perceptible grimace at the word "trousseau."

"O yes, quite warm," she assured him. Unfortunately, she shivered involuntarily just as she said this, not so much from the weather (although it was quite chilly) as from the thought of what he might do to warm her.

"But you are cold," said he, perceiving the shiver. "Let me—"

"No!" she exclaimed, without meaning to.

"I was about to say, let me offer you this lap robe," he continued, obviously amused at her distress. He pointed to the robe, which was folded up at her feet.

"I assure you, I am not in the least cold," she said firmly.

"As you say," he answered, with a slight bow. "Mrs. Blackwood," he resumed, when they had travelled about a hundred feet, "I hope you are not still angry with me?"

"O no, not at all. Not at all," she repeated, as her words sounded rather weak in her own ears.

"I had hoped—foolishly perhaps—" he began, in persuasive, sincere accents, "I had hoped we might become friends, now that you are indeed married. One of the advantages to marriage for a lady, you know, is the greater freedom it allows her in forming such connexions. I have always aspired to your confidence," he went on, "and I do not cease to do so now."

Honoria, hearing these words, felt ashamed of the improper sentiments she had (in her mind only) been ascribing to him. He was quite in the right of it, of course; as Mrs. Blackwood, no one could take exception to her pursuing an acquaintance with Mr. Kemp—so long as it remained within certain bounds, that is. She felt that she had been unfair to Claude. "You are most kind to offer your friendship," she said gently, "and I am delighted to accept it. I hope you will do me the honour to take me into your confidence as well."

Claude smiled his handsome, mirthless smile. "I may call upon you then sometime?" he said.

"Please, anytime," she returned, on a generous impulse. "I am sure the Blackwoods will be glad to see you as well."

"Do you mean to reside at Sweet's Folly permanently?" he inquired, on a conversational note.

"O no, we will remove to Stonebur Cottage quite soon," she said. "It is only a question now of transferring our things from one place to the next. All the servants and so forth have been engaged . . ." She enlarged upon this topic at length, thinking it a comfortably neutral one, and they drew up presently into the drive of Sweet's Folly. "Should you like to come in?" she said.

Mr. Kemp smiled again—as it seemed to her, a trifle ironically.

"I thank you very much," he said, "but no. Not but what I am most anxious to see Mrs. Blackwood—your mother-in-law, that is—and her agreeable children again, but I think my father awaits my return somewhat impatiently, and would not wish me to stop away too long. It is long since he and I have talked, you know," he explained. "Pray convey my compliments to all your new family, however."

Honoria assured him that she would do so, and quitted his phaeton with relief. Jepston admitted her to the house, welcoming her and informing her that Miss Blackwood had requested she join her in her sitting-room as soon as she arrived. As this was exactly what Honor desired to do, she hastened to her friend and sister directly.

Formal enquiries were exchanged as to the healths of those here and at Colworth Park, but these were soon done with and the two young women sat down beside one another to discuss what concerned them more closely. "The most exciting thing!" said Emily, her blue eyes shining. "I have had a letter from the academy in London, and—"

"You've won!" Honor broke in.

"Well, no, not won . . . but I have not lost; that is the great thing.

It was to say that my picture would be among those submitted to final judging." She felt her news sounded disappointing after the conclusion Honoria had jumped to, and was a little hurt.

"But that is wonderful," her friend replied, sensing Emily's slight injury. "I know you will win, I just know it!"

"But there is more," Miss Blackwood said. "It is certain at least to be on exhibition in London, no matter what happens. All the finalists are."

"Emily, I am so proud of you," said Honoria, squeezing her hand. Then, lowering her voice somewhat, she went on, "Emily, I must ask you something and you must promise to answer truthfully. It is important to me, and you mustn't spare my feelings."

Emily vowed she would be as honest as possible.

"The letter Alexander sent to me at Colworth—did you—was it your idea? Did you tell him to write, or tell him what to write?"

Miss Blackwood appeared puzzled. "Did he send you a letter then? I had no notion."

"But he referred to you in the postscript," Honor objected. "He said you desired me to sit again for my portrait."

"Did he, indeed?" Emily mused. "I said so at breakfast today. I am astonished—he must have been listening!"

"But it is more than that—!" Honoria exclaimed, and stopped, at a loss for how to continue. It seemed ridiculous for a wife to rejoice at a note from her husband but Emily must understand.

"I am very glad he wrote to you," she said, proving that she did indeed understand. "Was it—did he say anything—?"

"It was rather a formal note," Honoria confessed, realizing what her friend wished to ask. "But a note all the same. Emily, it is the first."

"Well, my dear, this is progress, indeed," Miss Blackwood said briskly. "I suppose he sent it with my father?"

"Yes . . . Em, you don't think your father might have told him to write it?" Honor asked dubiously. She had much rather believe it was Alex's idea, but the truth had to be known.

"Well, no," Emily said decisively, after some thought. "My father was called out to the Higgins' last night, and did not come home until well after midnight. Naturally, he went directly to bed, and he slept through breakfast. I am sure he did not leave his room until just before driving to Colworth. Alex would not have had time to write to you then; it takes him such an age!"

Honoria's smile was perfectly blissful. "Then it was—" she began, and broke off suddenly. The cause of this interruption was the sound of a knock on the door, and the appearance, immediately afterwards of her husband.

"May I come in," he asked, entering at the same time. "Honor, you are here! I thought I heard a carriage in the drive." To both the girls' surprise, these words were uttered almost fondly, and Alex advanced into the room as he said them until he had gained Honoria's side. He took her hand—a little awkwardly, but nonetheless—and kissed it gently.

Honor was so amazed, she could think of nothing to say but "Alexander," which she said in a tone so low as to be barely audible.

"I wish you had not stopped away so long," he continued reproachfully. "Of course, you had a perfect right to do so, but I hardly slept for wondering how you were."

Both young women gaped as if Alexander's mere presence constituted a miracle, which it did rather, for he never quitted his study during the afternoon, and he had certainly never addressed his wife so tenderly, either in public or alone. All at once, however, their surprise seemed to infect him, and he stopped speaking, obviously ill at ease. Gracelessly, he fell into an armchair opposite them, and began to stare at Emily distractedly.

"Had I known it would disturb you, I should not have stopped the night there," his wife said, when she had recovered herself somewhat.

Alexander shrugged his shoulders as if the topic were indifferent to him. With a pang, Honor realized that it was her own slowness to react that had embarrassed him. "I am quite well," she assured him timidly. "You look a bit tired."

Alex shrugged again. "As I say, I slept badly. I oughtn't to have burst in here, I suppose. My apologies, Emily," he said to his sister, and rose again.

Both girls started to assure him he was welcome, but he had already reached the door and opened it. "We must discuss some domestic matters at tea," he said to Honoria, "as I told you in my note."

"O yes, your note—I was so happy to get it!" she exclaimed, but it was all too late. Alexander had not stayed for her answer, and it was doubtful whether he had heard her last words. Vexed past bearing with herself, Honor angrily dashed away a tear that had somehow stolen onto her cheek, and clasped her hands rigidly in her lap.

"You see what I have done," she said at last. "If he never speaks to me again, it will be my fault."

"Honor, really, you make too much of it. It does not signify—"

But Honor's fury with herself was increasing, and she broke in, "All my fault, my fault! His first husbandlike words to me, and I ignored them. O, I deserve his neglect," she cried hotly.

Emily, surprised at the wrath her gentle friend now displayed, sought to calm her. "Well you mustn't fly into alt about it, my dear; that will certainly serve no purpose. Follow him, if you like. He will still listen to you."

Honoria refused to be comforted. With a stoically flat tone in her voice, she replied, "You may as well paint me now, if you need to. At least I cannot spoil that."

Emily laughed quietly, hoping her friend would join her. "I can't very well paint you as you are now," she objected. "You look as sour and enraged as a wicked witch whose plans are thwarted."

But instead of laughing, Honoria exclaimed even more vehemently than before, "That is exactly what I am! Exactly!" And she leapt up from the little sofa, upsetting a candlestick as she did so, and ran from the room without another word. When she reached her own chamber, she threw herself on the bed and sobbed for all she was worth, lost in a fit of self-dislike.

At Colworth Park, another kind of storm was raging. At about five o'clock, Prudence Deverell, having assured herself that all her troops were ready, crept out of Mercy's bed-chamber, Fido at her side. Patting his massive head now and then, she tip-toed carefully down the broad steps that led into the front hall. There she found Boothby who, startled by her unexpected appearance, asked in a rather loud voice, "Is anything wanting, Miss Deverell? May I help you?"

Prudence raised her finger to her lips and emitted a sibilant "Shhh!" Boothby, taken aback, said nothing. "Where is your master?" Prudence demanded in a harsh whisper.

"I'll take you to—"

"Shhh!" she repeated. "Quietly, quietly, my good man. I do not wish to be taken to him. Point him out to me, that's all."

Really, the Deverell sisters were just as queer as people said, Boothby concluded to himself; this one at least appeared to be half-mad. Stealing about in other people's houses! And with that mongrel—! Mr. Boothby, accustomed to do so from long years of service to the Kemps, refrained from voicing any of these opinions and merely said (in an obliging whisper), "Just as you say, madam."

"That's better," Prudence muttered, and began to follow him down a narrow, high-ceilinged corridor. At the end of it, Boothby pointed to a closed door.

"There—in the study," he mouthed silently. "With Mr. Claude."

Impatiently, Prudence gestured to him to be quiet and go away, waving him off as one would a fly. Mr. Boothby retreated discreetly to the opposite end of the corridor. "Now for it!" she whispered to Fido. Cautiously and without a sound, she turned the handle of the door, not so far that it opened, but so the bolt held back and no longer barred the way. "Forward!" she hissed in the dog's ear, and immediately feigned an enormous exaggerated sneeze: "Ah-chooo!"

Fido, dragging his useless leash behind him, burst ahead through the door with a mighty bound. Barking and jumping with frenetic excitement, he knocked first against Claude (who had been standing, pouring a glass of wine), bowling him over, and then against Squire Kemp, who sat as always before the fire. Instants later, Prudence pursued him, panting as if from exertion and exclaiming in a weak voice, "Fido! Fido! Good boy. Down, boy!" The hitherto quiet study was, for the next few minutes, the scene of uncontrollable havoc. Fido leapt gaily onto Claude—who still lay in semi-recumbent posture on the floor—mashing him with his large paws; then grew weary of that amusement and threw himself affectionately on the squire. Prudence stood gazing, as if paralyzed with dismay, at the broken wine decanter for several moments, and resumed her feeble cry of "Down, boy!" ever and anon. At last Claude recovered himself and got up upon his feet, rushed over to the dog, and grabbed him firmly by the collar. Both gentlemen, who until then had said nothing more interesting than "Hah!" and "Hold!" suddenly left off speaking altogether and stared intently at Miss Deverell.

She too was silent for some time. Then, dropping a pretty curtsey and addressing the squire, she said, "Dear sir! It seems an age since I have seen you. Still well, I trust?"

"Damnation, woman!" the baronet thundered suddenly. "What is the meaning of this?"

"The meaning—?" she inquired gently.

"This beast, this mongrel, this cur!" he roared. "Damme, you shall pay for this!"

Prudence returned his gaze as if with mild surprise. "Why, naturally I shall," she agreed. "I am so very sorry. You see, I was taking dear Fido to see my poor sister, when all at once I sneezed. Terribly draughty corridor, I am afraid! My sneeze caused me to lose my grip on Fido's leash, and the poor dear simply jumped away from me at once. I suppose the sneeze upset him; perhaps he thought I was taking a cold. He's terribly sweet."

"My good woman—" the squire began with an angry snort, and continued after a moment, "Perhaps you will have the goodness to tell me how, if you were taking your cur upstairs, you happened to be in this particular draughty corridor?"

Prudence smiled radiantly. "I suppose I lost my way," she said sweetly. "Does this corridor not lead to a stairway?"

"What the devil—damnation!" the baronet bellowed again, seeing it was ridiculous to unloose any more spleen upon so innocent an object. "Get him out of here," he said, his fine head of white hair trembling with anger.

"Of course I shall, if you do not like him," Prudence said naïvely. "I am so sorry about the decanter, you know—and that lamp," she added, catching sight of a number of glass shards scattered under a table. "It must have been quite a pretty lamp," she continued, musingly.

Squire Kemp said "Hah!" in a loud voice.

"Isn't it the oddest thing," Prudence continued, while she went to Claude and took the dog from him, "I suppose you gentlemen are having your after-dinner conversation, aren't you? Now is the time when ladies withdraw to the drawing-room, is it not? And I never in all my years entered the room while the gentlemen were talking. Isn't that the oddest thing?" she repeated winningly.

As his father seemed about to say something rude again, Claude interrupted. "Very odd, ma'am," he said. "I am afraid you have somewhat startled us, however—perhaps—"

"My goodness, it's Claude!" Prudence declared. "I almost did not recognize you: the holidays have done you good, I can see. Not but what you weren't always a strapping, healthy lad; I often said so to Honoria, you know, when you used to come calling."

Claude, annoyed at this mention of his failed courtship, was obliged to check himself for a moment. "I hope you will forgive us," he said at length, "but my father and I were indeed engaged in—in the sort of discussion you describe, and I hope you will not think it unkind of me if I ask you to—perhaps I may ring for Boothby to escort you back to your sister?"

"O no, not in the least necessary," said the old lady, hugging Fido as she spoke. "I know my way well enough now. There is only one thing, just one thing, and then I will disturb you no longer: I wonder, do you have a chess set about? My sister is simply aching to play chess; she says nothing else can distract her from her pain—"

"Yes, yes," the squire interrupted suddenly, eager to be rid of the intruders. "In the buffet, there—Claude, fetch it for her."

Mr. Kemp opened the cupboard indicated and drew out a board and a set of ornate, carved-ivory chess pieces. "Will this answer?" he said, handing the game to her.

"O yes, this is just the thing. These are chess pieces, are they not?" she inquired, in an anxious afterthought. "I am sure I would not know."

The squire confirmed that they were.

"O, thank you so much. You are too kind. You see, whereas Mercy is simply mad for chess, I do not know the first thing about it. Dear Honoria was used to play with her, when we all lived in Bench Street, but now . . . O my! That makes me wonder: who will play with her? I know I cannot!"

She looked helplessly at her host, smiling all the while.

"I don't suppose you play, sir?" she asked, when he failed to respond.

"What's that? I play," he said gruffly.

"Then, will you have a round of it with Mercy? After tea perhaps? She would be so thankful; it's the only thing to distract her she says, and I—"

"Yes, yes! Yes, and to the devil with you," Squire Kemp burst out. "I'll play with her—anything—only get away now, get away."

"O sir, I am sure you are all kindness," Prudence said, bobbing another curtsey, and babbling on, "Mercy will be simply delighted, I know it; she said it was the only thing . . ." and she continued to prattle on in this vein even as she turned and led Fido back down the hall, not ceasing to chatter until she was well on her way upstairs.

Once safely arrived again in Mercy's bed-chamber, Prudence exultantly recounted all the details of this battle, as well as her eventual victory. "The campaign is brilliant, Mercy, brilliant, if I say so myself!"

Mercy, though not understanding quite what had occurred, was only too eager to congratulate her clever sister, and did so with many expressions of fondness and praise.

"You must congratulate Fido as well," Prudence reminded her. "Hasn't he been a fine doggie? O, he has!" she exclaimed, and hugged the mongrel closely, kissing the top of his shaggy head. "I'll have Mrs. Cafferleigh bring him a bone, and when the hospital is built, he will have first choice of lodgings there. Anywhere you like, my sweet pup," she told him, kissing him once more.

The squire had several hours between the time of the calamity and tea in which to calm himself. It crossed his mind that he might send a note upstairs crying off from the promised chess game, and he very nearly did so; but there was something cowardly in this course of action that he could not like, and he restrained himself. At the appointed time, therefore, he stood before the door of Mercy's bed-chamber and rapped briskly.

A sweet voice pealed from within, "Who is it?"

"Kemp," he muttered.

"Sir Proctor? O, do pray come in," the voice replied, and he entered. He was wearing boots and breeches, as he always did, for he declared it nonsense to dress in his own home. Prudence had rather hoped he would feel the propriety of attiring himself at least in pantaloons, if not in silk stockings and pumps, but she found herself disappointed. Mercy, on the other hand, was dressed quite to the nines. She wore a blue robe of fine muslin, threaded richly with white ribbons, and a cap (thickly frilled) to match. Her long sleeves, drawn tight above and below the elbows, were pulled up just ever so slightly, to reveal a pair of neat, delicate wrists. Prudence had spent nearly half an hour arranging her coiffure, and had been rewarded by a very pleasing effect. Fresh linens covered the pillows that were plumped up behind her silvery head, and all in all she made a very attractive sort of invalid. When Proctor Kemp came in, she turned her head towards him and smiled her sweet, mild smile, reminding herself at the same time that she must flirt well with him or all was lost.

"I am so glad to see you, sir," she began, "and especially to have an opportunity to thank you for your many kindnesses." Though the baronet showed not the least interest in being thanked, she went on in this way for quite some time, mentioning good Mrs. Cafferleigh, his own heroism and hospitality, and enlarging upon these themes at length.

The squire interjected an occasional grunt, and now and then a characteristic "Hah!" but said nothing of any note. He would have liked to turn the conversation, but could not think of anything to say, so instead he merely began to set out the chess pieces on a small table drawn up to her bedside for that purpose. When at last she paused for breath, he broke in saying, "Shall we play, madam?"

"O yes, indeed! Chess is so amusing, don't you think?"

"Eh, what's that? Amusing. Hah!" said he. He had given her the white pieces, and sat waiting for her to make her first move, but she only rattled on about the weather. At last he interrupted again, and begged her to begin.

"O, is it my go first?" she inquired innocently.

The squire indicated the board. Mercy, though she did not know why, understood that she was indeed to begin, and moved a pawn forward. The baronet snorted and countered.

To Prudence's great relief, the game was successfully begun. She remembered suddenly, and with a tiny gasp, that she had never instructed her sister to be silent during the game, and was much afraid that Mercy might chatter on aimlessly all through it. As it happened, however, Mercy became very quiet once they started, and looked quite appropriately absorbed in the moves. In fact, Prudence noted (with agreeable surprise), she fairly frowned with concentration. Reassured, Prudence sat back and opened her work-box, and found some embroidery she had begun long ago and long since forgot. The bed-chamber gradually sank into utter silence, and remained so for many hours. During this time, the elder Miss Deverell somehow nodded off to sleep—how, she could never tell—and when she opened her eyes again it was on hearing a triumphant, sharp "Checkmate!" from her sister.

"Eh? What's that?" the baronet barked immediately. "It's no such thing, I'll lay wager—" He leaned forward, scrutinising the board. "I don't—damme, she's really done it!" he exclaimed at last, too startled to be displeased. "Well, I'd never have guessed it in a million years."

Prudence, rapidly taking in the situation, sat helpless in incredulous dismay. What on earth had Mercy done? But before she could think of something to say, the squire was up on his feet, extending a hand to Mercy and shaking hers vigorously.

"I never thought a woman could beat me," he said, with evident approval. "Never thought anyone could beat me," he added. "Congratulations, Miss Mercy, you're a fine player."

Mercy, almost as astonished at her victory as anyone else, accepted his tribute with a blush and a humble, "I hope you enjoyed the game, sir."

"Enjoyed it very much, very much," said the squire, who (being a just man at heart) admired ability in anyone wherever he found it. "Have a game with you tomorrow if you like."

Mercy was about to answer, but Prudence, horrified at the thought of further humiliations for the old man, interjected, "O no, I think it has been abominably tiring for my sister. Aren't you tired, dear?"

"If you say, Prue—" Mercy began dubiously.

"She ain't tired!" Sir Proctor growled. "Look at her—her cheeks are glowing like a baby's. And very pretty cheeks, too," he added with a bow.

Mercy, unspeakably pleased, only coloured more deeply.

"Tomorrow, then, madam," said the squire; "and good night to you both for now." It was a great satisfaction to him to find a player who could challenge him: his son never would attend to the game closely enough, and consequently always lost. With a feeling of pleasurable anticipation of the morrow—which he had not felt for a long time—he bowed again smartly to the ladies, and withdrew. Prudence began to speak as soon as he shut the door.

"What have you done?" she demanded. "How could you have won?"

Mercy shrugged her shoulders. "I am not certain," she said, "but there is a game I play, Prue, with the cats. I never mentioned it to you, as it seems too silly, but I play it in my head all the time. It has to do with which cat will sit where, and so forth. If I put Muffin here, which means Snowflake will take her kittens away, where will Tiger go? Things like that, you see. Anyway, this chess is very much like my game. Easier, in fact. I suppose I won because of that," she ended, shrugging again. "Was it very dreadful of me to win? I know you did not mean for me to," she asked anxiously.

Prudence looked at her, hard put for what to say. On the one hand, things had turned out amazingly well; on the other, they had not followed her plans. As a matter of policy, she could not approve anything that went contrary to her schemes; but still . . . She finally told Mercy she had done her best, and that was as much as anybody could ask. A little while later they had supper, and sat up chatting with Mrs. Cafferleigh for a bit. Quite early in the evening, as was the routine at Colworth Park, Prudence took to her bed, kissing Mercy first, of course, and directing her to sleep well. Mercy made sure to carry out this instruction precisely.

The inhabitants of Sweet's Folly retired, as a rule, somewhat later than those of Colworth. Honoria had emerged briefly from her room at tea-time but disappeared again shortly afterwards, having agreed with all her mother-in-law's suggestions concerning the choice and placement of furnishings for Stonebur Cottage. To Dr. Blackwood's enquiry whether she might be ready to take up residence there herself at the end of the week, she replied with a nod and a rather indifferent "Certainly." Alex had not come down to tea, after all, and so he took no part in these decisions. Honor, murmuring something about a headache, asked to take supper in her room, to which retreat she presently retired. Her fury with herself had subsided into a dull dissatisfaction, which yet unsettled her so that she could not sleep, and she lay awake whispering to Amber until well past midnight. At about one o'clock, a new thought occurred to her; she debated with herself for a while, then rose and robed herself in a ribboned matinee. Taking a candle, she crept silently out of her room and through the darkened halls of Sweet's Folly to the kitchens. Still later she appeared again, bearing the candle and a glass, at the door to Alexander's study. She knocked but received no answer. Hesitantly, she set the candle down at her feet and turned the knob, opening the door just slightly and peeking in.

Her husband sat staring at a paper on his desk, his soft blond hair twisted through the long fingers that supported his head on either side. Evidently he was deep in thought, for he did not notice her even now. Leaving the candle behind (for the study was adequately illuminated by several lamps and a moribund fire), she advanced several paces into the room. Still, Alex did not look up. For a moment she stood silently, the warm tumbler in her hand, gazing at his fine, clear features and admiring the gracefulness of his neck, bent now in an attitude of heedless absorption. The red light of the dying fire created a glow that his fair hair caught and reflected, rendering him more handsome than she had ever seen him. At once she felt envious of the papers that so captured his attention, and wished hopelessly that his regard might someday be focused as powerfully on herself. Thinking this, she sighed, and the sigh—for some reason—penetrated his concentration and shattered it.

Inordinately startled, he looked up abruptly and dropped his hands at the same moment, covering the papers with them awkwardly. His surprise communicated itself immediately to her, and she suddenly felt cumbersome and foolish, standing in the middle of his study in the dead of night, a glass of warm milk in her hands. She forgot what she meant to say, and blurted out, "I brought you some milk. Here—" She set it on the desk with a conscious, jerky motion, spilling some of the warm liquid. Alex looked at it. "I thought you might like it," she went on. "I thought you might be tense, with all your work. It will relax you."

Alexander, smiling now that he understood what had made him start, said, "Thank you. Isn't it terribly late for you, Honoria?"

She interpreted this immediately as a reproach, and spoke defensively. "I suppose I may keep what hours I like."

"Indeed, of course," he replied in mild accents. "It is only—goodness, you startled me!" he exclaimed suddenly, recognising again how oddly he had jumped, as if there were something to be afraid of in Sweet's Folly. "I was so lost in what I was doing," he began, gesturing widely at the papers before him, "I suppose I never expected—no one ever comes in, you see—"

Alexander was trying to explain to her the reason of his unnatural surprise at her entrance, so that she would not feel offended by it. She, however, misunderstood him utterly, and supposed his words were meant to rebuke her, and to caution her not to repeat such a foolish act. Consequently, she shrank towards the door and stood poised on the threshold, intent upon removing herself from his sight as soon as possible. "I shan't do it again," she said, in a low voice. "Good night."

"But it was very kind in you—" he commenced. Unfortunately, Honoria had run away, and could not hear him for the despairing sobs that were already breaking from her. More miserable even than before, she gained her room again and flung herself under the covers, scaring poor Amber half to death. The frightened kitten leapt off the bed and scrambled to the farthest corner, whence he watched with round eyes as his mistress wept and sighed. For many minutes this scene continued; it did not cease till Honoria, still wretched but exhausted, wearily extinguished her candle and went to sleep at last.

Chapter VI

Emily drew her sister-in-law to a far corner of the drawing-room and spoke in a fierce whisper: "I never was more mortified in my life," she said. "What on earth does my father think to do?"

"I am afraid that is only too clear," Honoria replied. "My question is, what does Mr. Kemp mean to do? His behaviour has been simply too vile! I can scarcely credit it."

"Nor I, but it is my father who amazes me more. I declare, I may never speak to him again," she hissed, with a mutinous look at the company in general. The two women were not at liberty to continue this private colloquy for long; Mrs. Blackwood soon interrupted them, taking Honoria by the hand and requesting her to play a bit on the pianoforte to entertain Mrs. Drinkwater. Mrs. Drinkwater, a childless matron of uncertain years, who had been the Blackwoods' neighbour for decades, heartily seconded this proposal, and Honoria was obliged to comply. Without warning, she broke into a vigorous rendition of Beethoven's *Sonate Pathétique*, a choleric composition that she normally reserved for occasions when no one could hear her. Now, however, she was so angered by what had passed at dinner that she did not care at all whether the ladies knew it or not.

"The ladies" consisted only of Mrs. Blackwood, Mrs. Drinkwater, Emily, and herself. Dinner had just recently ended, and the four women had removed themselves to the drawing-room as was usual on such occasions, to amuse themselves while the gentlemen smoked and drank at table. The family party were joined this afternoon by three guests—Captain and Mrs. Drinkwater, and Mr. Claude Kemp— because Dr. Blackwood meant to give the repast a slightly festive air. It was to be Honoria's and Alexander's last dinner at Sweet's Folly; to-morrow they would take up residence at Stonebur Cottage. Such an

event in the life of his family seemed to Dr. Blackwood to call for
some little celebration, and so the guests had been invited. Squire
Kemp had been asked as well, but had declined to attend. His son
therefore arrived alone.

What had so outraged Miss Blackwood in her father's behaviour
was this: Dr. Blackwood was eager for his daughter to marry. He knew
dimly that there had once been some question of Claude's offering for
Honoria, but quite reasonably assumed, in light of recent develop-
ments, that that possibility was now obsolete and forgotten. Therefore he saw no cause why Mr. Kemp might not be interested in his
daughter, and was resolved to do everything possible to throw the two
of them together. He directed his wife to seat them next one another
at the dinner-table, which she did, and took every opportunity of in-
timating to one or the other of them that they might be romantically
linked. Unfortunately, his hints were a bit broad. They were far too
obvious, in fact, to escape Claude's subtle powers of observation, and
they were entirely distinct to Emily. In Claude they evoked a vague
amusement; in Emily, the fury that now caused her to look so mur-
derous.

There was worse, however, and this was what so concerned Honoria. Dr. Blackwood had assumed Claude's intentions towards her
were obsolete and forgotten. In this he was only partially correct: they
were obsolete, of course—but they were hardly forgotten. On the contrary, Claude had never ceased to entertain plans for winning Honor's
confidence and her love. The inevitable result, that this would also
sully her virtue and render her life miserable, troubled him not a
whit. Once having set his sights on an object, Mr. Kemp never faltered in its pursuit, and that fact had become excessively clear to
Honoria tonight. For instead of responding to Dr. Blackwood's hints,
and treating Emily attentively—instead even of ignoring his host and
persisting in a neutral position—Mr. Claude Kemp had displayed the
most unmistakable interest in Honoria herself, under the very noses of
her husband and his family.

She sat opposite to him at table, next Alexander, and all during the
meal Claude did not cease to shower upon her a veritable flood of
kindnesses, gallantries, and flirtatious observations. Honoria was delightful, she was so witty, she struck one by her beauty more than any
young woman in the neighbourhood—did not Alexander agree? For it
was this that was most outrageous of all: these remarks were not
addressed solely to Honoria, but to Alex as well. Poor Alex, still terribly uncomfortable beside his bride, and distracted anyway by the so-

lution of a particular geometrical enigma, seemed neither to notice nor to care what impertinent comments were made regarding his wife. He said nothing at all unless pressed to do so. When at length Mr. Kemp would check his flow of remarks to ask, "Don't you agree, Alexander? Is it not so?" Alex could think of nothing better to say than yes. Consequently, Honoria had been subjected all through dinner to the most humiliating attack of improper flirtation imaginable, while her husband sat by doing nothing. Recalling this, she struck the ivory keys with all the force of her pent-up rage.

It was the more frustrating because she saw what Dr. Blackwood wished Claude to do—that is, she saw that Emily was meant to be the object of this extraordinary attention, and that instead her friend was soundly ignored. Except for asking her once for butter, and once for a confirmation of Honoria's charms, Mr. Kemp said absolutely nothing to her during the whole repast. Dr. Blackwood, in no case a perceptive man, and on this occasion somewhat blinded by wine, remained entirely unaware of this impossible situation, and continually made it more painful by calling out gay encouragements to the animated Claude. All in all, it was the most dreadful repast either young woman had ever taken, and it was with the utmost relief that both fled to the drawing-room at its end.

Mrs. Drinkwater and her hostess were both somewhat startled at the violence with which Honoria played the pianoforte, but they made nothing of it and thanked her for her performance just the same. Honoria rose from the little stool feeling slightly calmed by this release of her inflamed emotions, and immediately resumed her seat beside Emily. "Shall we walk up and down the room a bit?" she asked her in a low voice.

Miss Blackwood consented and the two women, side by side, began to pace rather rapidly the length of the drawing-room. "I assure you, I did all I could to make him stop," said Honor, a little fearful lest her friend think she was pleased by Claude's attentions.

"I am certain you did," said Emily. "I always said Claude was a boor. Do you recall what I told you when you considered marrying him? The most conceited, despicable—and I believe I mentioned he seemed sinister to me—well, now I am sure of it. We have proof in abundance, in fact."

"Proof?" Honoria inquired, still hoping for the best.

"If he does not mean to destroy your marriage with Alex, I am not an artist and my father is not a fool. It is only too clear."

"Emmy, really, you must not think your father a fool merely because—"

But Emily cut her off with a virulent, "Nonsense! My father makes a cake of himself, of me, and of Alexander—not that Alexander needed any assistance." Her tone changed slightly as she added, "I knew my brother was a child, but I had no notion he was so feeble as all that! If I had, I promise you I should never have suggested your marriage to him. You were far better off in Bench Street: at least there you were free to defend yourself from Claude, instead of being obliged to place yourself in the hands of such a powerless protector as my miserable brother. I am very, very sorry. I gave you false counsel."

"Emily, I pray—! Do not say so, please. You may regret your hand in the affair, but I am not at all sorry to be—to be my husband's wife. It is painful, yes, at times—and I do not see what will come of it all just now—but far better to be married to him than not—far better!"

Honoria's voice was so soft and pleading as she said these words, so entirely sincere and passionate, that Emily looked up at her and scrutinised her eyes with the full force of her perceptiveness. What she saw there surprised her, but was undeniable: young Mrs. Blackwood had fallen in love with her husband. For what cause, Emily could not possibly have said, but she was too clear-sighted not to see it, and too pragmatic to ignore it. When she spoke again her voice was altered, and her words flowed less freely: "I am glad to know it," she said hesitantly. "I apologise for not having guessed before. You are a wonderful woman, Honoria, and I admire you more than I ever did before."

Honoria was spared the necessity of replying to this praise by the sudden entrance of the gentlemen into the room. Dr. Blackwood and the rather simple Captain Drinkwater, long a drinking companion of the physician's, were evidently a trifle foxed at least. Mr. Kemp was flushed, but exhibited his inebriation in no other manner. Alexander was quiet and withdrawn, as usual. Looking about himself absently, he spied an unoccupied hassock in a remote corner of the drawing-room, and seated himself there alone. He did not stir from this position during the whole of the next hour. Dr. Blackwood, even more jovial than when he visited his patients, pulled a chair up to where his wife and Mrs. Drinkwater sat, and set about flirting mildly with that middle-aged lady, in inoffensive and good-humoured style. His wife, accustomed to such displays of playfulness when her husband was in his cups, was not in the least disturbed, but rather turned calmly to Captain Drinkwater and engaged him in a discussion of Napoleon's present whereabouts. Captain Drinkwater, though retired from the army, had never ceased to concern himself about England's military and political position, and he answered her questions and suggestions

with ardent enthusiasm. All of which left Claude perfectly at liberty
to attach himself to the young ladies, which he did directly, harassing
them almost beyond toleration.

"Your Aunt Mercy displays the most astonishing talent for chess,"
he informed Honoria conversationally. "I understand, though, that
Miss Prudence does not play at all. I trust it was you who partnered
her in Bench Street, clever as you are?"

"No, sir, I did not," Honor returned evenly. She felt she was acting
very rudely in saying no more on that point, but Emily's predicament
swayed her and she immediately turned to her friend saying, "You
must let me come back to Sweet's Folly some time soon, so I may sit
for you again. I am frightfully eager to see how my portrait will be
finished: I know it will be very true—"

"And consequently very beautiful," Claude interrupted. Honoria
was most dismayed by this interjection, for she thought she had hit
upon a topic to which he would have nothing to say. Taking a deep
breath, she tried again.

"My husband is half-way through his monograph," she began,
addressing Emily again. "He hinted once he might let me edit it—not
the mathematics, of course, but the grammar and so forth. I should be
so glad to think I had a hand in it somehow."

"I am sure you have already had a hand in it," Claude said wick-
edly, since he knew what he said was extremely unlikely to be true.
"No husband could fail to be inspired by a wife such as yourself."

Honoria, aware of his unpleasant intention in saying this—for she
was too shrewd to imagine he had not noticed Alex's utter disregard
of her—blushed deeply and said nothing.

"I have frequently felt the same," Emily said, and though this was
known by all three of them to be perfectly false, even ridiculous, she
said it with such pride and dignity that the subject was let drop.

"I hope my aunt is well?" Honor said, when the silence that had
ensued among them at last became unbearable. "It seemed to me her
colour was not quite what it once was, when I visited yesterday," she
added, for she had indeed gone to call on Mercy almost every day
since the accident. Mr. Kemp had, of course, taken advantage of these
visits to pursue his friendship with her—and he had sometimes become
insolent, she thought—but he had never been so brazen and offensive
as he had shown himself tonight in front of Alex. Not the least of
Honor's worries was that Alex might think his wife willingly permitted
Mr. Kemp to take such liberties with her, and refrained from inter-
vening in deference to her supposed feelings. Her common sense,
however, told her that it was more likely Alexander simply had not

noticed Claude's untoward conduct, and though this reflection was small comfort, it was something.

"She improves daily," Mr. Kemp now assured her. "I believe I shall have the honour of conveying her back to Bench Street tomorrow or the following day. My father seems to have taken quite a fancy to her, by the by; it must be an affinity in the blood of the two families," he closed, staring at her with an intense, admiring expression.

"I am sure I do not know," Honor murmured weakly. The threesome again lapsed into silence. They continued thus—brief spurts of conversation followed by periods of wordlessness, during which time Claude never failed to gaze rapturously and ardently at Honoria—for about an hour, at which time Dr. Blackwood proposed billiards to the male company, and the four men once more left the ladies. This time both Emily and her friend were too absorbed in their own musings to converse much: Honor resumed her place at the pianoforte, playing a few rather melancholy airs by Bach, while Emily sat listening, her hands folded loosely in her lap. When the gentlemen returned it was almost dusk. Mrs. Blackwood offered them tea, but Captain Drinkwater thought it wise to depart before night fell completely, and Mr. Kemp was more or less obliged to follow his lead by agreeing with the wisdom of this. When the guests were gone at last, the family retired severally to different parts of Sweet's Folly, each with his own concerns and sentiments, and did not meet again until supper. Honor took to her bedroom early, for the following day she was to move to Stonebur, and she would need her rest.

Meantime, at Colworth, Mercy Deverell's health was improving with what seemed to her sister to be alarming rapidity. "If only that nasty Charles Blackwood would not be so loud and cheerful about your progress," she complained sourly, "Sir Proctor would have no idea of your mending so well. As it is, he will expect us to take our leave at any moment. O, do not try to walk, Mercy," she added, as she noticed her sister trying her ankle gingerly. "You will only make matters worse."

Reluctantly, for as her health improved she had begun to grow restless, Mercy sank back again into the pillows. "Dear Prue," she began timidly, after a moment, "are you certain matters are really so bleak? They do not appear so to me—"

"Much though I love you, my pet," her sister replied, with rather more candour than usual, "you have never distinguished yourself by the penetration of your mind. Pray do not concern yourself with assessing our success thus far; I can do that alone more than adequately."

Much less discouragement than this would have sufficed to silence Mercy. With a fretful pout, she turned her attention to the pattern embroidered into the edge of her bed-linens, tracing her finger along the intricate design. After several minutes had passed, Prudence addressed her again.

"Of course, you are not to blame, my love," she said, "but your acquaintanceship with Kemp is not at all what I hoped it would be. You were meant to win his heart; instead, you are become a sort of playmate, a companion who might as well be a man as a woman. I know men: the only way to persuade them to act generously is to incite in them that state of temporary madness called love. They are friendly to their friends, but they do not do favours for them as women do. No," she added, shaking her grey head firmly, "it will not answer. You must endeavour again to win his affections, Mercy. You must attempt to seduce him."

"I must?" asked Mercy, with a gasp of surprise.

"For our small friends," the other returned solemnly.

"That is all very well for you to say, Prue," Mercy began petulantly, but stopped as she saw the look of righteous wrath that had begun to cloud her sister's face. After a very little more discussion between them, it was settled. When Squire Kemp arrived that evening to play his customary game of chess with Miss Mercy, Prudence would quit the room on a pretext and leave them alone. From that time, it was up to Mercy to employ all her wiles to provoke and secure his tenderest regard.

Consequently, just as twilight fell on the wintry landscape outside, Miss Prudence Deverell rose from her embroidery and announced to her sister and the squire that she begged to be excused, but there was some correspondence she simply must attend to in her own room. The squire, his whole attention concentrated on the chess board, merely nodded absently in answer. Prudence left the room, pausing at the door to make a silent gesture to her anxious sister, a gesture that was intended both to reassure her and to urge her to battle. Then she left.

Mercy permitted a few more minutes to pass by quietly, but when the squire at last made his move, she uttered a pitiful "O!" and put a hand to her forehead as if something troubled her. The squire, still intent on the board, said nothing. "O!" Mercy repeated, this time more audibly.

"Is something the matter?" Sir Proctor asked finally.

"O, I am—it is nothing, I suppose," she murmured, with a charming, rather mournful smile.

Proctor Kemp appeared satisfied with this explanation and seemed about to resume his thoughts about his remaining bishop. To prevent this, Mercy again cried, "O!" aloud, and this time put both her hands to her forehead.

"What is it, eh?" he inquired. "Foot troubling you?"

With the same mournful smile, she gazed dolefully at him and shook her head softly. "Sir Proctor," she commenced in a faint voice, "Sir Proctor . . ." Hardly knowing where she found the courage, she put a frail hand out to him and touched his arm gently. Her hand immobile on his sleeve, she whispered, "It is so long since I had a friend I could trust, I hardly know how to begin. But may I—my dear sir, may I speak to you as a friend? May I presume so upon your goodness?"

The elderly gentleman, not a little surprised, merely stared back at the fragile woman who so importuned him.

"You are so—so strong, dear sir, and kind. You ask if there is something troubling me: I must admit—in confidence, of course—that there is." Then, with a sudden graceful turn of her silvery head, she withdrew her hand and continued apologetically, "But I must not burden you with my sorrows. They are mine to bear alone, as they always have been. Forgive me for speaking."

She had succeeded in rousing his curiosity, and he answered, "Now, now, my dear madam, if there is anything I can put right, you must tell me. Eh?"

Smiling tremulously at him, Mercy replied, "You are all kindness, all kindness! But no, there is nothing to be done. I only thought perhaps if I might confide my poor worries to someone, perhaps the load would seem lighter. No, nothing could be done," she murmured gently, allowing her voice to fade away.

Sir Proctor said nothing.

Miss Mercy permitted a single tear to course down her careworn cheek.

Sir Proctor entreated her to rely upon his confidence and share her woes with him.

Miss Mercy relented. "O sir, since you are so good, I do not know how to refuse you. It is my sister, sir, my poor, dear sister!"

"Your sister—?" the squire prompted.

"Yes, yes," she went on, in a faltering voice. "She is—she had always been my everything, my all—my one companion and dearest friend, you see—and now—!"

"And now—?" he urged again.

"And now she grows so old!" Mercy wailed piteously. "She loses her memory, forgets the simplest things—it is natural, of course, but you see, sir, when Prudence believes she is right, and finds herself contradicted—O, she gets so very cross! She shouts at me and is harsh, harsh—!" Her voice broke on a sob. As if struggling to maintain her composure, she breathed rapidly a few times and continued at last, "So, you see, it is often very hard on me. Prudence says we must have supper—I reply that we just did have supper—she says but of course we did not (for she has forgot it entirely) and I am obliged either to submit to her temper or to go and fetch supper all over again. It is very very hard. When Honoria was with us, it was better, for then I had another witness as it were. But now, I am all alone with her, and bear the brunt of her anger." She lapsed into silence once more, tracing again the design of the embroidered edging. "You are very good to listen to me," she said, finally looking up with a smile, and laying her hand over his. The charming, mournful smile once more appeared on her countenance as she concluded, "But, you see, there is nothing to be done."

Sir Proctor, an eminently practical man, was not quite convinced that this was so. Miss Mercy's plight seemed to him uncomfortable, but her tears and sighings did not strike him as picturesque. Consequently, he spoke to her as he might have to anyone who had come to him with a problem, and since he was magistrate of the district, people did frequently bring their grievances to him. In the brisk, terse language of common sense, he said, "Seems to me you might easily overcome such a difficulty. Why don't you hire a companion, somebody young like your niece? She'll keep peace between you."

By the tone of his voice, poor Mercy realized immediately that she had failed to evoke any tender passion in the gentleman. The situation she had confessed to him was pure fabrication: if anything, it was Mercy who forgot things and Prudence who recalled them. However, it seemed to her that if her tale were true, what the squire suggested would be precisely the most reasonable, direct, and practical solution. Though she wondered how she had failed to move him, she admired his immediate grasp of the imaginary situation. Her intention to appear pathetic having proven quite useless, she replied in the same calm, businesslike tones he had used, "Thank you, sir. I see, you are very right. That would be the simplest answer, indeed! I wonder I never thought of it."

The squire took her hand, which was still resting gently on his own, and shook it briskly. "There—if you played chess as foolishly as you managed your life, I wouldn't have a partner, now would I?" Since he had in fact grown quite fond of her, there was no hint of annoyance in his voice; on the contrary, he spoke very kindly. He restored her hand to her adroitly and dismissed the entire episode from his mind at once. "It's your go," he reminded her, adding craftily, "I shouldn't be so sure of my knight, if I were you, Miss Mercy!"

And so the game continued from where it had been left off. Prudence, who entered Mercy's room as soon as the squire quitted it several hours later, was excessively displeased by her sister's account of what had passed.

"I promise you, I looked just as pretty and pleading as possible," Mercy defended herself. "He simply did not care for it."

Prudence frowned with disapprobation. "Now he will think I forget things, in addition to all our other difficulties. This is very bad, Mercy. He will be all the more inclined to think my hospital scheme merely the whim of an infirm mind. I cannot like it."

"Well, I am very sorry—" Mercy began, with more than a touch of plaintiveness, but her elder sister interrupted her.

"Never mind now, shhh, please! I must think of another scheme." And refusing either to forgive Mercy or to scold her, she sat quite still in severe silence for many minutes, debating and deciding within herself.

Stonebur Cottage, if anyone had had high hopes of it (and Dr. Blackwood had at least), must be confessed to have proved a disappointment. It had been the physician's expectation that his son and daughter-in-law, once isolated within its sturdy walls, would become better acquainted with one another and make of their marriage what a marriage should be. Unhappily, the first night of their residence there was very inauspicious, indeed, and extremely disagreeable both to Alex and to Honoria.

The cottage, though it was called so, was really not a cottage at all, but rather a cottage *ornée*—which is to say, a house of substantial size masquerading as a peasant's dwelling. Sheltered from the road by a fair lawn and a low stone fence, the house was situated very pleasantly at no great distance from Sweet's Folly. The downstairs consisted of two small kitchens, one rather large bed-room, and a dining-parlour. Upstairs were the drawing-room—or rather, parlour—a tiny library, and a sitting-room that contained a pianoforte. Above this were four very small chambers with sloped ceilings; these were the servants' quarters. French doors opened from the back of the dining-room onto a pretty, terraced garden; a meadow lay beyond. Mrs. Stonebur's sense of elegance was not much above the common, but she had evidenced reasonable taste in her choice of carpets and draperies, and not much had had to be altered before the Blackwoods moved in. The cottage was above all cheerful, with large windows everywhere and a pleasant southern exposure in most of the principal rooms. Honoria had, of course, seen it—as everyone in Pittering had seen everything in Pittering—but she had never been inside until after her marriage, and it struck her as a quite delightful place. Alexander, previous to their moving, had also expressed his satisfaction with it, and so one might think that their first evening there would be passed tolerably well.

However, it was not. They had dined at Sweet's Folly—another fare-well celebration—and did not find themselves alone at Stonebur until well past six o'clock. Emily and Honoria, despite the fact that they were sure to see one another nearly every day, and were now in closer proximity to each other than when Honor had lived in Bench Street, had exchanged quite a tearful good-by. The elder Blackwoods took leave of the couple rather more calmly, though one might have ob-served a tear in Mrs. Blackwood's eye as she embraced her son. Alex-ander, as usual, appeared not to know what was happening, and said good-by affably when he was told to. A small, neat carriage and pair, which had been a belated wedding-present to the couple from the doctor, bore them away to Stonebur, driven by a man named Wattles who was to function as coachman, ostler, and general odd-jobs man for them. The drive was very brief, and neither Alex nor Honor felt the need of making much conversation; it was when they had been admitted into their new abode that the discomfort began.

They were let into the house by Mr. and Mrs. Traubin, who had been engaged several weeks previously to share between them the duties of butler, housekeeper, and cook. Both these good people wel-comed their master and mistress profusely, though they had all seen one another upwards of a score of times during the bustle of the past se'ennight. Mrs. Traubin, though otherwise a pleasant enough woman, had rather a fishy look about her eyes that made Honor nervous. Traubin, middle-aged like his wife, seemed to make a study of appear-ing utterly noncommittal and bland, a thing that he did to perfection. They were ushered from the foyer up the carpeted stairs, and begged to wait in the parlour while tea was prepared for them. "For I'm sure you've had a day of it, ma'am; I'm sure you have," Mrs. Traubin told her with a curtsey, "and a cup of tea is always just what's wanting." Honoria was grateful for her kindness, but she could not bear to look long into those wide, watery eyes, and she was glad when the Trau-bins disappeared again.

Unfortunately, their departure left the young Blackwoods alone. For a moment, both stood near the doorway, looking round the room as if to get acquainted with it. Then Honor chose an armchair near the fireplace, and started towards it. At the same instant, Alex also chose that armchair and approached it. They bumped into one another in the middle of the room, and both jumped back, apologizing and smiling strained smiles. Honoria was uncomfortably conscious that such a ridiculous accident would never have occurred if she and Alex dared to look directly at each other more frequently. For several seconds they stood together wordlessly, each gesturing at the chair as if to invite the other to sit down. In the end, neither of them took it, and they settled opposite one another on wooden chairs that looked, and were in fact, much less agreeable than the disputed one.

In short while it became necessary to say something.

"What a cheerful fire that is!" Honor remarked, looking into the blaze. "How good of the Traubins to think of it."

"Yes, very cheerful," said Alex, nodding at it and stretching his hands out towards the grate with an exaggerated gesture. "Warm, too," he added, smiling.

"O, very warm, I'm sure," Honor replied, and wondered how it was that she never ever was reduced to such inanities, except with her husband. "And tea in a moment! So very kind of them. Just what one needs with all this wet." For it had continued grey and rainy for above a month now.

"O yes, tea is the perfect beverage," said Alex. "It has indeed been very wet. Cold, too."

Conversation wavered between high points such as this one and low points where nothing was said at all between them for minutes together, until finally tea had come, and had been drunk, and had been cleared, and had been forgot. Honoria, pasting a bright smile on her unwilling lips, felt it time at last to rise and she stood, saying, "I must go and tidy my things. Do remember, won't you, supper at eight-thirty."

"O yes, supper," said he amiably. "We shall want it by then, won't we? I'll go off and have a look round the library again. My desk must be set in order if I am to work tonight."

The two of them left the parlour, Honoria reflecting that although it was most discouraging to know her husband meant to work tonight as usual, it was probably a good deal better than if he knew no way of distracting himself at all. She descended the stairs and turned into the bed-chamber, which contained among other things one very large, postered bed, and one rather narrow couch. She had been aware there was only one bed-room in Stonebur Cottage from the first, and the thought of what that meant had troubled her all during the move, but on each occasion of its recurrence she had reminded herself severely that they must face up to this facet of marriage sooner or later, and it was probably better to do so sooner. Alexander had said nothing about having to share a chamber with her as yet, so she assumed that he must have no objection, at least. In this she was not quite correct.

The hours they spent apart from one another that evening passed industriously and quickly enough. They met for supper at eight-thirty in the dining-parlour, to engage in a conversation that was so obviously stilted and awkward that the fact of Traubin's witnessing most of it quite embarrassed poor Honor. After supper Mrs. Traubin suggested coffee in the parlour, and they accordingly reentered that apartment together. The next half-hour, with nothing to do but sip coffee, and conversation utterly impossible, seemed to Honor the most tedious of her whole life. How things would get better, she did not know, but get better they must, she thought.

"Alexander," she said at last, introducing an intimate topic more from despair than from daring, "do you mean to sit up late to work, as you did at Sweet's Folly?"

"I had intended to," said he obligingly, "but if there is any thing you would prefer—"

"O no, you must do your work, of course. But it occurs to me to tell you—in case you should like to know—that I can sleep quite well with a candle lit, or a lamp. What I mean is, I shall probably be asleep already by the time you come—you come to bed"—she said these last words in a faltering, dying whisper—"and you might be afraid to disturb me when you enter. But you are very unlikely to—you see . . ." Her words hesitated and halted.

"Have we but one bed-chamber then?" asked Alex, as if surprised. "But this is very bad; I shall be certain to inconvenience you, no matter what you say. Poor Honor! How kind you are to pretend it doesn't matter—"

"But it doesn't!" said she, horrified at the thought of what he might say next. "It doesn't at all!"

"But it must," he insisted. "I shall sleep upstairs, with the servants."

"You can't," she gasped, adding lamely, "There are only just rooms enough for them as it is."

"Then I shall stay right here," said he cheerfully, patting a cushion of the sofa on which he sat as if to try its firmness. "I've often thought I should like to sleep on a sofa," he went on, with a gallant smile.

"But no—Alexander, please! Whatever should Mrs. Traubin think?" These words escaped her without her quite meaning to say them.

"Well, I don't think she would think of it at all," he began.

"Please, I beg of you," she broke in. "It—it distresses me too much."

Alex, perceiving at last that her dismay was real, agreed to sleep in the bed-chamber. "But I shan't wake you up by climbing into—no, no. There is a couch in there, is there not? I shall sleep there," he said firmly.

This seemed so vastly preferable to the alternatives he had suggested that she agreed to it with alacrity. They parted again, Alex to do his work, Honoria to become familiar with the kitchens, and to make the acquaintance of the fourth servant, a young girl named Maria who was to help out everywhere. She would have liked to play on the pianoforte, but was afraid this would disturb her husband, and at last decided to retire at eleven o'clock. Alex came in some two hours later. She was awake, but dared not say anything to him, so she shut her eyes tightly and tried to breathe evenly. A few minutes after he had entered, she was aware of a red glow inside her eyelids, as if someone held a candle before her face, but she was afraid of further awkwardness with her husband and still pretended to sleep.

In a moment the glow disappeared. It had been Alex, cautiously holding a candle aloft to illuminate his wife's sweet countenance. He had wished to see her once more that night. However, Honoria had no means of knowing this.

Chapter VII

"Good riddance to the both of them," Sir Proctor muttered gruffly to Boothby, who stood waiting in the doorway for permission to leave his master.

Mr. Boothby bowed.

"The lot of them, I should say," the baronet continued. "Dogs, females . . . Hah! Like to turn this household on its ears, that's what."

Mr. Boothby bowed again.

"But you say they're quite gone?" Sir Proctor demanded.

"Quite gone, sir."

"And the carriage we sent them home in? Has it returned?"

"Not yet, sir."

"Well, let me know when it has," said the squire. "I won't rest easy till I know. Pack of screaming females . . . idiotic. Not keeping a carriage, either—what are they about? Madness, not keeping a carriage. Every tradesman's wife in Pittering keeps a carriage!"

"I believe the Deverells' circumstances are somewhat straitened," Mr. Boothby said patiently, thinking briefly of the dinner waiting for him in the kitchen. It seemed to him Sir Proctor was making even more of a fuss over the departure of the guests than he had over their arrival, a fact that struck him as odd, at first. A little reflection, however, resulted in a strong suspicion that the baronet—despite his testy professions of relief—was rather sorry to see the sisters leave. Poor man! He'd made such a nasty old institution of himself; no doubt he felt positively embarrassed at discovering a taste for company. These charitable thoughts on Mr. Boothby's part were rudely interrupted by their subject.

"Well, then, go on, go on, can't you? Off about your business, man! You may have all day to loiter about chatting, but I certainly have not. Hah! Rascals and rogues," the old gentleman expostulated, while Boothby made his most obsequious bow and disappeared. Left alone, Sir Proctor cleared his throat. "Chess at tea-time, doggies in the parlour . . . enough to make a well man sick," he said disgustedly, for the benefit of no one in particular. He continued to mutter complaints for several minutes, and indeed took up the refrain once more when word was brought him that the borrowed carriage had been returned. He really was quite lonely.

The borrowers of that coach, meantime, were in the midst of a most happy return to their home in Bench Street. Miss Prudence had once absented herself from Colworth Park to visit her dear small friends, but Mercy, of course, had been unable to do so. Consequently, though the sight of her beloved house alone was enough to bring tears to her eyes, her reunion with its furry occupants was enough to make nearly anyone cry.

"O, my dear Zeus!" cried she to the sheep-dog who jumped on her first. "And Apollo, and Pandora! Niobe! (Some three years before this time the Deverell sisters had grown tired of thinking of names for their pets, and had called them all after mythological figures. They had grown weary of that, too, within five or six months, and had returned to more traditional methods.) Come and kiss your poor auntie! O, yes, please do." She opened her frail arms to all of them, kneeling on the floor, and rose only when Prudence reminded her there were the cats to be said hello to as well. Then she went into the tiny parlour, and kissed every feline in turn.

"Ah, my dear sister! Muffin has got quite fat! Look how fat Muffin has got!" she exclaimed similarly on each cat and kitten to Prudence, who was also engaged in greeting and caressing all members of the menagerie.

"Did I kiss Tiger?" Mercy asked, after nearly half an hour of this. "I think I did kiss Tiger. I think I kissed them all, the darling soft things. O, I could kiss them again, all day. I declare I did not know till this moment how much I missed them."

Prudence, though she was enjoying her home-coming almost as much as her sister, settled herself on the ancient Confidante and invited Miss Mercy to do the same. "For you can't go on saying hello all day," she said, "even though you would like to. We've work to do, you know," she added rather sternly.

Mercy sighed a little and bowed to the elder's will. "Muffin, you sit on my lap now, won't you? What sort of work have we to do?" she added.

"But our campaign," said Prudence. "You haven't forgot, have you? The welfare of these innocents—we must attend to it."

"O yes," said the other, a little sadly. "It isn't proceeding too very well after all, is it?"

"Certainly not as we had hoped."

"No, certainly not. Not at all. Certainly not," Mercy repeated, in order to say something on the topic her sister wished to discuss. "Not at all. Certainly not—"

"No, not at all," Prudence interrupted impatiently. "But lamenting it won't help things, now, will it?"

"Not if you say it won't," Mercy replied obligingly.

"Not at all!" said Prudence.

"No, not at all. Certainly not—"

"Pray, Mercy! Do be quiet for a moment."

"O. Yes! Quiet for a moment," Mercy answered. These campaign deliberations frightened her; she always felt she was expected to say something, and she never knew anything to say. "Certainly."

"Mercy, hush!"

Tears crept into Mercy's eyes, but she blinked them back. Really, she would be very happy when all this nonsense was settled.

"I think our original scheme has failed, and must be abandoned," Prudence began musingly.

"O, certainly! A terrible failure," said Mercy, who could not entirely recall what the original scheme had been.

"So we must devise another," the elder sister continued.

"O, another! The very thing. I protest, Prue, you make my head swim when you think so—so decisively."

"Now we have attempted to gain Sir Proctor's support by involving him romantically with you."

"So we did, indeed," Mercy said promptly. "But do you know, Prudence, I don't quite think we achieved our object—"

"No, we did not! Naturally not. That is what I just said."

"O," the younger sister answered, somewhat taken aback. "No, naturally not. No, it is quite natural when you think of it. We did not achieve our goal, naturally. We attempted—"

"Therefore we must find another means to induce the squire to attach himself to our cause," said Prudence, ignoring her completely this time. "And I believe our best hope is to win his affections through our small friends themselves. That is most direct, and may yet be possible."

"O, it may, it may. Indeed! It may yet be possible," Mercy seconded enthusiastically. "Our best hope, doubtless. The most direct . . ." she continued, adding, "I don't suppose you would wish to—would you explain that once more, my dear?"

"We must teach the squire to love our small friends," said Prudence, obliging her sister in spite of the fact that she had not listened to her. "Somehow . . . Do you think he liked Fido?"

"The squire? But most certainly he liked Fido. Naturally he did. I like Fido, too. Fido is a good dog, a very good doggie. I like Fido. Sir Proctor likes Fido—"

"Then we shall encourage the acquaintanceship," Prudence broke in.

"Excellent thought! Prudence! You do astound me," said Mercy. "And how—how precisely shall we do so?"

"We must think of a way," Prudence responded.

"O, think of one. Yes, dear Prue! Very good. Think of one."

"Think," Prudence repeated, and the two old ladies sat and thought for a very good long while, Mercy continually punctuating their silence with "Ummms" and "Ahs" in order to let her sister know that she was thinking her hardest.

The very first person to call on Mrs. Blackwood of Stonebur Cottage was the last person that lady wished to see. Mr. Claude Kemp, Esquire, visited the young Blackwoods on the day following their removal to Stonebur, and succeeded (if such was his object) in disturbing the mistress of that place quite thoroughly.

"Traubin has taken your cloak, I see," said Honoria, upon being summoned to the hall. She was rather in a pucker at that moment, having come directly from an interview with Maria, the young woman who had been engaged to serve as her abigail and to help the Traubins. It seemed Maria was frightened of the dark. Mrs. Traubin had given her a single candle for her room last night, and had forbidden her to take another; as a consequence, Maria had slept very ill, indeed, if at all. She considered nothing could be more cruel than Mrs. Traubin's behaviour (Honoria secretly agreed) and, driven by despair, had dared to address the mistress directly with her grievance. It was left to poor Honor—who had not slept well herself—to console Maria and assure her of a generous supply of candles in future, and then to conciliate Mrs. Traubin, who considered that she had acted only in her employers' interests, and was not at all pleased to learn of Maria's bold application to Mrs. Blackwood. Though she had done all she could, Honoria feared that Mrs. Traubin might hold a grudge against the girl on account of the incident, and make her life at Stonebur unpleasant. This was on her mind as she greeted Mr. Kemp.

"Your butler was most hospitable," said Kemp, smiling his cheerless smile. "In fact, I had meant only to leave my card, yet he welcomed me so congenially, I felt I might step in after all."

"I am so glad you did," Honoria lied, knowing nothing else to do. "Please come up to the parlour," she added, leading the way.

"A charming little house," he remarked as they climbed the steps, stressing the word "little." Honoria noticed the emphasis, and thought it unnecessary.

"Shall I go and call Alexander?" she inquired.

"But he must be at his studies, I think," Mr. Kemp objected smoothly. "I could not think of breaking in upon him so rudely."

"I could," Honoria muttered, made brave by her annoyance. She had never before disturbed her husband at his work—except that ill-fated night at Sweet's Folly—but such was her dislike of being alone with Claude that she was willing to do so now.

"I beg your pardon?"

"Nothing at all," she said, for she instantly regretted her words. "May I get you some coffee?" she asked. "Perhaps some tea? Or sherry—"

"Coffee will be delightful," he broke in. "Will you join me?"

"Join—? O, yes, if you like," she said distractedly. It worried her to be alone with Kemp; now she wondered what Alex would think, were he to enter unexpectedly. "And Alexander, too, I think he must take coffee as well; he will like a respite from his monograph."

"As you like," said Claude, bowing. "However, there was a matter I hoped to discuss—" he began, and paused, ending, "but it will wait."

Honoria had risen to ring for coffee, and was returning to her chair. She turned in her way and looked at him inquiringly.

"You look very well today," said Claude, one of the few truthful statements he had made since entering the cottage. Despite her restless night, and her anxieties, Honoria's appearance really was charming. She wore a dove-grey morning gown with ivory edging round the cuffs and hem, the long sleeves drawn in tight at the elbows and wrists, and the collar becomingly trimmed with lace. Her agitation had only increased the rosiness of her cheeks, and sleeplessness had given her a hint of languor that did not detract from her looks.

"Thank you," she said, a trifle peevishly, for she was aware he had purposely piqued her curiosity and then declined to satisfy it. Traubin arrived in response to the bell and was directed to bring coffee for three. "You mention something you wished—to discuss, perhaps, with me?" she said, prompting him though she felt it would be wiser not to.

"O, yes, that. But if you wish to see Mr. Blackwood—" he said, with a wave of the hand to indicate that he was entirely at her disposal.

"I do wish to see him," she said. She felt she was being drawn into a kind of verbal joust, which she could not like; but she did not know how to escape from it. "But if this matter troubles you, pray reveal it."

"It does not trouble me in the least, I assure you. Kindly forget I mentioned it at all."

She was about to rejoin with something equally useless, when suddenly she laughed. It had occurred to her that she and Kemp were behaving for all the world like two people who stand at a door-way, waving one another inside and bowing, "After you, dear sir," and "No, after you."

"Have I said something to amuse you?" he asked uncomfortably. "If so, I am most glad."

"No, it is—" She sat down, still smiling, and leaned towards him straightforwardly. All at once it seemed ludicrous to fear Mr. Kemp's company so much. What, after all, could he do? "Please do tell me what is on your mind," she invited. "I should like to know."

"Well, then, it is this," he began. "Your aunts—the Misses Deverell—have made known to my father . . ." For no apparent reason, he stopped here.

"Yes? Pray, speak frankly."

"Well, then, the whole neighbourhood is aware of the Misses Deverell's kindness to animals, of course . . ."

"Of course."

"And several months ago—three or four, I believe—your Aunt Prudence made it known to my father that she wished to—" He stopped this time because Traubin had arrived with the coffee. After the tray had been set down, and the business of pouring and so forth duly carried out, Honoria begged her guest to continue.

"Well, it appears your aunts desire to found an—an animal shelter of sorts," he said finally. "No doubt you are familiar with the project?"

"An animal shelter?" she repeated. "No, I am not—not quite certain I understand you. An animal shelter of what sort?"

"A hospital, I believe. And a home. For the care of, ah, stray dogs and cats." He spoke hesitantly because he felt more than a little abashed; his father had said no Kemp was ever obliged to bribe a lady in order to win her regard, yet that was more or less what he was attempting to do now. A faintly discernible flush rose on his neck as this fact crossed his mind; he suppressed it and resolved to regulate his thoughts more sternly.

"I must confess, this is the first I have heard of such a scheme," she replied. "You say they applied to your father. When?"

"Some three or four months ago, I think. It is of no moment," he said, and was about to continue when she interrupted him.

"I beg your pardon, sir, but it may be of some moment to me. Can you recall precisely when they visited Sir Proctor?"

"Well, it was not both of them," he replied, "but your Aunt Prudence only. I think she is the more business-minded of the two . . ."

"Yes, but when?" she repeated impatiently. Suddenly this question had come to signify a great deal to her. She forced herself to recall all the details of the conversation she had overheard in the hall-way at Bench Street that evening (so long ago, it seemed now!) when Claude had made his last offer for her.

Mr. Kemp now sat frowning in thought. "I believe—it must have been not long before I—before I went into Wiltshire at Christmas." He had been about to refer to the evening of his offer, but immediately decided he did not care to mention it.

"Before you went into Wiltshire!" she cried. Her consternation was clearly visible in her large, liquid eyes, and her hands flew instinctively up to her mouth, covering her lips as if to prevent them from uttering a terrible truth.

"Is any thing the matter?" he inquired solicitously. He had not expected such a reaction from her.

"O no! O yes! O dear," she exclaimed without thinking. "O dear!"

"Something distresses you," he said, rising swiftly from his chair and hastening to her side. He stood above her, bending a little as if to peer into her face, which was now completely hidden in her hands. "Shall I call a servant? Some ratafia perhaps—?"

"O no, no. Call for nothing," she said, in great agitation. "It is only that—my aunts—did they ask your father for money? Was that it?"

"Yes," he said, evidently puzzled. "I believe they did, but it is nothing to fret about. They wished to establish it as a public charity, I think."

"Nothing to fret about!" she exclaimed into her hands, now wet with tears. "My life! My life, that is all." Her mind raced as she reviewed the many results of her eavesdropping that night. No wonder they had not been grateful for her departure! No wonder Aunt Prudence had said they could not afford it! "O, what an idiot I have been!" she cried all at once. "What a fool, fool, fool!"

"My dear Mrs. Blackwood," he said, quite alarmed by now. "I had no notion this scheme was unknown to you—or that it would provoke such sentiments in you. Pray, I am profoundly grieved to have brought this about—" And he really was grieved, in a sense: it was dreadfully vexatious to have made Honor cry when he had meant to please her, particularly as he had no idea what he had done.

"But why did they not tell me?" she demanded, apparently of the bewildered Kemp. "Why did they not ask me? I should have helped them, and I should not have had to marry at all! And now I am married for ever, and all for nothing," she ended on a sob. She cried not because she was sorry to be Mrs. Blackwood, precisely, but because she realized now that her marriage had been precipitated by a foolish and unnecessary misunderstanding. Besides, she had begun to think she would never make Alexander happy—in fact, that she would always make him unhappy.

This last utterance on her part was music to Mr. Kemp's ears; he dropped immediately to his knees and sought to take her hand. Hardly even aware of him, she let him take it. He held it between both his own, and said softly, "Did you not wish to marry, then? Poor Honoria! What sufferings you must have undergone." So saying, he kissed the hand she had granted him.

At this moment Honoria looked up, and perceived through a mist of tears her husband standing in the door-way.

"Alex," she gasped, "what are you doing here?" Though she said this only because she was confused, her tone of voice was exactly that of a woman caught in a guilty act.

Alexander surveyed the scene before him—his wife sobbing, another man on his knees kissing her hand—and recalled the words he had just overheard by accident. He looked startled, gentle, and at the same time rather pathetic. "I live here," he said quietly. "I beg your pardon. I appear to have intruded at an awkward moment."

"But no—stay. Do not go," she implored, as he bowed slightly, evidently about to take his leave. She noticed for the first time that Mr. Kemp held her hand, and removed it from his grasp rather roughly.

Alexander merely bowed again, and retreated into the corridor.

"Alex!" she cried.

He shut the door.

"O, Alex," she breathed broken-heartedly. She was thoroughly miserable now, and even more thoroughly confounded.

"Your husband appears as unhappy with the present state of affairs as you are," said Claude, hoping to press his advantage home. He attempted to possess himself once more of her hand, but she tore it away angrily. "I beg you will trust me," he said after a pause. "I have entreated you before to take me into your confidence, and to think of me as a friend."

"A friend!" she exclaimed. "But you are the one who—" She had been about to pour a torrent of abuse onto his head; for an instant it appeared to her that he had been the cause of all this unhappiness. She recovered herself in time, however, and recognised that all he had done had been to inform her of her own folly. He was not to blame in this, she told herself, and struggled to regain her composure.

"I owe you an explanation," she said at last, in low, trembling accents. She was still very much overset, but it was both her nature and her habit to consider other people before she thought of herself, and the more she deliberated, the more unseemly and unkind did her recent behaviour towards him appear. She ought never to have shown her discomposure at all; she ought to have been able to govern herself more successfully. She might have heard him out calmly and reflected later upon the meaning of his revelations; instead she had panicked, and behold the unhappy result. "I am dreadfully sorry," she added, full of guilt and repentance.

"Not at all," he assured her, still kneeling at her side. "If friends cannot be easy with one another, what use are they?"

"You are too good," she murmured, feeling he was.

"You flatter me." He inclined his blond head slightly, as if to signify a bow. She gazed down at his pale, gleaming hair, and felt with a tremble that she had misjudged him. Many another man would long ago have fled from a scene like this, she thought (forgetting that such a course would also have been by far more gentlemanly). His attachment to her must indeed be very tender, and he must be very brave, for he not only stood by her while she wept and raged, but submitted to her abuse (in her mind she had as good as said aloud everything she had thought of him) and waited patiently to hear whatever she might tell him now. She felt unworthy to receive such goodness, and consequently was doubly wretched.

"I must and will explain my conduct to you, sir," she said. He raised his head again and looked up into her dark eyes. "Only allow me to compose myself a little. Will you wait a moment?"

"Years," he answered lightly. "Decades."

She smiled a little, as she knew she was meant to. Now that she was a trifle calmer, she felt the awkwardness of his kneeling next her chair. "Pray, be comfortable," she said, gesturing towards a sofa. "Another cup of coffee?" she added, as he failed to move. She had to rise to reach the tray, an action that left him on his knees by an empty chair. Then he stood immediately.

They drank coffee in silence, she avoiding the steadfast gaze he lavished upon her. She was aching to fly to Alexander, to explain to

him what he had seen—if it could ever be explained—but she felt instinctively that Claude, being a guest in their house, was the first matter to be seen to. That was her duty, both as mistress of Stonebur and
as Alexander's wife. Alexander would not disappear, in any case, and
it would be as well to have reflected a bit in solitude before she
approached him. Therefore, as soon as she felt capable of speaking
smoothly, she addressed Mr. Kemp as follows:

"You wonder, no doubt, what you did to precipitate so much excitement, dear sir—"

"I admit," he agreed, "the question did cross my mind."

"Of course. I ought to begin by informing you that the project that
my aunts hope to accomplish was not known to me before you referred to it today."

"Yes—?"

"But I had heard them discuss it—without knowing what they spoke
of. It was on the day . . ." She hesitated here, wondering first whether
to allude to his offer, and then whether to tell him all the truth. "It
was on the last occasion when you were so good as to honour me by
an offer of marriage," she continued, whispering by the time she
reached the word "marriage." She had decided to tell him all the truth
up until the point when she determined to marry the first man to ask
her, and to gloss over the rest as vaguely as possible. That part
touched Alexander too nearly, and she did not like to disclose it.

He listened to her in the most attentive silence, only now and then
interjecting a "Yes" or an "Of course." When she had finally done he
sat wordless for a few minutes. "Then you might have married me,"
he remarked at length, almost without expression.

"Had you offered again," she affirmed.

"The world is a strange and ironical place," he said, adding, "And
your husband—he knows all this?"

"He knows—" she began, and was interrupted by a knock at the
door, followed immediately by the precipitous entrance of her sister-
in-law.

Emily burst through the door, her cheeks flushed with exertion (she
had run all the way from Sweet's Folly) and her eyes shining and
dancing as Honor had never seen them do. She looked excessively
pretty, especially as some of her blond hair had escaped her bonnet
and fell in wispy curls on her neck and brow. "I've won!" she cried,
running directly to Honoria and seizing both her hands. "I've won,
I've won, I've won!" She leaned down to Honor and was about to embrace her when she noticed that her friend was looking not at her but
at some other point in the room.

Then she turned and saw Claude Kemp.

"You here!" she exclaimed. "Damnation!"

"Emily!" gasped Honor, who had never heard her sister—or any other female, for that matter—use such a word before.

"Well for the love of Heaven," Emily said impatiently, "I do think it's a bit too much." She was infinitely annoyed at having to share this moment of triumph with anyone other than her dear friend; as far as she was concerned, Mr. Kemp was an intruder, whether he had been present first or not.

Scene after impossible scene! was all Honoria could think. How would she ever hold her head up before Mr. Kemp again? "Emily, pray—your news in a moment—but you really have been unkind to Mr. Kemp."

"O yes, very well. My sincerest apologies, sir," she muttered, at the same time hastily undoing the ribbons of her bonnet, and flinging it across the room. "Honor, when can we speak alone?" she continued, again grasping her hands.

Claude spoke before Honor could answer. "My congratulations, dear Miss Blackwood, on whatever it is you may have won. And naturally my acceptance of your thoughtful apologies. And lastly, you may be private with Mrs. Blackwood whenever you like; I could not think of remaining where I am *de trop*." He spoke in accents of the profoundest irony, and rose on his last words.

"O, for Heaven's sake," said Emily.

Mr. Kemp bowed, first to her and then to Honor. "Madam," he said.

"Mr. Kemp, pray—do not depart so—"

"I assure you, it does not signify. Your butler will show me out, I trust."

"Yes, but—"

"Pray, do not refine upon things so," he said. "I shall call upon you again when"—he glanced at Emily—"you are more at leisure."

Honoria, feeling that all this coming and going was too much for her to worry about, permitted him to leave without further protestation.

Emily forgot all about him the moment he had gone. "Felicitate me, my dear," she cried, throwing off her cloak with an exuberant gesture. "Reverence me. I am an artist!"

Honor gazed into her friend's rapt countenance and could not help but smile with her. "I knew you could do it," she said jubilantly. "I made sure of it! And did you win—" she paused.

"Top honours! The best, the winner—O, Honoria, I cannot tell you what this means to me, how unbearably happy I am."

"Someday all the world will know the name of Emily Blackwood," Honoria said proudly.

"Yes, someday . . ." Emily began, but her expression changed all at once and she concluded, "Well, not precisely Emily Blackwood, perhaps."

"I beg your pardon?"

"I did not—I entered—O dear, I may as well out with it. I did not enter quite under my own name."

"Whatever do you mean?" Honor queried.

"I entered—ah, the winner of the contest is Mr. Cedric Blackwood. I did not use my own name," she repeated.

"But why ever not?"

"Because I should most certainly have lost. I might even have been disqualified, Honoria; I am not sure the competition was even open to women."

"Not open—"

"I dared not enquire, for fear they should discover why the question concerned me. And I know positively—think of it Honor, and you shall see yourself—they would never have awarded a prize to a woman."

"Emily, I never thought of it," the other replied wonderingly.

"I did. And I am very glad I did," Emily exclaimed suddenly, pirouetting round a chair and knocking over a firescreen in the same movement. "Where is Alexander?" she demanded abruptly.

"In his library, I think. But are you certain you ought to—"

"It cannot remain a secret much longer."

"You did not tell your parents?" Honor asked, horrified at the thought.

"O no, no, of course not. I came directly to you. But Alex can be trusted—call him, won't you?"

"Yes. Yes, I will," she said, rising and pulling the bell-rope. Traubin appeared and was instructed to ask his master to come to the parlour.

"What will you do now?" Honoria asked as they waited.

"Do? But there is nothing more—O, you mean how shall I tell my parents, and persuade them to let me go, and so forth?"

"Precisely."

Emily sat for the first time since she had come in. "I don't know," she said finally. "In fact, I don't know at all."

"Well, we must certainly consider the question now," Honor was saying, when her husband entered the room.

"Madam," he said, bowing to his wife. He looked a trifle paler than was ordinary in him, which made him very pale indeed. "Emily," he added with a second bow to his sister.

"Alex, sit down," said this last, without observing either his pallor or his uncommon formality.

"If you say so," he said indifferently. He generally did say many things indifferently, yet this tone (like his complexion) was not quite his wonted one. Whereas his habitual remoteness appeared to stem from a pleasantly distracted mind, his dispassion now seemed to spring more from a determination to remain detached than from an inability to do otherwise. Honoria noticed his altered behaviour immediately, but Miss Blackwood did not see it at all.

"Prepare yourself for extraordinary news," she advised him, smiling broadly.

Her brother smiled, too, but with a touch of irony, as if to say that what was extraordinary to her was not likely to excite him that day.

Without further introduction, Emily apprised him of her excellent fortune, hastening back haphazardly now and then to explain how it had all come about, and referring hazily to her future plans only when it was necessary to do so. Alexander rose and embraced his sister with almost a stately motion, kissing her lightly on the brow.

"You don't think—" she said worriedly after he had done so, "you don't think my father will actually prevent me from turning this opportunity to good account?"

Alexander reflected briefly on his father's character, a thing he had seldom done before. "I haven't any idea," he answered finally.

"O, he could not," Honoria protested.

"I shouldn't say that," Alex returned, looking not quite at her but more through her. "I should think he could very easily."

"But *would* he?" Emily insisted.

"Impossible to say," Alex objected, and then corrected himself immediately, "No, not quite impossible. Certainly he would. Emily, my father has no great interest in your success as an artist, has he? Has he —he has not encouraged you much, has he?"

Emily replied no through compressed lips.

"In that case, you must put the question to him in order to know its answer." On these words Alexander rose, as if about to quit the parlour.

"Wait!" both Emily and Honor commanded simultaneously.

"Alexander, I must speak with you," Honoria continued.

"Alex, you must assist me," Emily said.

"What is this?" asked the party so applied to, raising his eyebrows and opening wide his green eyes. Something out of the common gleamed in these eyes as he added, "I am at your service, of course, ladies, but I know not how I may serve you."

"Well, you are a thinker," Emily flung at him. "Think!"

He seated himself again and inclined his head obligingly towards her. "Very well," he said politely.

"No, Emily, pray do not insist quite so imperiously just now," Honor remonstrated. "My husband has his work to do today, and oughtn't to be distracted in this wise. Perhaps the best thing to do will be to sleep on the question. Say nothing to your father this evening; I will discuss the matter with Alexander and call on you tomorrow."

"Say nothing . . . O, very well," Emily said in a disappointed voice. "But I must send my acceptance very soon; the committee expects to hear from me before the end of the week."

"Yes, yes, you shall know what to say by then," Honoria assured her, standing and walking to where Emily had tossed her cloak. She returned with it to her friend and bundled her into its folds. "Should you like the carriage to take you back to Sweet's Folly?" she enquired.

"Am I leaving?" said the other, much surprised.

"Yes, my dear," Honoria said firmly. "I am afraid you must." She knew Emily would have liked to stop longer and debate her situation with the only people acquainted with it, but Alexander's unusual manner made her feel she had more pressing things to attend to. Emily, perceiving that her presence was no longer wanted, tucked her hair into her bonnet and accepted the use of the carriage. In a few moments she was gone.

"My dear Alexander, the scene upon which you happened today—" Honoria began when they were alone.

"Madam, I beg you will not refer to that—that unfortunate accident. I assure you, I understand entirely."

"But you cannot understand!" Honor cried.

"Entirely," he repeated. "And really, it does not disturb me in the least."

"Not disturb you—! But—"

"Madam, ours was a marriage of convenience. Your convenience, and mine too perhaps. In any case I do not choose, and have never chosen, to assert any prerogative that our marriage contract may give me to scrutinise your sentiments, judge your actions, or—or anything," he ended with a slight flush, for he was thinking of the bed-chamber below them.

"But, my dear Alex, we cannot continue in this fashion," she protested. She was about to speak again, but he interrupted her.

"Do you find it too uncomfortable already?"

She gazed at him, evidently puzzled. "I am not certain I follow your meaning," she said.

"It is very simple, really. I ask if our present circumstances are too unpleasant for you to bear. I fully comprehend that my residence in this house may be too—too cumbersome and awkward for you to support. If that is the case, or when it is, you must inform me of it so that some more suitable arrangement may be made."

"But, Alex, I love you!" she cried in the utmost dismay. "You think you understand me, but you do not understand at all."

Alexander stood and addressed her more sternly than she had ever seen him do. His face had gone quite white and he held himself rigidly. "Madam, it is utterly unnecessary to go to such lengths to conciliate me. Utterly unnecessary, I tell you! You do not please me at all with such hypocrisy. Our marriage was made without pretence of love, and so it shall remain. To add lies and deceit to it all is too painful to me. Do we understand one another?" he demanded savagely.

Honoria had never heard him speak so, had never seen him look so, had never guessed at all that he was capable of such oratory. Entirely shaken, she responded in the weakest of whispers, "Yes, sir. We understand one another, I think."

His rage apparently somewhat diminished, he bowed curtly and said, "Very good, then. I shall go to my library now, where you may find me should any household matter require my attention."

"Yes," she murmured.

"And I think it will be better if we keep separate bed-chambers," he added deliberately, as he drew near the door. His tone grew less vigorous as he added, "It will be more comfortable for both of us."

"But where will you sleep?" she asked. Tears spilled from her eyes and coursed down her cheeks while she regarded him.

"There is a couch in the library," he said quietly. "It will answer for a while at least."

Honoria had not thought matters could get any worse than they had been on the previous evening, but she was compelled as her husband bowed again and shut the door behind him to conclude that she had erred. The gap between herself and her husband, which last night had been merely a lack of closeness, was now a definite rift, created and confirmed by words between them that could never be retracted. Positive damage had been done to their relationship that seemed to her to be past remedy, past reparation. In all her young life she had not felt so desolately alone, and as she sobbed into her pillow that night— freely, for Alexander was too far from her to hear her—she almost wished to be back in Bench Street, and longed for the comforting nonsense of her dear, dear aunts.

Chapter VIII

The morrow brought no answers. Emily, greeting her sister in the front hall at Sweet's Folly, looked anxiously at her to discover if Honoria had brought the solution to her dilemma. She saw at once that she had not.

"Nothing at all?" she whispered into her ear as they mounted the staircase to Miss Blackwood's sitting-room.

"Nothing," poor Honor confirmed.

"But you did talk it over with Alexander? He had no suggestions?"

"No," said Honor, and left it at that.

"Then I must simply tell them," Emily concluded flatly. "I thought as much last night." As Honoria said nothing, she continued with an offer of tea.

"Please, my dear." When the soothing liquid had been brought and drunk, and some of Honoria's calm restored, she was able to address her friend more sympathetically.

"Dear Em," she began, "I know you must be frightened now. I should not like to be obliged to inform your father of news of so—so explosive a nature."

"Yes. I am a little frightened," Emily confessed. "It is very odd, Honor, but do you know, I never felt frightened before? Never once, in my whole life?"

"Never at all?" gasped she, who spent half her days in fear of one thing or another.

"Not since I was a little, little girl. It is a—a terribly distressing sentiment, is it not?"

"O yes," Honor agreed fervently.

"I don't—Honor, I do not know what to do!" Emily cried all at once, and instantly began weeping as well. Honoria had seen her friend weep for joy, she had observed tears of sympathy in her, or of pity, but never had she heard these long-drawn, racking sobs, this dry, desperate, piteous moan! "My poor dear," she exclaimed, and threw her arms round Emily's crumpled figure.

"I am terrified," said Emily, when she could speak at all.

Honor soothed and comforted her as best she could. "This is the worst of it, believe me," she assured her, speaking from long experience. "The anticipation torments—much more than the actuality." But on these words the thought of her own situation recurred to her. Suddenly she doubted of what she had said, and began to weep as well.

"Look at the pair of us!" Emily said, with half a smile.

"Ridiculous," Honor agreed, sniffling. "Come, come, handkerchiefs, please. We must do better than this," she said resolutely.

"I haven't got one," Emily said, laughing in a strangled sort of fashion.

"Never mind, dear; I have." The young Mrs. Blackwood was forcing herself to be calm. She was more familiar with fear than poor Emily; therefore, she must take the lead now in setting matters straight.

"Now, I promise you," she said warmly, while wiping the tears from her sister's cheeks, "you cannot but feel better once it is all over. You will go to your father and tell him outright what it is you have done, and what you wish to do. It is the only thing to do, and believe me, you will feel relieved instantly. No matter what he says," she added, hoping devoutly this was true.

"Very well. Yes, of course, you are quite in the right of it," Emily agreed. She paused to blow her nose. "I am dreadfully ashamed of myself," she continued when she had done so. "Bawling like a brat, that's what it is. Serves absolutely no purpose."

"No, naturally it does not. But it is quite understandable," Honoria assured her. "You needn't feel ashamed. Only follow the course we have settled upon."

The interview concluded with many expressions of gratitude on Miss Blackwood's part, and a comparable number of shrugs from Honoria's shoulders. Emily was resolved to address her father as soon as he should return from his professional calls. Honoria, though she might have liked to remain at Sweet's Folly and support her friend through that scene, decided she preferred for her own comfort to visit her aunts in Bench Street. She had not seen them since before their quitting Colworth Park, and missed them now sadly.

Her arrival at their little house interrupted a conference that, like so many others lately, had been something of a trial to Mercy. Prudence would not be quiet about the shelter for their small friends; at break-fast, dinner, tea-time, supper—at every opportunity, and there were many—she insisted on debating and discussing strategy. Just previous to Honor's knock on the door, the following discussion had taken place.

"Resolved," Prudence had said, pacing the room as best she could, for so many cats intruded in her path that the exercise could hardly be relaxing, "that the best way to win Squire Kemp's support is to excite and cultivate in him a fondness for our small friends."

Mercy, who was trying to ignore the aimless gyrations of her sister as she wandered through the room, and instead turn her attention to her embroidery, said yes.

"Further resolved, that in order to do so, we must bring said squire together with said small friends."

"Yes, yes," said Mercy.

"Concluded, that we must invite the squire to Bench Street, where the greatest number of said friends may be seen most easily and in the best light."

"Is that true?" Mercy inquired wonderingly.

"Yes, yes, it is true," said Prudence irritably. She was always irrita-ble these days.

"Of course, if you say it is true, I know it must be true," Mercy said amicably, "though I am certain I should never have—what did you say?—concluded it myself. You are so logical, and I such a chop-logic! I often wonder we should have been born to the same parents. And yet we were; that much is undeniable, is not it?"

"Certainly undeniable."

"Undeniable and resolved," said Mercy, with satisfaction. She en-joyed utilising herself what she imagined to be the language of logic her sister had introduced.

"Yes, resolved, my dear," Prudence said, at last smiling upon her. Mercy's foolishness had annoyed her more of late than was usual, but she did still love her, for all that. "So let us send a note round to the squire, shall we?"

"Resolved!" Mercy cried enthusiastically.

"And invite him to dine and to play chess with you here."

"Resolved and concluded!" exclaimed the other, who had begun to like playing chess. "But when, precisely?"

"This afternoon is as good as any other," said the elder. "I do not imagine our dear squire has many other engagements to prevent his coming."

"Don't you?" Mercy enquired, adding stoutly, "Then I shan't imagine so either."

"But there is more," Prudence continued. She smiled rather mysteriously and waited to be asked what she referred to. Mercy continued her embroidery. "There is yet the *coup de grâce*," Prudence said, still waiting for the eager inquiry she expected.

"What does *coup de grâce* signify?"

"It signifies—it signifies the finishing touch," said Miss Deverell. "It is French."

"Ah!" cried she, apparently satisfied with this explanation. She returned her concentration to her needle-work.

"Don't you wish to know what it is?" said Prudence, despairing a little of this attempt to arouse her sister's curiosity.

"Wish to know what it is?" Mercy repeated blankly. "But I do know. It is a French finishing touch. You just said so yourself, Prue," she added reproachfully. "My dear, I do believe you may be growing just as forgetful as I told the squire you were."

"No, no, you don't see. I mean there is one more stroke in our scheme that you do not know about. A brilliant stroke."

"Then why do you not tell me?" Mercy asked, feeling a bit hurt at being excluded from her sister's confidence.

"Well, I will tell you then!" Prudence exclaimed in exasperation.

"There is no need to shout," Mercy admonished mildly.

"O dear, never mind. It is this. In order to establish the closest of all possible ties between the squire and our small friends, we shall conceal one of said friends—Fido, I think—in his carriage. Then it will appear to Sir Proctor that Fido so liked him that he ran off back to Colworth and hid himself expressly to be close to the squire. Since he will be coming to Bench Street anyhow, we shan't have to do without Fido for long," she concluded triumphantly. "What do you think?"

"I think—is Sir Proctor really so foolish as all that?" Mercy asked.

"So foolish as all what?"

"Prue dear, don't become disagreeable—so foolish as to believe Fido would do such a thing."

"It is not so difficult to believe."

"I find it difficult. I am sure *I* should never conceal myself in Squire Kemp's carriage merely to further my acquaintance with him. Why should Fido?"

"Because he is a dog!" the other cried, profoundly irritated.

"Prudence! I wish you will not say such things."

"But it is true," she insisted.

"Fido would be dreadfully hurt," said Mercy, shaking her head sadly. "Hurt and offended. Dear Prudence, really you must not abuse him so."

"But my dear sister, he is a dog."

"He is a friend," Mercy said loyally.

"He is a friend who is a dog."

Mercy looked very sorrowful, indeed. "If you say so," she answered in a small voice.

Miss Deverell was spared the necessity of replying by Honoria's arrival, and the discussion was thus brought to a close. Honoria, who had hoped to find some solace in her aunts' company, instead found them strangely distracted. She stopped but a short while, and returned afterwards to Stonebur Cottage, where she shut herself into the parlour to deliberate in solitude.

The result of this meditation was a note, received several hours later, by Mr. Claude Kemp, Esquire, Colworth Park. Boothby handed it in to the young master, and he turned it over thoughtfully before opening it. The hand was unknown to him, though distinctly feminine. Curious, he broke the seal and scanned the letter rapidly.

"Sir," it read,

"Your yesterday's call at Stonebur having been distressingly interrupted by so many untoward incidents, and having been curtailed so abruptly, I desire you will do me the honour to call upon me again at your earliest possible convenience. I assure you, dear sir, my conscience will give me no rest until I have had some opportunity of undisturbed discourse with you.

"I am, dear sir, your, etc.,

"H.B."

Mr. Kemp folded up the letter again, a curious smile on his sharply modelled lips. He was beginning (alas for Honor!) to understand his quarry. Her affection was not to be won by courtesy, nor by a show of wit or talent, nor by humble protestations of esteem. Her regard, he saw at last, was best gained by inspiring in her a sense of guilt. Then she softened; then she was ardent to meet the offended party again! In future he would take care to make her feel at fault whenever he could. The odd smile on his lips broadened.

"Will there be any answer?" Boothby asked, who had stood waiting while the young master so reflected.

"No," he said at first, for he planned to drive to Stonebur at once. Then, "Yes," he amended, concluding it would be as well to allow Honoria's sense of culpability to ferment just a bit longer. He went to a writing desk and scrawled a note saying he should be at Stonebur in several hours. As he was handing it to Boothby, however, he changed his mind one last time. "No," he said, crumpling the note in his hand. "No. There is no answer."

"As you like, sir."

"That other note you hold," Claude continued, "is it for me as well?"

"It is for your father, sir," Boothby corrected. "From the Misses Deverell, I think. No doubt a word of thanks for his hospitality."

"Very well, then," said Claude. "Well, be off! I am sure my father does not care to await your pleasure in receiving his correspondence."

Mr. Boothby bowed, too enured to Mr. Kemp's ill-treatment even to feel offended. As he departed, Mr. Kemp took a book from the writing desk and sat down with it to read. He would keep Mrs. Blackwood waiting a few hours, he thought. No doubt her anxiety would prove useful to him.

Mr. Boothby had been correct in guessing the origin of the second note he held, but he little suspected that its senders were at that moment in the coach-house of Colworth Park, engaged in persuading a rather large dog to lie under a lap-robe on the floor of a carriage.

"But there are so many carriages!" Mercy had cried when they entered the cavernous structure. Large, shadowy coaches surrounded them, several covered with cloths and evidently in disuse, but three quite prepared for an excursion. "Are you quite certain this is the one he will take?"

"Not quite certain," Prudence admitted, "but it does seem the most likely. Don't you agree? It is not the most formal, nor yet the rudest."

"If you say so," she returned fretfully.

"I say so. Now, Fido," Prudence went on, giving a mighty shove to the animal, "this is where you must stay. We agreed upon it!" she added, for she had had a long talk with Fido regarding his mission before they had left Bench Street.

"He does not seem to care for it," Mercy observed.

"Obstinate thing! Go on, go on!"

"Prudence!" Mercy simply hated to see anyone pushed to do anything. She never had been able to do it.

"He will go," Prudence muttered grimly, shoving at the beast again. "He will and he will and he will! Now, won't you, dear Fido?"

The poor beast stared dumbly at her, then yelped twice.

"I know, I know—but we've been through all that already," Prudence wheedled. "You will be home tonight, my dearest; I promise you."

"Is he worried?" Mercy said.

"He dislikes being from home again, and especially here. That nasty butler left him in this very coach-house for hours and hours, until I saved him."

"You mustn't mind, Fido," Mercy coaxed reassuringly. "It really is for a very good cause, and—and I'll have Mr. Morley prepare a special bone for you, with a ribbon on it, if you'll cooperate."

Fido jumped into the carriage and lay down.

"Now the lap-robe," Prudence said, arranging it over the dog. "Don't whimper, poor thing."

"No, don't," said Mercy, and kissed his nose before it disappeared under the robe.

"Just remember to stay where you are until the carriage has gone some ways—a mile or two, at least. It won't do to have Sir Proctor find you until he's too far from home to leave you behind. Do you understand?"

Fido's tail thumped up and down several times, which looked quite comical as he was now completely covered with the lap-robe.

"There's a dear doggie," Prudence said. She was about to continue, but Mercy thought she heard something, and the two old ladies lifted their skirts and fled the place precipitously. They were lucky enough to escape detection, and went home together to ready the house for Squire Kemp's expected visit. He had not yet answered their note, but they felt sure he would not fail them.

The household of Sweet's Folly, far from being prepared for visitors, was at that moment quite on its ears, and threatened to remain in such condition for a good long while. Emily Blackwood, locked into the sitting-room adjacent to her bed-chamber, yet held her hands over her ears in an instinctive (and, of course, fruitless) effort to keep from hearing her father's words reverberate in her mind. Poor Mrs. Blackwood, the weary look in her eyes more noticeable now than ever, hovered fretfully near the door of her husband's study, hoping to catch some hint of his humour (or at least some sign of life) from within. Dr. Blackwood had been closeted alone (and apparently idle) in that apartment for some thirty minutes now, ever since he had dismissed Emily so explosively. Mrs. Blackwood would have visited her daughter, rather than hanging about uselessly at this closed door, but she had been forbidden to do so. The hour for dinner was approaching, and she did not know what to tell the cook. She had not been present at the interview that had begun all this, nor did she know what matter it had been concerned with; she only knew that there had been a storm, and that now both husband and daughter were barred to her.

Dr. Blackwood had no particular reason for concealing from his wife the cause of the uproar. In due time he would tell her; only now his fury was such that he did not care to do so. He had instructed her to stay away from Emily only because he desired to punish that young lady, and he did not wish her to be comforted by her mother's consolations. The discussion he had had with Emily had gone ill almost from the very start: there was no detail of her covert actions—from entering the competition to doing so under an alias—that did not enrage him thoroughly. It had been difficult enough while she confessed what she had already done; when she revealed what her hopes were at present, a genuine tempest had arisen.

"Am I to understand, miss, that now, having committed outrage upon outrage, you petition me for permission actually to go to London and avail yourself of this—prize, or scholarship, or whatever you may call it?"

Emily had recovered some of her courage; she was too busy to be frightened at the moment. "Yes, sir," she said evenly.

"You have the impudence, the audacity, the—thundering heavens, the stupidity to make such a request?" he bellowed. He rose from the chair behind his writing-table, where he had hitherto been seated, and stood towering over his daughter. She met his eye squarely, which was a brave, but perhaps not a prudent, thing to do, since it only infuriated her father the more. "Allow me to remind you of several trifles, my good miss," he continued, still shouting. "Your education—your music lessons, and dancing lessons, and elocution and drawing and French lessons—these were not paid for so that you might lavish your talents on a roomful of idle, smocked daubers. Your masters and mistresses and governesses were not engaged to keep you safe and sound until such time as you should choose to abandon good society for the ranks of scapegrace artificers! Your wardrobe, the dressing of your hair, the polishing of your manner, and a thousand other details of your up-bringing were not intended to convey you gracefully into the very depths of Bohemia! Perhaps you thought they were, Mademoiselle Artiste (and the word 'artiste' oozed from his lips as if it were covered with slime), but they were not! Not, I tell you! NOT!"

Miss Blackwood said nothing for some moments, hoping her father would turn the time to good account by composing himself somewhat.

"With all due respect, sir," she began—though here her father interrupted her to say "Bah"—"if you did not desire me to become an artist, for what reason did you provide me with drawing instruction?"

"You talk like a child," he said disgustedly, apparently not in the least calmer. "Every young lady of breeding learns to draw. It is one of the accomplishments expected in a wife, as you perfectly well know."

"And pray, of what use is the cultivation of such a talent in a female if she is destined only to keep house and have babies?"

"It is—it is—I don't know what use it is, but damn, every lady at Almack's can draw, and play and sing as well. It makes no difference if she never once picks up a pencil or sits to a virginal or opens her mouth after she is married. They are accomplishments; they are expected and an end unto themselves."

"Then is it not cruel to encourage these ladies to dabble in art, yet not to allow them to study it seriously?"

"Miss Blackwood, I feel under no compulsion to explain to you the conventions of society. They are what they are and we bend to them. A young woman of the *ton* who steps a quadrille most neatly does not become an opera-dancer; no more does she who can pen a ditty run off with Lord Byron. Thus it is and thus it has ever been, for all I know, and I'll be hanged before I see you turned into a gypsy!"

"An artist is not a gypsy, sir," said Emily, with some dignity. "Miss Linwood of Leicester Square exhibits her art-work to all manner of gentry, and nobility too, and is in no wise despised by them."

"Miss Linwood of Leicester Square is not my daughter," he countered, reverting to a line of argument that has doubtless been used by parents to their children since the Flood, at least. "What she does is not my concern. What you do, on the other hand, is my intimate concern, and by God I'll see you married and with child before this year is out. That will stop your damned painting!"

Emily drew a long breath: this was worse than anything she had expected. She had been prepared for a refusal, but not for a plan that would otherwise encroach upon her freedom. "Whom shall I marry, sir?" she asked rather grimly.

"You may marry Claude Kemp," he returned.

"Claude Kemp abominates me."

"Ridiculous!"

"Not at all ridiculous. He loathes me, and is dangling after Honoria as plainly as can be."

"Well and no wonder," he roared all at once. "Honoria is what a woman should be—quiet, neat, pretty, and refined. While you, with your wild schemes, and won't dress your hair, and streaked with paint head to toe, and smelling to heaven of turpentine—" Dr. Blackwood's objections to his daughter's habits poured out in a steady stream, leaving grammar and common sense far behind. Emily bore it as patiently as she could. It was no matter to her; at least she knew for certain that Mr. Kemp would never do anything like marry her. This was not the point, anyway. She only wanted to go to London. She let her father rave without listening to him.

". . . and he *will* dangle after you," he was saying, when she finally began to heed him again. "There's nothing wrong with you some care and clothing won't correct. He'll dangle and offer and be your husband—that he will or my name's not Charles Blackwood!"

Emily had not heard enough of this last to respond to it. However, she saw no way of turning the argument back to its original head—and no advantage to herself even if she did so—and so she merely stood before her father in silence.

"I trust I will never hear a word of this nonsense again," Dr. Blackwood said severely.

Emily said nothing.

"Miss—?" he said, waiting with glaring eyes and a terrible frown.

Emily remained silent.

Dr. Blackwood came very near striking her, but checked himself at the last moment. "Go to your room, obstinate, fool-hardy girl. And keep to it until you are ready with a promise and an apology. You will take your meals there until you do—alone."

And thus the interview had terminated, both parties forming solitary armed camps in opposite parts of Sweet's Folly.

The gentleman whose name they had mentioned, meantime, was enjoying himself much better than did these two. He had called upon Honoria shortly past two, and had contrived to persuade her that they must take an outing in his carriage, in order to ensure that their colloquy would not be interrupted.

"I am not quite certain—" Honor had said anxiously, her brow wrinkling as she thought of Alexander.

"Please, Mrs. Blackwood. You do not look quite well, either, and I am sure some air will prove salubrious to you."

"Very well, if you think so," she agreed at last. Mr. Kemp smiled. He had driven over in the carriage expressly with this excursion in mind; generally he rode. The rain having stopped at last, and the weather open, all things in nature and in man appeared to him to conspire with his effort.

"I know you will feel better directly," he assured her. She directed Traubin to bring her her cloak and bonnet, wrote a brief note for Alexander in case he should ask for her, and set out with Mr. Kemp.

"I think nothing is more pleasant than a drive in mild weather," said he, when he had given his orders to the coachman. "Don't you?"

"It is very pleasant. I do enjoy riding, too, however . . . and an open carriage might be more suitable to an airing," she suggested. She had not realized he had brought a closed coach with him; it did not please her to find herself situated alone with him in a closed one.

"I am desolate that I did not take the calash," he lied. "We so rarely use it any more."

"It is of no moment," she murmured politely. "And how is your good father?"

"Very well, I think. He goes to your aunts' this evening, I believe. Did you know?"

"I did not. How very interesting. I suppose they must have formed a friendship, then. At least poor Aunt Mercy's accident had some good result."

"Yes. Accidents—and even more so, coincidences—are curious things. Are you quite warm? Not at all chilly?" he added.

She grew nervous, as she had before, at the thought of how he might try to warm her, and was about to reply with something unmistakably discouraging, when she seemed to notice some movement in a lap-robe that lay upon the floor. She had remarked before that it was not folded, as it ought to be, and had even thought she saw it twitch, but she had attributed this to the jolting motion of the coach. "I beg your pardon, sir," she said, "but is it possible there is something—or someone—under that lap-robe?"

"Under—? I should not think so!" he answered. To oblige her, however, he leaned down to the floor and pulled at a corner of the robe. The robe growled.

"This is extraordinary!" said Claude, tugging at the corner he held. The robe snarled, and resisted.

"But what on earth—?" He stooped and removed the lap-robe from the end that did not growl. Fido, of course, was revealed, though the silly dog did not realize it yet, his eyes being still covered and his mouth full of lap-robe.

"Fido!" cried Honoria gaily. She did not care how or why he had come to be there; she only knew she was happy to see him. She had regretted her drive in the closed carriage more with every yard they travelled. "What are you doing here, silly darling?"

Fido, recognizing her voice, let go the lap-robe and jumped up onto her knees, yelping joyfully.

"How in Heaven's name did he come to be here?" Claude asked, much vexed. His clearest remembrance of Fido was of the evening when the mongrel had bounded into the squire's study, all paws and tongue and waggling tail. His relationship with the beast had not improved from that time. Besides all that, it might prove extremely inconvenient to have an animal along on this particular outing—any animal, no matter how sweet. For Claude cherished a design that he had hoped to set into action very shortly.

"I can't imagine," Honor said truthfully. Fido was attempting to jump into her lap, for which feat he was rather too large and the carriage somewhat too small. "Now, now, dear doggie," she reproached him fondly, and put her arms round him as best she could.

Mr. Kemp groaned audibly.

"You are not frightened of him, I trust, sir?"

"O no—not frightened. Though I do think Fido and I are not on the best of terms. We had a falling out once, as it were. I did the lion's share of the falling myself."

"O, Fido, did you knock Mr. Kemp over? You bad dog! He's very strong," she added to Claude, who already knew it too well.

"Yes," he agreed. He drew away from the dog and leaned back into a corner of the carriage, placing his elbow on the window frame and leaning his handsome head on his hand. He regarded Fido and Honor warily from the corner of an eye, and endeavoured to determine what was best to do. All this while the carriage had not ceased to move, and especially to jolt, as the recent rains had revealed a number of rocks in the lane that the coachman evidently found himself unable to avoid. A particularly violent lurch interrupted Mr. Kemp's reflections rudely and threw him up against the joyous Fido.

"I beg your pardon," he was saying to the dog, as one begs pardon without thinking of a door-jamb or a lamp-post that has been encountered accidentally. Mr. Kemp's unnecessary courtesy, however, was repaid most discourteously by dear Fido who, taking umbrage at being squashed so suddenly, bit Mr. Kemp on the arm. There was more confusion now even than before in the carriage: Honoria began an instant and steady stream of apologies and inquiries; Fido, excited by whatever it was that was happening, barked monotonously and enthusiastically on a high pitch; and Mr. Claude Kemp became aware that his arm was bleeding.

"Damme, if this beast is rabid I'll shoot him," he exclaimed upon perceiving his wound. "I'll shoot him, anyway!"

"Are you hurt? What must I do? Coachman, coachman!" Honoria cried, beating furiously against the roof of the carriage to attract the driver's attention. "What can he be thinking of?" she demanded in exasperation, when the driver did not turn round.

"Damme, damme, and damnation!" Claude remarked. "A fine seduction this. He'll not answer you," he flung at last at the frantic Honoria.

"Why not?" asked she, at the same time reaching for Claude's arm in order to examine the bite.

Mr. Kemp pulled the arm from out of her grasp and muttered, "He has orders not to." Honoria was left to ponder this extraordinary explanation while Claude rapped loudly at the cab with his good arm, and called for a halt.

The coachman heard him and the vehicle slowed to a stop.

"Where are we?" asked Honoria, suddenly distracted by the unfamiliar landscape in which they had stopped. "This—this is the road to Tunbridge Wells, is not it? I thought we were to drive along the lanes near Pittering—"

"Never mind, enough of that now," Claude snapped. Everything had begun so propitiously! How had it all gone astray? "That dog," he said ominously, "that dog will hang before this day's work is done or my name's not—"

"Sir!" Honoria broke in. "He is not to blame at all. It was you who collided with him so startlingly. I am very sorry, and I hope you are not much hurt, but there is no sense in blaming Fido."

"Did you wish to get out, sir?" the coachman was asking through the window. "It's miles more to the Rose and Crown—"

"Stop that infernal yelping!" Claude commanded.

"But sir—" insisted the coachman, much stung.

"Not you, the dog—stop it! Be silent, I say!"

It was some while before order was restored in the ill-fated carriage, but at last, by dint of everybody's saying what to do at once a score of times or more, the situation was got into hand. Claude's arm was bandaged with the coachman's rather greasy cravat; Fido was restored to a state of relative calm on the floor of the carriage; the driver was instructed to turn round to Pittering and return directly to Stonebur Cottage; and Honoria was satisfied that she would soon be safe at home where she belonged. Of the four involved, the originator of the excursion was the least pleased with its outcome: he had had plans, not one of which had come right, and now his arm ached like the very devil.

"Well, that's outside of enough," he muttered as the arm began to feel stiff. "I shall have to see your saw-bones of a father-in-law," he added.

"We might go to Sweet's Folly first," Honoria offered with extraordinary generosity, extraordinary because for her own part she was extremely relieved to see the expedition at an end, for whatever reason, and the drive to Sweet's Folly would only delay her return home.

"No," said Claude, then "Yes," as he felt a pang travel from his forearm to his shoulder. "Tell the driver."

"Coachman! Coachman!" Honoria called again. Again there was no response.

"Damn that man's eyes!" Claude shouted. "Can't he see the game is off? Jimmy, you scoundrel, Jimmy!"

The driver answered his master's signal and was told to go to Sweet's Folly instead. From then it was only a matter of waiting until they arrived at their new destination, although at one point Honoria noticed the dressing on Claude's arm was proving inadequate.

"Blood," she pointed out faintly.

"Wrap it in my cravat," he directed; and so Honoria was obliged to untie the intricately knotted neck-cloth under Claude's chin, and to wrap it round the old bandage. Fido was about to take exception to this unwonted closeness between his young mistress and (so he perceived Claude) his rival in her affections, but Honoria silenced him with a sharp command before he could get too very excited. Minutes later they drew up before Sweet's Folly. Honoria sprang unattended from the carriage and ran inside to summon Jepston. Ten minutes later Mr. Kemp was submitting to examination by the doctor, and Honoria was consulting with her mother-in-law.

Mrs. Blackwood had drawn her new daughter into the breakfast-room, a handsomely panelled apartment that was yet rather too square to be elegant in its proportions. Mrs. Blackwood had furnished it with a round table in order to draw attention from this fault in the room's dimensions, and it was to this table that she now took Honoria, seating her on a chair next her own. Corinna Blackwood was far too overset herself to enquire, or even to wonder, by what chance Honor was in Mr. Kemp's company. On the contrary, she allowed Honoria to say no more than good-day before launching into an account of what events (so far as she could tell) had taken place that day in her home. "But I cannot imagine," she ended by saying, "I simply cannot imagine what in Heaven's name they might have quarrelled over. Can you, my dear?"

Honoria could imagine only too well. "I, think, madam . . . Might I speak with Emily?"

"But no, my dear!" the elder Mrs. Blackwood exclaimed in evident consternation. "I tell you she is locked up! Shut away, under strictest orders from my husband that she is not to receive visitors. There is the problem, you see," she repeated agitatedly.

"Clearly, the first matter for you, dear madam, is to calm yourself," Honor said. "It can serve no purpose to anyone to see you succumb to hysteria."

"I do not feel hysterical—" Mrs. Blackwood began, but she looked very much as if she did. "Perhaps you are right."

"I suggest some ratafia," Honor went on. "And then . . ." But she truly could not think what to advise other than a draught of the soothing liquor.

"Honoria, you know something about all this, do not you?" Mrs. Blackwood said, when the ratafia had been fetched and drunk.

"I—You must wait," said poor Honor, who was loth to say any more than she had to. "I am so terribly sorry; you will understand . . ." she murmured. "Might we not send to learn what has happened to Mr. Kemp?" she asked suddenly.

Information was accordingly sought, through the good offices of Mr. Jepston, and word received that Mr. Kemp's wound was a minor one, not to be fretted about. Owing, however, to his considerable loss of blood, Dr. Blackwood had administered a sedative and laid him temporarily to bed in one of the guest-chambers upstairs. Honoria, relieved to know there was no expectation of further complications, and particularly glad to find she could now do nothing for the unfortunate Mr. Kemp, asked her mother-in-law if she might be driven home by the Blackwoods' coachman. "For truly," she added, "Mr. Kemp's coachman is the most peculiar man I ever heard of, and would not answer a how-do-you-do from me."

Corinna Blackwood obliged her daughter-in-law unquestioningly, for she had given up hope of learning anything from Honor. That young lady therefore arrived at Stonebur Cottage some quarter of an hour later, handed Fido into the care of Mrs. Traubin, and learned (almost to her dismay) that so far as anyone knew, Mr. Alexander Blackwood had not yet even noticed his wife's prolonged absence.

"And no one has called? No word from—from Emily Blackwood perhaps?"

"Sorry, madam. Not a word from any quarter," said the housekeeper, her fishy eyes looking rather smug than sorry in spite of what she said. "Am I to feed this dog?" she inquired.

"Feed him, yes. I will send word to my aunts later," Honoria said rather vaguely as she drifted up the stairs towards Alexander's study.

The door was closed, as it always was of late, and she hesitated long before she entered. She braced herself, finally, with the reflection that Emily had no other hope of aid than from herself and Alex and, straightening her back with savage self-discipline, she knocked and went in to her husband.

Chapter IX

The Misses Deverell were entertaining, a thing they rarely did except between themselves. Tonight, however, a guest was within the little house in Bench Street—a guest, moreover, from the highest rank of local gentry.

"You do not think he will find our table wanting?" Mercy asked timidly, just after his acceptance of their invitation had been received.

"Wanting? But wanting what?" Prudence was in a fine humour; her scheme appeared to be working famously.

"Wanting variety," Mercy suggested promptly. "Or richness. Or imagination."

"Do you find it wanting?"

"O no!"

"Then he will not."

"That is very sensible, Prudence," said the other musingly. "I should never have thought of that. I do not, so he will not. It is very sensible. And symmetrical," she added. "I like that."

"Good, my dear. Then you run upstairs and prepare your toilette, while I confer with Mary. She must be reminded how to serve a dinner, I daresay. She appears to have forgot the proper fashion."

"Do you know, Prue, I thought that!" Mercy agreed, much struck. "Just yesterday she held out two dishes to me at once, and neither of them equipped with a ladle, and I said to myself, 'Mercy, I do believe Mary has forgot how to serve a proper dinner.' I said those very words, Prudence!" she went on, wondering mildly. "Though only to myself, naturally."

"Naturally, my dear."

"Naturally."

Miss Mercy mounted the stairs as she had been bidden, and descended not long after looking very fresh and trim in a light blue muslin gown. She was in plenty of time to greet the squire, which was well, since Prudence had forgot to dress until she heard his knock upon the door.

"Do come in," said Mercy cordially, leading the way into the cramped parlour. The squire looked about himself for a moment, searching for a person to whom he might hand his cape and hat and so forth.

"Harrumph," said he, regarding Mercy's heedless back as she left him to himself in the tiny entrance-way. "So there you are!" he cried, finally espying poor Mary, who stood cowering in a dim corner of the hall, alarmed at the magnificence of the gentleman before her. For Sir Proctor had chosen to dress formally for dinner this evening. He rarely went out, and therefore had no notion of distinguishing between a banquet provided by the local politicos for his benefit and a dinner for three cooked in homely fashion in Bench Street; he never went to London, nor perused any modish journal, and therefore had no notion whatever of trousers; and in consequence of all this, he was attired in the most correct of outfits—according to his lights. He wore knee-breeches, buff in colour, silk stockings, and shiny, buckled pumps. His white cravat was plainly but most neatly tied above a white waistcoat, and his coat was elegantly cut. With his superb head of snowy hair, he looked excessively handsome (though slightly out of place in the shabby little house) and rather like a fashion plate from a magazine ten years out of date. He handed Mary his things and hastened after his disappearing hostess.

"I look forward to our game of chess," said he, trying for the sake of politeness not to ejaculate something untoward about the cats. There were more of them than even he had expected, and he had been prepared for many. They mewed and cried and purred, rubbed their sleek backs against his silk stockings, pounced upon his pumps, and hurled themselves, when he sat, into his lap.

"So indeed do I, sir," Mercy replied, gazing fondly at her small friends. "That is Tiger on your knees, sir. Is not the weather fine? I so enjoy open weather. And how dull it was when I stopped at Colworth! Do you not recall, sir? The rain simply poured, and poured—and—poured," she rattled on, failing to find a verb other than pour. "You must find your daily ride more cheerful now the sun shines again. Though it is dreadfully chill, for all that . . . I so often wonder how it is that the fiercest sun in winter will not warm the earth half so much as the most leaden of summer skies. Do not you wonder, sir? I am sure

I have no notion. The oven in the kitchen, the fire in the fireplace—they do not burn less brightly in winter! On the contrary, I have frequently remarked that the warmth of a fire when one truly stands in need of it is even greater than when one might do without. Of course, we haven't nearly the number of fireplaces you have at Colworth. If we did, we'd have nothing *but* fireplaces! That is Muffin licking your pump, Sir Proctor. Taking little thing, is she not?"

"Very taking," he lied. Cat fur flew everywhere about him, it seemed; his clothes, impeccable when he had entered, now had grown quite woolly.

"Prudence will be down in a moment," Mercy continued pleasantly. "We have been so looking forward to your visit. And here you are! I find it so odd, the way we will anticipate events. All day Prudence and I—Prudence is my sister, you know—Prudence and I have been rushing about preparing one thing and another, saying, 'The squire will want this,' and 'The squire will like that,' and so forth, as if your arrival here signalled the start of a new century or—or something like that, and yet here you are! Here you are and the grandmother clock continues to tick just as it did before; the kittens still purr and the dogs yap . . . and you and I sit here just as if nothing at all were happening. And then, I am sure I never thought Prudence would take so long at her toilette; I am sure when I imagined your reception here I thought of Prudence welcoming you, and yet she is not here and life goes on very much without her! Is it not most peculiar?"

The squire agreed obligingly that it was most peculiar. For all he had been prepared, he was shocked at the shabbiness of the place. He had always lived in comfort, and though he was aware of poverty and squalor as things abstract and distinct from himself, he had never once considered how it would be to live in straitened circumstances. Miss Mercy Deverell seemed to him singularly cheerful for one confined to such uncomfortable quarters. His thoughts had run on this theme all through her prattle, and only broke off at the arrival of Miss Prudence.

"Sir Proctor, I am delighted to see you," said she, her hawkish nose wrinkling at the bridge as she smiled. She crossed the threshold into the tiny parlour and extended her hand towards him. He rose and bowed over it, murmuring his thanks for her invitation.

"And did you—did you arrive alone?" she asked coyly.

"I did, madam," he said puzzled. "Save for my coachman, I mean."

"And there was . . . you did not bring us any little gift?" she suggested, with a sly smile. She was thinking, naturally, of Fido.

"Prudence, what do you wish to say?" Mercy exclaimed reproachfully. She had utterly forgot about the dog, and was (for all intents and purposes) as ignorant of him as was Sir Proctor. "My sister is *very* odd sometimes," she explained to that gentleman. "She never has had any notion of propriety, either. Prudence, it is really too ill-bred of you to ask for gifts."

"I do not—" Prudence began, then broke off, glaring at Mercy. To say more would be to reveal what their scheme had been. Evidently it had miscarried; evidently too, Mercy no longer recalled what it was. Poor Prudence was forced to wonder in silence what had happened to her *coup de grâce*, and wonder she did, all through dinner and coffee and the tedious, tedious chess game. And it was most vexatious of Mercy to have forgot all about it—even more vexatious, perhaps, than the knowledge that it must have failed. Mercy and the squire were able to enjoy their dinner—in spite of the fact that it was awkwardly served, and rather poor fare to begin with—but Prudence could find nothing to like in the whole of the evening. It was all very frustrating. The elder Miss Deverell was exceedingly glad to see her much-anticipated guest depart.

"And stay away!" said she, when the front door had been shut upon the visitor.

"Prudence!"

Miss Deverell reminded her sister of Fido.

"O my! Is that not the oddest thing? Wherever can he be?"

Prudence muttered darkly of irresponsibility on the part of certain small friends.

"Well, it cannot be helped now," Mercy said calmly. "I am sure he will return tonight. He is a very good doggie."

"And what of Sir Proctor?"

"He is very good, too," she answered mildly. "O! You mean, will he return? I think he will. He said he would, Wednesday next." For the squire (in spite of his having been beaten again) had so liked his game with Mercy, he had settled with her to establish it as a weekly routine.

"I have a headache," Prudence announced severely.

"Poor dear! I am so dreadfully sorry. It must be the way Sir Proctor carried off my bishop so unexpectedly; it came very near giving me a headache as well. Do go to bed," she went on soothingly. "I shall wait up for Fido."

But Mercy had long to wait, since Honoria, in whose keeping Fido then was, found herself by far too abstracted in other matters to remember to send him to Bench Street. Alexander had received her into his library with that same exaggerated courtesy she had noticed in him the day before, and begged her politely to sit down.

"Thank you," she said, drawing up a small chair near to his desk and seating herself on its gold-and-blue brocaded cushion.

"There is some household matter you wished to discuss?" Alex began, a strangely cold, almost sardonic light showing in his green eyes. "Or, is this merely a social call?"

"Alex, please . . ."

He ran an unconscious hand through his fair curls. "Honoria?"

"My dear, this is neither a domestic conference nor an idle chat. Something dreadful has happened to Emily."

Alexander's interest was sparked now, and he dropped his affected manner at once. The chilling gleam went out of his eyes, to Honoria's great relief, as he turned his full attention to what she said. As rapidly as possible, she gave him an account of what her counsel to Emily had been, and how she guessed Dr. Blackwood had responded.

"And you say she is shut up alone?"

"Absolutely. Alex, I know she must ache for our help, but she is too proud to capitulate to my father-in-law. And too obstinate," she added regretfully.

"I do not see what we are to do," he returned flatly.

"We must go and speak with your father. *You* must go," she amended.

"What shall I say? He is quite right."

"Quite right!" she exclaimed indignantly. "Alexander, imagine your feelings if your work were taken from you. Imagine what your life would be had your father refused to send you to Cambridge. Imagine," she said hotly, "being obliged to plod along with your geometry in the deepest ignorance, the profoundest darkness, at the mercy of country schoolmasters and outmoded texts. And imagine being informed it was quite right that you should do so, all on account of your having been born of a certain sex, in a certain family! Quite right!" she nearly shouted. "Quite impossible!"

"I believe," Alexander said slowly, after a long silence during which she simply stared at him, "I believe you are correct. I am sorry for my former heedless statement. Life would be utterly intolerable without the possibility of achievement in my field. I will go to my father."

"Alex," she said anxiously, putting out a hand to check him as he began to rise from his desk. "Alex, tell your father we will take Emily to London. Tell him we will chaperon her, and be responsible for her."

"I do not see—"

"Tell him she will never be alone," she went on pleadingly. "Say I will be certain to find my parents' friends there, and to introduce her into good society." Her face became very sober and proud as she mentioned her parents. "I am not without friends, you know, though I have never met them."

"I will say so," Alex promised. He jumped from his desk and rang for Mrs. Traubin, then instructed her when she came to ready the carriage and have Traubin lay out his driving clothes.

"May I come with you?" Honor asked timidly.

"If you like." His tone had returned to one of utter indifference.

"I shall, then," said she, though her instincts generally forbade her to go where she might not be wanted.

They arrived together at Sweet's Folly just at dinner-time. "Where is my father?" Alex demanded of Jepston. The butler, justifiably startled by Mr. Blackwood's imperious tone and angry pallor, hesitated for a moment.

"In his study, sir," he said finally. "Shall I tell him you and Mrs. Blackwood are here?"

"No," said Alex, tossing his driving cape at the astonished Jepston and striding past him into the house. "I will go to him myself."

Honoria was left standing with the butler. "Is—is the young master quite well?" he dared to ask her, while helping her remove her pelisse.

Honoria smiled a peculiar, thoughtful smile. "Incredible, isn't it?" she murmured. "I will be in the drawing-room, should anyone wish to see me, Jepston. Emily—Miss Blackwood is still—?" she began inquiringly, and stumbled.

"Miss Blackwood remains in her room," he returned, comprehending her instantly. He bowed her into the drawing-room and went away to see if he could not eavesdrop on the master and his son.

"Let her out of her room," Alexander was commanding by this time. "No purpose can be served by her incarceration, sir. Let her out."

"Your sister is aware by what means she may regain her freedom," said Dr. Blackwood, but not as firmly as was his custom. The spectacle of his son, livid with rage and spewing directives, first surprised and then almost frightened him.

"She will go to London. We will take her, Father."

"We—?"

"My wife and myself." Alexander began to pace the room furiously, talking all the while as his father had never seen him do, and looking a very fine picture with his hands clenched into fists and his golden hair streaming. "Emily has done a remarkable thing. She had had the courage and the ability to succeed where not one woman in one million might have. She will go to London and we will take her. She will study all she likes and take full advantage of every opportunity offered to her by her instructors. In the meanwhile, Honor will see to it she comports herself as befits her birth and station, becomes familiar with the life of the *ton*, and meets as many eligible gentlemen as you may desire. There is no need for you to lift a finger. Now, have you any objections, sir?"

Dr. Blackwood was too stunned to reply.

"Send for her, have her fetched here," Alexander said, and rang the bell himself. Jepston answered with a swiftness surprising only if one did not take into account the fact that he had had his ear to the keyhole throughout the entire proceedings.

"Fetch my sister," Mr. Blackwood told him.

Mr. Jepston bowed and disappeared, not even taking the time to glance at his employer.

"It is not as simple as you say," that worthy had finally begun, when his daughter's entrance interrupted him.

"Alex—?"

"Jepston, send for my wife," said he.

In a few moments all the Blackwood family—including Mrs. Blackwood, who had got wind of the excitement through the thoughtfulness of Mr. Jepston—were assembled in the library at Sweet's Folly. There ensued an animated discussion—in which Alexander assumed and maintained the lead—regarding Miss Blackwood's future.

"I will go, too," said Corinna Blackwood.

"No one will go," her husband contradicted.

"You need not trouble to come," Honoria told her mother-in-law kindly. "I will see to her well-being."

"Honoria, if I may speak in my own house," the doctor began severely, "I should like to point out that neither you nor Alexander ever having been to London, you do not make suitable chaperons."

"I have been to London," Alex stated flatly, and then coloured crimson from his neck to his scalp.

A silence fell upon the room.

"When have you been to London?" his father demanded finally, as all eyes stared at Alex.

"While I was up at Cambridge. On several occasions."

"I can imagine for what purpose you went there," said his father slowly.

"No doubt you imagine correctly," his son returned. The blush receded from his cheeks and he went on evenly, "I am a man, grown now, and was then, and do not feel under compulsion to justify my mode of life."

Of all the occupants of the library, perhaps Honoria was most stunned by this news. She knew little of life at Cambridge, but she knew enough to guess that her husband's visits to London had much, in all likelihood, to do with women—and women, moreover, very different from herself. Honoria was not missish, but she fairly gasped now. It had never occurred to her that her husband might have had anything to do with passion.

"It will not be necessary to discuss this further in the presence of ladies," Dr. Blackwood pointed out stiffly. "The fact is, your having been to London on such a—such a mission still gives you no experience of the *ton.*"

"I must beg to contradict, sir," said Alexander, a very strange light blazing in his eyes.

"What on—Good Heavens, Alex!" Dr. Blackwood spluttered. "What are you trying to tell me?"

"It is neither here nor there, as you will doubtless agree. Suffice it to say that I am as familiar with the habits of good society as I need be to manage passably in London."

Emily, meanwhile, though she was burning with curiosity to know how on earth her brother had established a connexion (if indeed he had) within the *ton*, and when, and with whom, yet considered the problem to be of no immediate significance. "May the subject of this argument say something?" she inquired. Without waiting for permission, she continued, "I do not see how you can object, sir, to my going to London for the season under the aegis of my brother and his wife. On the contrary, I think you must be very pleased, especially as you are so eager to see me married. I have won the scholarship, whether you like it or no; I have business in London. I ought probably to have been sent there years ago, if such were your plans for me, as it is clear Claude Kemp will never offer for me; and he is the only eligible—"

At this juncture she was interrupted by a loud, male harrumph. All eyes turned from Miss Blackwood to the newcomer, who was soon seen to be Mr. Kemp himself.

"I hope I do not intrude," said he, in a voice still faintly gruff from his enforced nap. "I confess I am not quite awake, yet I thought to hear my name mentioned. I only came to take my leave of you, Dr. Blackwood, and to thank you for your services."

Emily flushed, and deemed it very rude of him to refer to what he had overheard.

"Keep to your bed when you get home," said Dr. Blackwood, "and let that arm of yours lie still when you can. How does it feel?"

"Much improved, thank you," Claude bowed. He perceived Honoria, sitting in a far corner on a green velvet settee, and crossed the room to her. "I regret very much that our *tête-à-tête* was ended so abruptly this afternoon," he murmured, bowing to her, "not only for the sake of my arm, but for the sake of our understanding one another better. May I hope to call upon you tomorrow?"

Honor glanced uneasily at Alex, whose face had suddenly turned—so it seemed—to stone. He would not meet her glance and only stared fixedly at the floor, as if refusing even to hear what Claude Kemp said.

"I may—I may be otherwise engaged tomorrow," she managed finally. "Perhaps another day."

"Mr. Kemp is always welcome at Stonebur Cottage," Alexander said suddenly, though still regarding the floor. He did not at all sound as if he meant what he said.

"You are everything that is kind, Alexander," Kemp returned lightly. "I hope I may have the honour of seeing you all again very soon," he added, bowing to the company. He wished all good-day and quitted the library.

"As I was saying, Father," Emily stated pointedly. No one except the principals had any idea of the exact meaning of the scene just enacted, but it suited Emily down to the ground, for it illustrated what she had been saying to a nicety. "I think I will fare better among strangers than I do at home."

Dr. Blackwood, forced now to take note of Kemp's encroaching familiarity with Honoria, finally admitted to himself that his son's marriage was in imminent danger. He folded his hands upon his desk, scrutinized them keenly, and said in a dull voice, "Go to London."

"My dear—" Mrs. Blackwood began.

"Go to London," he repeated.

The younger members of the party were too shocked to speak for a moment; then they broke into a prolonged series of whoops, huzzas, and mutual embracements. Emily's joy knew no bounds: she even kissed her father. Honor, who was to travel at last—at last!—was in ecstasies of gratitude to everyone. Only Alexander, who had no personal stake in the matter, remained calm in his victory.

"I do not think you will regret this, sir," he said to his father.

Dr. Blackwood shrugged. Fatigue showed everywhere in his features. "I hope you are right," was all he said, and then repaired alone to his bed-chamber. Mrs. Blackwood followed him presently.

The remainder of the party stopped in the library, scheming and suggesting, objecting and arguing, supposing and proposing and opposing one another. There were so many decisions to be made! Where they were to reside in London, how to hire a house, when they would journey there, what they would require, to whom they might apply . . . the list was endless, and every new difficulty an excitement. At length they discovered they were agreed at least on one thing: all were famished. Learning that the poor cook had been waiting dinner this past hour and more, they removed instantly to the dining-parlour and partook of a very pleasant meal. The elder Blackwoods dined alone, upstairs.

It was determined at last that Alexander would go by himself to London before the close of the coming se'ennight, to engage lodgings for them. Time was of the essence, for Emily's studies began scarcely a month from then, and continued throughout the coming year.

"I protest, Emily, that is a very awkward time to begin," Alexander remarked. "Just about the end of term for everyone else, I should think."

"I believe that is done on purpose," said she, glowing at the thought of her education. "They take the amateurs in when the others have gone home, so that by autumn, when everyone returns, we needn't be slowed by beginning in the first form, nor humiliated by lacking technique for the upper ones."

"In any case, it's a sticky time. London will be teeming with people hoping to engage apartments for the season."

"Alex, you are so worldly!" Honor could not help exclaiming. The cheerful aspect of her new prospects had almost made her forget how strained her relations with her husband were.

Alexander, unfortunately, had not forgot. "I am not an infant," he observed.

"No one suggested you were," Emily said rather sharply, and then softened at once. "I do love you both for escorting me! And I promise to be no trouble at all."

"How could you be?" Honor asked, embracing her fondly.

"How can she help it?" Alex took up immediately. "Emily my dear, there is one hitch in all this that no one has cared to mention as yet. Hadn't we best examine it?"

"And what is that?" she returned, frowning faintly.

"Mr. Cedric Blackwood," he answered succinctly.

"O. O dear," Emily said.

"O dear," chorused Honor.

"O dear, indeed," Alex resumed. "But 'O dear' won't help it. What, if anything, do you propose to do about him?"

"I suppose—" Emily began, and halted. "It seems cowardly, perhaps, but how will it be if we do nothing at all about him?"

"Don't you think the members of the academy will be just a trifle surprised at Master Cedric's gowns?" he suggested sceptically. "Not to mention his coiffure, his voice, and his rather effeminate address."

"Well, of course they must find out sooner or later."

"Of course."

"I only think it will be better if they find out later."

"When there is less time to object," he pursued.

"Precisely."

"If they learn now, they may have time to choose another winner," Honor agreed anxiously. "I believe Emily is right."

"All our plans may be overset in a moment," Alex warned. "You must prepare yourself for that, Em."

"I am prepared," she said grimly.

"More for a bloody battle than for a disappointment," Honoria observed, noticing her friend's clenched hands and stern tone.

"If need be," said she. The topic was let drop after this and the conversation turned upon other details of the forthcoming adventure, but the problem gave them all pause in the coming weeks. It seemed excessively unlikely that the judges would make no demur upon discovering Cedric to be Emily. However, there was nothing to be done about it at present, and a hundred other things occupied their minds.

Honoria was too weary, on returning to Stonebur that night, to do anything else than jump into bed. This was well, since had she had the energy to notice it, she might have sunk into the dismals again at her husband's present resumption of chilly formality in regard to her. As it was, she slept soundly and dreamt only of London's wonders. In the morning Mrs. Traubin brought her her chocolate in bed, and enquired of her what she was to do about the beast.

"The beast?"

"That mongrel. Fido, I believe you said."

"O dear! I have not thought of him once from that moment to this!" she cried as if stricken. "My poor aunts must be distracted with worry. Send him to Bench Street at once."

"On foot, or in the carriage?" Mrs. Traubin asked sarcastically.

"In the carriage, I think. Yes, silly though it seems."

"He seems to have taken your little Amber in aversion," the housekeeper went on, not quite necessarily.

"Has he? How odd! He lives with two score of cats, at least."

"Well, it's a blessing for your aunts he doesn't live with this one," she replied unpleasantly. "Nearly took her head off, Fido did."

"Well, I'm very glad he didn't," Honor said. She was eager to bring this discussion to a close, so that she might contemplate what was best to do next.

"Had to separate them myself," Mrs. Traubin continued, her fishy eyes gleaming malignantly.

"That was very good of you," said the young mistress.

"I should think so. I know I never engaged to work in a bear-garden—" the housekeeper took up threateningly. She was meaning to drift on in this vein—probably for ever—but Honor stopped her at last. "Thank you, Mrs. Traubin," she said curtly. "That will be all."

The elder lady, who had never before encountered the slightest resistance in her young employer, was too surprised to do anything but curtsey and depart. "Never seen her so disagreeable," thought she to herself, as she left the room. "A proper little tyrant is what I think," she added with satisfaction. She repeated these sentiments to her husband a few moments later, and resolved in future not to be so biddable with Mrs. Blackwood.

Honoria herself was a little surprised at what she had done. It was not like her to silence people when she could bear to listen to them. Yet, it had worked very well, and she did not really believe she had overstepped the bounds of courtesy too very much. It must be admitted, she did consider the possibility, but her conclusion was that she had acted properly. "For I can't be bullied by the servants," she remarked to Amber, who had strolled into the room, "even if she did save your sweet little head." This incident, trifling though it was, constituted a milestone for Honor, and provided a lesson she was to remind herself of repeatedly in the months to come.

Young Mrs. Blackwood passed that morning at the writing-table in the tiny sitting-room upstairs, composing letters to be sent to her parents' friends. They were awkward to phrase, since she had never met any one of these people—at least, not that she could remember. Through her aunts, however, she knew the names and styles of some three or four Londoners she might apply to, among them her godfather, Lord Sperling. To him she penned the longest letter, for though she did not know him, she had at least written to him before—quite recently, in fact. It had been to apprise him of her marriage, and his lordship had been kind enough to send a decanter and glasses of cut crystal, which now resided on the side-table in the dining-parlour. His remembering her on that occasion gave Honoria some hopes of his assistance when she arrived in London, for unless someone undertook their introduction into society, the little party from Pittering would be quite at sea. Lord Sperling was a widower, but his wife had left behind her a daughter, who must be grown to womanhood now. It seemed to Honoria that if their situations were reversed—if it were Miss Sperling who sought introduction to the *ton*, and Honoria who had dwelt within it all her life—Honoria would have no hesitation in doing her possible for the petitioner. She felt, therefore, quite optimistic about the prospects of the Blackwoods in London society.

These missives had just been sealed, and their directions inscribed on them, when a brisk rap at the door interrupted her, and Mrs. Traubin came in.

"Gentleman to see you, ma'am," said she, approaching to hand Honoria an engraved card.

It belonged to Claude Kemp. "Thank you, Mrs. Traubin. Ask him to wait in the parlour, if you please."

Mrs. Traubin grumbled something dark about tea.

"I shall ring if anything is wanted," said the mistress serenely. Mrs. Traubin sketched a curtsey and departed on her mission.

"Alex," Honoria called tentatively, a minute later, while knocking on the library door. "Alex?" She entered to find her husband reclining at his desk, his chair precariously leaning and his feet perched upon a half-open drawer. The book in his lap appeared to absorb all his attention. "Alex," she repeated, drawing nearer.

He looked up finally and asked what was wanted.

"Claude Kemp is here. Alex, I wish you will receive him with me."

"What on earth for?" he inquired, annoyed.

"For—because—" she faltered. "Because I wish you will, that is all."

"Honoria, this is doing it a bit too brown."

"I beg your pardon?"

"Receive him alone. There is nothing improper in it, and certainly no need to maintain a pretence of unity before him."

"But he frightens me," she protested sincerely.

Alexander's mouth pulled into a dissatisfied curve. "I am sure your fears are quite unfounded. Go and speak with him. I will come if you cry out."

"Alex, really," she said, ready to weep.

"Alex, really what?" he exclaimed, his voice breaking from its previous evenness. "My wife, go and visit with your friend. He is come to see you. And when you have done with him, there is a matter I wish to discuss with you regarding our future together."

"What is it? Tell me now," she begged anxiously.

"It will wait." His tone was positively grim, and she feared to provoke him further. She promised to come to him the moment Mr. Kemp had gone, and went to the parlour alone.

"Mrs. Blackwood, you look very well today," said Claude, with an exaggerated bow.

"And you seem in very high spirits, sir," she returned.

"I am; I am, madam. I perceive I may expect London to be gayer than ever this season. The prospect is delicious."

Here was something Dr. Blackwood did not know, or had forgot at least. Claude Kemp passed every season in London; in fact, kept a town-house there expressly for that purpose. The unfortunate doctor, instead of delivering his son and daughter-in-law from evil, had thrust them directly towards it.

"If you mean my husband's and my intention to escort Miss Blackwood there," she began, "then your—but how do you come to know of it?" she broke off. "It was decided only yesterday."

"Mr. Jepston of Sweet's Folly keeps in close communication with the doctor's tiger," he began, smiling his cheerless, intelligent smile. "That tiger, you see, is quite intimate with the second upstairs maid at Colworth. That maid, moreover, is the niece of our good Mrs. Cafferleigh, who for her part shares all her bits of gossip with our Boothby, who in turn occasionally transmits them to me. And so I had it from Boothby, as it were. It is an excellent intelligence-gathering system, I think, far better than what Wellington employs no doubt."

"I will take care to preserve my secrets from Mr. Jepston," said Honoria. "It is quite chilling."

"Pittering is a small place," Mr. Kemp reminded her, "as I believe I once observed to you."

This sidelong allusion to one of his offers for her reminded Honoria that she disliked Kemp's company, and had some reason to distrust him now as well. "How is your arm, sir?" she inquired civilly.

"A trifle tender, but much improved, thank you."

"I am glad to hear it."

"If it gladdens you, I will take care to mend even more quickly than I'd planned to."

She smiled woodenly at this gallantry and sat in silence.

"I am afraid our explanation was delayed yet again, yesterday," he observed.

"I trust it is no longer necessary."

He shrugged. "No, in fact it is not. The nature of the cause of Miss Blackwood's rather—ah, erratic behaviour is now known to me, and all the neighbourhood too, I should think. As for your husband's—well, I can guess."

"Mr. Kemp," Honor broke in hurriedly. "I do not wish to be rude, but may I ask what is the reason of your call today? I have many things to accomplish before we begin our journey to London."

"I would not keep you from them for the world," said he, smiling icily. "I merely wished to promise you my assistance, should you need any, in London, though perhaps," he added unkindly, "your husband's connexions there will see to your welfare adequately."

"Mr. Kemp, how long were you eavesdropping at that door?" she demanded sharply, burning with resentment and anger.

"I did not eavesdrop, but only waited for a convenient pause to enter," said he, with false dignity. "And I heard enough, if that is what you wonder."

"Enough for what?" she spat back at him.

"Enough to know why your relations with your husband might be—strained."

"Mr. Kemp, I must ask you to leave," she said, rising with an attempt at appearing threatening.

He looked rather amused than frightened. "I go down to London next week," he said calmly, standing when she did. "I will look forward to seeing you there, if I am not so happy as to do so here."

"Traubin will see you out," was all she said, and rang the bell.

"It will not be necessary," he returned airily. He bowed low once more and obligingly quitted the room, prudently omitting to kiss her hand. Honoria sat down to compose herself a moment forcing herself to breathe deeply and think with clarity. Really, it was too dreadful of him to behave so—so familiarly with her. She felt quite humiliated—degraded, almost—and decided at last that Emily's poor opinion of him was in no way exaggerated. She made shift to calm herself, but succeeded only in growing more and more outraged at his conduct. One thing was certain: Mr. Kemp should see neither hide nor hair of her in London. It was a very large place, from all she had heard, and she had no intention of frequenting the society he graced. That decision made, she was able to turn her thoughts to Alexander. She had no notion what he wished to discuss, but she thought it wise to prepare herself for something disagreeable. He had looked very ominous indeed when he requested the interview. However, her curiosity got the better of her before she could restore herself to serenity, and she hastened to the library and knocked as full of hope as one might expect a young woman to be—and not the least bit ready for what she heard.

Chapter X

"This affair of Emily's," Alexander commenced, when brief courtesies had been exchanged and Honoria comfortably settled in the velvet chair, "gives us an opportunity of implementing a plan I have been pondering some while." He paused, turning over a pencil in his hands and regarding it gravely.

"And what is that?" his wife prodded.

"That is, the establishment of separate households for you and myself."

"I beg your pardon?" She was certain she had misunderstood him.

"It has been borne in upon me increasingly, since our removal to this house, that the relations presently existing between you and me do not justify our sharing a residence," he explained tonelessly. "You requested me to marry you; I did marry you; in the eyes of the law we live together in a sanctified state of marriage. To less jaundiced eyes, however," he continued, with a rather cynical grimace, "it is quite clear we have no business doing so. My presence here only hampers your—amusements, and yours only obliges me to keep regular hours that are sometimes inconvenient to my studies. Quite simply, I propose to engage two sets of rooms in London: one for my sister and yourself, and one for me."

Honoria could do nothing but gasp while her eyes filled with tears.

"You say nothing," he observed. "Am I to conclude this scheme is acceptable to you? There is no need to apprise my parents of it," he added, "if that troubles you."

Honoria's first instinct was to bend to his will, accept his terms uncomplainingly, and comfort herself when she might be private again with a very great deal of crying. After all, if Alexander could no longer suffer her company, then what right had she to inflict it upon him? He had been very kind to marry her; she had stipulated no further obligations when that arrangement had been made; therefore to complain would be to assert privileges that she knew did not belong to her. She began to say, "as you like," in an exceedingly muffled voice, when all at once her experience of that morning—when Mrs. Traubin had been forced to cede to her own will—returned to her and checked her. "I cannot like it," she amended presently. "No doubt you have every right to institute such a state of affairs, but if you do so it will be in opposition to my desires—not at all, as you suggest, to oblige me."

It was Alexander's turn to be surprised. "If you speak sincerely, as indeed you seem to—I do not understand you, Honoria."

"It is not necessary that you understand me," she returned, a bit giddy with her new-found power. "It is only necessary that you hear what I say and believe it. If you suggest the establishment of separate households to oblige me, you mistake my sentiments."

"I thought you had been delighted!" he exclaimed.

"I am not a triangle, Alex," said she. "You cannot manipulate me so easily as you do your diagrams and figures."

"I do not seek to manipulate you," he countered, "but only to puzzle out your nature. When we married—"

"I fear my nature is not so constant as that of a point or a plane."

"Not above half," he replied. His voice and features had lost that grim expression they had had earlier. He ran his slender fingers through his golden locks, and lapsed into abstracted silence.

"What will you do?" Honor asked, when some time had gone by with nothing said between them. She began now to feel anxious: perhaps she would have done better, after all, to have bowed to his will quietly.

"Do?" he repeated, rousing himself from his meditation.

"About the rooms in London," she prompted, sounding bolder than she felt.

"O! I suppose I must take a single town-house," he answered. He looked at her with a wide, open regard, as if surprised that she should ask.

"O!" said she, her tone quite as startled as his. Now that she had got her way, she did not know what to do with it. It was the first time she had prevailed in a decision of any import: she found the experience frightening, and immediately began a retreat into her former, more wonted, mode of behaviour. "But you are quite certain?" she entreated. "I do not—my presence in the town-house will not embarrass you?" she added, and coloured deeply.

"Why should it?" he inquired.

This was all much, much too confusing for Honor. Not only had she imposed her will upon her husband, but it seemed now she was to receive no punishment for having done so. In fact, he looked not in the least displeased—only distracted, as he so often had in the past.

"I don't know," she said lamely. "I suppose I may as well see about dinner now, if you will excuse me."

"Of course; pray go on—" he murmured, gesturing vaguely towards the door. He was as perfectly confused as she, and had no notion what had passed between them, or what it meant about their marriage. His well-regulated mind, however, would not allow him to concentrate for long upon a problem containing so many variables, and he turned, in time, to his work, leaving the question still unsolved.

And so it was that when, in due course of time, Alexander quitted Pittering Village and journeyed alone to London, he did so with the intention of engaging a single town-house, suitable for a small family, in an acceptably modish quarter of London. A very brief period of enquiry satisfied him, however, that he could not be over-nice in what he considered a sufficiently stylish neighbourhood, for indeed the greater part of the more eligible houses had been engaged by earlier comers. By the time he returned to Pittering, however, he was able to assure all concerned that they were to dwell in a very snug little house in Albemarle Street, a house of no great dimensions, but well proportioned and appointed. This news was received with indifference by Emily, who cared not where they lived, so long as they lived in London; and with great pleasure by Honoria, whose godfather resided at no great distance from there. Alexander's departure had caused her some sorrow, but his absence was not prolonged and she had been more than adequately occupied during it. For one thing, Corinna Blackwood had insisted on visiting the local dressmaker repeatedly—Emily and Honor in tow—and having carried out for them a number of garments that, she emphasised, were indispensable in London. Neither girl had a ballgown fit to wear, for of course they had no occasion to wear one in Pittering; moreover, their bonnets were all of the chip-straw country type, and therefore had to be replaced by others at the milliner's. Mrs. Blackwood was astute enough, however, to realize that the bulk of the young ladies' wardrobes ought to be purchased in London itself, for no matter how carefully she chose, there could never be anything in Pittering equal in quality and style to what was available in London. Therefore she made sure to invite Honoria frequently to tea at Sweet's Folly, where she conducted a series of lectures designed to impress upon the girls the importance of proper dress and the means by which it might be achieved. In addition, she imparted to them what little she recalled of London customs and proprieties, for she had been to the great city once only, and that when she was a young girl.

"I protest, Mamma has grown more wearisome than the dancing master!" said Emily at the end of one of these edifying sessions. The master to whom she referred had been engaged to give the young ladies some concentrated instruction in the most recent ball-room figures.

"It will all be done soon enough," Honor comforted her. So long as it would end in her visiting London, Honoria was willing to go through fire and ice. Everything was proceeding very well, in her estimation: she had contrived somehow to avoid any interviews with Claude Kemp after their last, most disagreeable one, and now he was gone out of the neighbourhood for the season. Her godfather had replied to her letter with quite a cordial note, albeit a brief one, informing her that though he himself was too much engaged with government affairs to devote a great deal of time to her and her party, his daughter Lady Jane Sperling might be applied to with any enquiries or requests. Alexander had dropped his frigid formality since their rather peculiar colloquy in his library, and had reverted to his old distracted air, which, though it had once irked her excessively, she now found most comforting in its familiarity. Naturally he still kept to his couch in the study, but this seemed a positively cheerful arrangement when contrasted with the one he had threatened.

What with one thing and another, the month allotted to them in which to prepare for their sojourn simply flew by. The trunks were packed and sent; Maria and the Traubins, who were to serve the party in London, were dispatched some days before the Blackwoods' departure; Alex and Honoria stopped at Sweet's Folly in the interim, where they were somewhat gloomily welcomed and entertained by Dr. Blackwood.

"I suppose you think London is all gaiety and uproar," he grumbled one morning at breakfast. He stared with saturnine solemnity at Honor, and continued, "It is not. A very great deal of town-life consists of dirt, and noise, and unpleasant sights such as you've never witnessed here in the country. And you will find yourself obliged to wait upon people you despise—and be courteous to them, too—and welcome them into your home."

The doctor's moroseness could not depress his daughter-in-law, however. "I expect all things have their good and bad qualities," she replied lightly.

The good doctor said, "Humph," and continued to warn her of how disagreeable town was likely to be until she excused herself to visit her aunts. "For we shall be gone scarcely a day from now, and I fear I shall have no other opportunity of telling them good-by," she said apologetically.

Dr. Blackwood popped the final morsel of a biscuit into his mouth, and waved her away irritably.

"Till dinner," she said cheerfully, with a graceful curtsey, but he was too dissatisfied with the state of things to be coaxed out of his bad humour so easily.

Prudence and Mercy Deverell had taken the news of their niece's present departure with their customary equanimity, and they continued to appear tolerably unruffled during this last farewell call.

"What is she come for?" Mercy asked sweetly of her sister, when Honoria had been admitted to the cramped parlour and given a cup of tea. "Don't gnaw at my skirt, Muffin—there's a dear thing."

"She says she is going to London," Prudence told her.

"I know she is going to London," said Mercy. "She informed us of that very thing not three weeks ago. Honoria, have you forgot? You told us you were going to London," she concluded, with the mildest tone of reproach possible.

"I do remember, Aunt Mercy," Honor assured her. "I only came to say good-by, this time, for we leave on the day after tomorrow."

"O! Is that all, then? Well, good-by, my dear," said Mercy obligingly, casting a side-long glance at Prudence as if to say, "I think our dear Honoria's wits are failing her."

"Good-by," Honor said uncomfortably; now she felt as if she ought to get up and depart immediately, even though she had just come. She too turned her eyes towards Prudence.

"That nice Kemp boy will be in London by now," said that lady, perceiving that some remark was wanted from her. On an impulse, she added persuasively, "Honor dear, are you very certain you hadn't rather marry him than Alexander Blackwood?"

"But I *have* married Alexander Blackwood!" she objected.

"O! So you have. Ah, well," Prudence went on, gesturing vaguely, "it was only a passing thought, after all." She had been thinking, of course, of how to win her way into Squire Kemp's coffers.

"Aunt Prudence, I must say—well, what a very peculiar question!" she ended, feeling more and more unsettled by this curious conversation. The little household in Bench Street had never seemed half so odd when she lived in it as it did now.

"Not a peculiar question at all," Mercy spoke up suddenly, feeling that she must fly to the defence of her sister, even against so gentle an attacker as Honoria. "A very straightforward question, on the contrary. Hadn't you rather marry Claude than Alex? So very clear! So elegantly phrased!"

Young Mrs. Blackwood gazed in astonishment at her aunts, but said nothing.

"Claude's hair is of a purer gold than Alexander's," Mercy went on, as if this somehow explained her sister's question. Nor would she be silent until she had had an answer of Honoria. "Well, is not it?" she demanded.

"Yes, it is," the poor girl assented, "but that is not a reason to marry one or the other of them!"

"Isn't it?" Mercy sniffed an eloquent sniff. "I don't know," she added airily.

Mrs. Blackwood thought with blissful anticipation of the time when she would be released from such conversations as this one, for a while at least. She took leave of her aunts presently, gratefully abandoning the attempt to comprehend them, but even then it seemed as if the eight-and-forty hours still remaining before their departure would never pass. So many last-minute promises and provisions; so many people to say good-by to; so much fret and bother! She was certain she would die before they came to an end of it; but she did not die, of course. In due time every possible detail had been taken care of; farewell embraces had been performed, and reperformed, and tears necessarily shed; the carriage had been laden with baggage and started off; it had returned five minutes later to collect what had been left behind; it had started off again, and had gone too far this time to be stopped when Emily's handkerchiefs were remembered at last to have been forgot.

"Then we are truly gone!" cried Emily, with amazement.

"O, most truly! Most distinctly, most unequivocally, most definitely gone!" Honor agreed, and the two girls set up a joyous shout so noisy and alarming that the coachman turned round to see what could be wanted.

Naturally, just as every painful moment had had to be lived through between their decision to go and their actual going, now every single inch of road between Pittering Village and the great metropolis had to be traversed, "crawled over, I think," Emily whispered to Honor, for (though she did not wish to hurt the driver's feelings) it appeared to her they went at a pitiful snail's pace. Yet, even this ordeal was done at last. Dinner was taken hastily at an inn about thirty miles from London, while the horses were changed, and just as dusk began to fall the landscape visible through the carriage windows—hitherto an un-relieved monotony of tree-dotted slopes and tiny villages—changed into that scene for which Honoria's eyes had hungered so long. Not a min-ute went by without an "Oooh" or "Ahhh" from one of the young la-dies until they had reached Albemarle Street, where they had to be rather dragged than escorted from the enchanted foot-path into the house, which was, as Emily reminded her brother, "only a house after all, and no doubt very like any other."

Once inside its doors, however, and reunited with Maria and the Traubins, the girls were able to forget for a moment the extraordinary mysteries still to be discovered in London and to turn their attention to what was to be their home. "It's very sweet," said Honoria approv-ingly to Alex, and Emily agreed whole-heartedly.

The house had two stories above the ground floor, besides garrets for the servants. The front doors led into a well-proportioned entrance hall, from which two other doors and the stairway were visible. These two doors opened, the one into a smartly furnished dining-parlour, the other into a breakfast-room. Long windows looked out onto the street, and similar windows appeared in the drawing-room on the floor above. Honor did not know quite what to make of the curious Egyp-tian motif this apartment seemed to suggest, but she heartily approved the pleasant study that shared the floor with the drawing-room. Up the next flight of stairs were four bed-chambers, two adjoining each other for the master and mistress of the house; and an excessively cosy little sitting-room done up in reds and roses. The ladies flew up and down the stairs, exclaiming now over the cheeriness of the breakfast-parlour, now at the chilly formality of the drawing-room. Honoria made a brief tour of the kitchens, heard the cook's complaints of them, and forgot them altogether, for if there was one thing she made sure of, it was that very little of her time would be passed *there*. The party at last reassembled in the dining-parlour, where Mrs. Traubin had caused an extensive cold collation to be laid out, to refresh the way-farers after their journey.

"Did you sit upon one of the benches in the drawing-room?" Emily enquired, adding, "For I cannot call them couches. How impossibly uncomfortable they are!"

"Well, we shan't use that apartment very often," Honor assured her. "At least, I hope not. It *is* most peculiar, is it not?" asked she, who had no notion of the Egyptian motif being quite the rage just then.

"Many another hostess would be green with envy," Alex broke in suddenly. He had not appeared to have been attending, but evidently he was. "It's excessively modish. I rather like it myself, though not particularly to sit in."

"Well, you would like it, naturally," said Emily to her brother, while Honor wondered again at her husband's familiarity with London vogues. "It's dreadfully geometrical."

"It wants some of your paintings," Alex offered gallantly.

"They would look quite absurd there," she objected.

Honoria began to be afraid her husband might think them ungrateful, so she broke in, "The house is perfect, Alexander, absolutely perfect. I am certain there is not another house in London that would suit us so well."

All at once, without the slightest warning, Alex grinned his delightful, crooked grin, an expression Honoria had not seen upon his features for aeons, it seemed. "You must keep your judgement of Albemarle Street until you have seen something to compare with it," he advised his wife.

"It is much more elegant than Sweet's Folly!" Honor protested. "And by far more pleasant than Colworth—"

"Wait until you have visited your godfather," he interrupted, still grinning. "I expect you will find that a very interesting experience."

Honoria was too glad to see him smiling to care to protest further, and the conversation turned on other schemes and topics until, at length, Emily pointed out sensibly that if they did not retire presently they would be unfit to do anything at all on the morrow. Soon after this she took herself off to the bed-chamber she had chosen; Alex and Honor removed to their adjoining rooms; and Alex, carelessly wishing his bride a good night, shut the door that connected their apartments. For several seconds Honoria waited, in dreadful suspense, to hear if he would turn the key in the lock, but he did not. Well, there was that to be thankful for at least, she told herself, and was very shortly afterwards (in spite of the din that seemed to echo ceaselessly in the streets of London) quite peacefully asleep.

Alexander had been correct about the visit to Lord Sperling's residence: it was an extremely interesting experience. Honoria and Emily were loth to enter the carriage again—they had much rather have walked—but Alexander dismissed this suggestion as being impossibly countrified, and so they drove instead. The drive was brief, but even so Honor was struck again, not so much by the buildings and monuments of London—though these were wonderful—as by the extraordinary throngs of people to be seen everywhere, and the press of carriages on the streets. Tunbridge Wells was nothing to it: there seemed to be more of people in London than there was of anything else. She and Emily resumed the chorus of exclamations that their arrival in the great city had inspired in them yesterday; Alexander did not join them, but sat with his old distracted look upon his countenance, neither laughing at nor looking down upon his companions, but rather utterly unaware of them.

The drive to Berkeley Square, where Oliver Brayden, Lord Sperling, had resided since his birth, was over all too quickly. Honoria would have sprung from the carriage directly they halted, had not her husband reminded her she must wait to be handed down. "These town proprieties begin to grow tiresome," she remarked almost pettishly to Emily. "I suppose we are fortunate to be allowed to breathe for ourselves."

"Did I omit to mention that?" enquired Alex, who by this time had descended to the pavement and was offering her his arm. "You are *not* permitted to breathe for yourself—at least, not until your host has invited you to do so."

"O Alex," she cried, striving for a complaining tone, but hardly succeeding, so delightful was it for her to hear him tease her and to see his crooked grin appear again.

"Well, you mustn't blame me," he said as he conducted her towards the enormous front doors. "I only tell you the customs—I do not invent them."

She had no time to reply, for at that moment a butler appeared at the door and whisked them into a drawing-room, where they were to wait while their card was handed in. The little party took advantage of these few minutes to stare, in growing wonder, at the opulence surrounding them. At least, the ladies stared; Alexander seemed quite composed. "I have never seen such a tapestry!" Emily exclaimed, examining a vast, antique hanging that represented the risen Christ appearing to Mary Magdalene. She dared to finger a bit of the stuff with her hands, and cried out again, "Marvelous!"

"And the hearth!" said Honoria, admiring its rich carvings and awed at its sheer largeness. "I protest I never knew I had such a godfather."

"I dareswear he is worth millions," Emily agreed whole-heartedly.

"Not quite millions," came a cool feminine voice from the door-way.

Emily scurried to a seat near her brother, while Honor stood blushing furiously at what had just been overheard. A rather tall, dashingly dressed young woman stood between the double doors of the drawing-room surveying the visitors impassively. The strong, clean lines of her features were almost too severe to permit of her being beautiful— almost, but not quite. With her dark hair coiffed high and an ostrich feather in her bonnet, she made a most striking picture. "I have just been riding," the lady continued, indicating her sharply-cut, luxuriantly-trained riding habit. "I hope you will excuse my dress." No one said anything; the ladies were too conscious, and Alexander too distracted. "You, I perceive, must be my father's god-daughter," said she to Honor, with a curtsey. "My father would receive you himself, except he is at Parliament, or some such thing. Permit me to present myself; I am Lady Jane Sperling."

Honoria had by this time collected herself sufficiently to reply with adequate grace, and to present her husband and her sister-in-law. The appropriate queries as to their journey were put and answered; Lady Jane rang for tea, which appeared presently; and all sat down near a long, low, parcel-gilt table in one corner of the huge drawing-room, where Lady Jane poured a steaming brew from a Sèvres pot into exquisite Sèvres cups. "I have never," said she pleasantly, while handing the cups round, "been at all at ease in this room—save in this corner, that is. I cannot think what possessed the architect to plan a drawing-room so vast. Do you know, before that tapestry was hung it positively echoed!" She smiled that sort of smile that is encountered only within the *ton*, and that is generally described as "brilliant."

"I am very glad to hear you say so," Honoria confided; "I had begun to think all London drawing-rooms were like this."

"O no! How perfectly abominable that would be! But I do like this little corner; I think of it as a bit of habitable land, in the midst of an open plain. I frequently tell Father that if the ceiling were but one foot higher, it might well rain in here—and where would his cherished tapestry be then?"

"Then it is Lord Sperling who is the art-fancier?" Emily enquired.

"Fancier! I should say so. He simply dotes on it. Are you the same, Miss Blackwood?"

Emily coloured a little and replied, "Rather." This interest of Lord Sperling's might prove helpful to her, though she did not care to say more to Lady Jane.

"And you, Mr. Blackwood, do you share your sister's passion?"

Alexander, who had been contemplating the geometrical inlay in the arm of his chair, roused himself to say, "Yes. Well, no. Not extremely."

"How interesting," the hostess said politely, and turned her attention towards Honor.

"My husband is a geometrician," that young lady was saying. She added in a whisper (which she feared might be considered rude, but which Lady Jane, on the contrary found quite winning), "You mustn't mind his distraction. He is always like that."

"I don't mind in the least," Lady Jane hissed back, dimpling with a smile. "I expect you are all impatience to see the sights of London," she went on more audibly.

This was eagerly agreed to.

"If you like, I shall arrange for Trevor—that's my coachman—to drive you round tomorrow. He's a splendid guide."

"How very kind of you!"

"O, not at all," she disclaimed. "And tonight—unless you are too fatigued—I hope you will all join my party at the opera. It is only Lord Strougham, and that tiresome sister of his, but I daresay you will enjoy the performance. It is Handel," she added.

"But you must not—" Honoria broke off in some consternation. "I beg you will not incommode yourself for our sakes. I am certain we ought not intrude upon your evening so rudely."

But Lady Jane broke into a peal of laughter at this courtesy, replying frankly, "My dear, you have no notion what a welcome diversion your coming constitutes. This is my fourth season in London—mark that—my fourth, and my weariness with all of it surpasses everything. Year in and year out the same eligible bachelors quizzing me through their glasses, this year with their cravats *à la Byron*, next year *à la Bergami*, this one with his side-curls long, the next with his whiskers cropped: I promise you, that is all the variation you will discover among them. Only the ladies change: one year she is Miss Jessop, the next Lady Brackhurst—hardly a stunning alteration, if you ask me! And with each passing year, my father regards me more sadly. Will I never marry? is the question that haunts him. I myself have not thought of it this age, but that is a different matter. My point is simply this: you are far more likely to find *my* presence troublesome than I to find yours so."

This, naturally, was music to the ears that heard her. Honoria was quite overcome with gratitude; yet, a guilty feeling nagged at her. "Lady Jane, I must beg you," said she, "I must implore you to overlook the odious things you heard myself and Miss Blackwood say earlier. Pray believe me, we meant no rudeness by them—only—we were somewhat overwhelmed—" she ended lamely.

"Apologetic little thing, is she not?" Lady Jane demanded gaily of Miss Blackwood. "Is she this way all the time?"

Emily laughed and said she was afraid she was.

"Well, it cannot endure long in London," said their hostess. "No

one is humble in the *ton*, though the girls make a show of being biddable for their first season."

Honoria smiled at this and said she "hoped Lady Jane would not
set her down an utter widgeon."

"My Heavens, she *is* always like that!" cried the lady so applied to,
and broke into another peal of laughter. "In any case, your apology is
accepted and accepted again, and all future apologies are accepted as
well—provided you refrain from making them whenever you may. I
am certain you are incapable of really offending anyone."

"Emily," Honoria protested, "do tell her I am not *quite* a jelly-fish!
I am not quite a jelly-fish," she informed Lady Jane herself.

"No, of course you are not," said Lady Jane, with a consoling pat to
Honor's hand, and an arch elevation of the eyebrows to Emily. "Now,
tell me, Miss Blackwood: what precisely has brought you to London?
Not looking for a husband, I hope; you appear much more sensible
than that."

"I am, indeed," the other confirmed. "I wish you will call me
Emily."

Lady Jane nodded agreeably. "Well then, Emily, if not a husband—
what?"

Miss Blackwood glanced round uneasily, for she felt it might be
best to say nothing of her purpose until she had settled squarely with
the academy.

"My sister is an artist," Alexander said suddenly. As it happened,
his remark was very timely—but this was only by the merest chance.
He had been lost in a muse ever since the last time he spoke, and had
no idea the conversation had wandered so widely afterwards. He
made his comment in the belief they were still discussing art-fanciers.

Having made this disclosure, Alexander relapsed into silence, leaving Emily to explain its bearing upon Lady Jane's enquiry. She did
this—first requesting that the intelligence be kept in strictest
confidence—with both modesty and succinctness, and left Lady Jane
looking thoughtful as she closed.

"Now, this *is* a difficulty," the older lady said reflectively. "I must
say I was not prepared to help you with such a project as that! The
judges are certain to squawk when they learn of their deception."

"I fear it," Emily assented, her hands clenching and unfolding unconsciously.

"I must ponder this further," said Lady Jane decisively. "But how
perfectly wonderful, anyhow!"

The guests did not stop much longer, for Alexander was eager to unpack his books, and Emily and Honor would be obliged to make certain purchases if they were to attend the opera that night.

"But you must let me accompany you!" cried Lady Jane, when she heard that their next destination was the milliner's.

Honoria protested again that Lady Jane was too good, was again told bluntly to give over apologising, and the party of ladies set off together in the Sperlings' coach, leaving Alex to go home and amuse himself as he might with his library.

The afternoon was passed very agreeably indeed, Lady Jane animatedly supervising the purchases the younger women made, and advising them most usefully on what sort of garments they must commission the dress-maker to carry out for them. She wisely chose for them much less daring fashions than those she herself wore, and limited Emily to whites and pale colours. "For an unmarried young woman in her first season simply must restrict herself to such insipid shades," she remarked, "though it is a dreadful shame. With your figure, you might carry off the most stunning crimsons, but it is far too dangerous." She sighed, feeling sadly thwarted in her efforts to make Emily into the dasher she could be. Honoria, though she was eligible for brighter colours, was by far too meek to wear them. Even the red-and-green plaid they contemplated for a walking-dress for her overpowered the little thing. It was a terrible shame, for plaid was certain to be all the rage this year.

The girls returned to the house in Albemarle Street exceedingly pleased with themselves and even more exceedingly famished, only to learn from Alexander that no one in London dined before eight.

"Eight!" cried Emily, scandalised. "But we shall die!"

"It does seem a bit late," said Honoria seriously.

"A bit late!" exclaimed the other. "It is positively barbaric! And what, pray, are we to do with our hunger?"

Alexander looked amused. "You might take a nuncheon," he suggested, "but I do think you ought to adjust your appetites to new hours as soon as possible. Otherwise you will be starved indeed at a ball."

"And why, pray tell?"

"Because supper is not served till past mid-night," he replied, delighting in the indignant reaction he knew this would provoke.

It came, and did not disappoint him. Emily stated flatly that in her opinion, a group of people who could find no better hours than those for the taking of their meals deserved to starve, and to die of it.

"No doubt we shall soon become reconciled to it," Honoria soothed her.

"No doubt," said Miss Blackwood sarcastically. "I am told prisoners become reconciled to bread and water, too, if it is all they receive."

"I shall have the cook fetch us a collation of some sort," Honoria said, ringing the bell.

"Of a large sort, please," Emily insisted.

"And after your nuncheon," Alexander interrupted, "I prescribe bed. A nap will be necessary if you are to keep awake through the opera."

"On our first day in London!" Emily protested.

Alexander shrugged. "As you like. But *I* am going to rest, whether you choose to or no."

With this he sauntered out of the room, his stomach apparently indifferent to its altered schedule. Honoria had hardly seen him in such good spirits, and she lay down upon her bed a little time later feeling contented, indeed. Lady Jane had promised to procure them invitations to some balls or other (as she phrased it), or at least a rout or two. The girls—particularly Emily—ought properly to be presented before they indulged in such amusements; but Lady Jane did not think it would matter much. Besides, she was bent upon giving a come-out for Miss Blackwood at her own house in Berkeley Square: she had been counting on it since Honoria's letter arrived, and had even chosen a date.

"It is to be Thursday week," she had informed them. "Just a dinner, you know, and perhaps some whist afterwards. Too tedious, I am afraid; but if we are not to do it up completely with a ball, I think it will be best to go it mildly. Very dull, you know, which is another way of saying very proper."

Such tidings as these could not but delight young Mrs. Blackwood, and Emily consented to submit to the ritual, since she had promised her father she would seek a husband earnestly. It was a promise made under duress, and with less than half a will, but she liked to keep her word and did not regard it lightly. For her own part, she was nearly dead with anxiety to go to Somerset Place, where the pictures of the Royal Academy were hung, and had much rather have passed her time there than fretting about a come-out, but there would be time for both things, as Honor assured her, and the pictures must wait a bit longer. The exhibition in which her own painting was to hang would not take place for weeks and weeks, so she had no choice but to wait for that.

Chapter XI

The opera in no way disappointed the young ladies, nor did the rout party they attended later in the week. The theatre that was the scene of the first event proved properly large and brilliant; their party was made cheerful enough by the presence of Lady Jane (though they were obliged to agree with her, afterwards, that Lord Strougham's sister *was* a rather wearisome rattle); the supper of which they partook at the close of the performance was most elegant—and most satisfying to Emily, who was famished. The latter festivity, Lady Drayton's rout, was as uncomfortably over-crowded as anybody might possibly desire: through the good offices of Lady Jane, the Blackwood party made the acquaintance of so many ladies and gentlemen as to make it utterly inconceivable that they should remember the name of any one of them; and in fact, a lengthy discussion took place among the three at breakfast the next morning, as to whether or not they had ever been presented to the hostess. This, their patroness informed them, was precisely as it should be: a rout that was not a hopeless squeeze was no rout at all, and she should have been most distressed to find her friends from Pittering otherwise than confused about the evening.

"Your come-out, however," she continued to Emily, "is a different matter. I am sorry to inform you that it will be your duty, on that occasion, to commit as much to memory as **you** possibly may. Some of London's first hostesses will be attending, **and** several of the *ton*'s most important gentlemen: without the patronage of these personages—or a few of them at least—your entrée into society will be very difficult to contrive. So do endeavour, my dear, to learn all their names, and a little about their interests if you can. Do not be afraid to flatter them, either; they dote on it, I assure you."

"Flattery has never been my forte," said Emily diffidently, "but I promise to make shift somehow or other." She was listening to Lady Jane with only half an ear, anyway; the chief of her attention was focussed upon the visit she and Honoria were to make that morning. This was to the academy, for they had naturally written to that establishment as soon as ever they had reached London, and the director there had been kind enough to send a note in return, expressing his desire to meet with the gifted Mr. Cedric Blackwood at his earliest convenience. "Do you think I look plain enough?" Miss Blackwood now demanded of her sister-in-law for the three ladies were situated in Emily's bed-chamber and were supervising her toilette.

"Perhaps you might expose your ears entirely," Honor suggested, surveying her friend's image in the looking-glass. It had been agreed among them that Emily must look as severe as possible for her interview, in order that the director should not think her frivolous.

Miss Blackwood adjusted her coiffure accordingly, and nodded with satisfaction at her reflection. "That *is* most unattractive," she remarked.

"My goodness, so it is indeed!" said Lady Jane. "My dear Emily, what you have been hiding from us all this time!"—for Emily's ears, generally invisible under curls and bonnets, were genuinely disfiguring when revealed. "How very kind of Providence to provide you with such convenient features—and particularly, with the means to cover them up."

Miss Blackwood, who had no trace of vanity anywhere in her character, took not the least offence at these observations, but instead was quite pleased that Lady Jane should think her so ugly. "I thank you, ma'am," said she. "You give me confidence that no gentleman—no matter how lacking in discernment—could consider me a pretty, foolish dilettante. And I thank you, dear Honor, for your inspired suggestion. I had quite forgot how startlingly hideous my ears are."

Garments correspondingly unappealing having been chosen and donned by Miss Blackwood, the young ladies judged themselves ready to depart. Alexander, who was to accompany them for the sake of greater propriety, was summoned and appeared presently; naturally he noticed neither his sister's uncommon homeliness, nor his wife's enhanced beauty (for she wore a newly purchased walking dress of *bleu celeste* velour, lace-trimmed and with a bonnet of the same material, which set off the sweetness of her countenance quite to perfection); but then, he never was expected to notice such things, and no one was especially disappointed. Lady Jane wished Miss Blackwood much good fortune, embraced her fondly, and drove off in her carriage only a few moments before the Blackwoods themselves departed. Alexander, ever absent-minded, politely wished Lady Jane equal good fortune, and handed his wife and sister into their coach.

Happily, the situation of the academy did not oblige the Blackwoods to drive to any undesirable quarter of town. On the contrary, the directors' offices and the studios both were located nearby in a large town-house in Bond Street. Thither they drove, Emily's excitement mounting at each moment, and there they descended. A butler met them at the great front door—which was painted black, with brass handles, and was consequently very imposing—received Mr. Blackwood's card, and begged the party to wait an instant in a small, elegant parlour. They had barely time to observe the many paintings with which that apartment was hung when the butler returned to lead the trio up the stairs and into a spacious, well-proportioned room. This chamber had evidently been meant for a study or library of sorts, but was now converted into an office. It was, they soon learned, the place of business of the chief director of the academy, Sir Geoffrey Penningdon. That gentleman, who had been seated behind a mahogany desk of quite mammoth proportions, rose hastily on the entrance of the little party and began chattering furiously at once.

"I am so pleased to meet you. You must be Mr. Blackwood—and these ladies I trust are your wife—or perhaps—? Our committee was quite delighted with your painting, we are aching to show it to London, and have no doubt of its most brilliant reception in all quarters; although the taste of the public has its vagaries, it is to be admitted, and perhaps—However, only time can tell what will come of it; the principal point is to cultivate even further your tremendous abilities, if they *may* be cultivated further! and to introduce you to these established masters whom the academy has the honour of . . ." And so he rattled on for a good ten minutes, all the time mistaking Alexander for the imaginary Mr. Cedric, and behaving as ingratiatingly and excitedly as possible. He was a smallish man, of middle age, entirely bald for some time now, but with such generous, unaffected manners as made him instantly likeable. The poor fellow, who had not a trace of talent of any sort to call his own, was yet such an avid admirer of ability in others that he stood almost in awe of the very people whose patron he was. He bobbed up and down unceasingly as he talked, in a sort of incidental half-bow, and wiped his quizzing-glass ever and anon, though he never used it. As chief administrator of the academy, Sir Geoffrey wielded considerable power over the lives of his beneficiaries, but an uninformed observer could not possibly have guessed this, so obliging—almost obsequious, indeed—was his address.

After a very great deal of inconsequent prattle, the director checked himself at last, resumed his seat at the desk, invited his visitors to sit also, and consented to listen to them. "Sir Geoffrey," Alexander began, evidently labouring to keep his mind on the business at hand, "I must beg to disabuse you of a misapprehension you have apparently formed—quite understandably, of course—yet still a misapprehension. I am not Mr. Cedric Blackwood; I am Mr. Alexander Blackwood. This lady" (indicating Honor) "is my wife, Mrs. Blackwood, and this lady is—ah, my sister. My sister, ah—Mr. Cedric Blackwood."

Sir Geoffrey very naturally did not understand.

"My sister's name is not really Cedric, you see; in fact, it is Emily. However, it is she who painted the portrait—" Alexander said, but Emily interrupted him here and explained the entire matter herself. In the frankest and most lucid terms, she described the deception she had perpetrated on the judges of the competition, enlarged a bit on why she had done so, and implored Sir Geoffrey to consider the reasons of her behaviour and not to act rashly.

Sir Geoffrey was very much taken aback. "I do not recollect such a thing ever to have happened before," said he. "No woman has ever studied under the auspices of the academy; it is most irregular. Of course, since you are the painter of the portrait—this is most upsetting! —of course, I must consult with the other directors. However, I do not think—you see, it would be most surprising, most unnatural—and yet, it seems hardly fair. On the other hand, the directors of the academy cannot be expected to—a most astonishing deception—we are not in a position to risk the censure—however," said Sir Geoffrey, and continued in this vein above a quarter of an hour, giving his listeners to understand that while Miss Blackwood *might* be accepted, it seemed extremely doubtful.

This was better, in truth, than any of them had expected, and though to Emily it seemed insufferably cruel to be obliged to wait yet longer for a verdict, she felt at least that there was still some hope. Sir Geoffrey was sufficiently good, before they quitted Bond Street, to give them a brief tour of the academy, the different branches of which were mainly situated within the capacious town-house. In one wing were the offices of the directors, among them Sir Geoffrey's; in another were a gallery and an extensive library comprised entirely of works and treatises on art. The top story of the house consisted of two gigantic apartments, the studios where instruction took place. The garrets that would normally have been found above these had been demolished in order to make the two stories into one. As a result, the studios were enormously lofty, and well provided with natural light, which streamed in through windows in the ceiling as well as the walls. Poor Emily, who had frequently been obliged either to restrict her painting to the briefest hours, or to work by lamp-light, was in raptures at this, so much so that she squeezed Honoria's hand quite painfully.

"Can you imagine?" she breathed; "All day to work in—all day!" One of the studios was empty at the time they visited it; the other, however, was the scene of a class in progress. A still-life made up of a silver bowl of fruit, an engraved silver pitcher, and a gleaming knife had been arranged on a table at the centre of the room. Four or five young gentlemen, of various ages and types, stood painting it at easels set up round the room, while a middle-aged gentleman (evidently the master) visited each of them and inspected their efforts. Other than these, there was no one in the great hall except a very young servant girl, whose business it was, apparently, to see that no one wanted colours, or brushes, or rags, and to perform whatever other menial duties the gentlemen required. This girl would not have attracted the attention of any of the visitors, had it not been for an incident that chanced to take place just as they were about to depart. One of the young artists had murmured something to her, apparently sending her on an errand that took her to the other end of the room, her thin arms full of brushes and soiled cloths. The unfortunate girl, being something confused by the urgency of her instructions—and not very clever to begin with—crossed through the middle of the room, instead of skirting round its edges. An instant cry went up of "Out of the way! Blast the wench! Mary, what are you about?" in excessively impatient voices. This naturally only increased her perturbation, and she contrived somehow, as she neared the table on which the still-life was arranged, to trip on her own skirts and knock over both pitcher and fruit. Oranges and apples rolled about; the brushes she carried fell to the floor, leaving coloured patches everywhere; the pitcher fell with a clang that almost certainly heralded the present discovery of a sizable dent in its side. Mary's distress was now immeasurable: the poor girl broke into sobs at once, and could hardly contrive to regain her feet. Her pitiful predicament, however, aroused no tenderness in the breasts of the artists, but only wrath.

"Mary!" shouted the master. "This is the end! I have told you repeatedly, never go near the centre of the room—never cross before the students—never never never! Here is what comes of it!" He read her quite a lecture, all of which was witnessed by the Blackwoods, and finished (alas for Mary) by turning her away. "And without a reference!" he closed stormily, and sent the poor girl weeping out of the studio, away from the academy for ever.

Sir Geoffrey was, of course, all apology. He was devastated that such a scene had imposed itself upon his guests; he assured them such explosions were not ordinary in the academy; he expatiated lengthily on the difficulty of finding girls intelligent enough to wait upon the artists, and yet willing to perform such dreary labour. This was the fourth wench turned away this twelvemonth, and he did not know where to find another. The visitors (when they could get a word in) prayed he would not be anxious on their account, rapidly completed their inspection of the house in Bond Street, and were soon in the carriage on their way home. Sir Geoffrey had engaged to confer with his colleagues in a day or two at most, and to inform Miss Blackwood of their decision the moment it was taken.

The reader may easily imagine, that during the next eight-and-forty hours, Miss Emily Blackwood talked, dreamed, and thought of nothing but her education. Lady Jane Sperling sought in vain to acquaint her with the guest list for her come-out; Honoria tired, after some two or three hours of obliging speculation, of wondering how the committee might decide, but she could not persuade her sister to take up any other topic: now that her fate was so soon to be determined, nothing else could interest Emily.

The answer came on the morning of the third day, in the form of a letter from Sir Geoffrey. The directors were very sorry. The committee had discussed Miss Blackwood's case from every vantage point. The rules of the academy had been examined thoroughly, and interpreted in every conceivable light; even the notion of casting them aside had been pondered. It was most lamentable; Sir Geoffrey did not know how to express his desolation; but there was no possibility of Miss Blackwood's being accepted into the institute. It was all he could do to persuade the judges to permit her prize picture to hang in the exhibit—and even that, he was obliged to inform her, could only be done under the pseudonym she had devised. As for the development of her considerable abilities, Sir Geoffrey sincerely hoped she would find some private instructor—perhaps some established artist who would take her in—to give her that assistance without which her gift might remain but half-discovered.

Miss Emily Blackwood read this and said absolutely nothing. Her face went white, her hands clenched angrily, she turned on her heel and marched wordlessly to her bed-chamber, whence she did not emerge until nearly three hours later. When she did come out, it was not to accept the lavish comfort proffered by her sister-in-law, but

rather to exchange a series of the tersest and most businesslike remarks. "I am going out," said she, "alone. You must not ask me why,
nor mention my absence to Alex. You must not accompany or even
seek to observe me. I have an errand that I *must* accomplish, and I
earnestly entreat you to grant these conditions."

"If you think so—" Honoria began anxiously, her brow wrinkled
with doubt. "But you will not expose yourself to any—impropriety,
will you? I promised your father—"

"The less we say of this the better," returned Miss Blackwood. "So
long as no one interferes, I guarantee no harm will come of this. I
shall be home in an hour or two," she added, and with that—and a
brief embrace—disappeared. The nature of her mission, and its satis-
factory or unsatisfactory conclusion, Honoria did not discover for
many weeks. Emily did seem in better spirits that evening, however,
and cautioned Honoria she would repeat her excursion the next day.
Honoria must not look for her, nor expect to hear from her until dinner. And indeed, Emily was gone all next day, and all the next as well,
and would not say a word to anyone of where she had been, or what
occupied her.

Her absence could not have been accomplished nearly so easily in
any other household than her own, of course, for it required the utter
inattention of her brother. Inattention being Alexander's most salient
trait, however, only Honoria fretted over Emily's unaccountable behaviour. That it was connected with the academy she had no doubt, but
how or why or what exactly, she could not have guessed—nor did
Emily wish her to. Mrs. Traubin, whose fishy eye observed everything,
was yet in no position to enquire into matters too closely, and was
obliged to make do with her mistress's firm, if brief, explanation that
Miss Emily was "not at home." And so things continued three days,
until the evening of Miss Blackwood's come-out.

That event even Emily knew she must attend, and she arrived at
the house in Albemarle Street somewhat earlier that day than had become her wont. Even so, Lady Jane Sperling had been waiting for her
there above an hour, and met her with the greatest impatience.

"My very dear Miss Blackwood," said she, with mock excess of
civility. "I do hope your debut does not intrude upon your schedule
too very awkwardly." Her handsome mouth dimpled into that brilliant
smile for which the ladies of the *ton* are renowned, and she regarded
her young charges archly.

"Not at all," Emily replied, purposely ignoring the sally. "I am
excessively obliged to you, too, for coming this evening. I suppose you
mean to make me beautiful?"

"Something of the kind," Lady Jane confessed, "though really, not much more is necessary than the covering of your ears, and I see you have been prudent enough to do that already. Really, you can have no notion how diverting this is to me! Introducing a handsome young girl into society—and to my father as well, now I come to think of it. He has given me his word he will be there—and I ought to warn you—he is something of an admirer of women."

"He must be a very busy gentleman," observed Miss Blackwood, "to admire both ladies and art—*and* to pursue politics simultaneously." She had been throwing off her cloak and bonnet while she spoke, and now turned to greet Honoria, who had hastened into the front hall at the sound of her voice.

"My dear," said young Mrs. Blackwood, embracing her, "you look—goodness, you look fatigued! And your hands smell like . . ."—she possessed herself of one of these and sniffed it curiously—"like turp—"

"Shhh!" Emily interrupted her. "It is no matter. Come, come my maidens, to my boudoir, and let us transform this sensible-looking young woman into a ravishing innocent. We'll have plenty of work to do that!"

Further questions thus stilled, Honoria and Lady Jane followed Miss Blackwood up to her bed-chamber, where an hour of choosing, arranging, and general primping ensued. At its end, Emily stood arrayed in a flowing gown of white, quite simple in its lines, but adorned with a delicate, lacy fichu as demure as it was flattering. Tiny white slippers peeped out from under the lace-trimmed hem. The only element in the entire toilette that even hinted at daring were the puffed sleeves of the gown, for they were quite short. What they revealed, however, long kid gloves were soon to cover up, and so no more modestly clad young lady could have been found in London that evening than Miss Emily Blackwood. At least, that was what Lady Jane said, and pronounced herself very satisfied. "You see—I must point this out to you, my dears, for it is quite a marvel of taste on my part, and you are too inexperienced to notice it yourselves—I have contrived to make Emily appear both elegant and sweet, and yet without resorting once to any of those missish frills and fripperies so many young ladies disguise themselves in. You look very handsome, my love, and owe a great deal to me."

"Then I thank you," said Emily, smiling.

"You do not think it was an error to take all those flowers from her hair?" Honoria asked anxiously, indicating a pile of discarded artificial blooms. Only one of the dozen originally planned had been left on Emily's head.

"O no, not at all! She looks much smarter this way. It was a mistake to purchase them in the first place. Now, Emily," she continued, "you do know how to drape a shawl, I trust? It does you no good to wear such a lovely lace one, if you cannot use it properly."

Miss Blackwood assured her she could manage a shawl.

"And your fan? You won't make too much use of it, will you? Simpering is not your style; you needn't affect it."

Miss Blackwood engaged not to simper all evening.

"Then I believe we are finished," said Lady Jane, turning upon Honoria. "My dear mouse, you are next. And Emily, don't you dare sit down, or breathe, or blink, until we are safely arrived in Berkeley Square."

Miss Blackwood swore she should be indistinguishable from a corpse, until she had set foot in Lord Sperling's residence.

"That is fine," said Lady Jane. The next hour was devoted to Mrs. Blackwood's toilette, not nearly so difficult to achieve, as Lady Jane pointed out, since Honoria's natural looks agreed perfectly with the current modes. She emerged from her bed-chamber with her hair becomingly coiffed *à la Titus,* the crown bound with a simple gold fillet; a velvet gown of the palest rose, its unexceptionable *décolletage* oval in shape, draped her graceful figure; and a wide, intricately embroidered shawl sat lightly upon her shoulders.

"But, Alexander!" she cried all at once. "Who has told him what to wear?"

Consternation was instantly general among the ladies, and while Emily informed Lady Jane of her conviction that her brother did not know a cravat from a handkerchief, Honoria hastened fretfully into her husband's library.

"He isn't there!" she reported, returning to the door-way of her own room after a moment. "O, where can he be? Why did I not think of this before?" she berated herself, wringing her hands with vexation. "Mrs. Traubin," she called, at the same time ringing the bell for that lady. "Mrs. Traubin!"

Mrs. Traubin appeared behind her, startling her with a strident, "Yes, madam."

"Mrs. Traubin, where is Mr. Blackwood? Where is my husband?"

"I believe, ma'am," she returned, with none of her mistress's perturbation, "he is waiting for you in the drawing-room."

"Waiting for—us?" This was extraordinary indeed, if true.

"I think so, ma'am," with a curtsey more insolent than anything else.

"But do you mean—he remembered we are going out?"

"Apparently, ma'am. At least, his attire seemed to indicate an intention to go out."

"What can it possibly be?" asked Honoria, of no one in particular, and ran down the stairs to the drawing-room.

"Buskins and top-boots; I shouldn't be the least surprised," Emily predicted grimly to Lady Jane, as they followed in Honor's steps.

But Miss Blackwood, for once, was wrong—quite entirely wrong, indeed. Alexander, when he rose at his wife's entrance, did so in the neatest, most correct raiment possible. He wore ankle-length trousers, a smart waist-coat with modish horizontal stripes, a snowy cravat carefully bound beneath an excessively high, perfectly starched collar, and a dark *frac* cut to perfection. His low pumps could not have been shinier, nor the high top-hat that he held in his hand more carefully brushed. "Alex!" was all his wife could think to say.

"My dear, I have been waiting for you this age," he replied. "Hadn't Lady Jane best return to Berkeley Square soon? I should think she had any number of things to attend to there, and no doubt wishes you to be present."

"Alex—!" was repeated.

But Mr. Blackwood steadfastly refused to regard either his promptitude or his dress as anything remarkable, even when his sister joined his wife in her surprise. Lady Jane said nothing, only agreeing that they had best be off, and so they entered their carriages and drove away.

"But doesn't Alexander look handsome!" Honoria whispered to Emily as they passed through the streets, while the subject of her remark gazed distractedly through a window.

Emily, though unaccustomed to view her brother in such a light, had to admit it was so.

"I am certain any lady might lose her heart to him," said Honor, and felt with a pang that she herself had done so six or seven times already.

"If he had any conversation," Emily returned diffidently. Their colloquy was interrupted by their arrival in Berkeley Square, and Alexander's apparent return to full consciousness.

Once inside, Lady Jane excused herself to accomplish her own toilette, and committed them into the care of her father—who, she assured them, would join them momentarily. Honoria had been looking forward to this meeting with some trepidation: by all Lady Jane's accounts, Lord Sperling was a kind and most unalarming man; however, Honoria felt so much in his debt—and further, knew so well that he was a man of fortune and of consequence—that she could not help but be frightened of him. Her fears vanished (as Emily had predicted they would) directly he entered the drawing-room.

"Ah," said he, going up to her immediately and holding her face between his hands, "I perceive this is the mouse my daughter spoke of. How do you do, Mrs. Honoria? You look exactly like your mother."

"Do I? I did not—how do you do, sir?" she finished, remembering suddenly to curtsey.

"Very well, indeed," he answered with a low bow. He turned to Emily, his broad face smiling with genuine pleasure. "If this is my god-daughter, then you must be Miss Emily," said he, and kissed her hand. "You see, I know you all. Mr. Blackwood, I hope you will not be angry with me for embracing your wife; we are nearly kin, you know."

Lord Sperling stepped back now to have a better look at his new acquaintances and gave them an opportunity of surveying him as well. He was a tall, sturdy man of robust middle age, his cheeks as fresh and pink as any member of Parliament's, his smile as engaging—in its masculine way—as his daughter's. It was easy to see Lady Jane had inherited her height from him—though not, fortunately for her, his girth, since he was so muscular as to appear burly. He was a remarkable gentleman. Everything, in general, amused him; everything was to his taste, though particularly politics. He never permitted himself to forget what pleasures and happinesses had already been his, and so never ceased to find more. Every one of his acquaintance envied him his health and cheerfulness, yet he had no enemy in all England. The Blackwoods, like everyone else who met him, were immediate converts.

Honoria naturally began her converse with him by thanking him profusely for the kindness he had showered upon them, for his daughter's goodness, for his generosity, for his—

"Stop, stop, I pray! Jane told me you were the soul of gratitude, but I was not prepared for this!" he interrupted. "Your thanks are entirely superfluous, as you must know, and as for the apologies I am warned to expect from you, kindly suppress those as well, whatever may be their cause or matter. Does she behave so with you, too, Alex?" he went on, eyeing that young man roguishly. "I suppose you hardly dare to hand her the butter at table, for fear you will hear of your kindness all through dinner, eh?" His lordship laughed heartily at his own joke—for he never saw harm in laughing at whatever seemed diverting, no matter if he himself were the source—and Alex (to the surprise of the ladies) laughed with him.

Other than sharing the laughter, however, he made no answer.

"Well, then, Miss Blackwood, I am told you are a proficient with a brush. You have seen our gallery, I trust?" he said to Emily, and proceeded to engage her in a very well-informed discussion of the most recent movements in art. This enlightened discourse was brought to a close, to Emily's great sorrow, by the entrance into the vast drawing-room of Lady Jane, whose toilette, now complete, was as bold and striking as the younger ladies' were mild.

"You are in prime twig, my dear," said her father to her, rising and kissing her hand with a gallant flourish.

"As are you, sir," she answered, adding a sweeping curtsey.

"And just in time, I think," said Lord Sperling, for at that moment the sounds of the first guests arriving became audible, and a couple—presented to the Blackwoods as Sir Malcolm and Lady Margaret Rowley—entered the room. During the next four or five hours, Lady Jane gave herself over entirely to the role of hostess, a part she performed so excellently that the Blackwoods had no difficulty in assuming the behaviour correct to them. Lady Jane introduced and informed, curtsied and bantered, gathered and dispersed her guests with an expert manipulation quite beautiful to behold. When some dozen of people had come, dinner was served: everyone went to the table escorted by his perfect complement; conversation continued easy and pleasant throughout three removes and the sweets; and when the ladies removed to the drawing-room, they did so in the highest good spirits. Even Honoria found her consciousness melting away: once or twice, she actually welcomed the opportunity of speaking with a stranger. Only one thing disturbed her: a young man, the last of the guests to arrive, had been introduced to her as Mr. Ambrose Tayt. This gentleman, amiably open in his address, his hair combed into careless *coups de vent,* and wearing a flowing cravat *à la Byron,* struck her as being somehow familiar to her. She knew this to be most unlikely, and was quite certain at least that she had never heard his name; yet, when Emily was presented to him, she too had seemed to recognise him, and in fact started visibly. If Miss Blackwood knew him, however, she said nothing of it, for Honoria distinctly heard her declare her pleasure at making his acquaintance. Yet, the affair continued to puzzle her, since—though unable now to judge objectively—she could not help but feel that Mr. Tayt observed Miss Blackwood most particularly. She resolved finally to put the matter out of her mind until such time as she could discuss it with Emily.

Alexander's behaviour, which had become thoroughly and maddeningly unpredictable ever since the journey to London had first been spoke of, proved entirely unexceptionable that evening. Far from appearing distant and distrait, as had been Honor's fear, Mr. Blackwood seemed transformed by the entrance of the first visitor from an absent, brooding scholar into a gay, witty, young tulip. Lady Agatha Huffle found him simply charming; Miss Cynthia Huffle, her daughter, was more than once surprised into a blush by Mr. Blackwood's elegant sallies; Lord Sperling invited the young man to join him next day in a proposed visit to Gentleman Jackson's Saloon. If Miss Blackwood was found to be of no more than passable beauty and manners, her brother was unanimously set down a genuine addition to the season's ranks of gentlemen.

"And his wife is rather sweet, too," whispered Lord Huffle to his lady, "in all fairness."

Lady Huffle yawned behind her fan and owned that Mrs. Blackwood was adequately sweet. "Still, she could not have caught him if they'd met here in town, I dareswear. Pitterling Village must be frightfully small, to have convinced Mr. Blackwood he could do no better than that."

"It is Pittering, I believe, my dear; not Pitterling. In any case, she is very pretty, and no doubt worships her husband most gratifyingly."

"I suppose that is what gentlemen desire," said she, stifling another yawn. "A shame, really. He is precisely the sort of match I want for Cynthia."

"I *knew* your indifference to Mrs. Blackwood had personal motives!" cried Lord Huffle. "Ah, well; I daresay a dozen match-making mammas will feel the same." His lordship then joined his lady wife in a yawn, for it was growing rather late; whist had long since been dispensed with, and supper, too. In a very little while the Huffles were making their adieux, and shepherding a reluctant Cynthia away from the company. Their going reminded others of the hour, and the soirée was presently at a positive end.

"I protest I am exhausted," exclaimed Lady Jane, as the front door closed upon the last guest to depart. She sank gracefully into a carved mahogany arm-chair, and dropped there in exaggerated languor.

"We ought to be going," said Honor at once.

"O, the mouse! You needn't run away. You all did so very well, did not they, Papa? You will be overrun with cards and invitations before tomorrow night, I promise."

The Blackwoods thanked their good friends civilly, made a few arrangements regarding their next meeting, and took themselves off to home and bed. In the morning Miss Blackwood was gone again, and did not reappear until seven of the evening.

Honoria, who had had all day to gird herself to the task, was ready with remonstrances when her sister-in-law at last returned. "You cannot do it, Emily," said she severely (or as severely as her mild looks and gentle voice allowed). She had cornered Miss Blackwood in the cosy upstairs sitting-room, and now walked up and down that apartment glancing ever and anon towards Emily's chair. "I simply cannot permit it! I do not know where you go, nor what you do; Lady Jane was right about the invitations; there seem to be scores of them, and at least half are for the mornings. Your father would never speak to me again if he knew of it, and moreover, you look quite dead with fatigue. I have never seen you look so ghastly. Why, you *cannot* have had more than three hours sleep last night—it is not human! It is not possible! Emily, tell me what you are about at once, or I shall take the matter to Alex."

Emily, who really did look weary, shrugged and said dispassionately, "Then take it to him. I appreciate your concern, Honor; really I do. But I dare not tell you what I am doing. If my assurances of its security are not enough for you—well, then . . ." She shrugged again.

Her small supply of sternness quite spent, Honoria now dropped to her knees by Emily's chair and employed her more customary method of persuasion. "Please, my dear Em," said she, taking her friend's hand, "whatever you are doing, it cannot be good for you. Look at you! So pale and drawn . . . and your hands are quite—well they are chapped, to say truth, and red. Anyone who met you could see in a moment you do not lead the life of a gentlewoman; your hands tell that story at once, to say nothing of your pallor!"

"I shall wear gloves," returned the other.

"Of course, you will, but—O Emily, do think what a position you put me in. You are under my care, and I do not know your whereabouts ten hours out of the day!"

Miss Blackwood, who wished more than anything to see this interview at a close, left off her indifferent tone and brought out her best weapon at once. "Let us all go home to Pittering, then," said she.

"Go home! But we've only just come," cried Mrs. Blackwood, failing utterly to see what sort of psychology was being practised upon her. "And just this morning a note arrived from your father, saying he is delighted to hear of the academy's decision, and advising us to stop on in London since we are here—to stop on with his full blessings, Emily. It is an opportunity we may never have again!"

Miss Blackwood smiled more gently than was her wont and returned her sister's warm grasp of her hand. "Then let us stay," said she; "but don't let's have any more of this interrogation, I beg you. Things are difficult enough without your flying into alt every afternoon. Now, I promise to be home early tomorrow, and home all day on Sunday. Will you promise in return to forget about this nonsense?"

Honoria, who felt she would die if her only visit to London was curtailed within a fortnight, was obliged to give her word, and only begged Miss Blackwood one more time to be as heedful of her reputation as she might. The topic then turned to more cheerful matters—at least, Mrs. Blackwood thought them more cheerful—for among the invitations received in the morning's post had been one to a ball tonight, and Honoria (unable to resist) had accepted at once.

"It is at Lord and Lady Throstle's—you remember Lady Throstle, the tall lady with the brocaded turban?—and only fancy, it does not *begin* until half past ten! Everyone in Pittering will be asleep by then, and we shall be dancing and supping and—"

"I must say, everyone in Pittering may not have a very bad notion about bed-times," Emily interrupted with a yawn. "Do you think I might nap a bit now? I am sure I need sleep more than I do my dinner."

"O," said Honor, immediately anxious. "Yes, naturally. You go lie down, and I will have a tray sent up to you. Alex and I will dine alone," she added, and this prospect at once absorbed half her attention and agitation. She had not been alone with Alexander since they had come to London, for he did not take breakfast except a cup of chocolate in bed, and Emily was present at their other repasts. She was all curiosity to see how he would conduct himself towards her, whether as the sprig of fashion he had been last night, or the awkward young fellow she had married. The remainder of her thoughts wandered continually towards the ball they would attend that evening: how she would compare to the other young ladies, who would ask her to stand up, whether the assembly would be very large indeed, and if they would be acquainted with anybody there besides the Throstles.

"No doubt we shall see some of our acquaintance of last night," said Emily with a yawn, when Honoria (in the act of helping her to bed) put this last question to her. "However, it seems most unlikely we shall meet anyone more interesting than that." With this prediction Emily shut her eyes, and fell instantly to sleep, hearing Honoria's disappointed "I suppose you are right" only as a dreamy echo.

But Emily was not right, after all. There were in fact two personages invited to the Throstles' that evening, whose lives were most intimately connected with those of the Blackwoods—the two personages in the world, perhaps, whom Honoria might hope least to meet.

Chapter XII

Dinner alone with Alex proved a melancholy affair, at least for Honoria. He arrived at table dressed as carelessly as ever he had been in Pittering; his conversation consisted entirely in commonplaces, and those disjointed and few; and his general manner towards his wife appeared to indicate his utter indifference to her presence or absence. "We might take our coffee in the sitting-room upstairs," Honoria suggested timidly across the huge length of the dining-table. "I am sure we will be more comfortable sitting by the fireside up there, than we could be here, even if it is dreadfully rustic behaviour."

"If you like," said her husband. The Blackwoods did not, as a rule, observe the custom of the ladies' withdrawal from the table when they dined at home, for the simple reason that Alexander did not smoke, and drank after dinner only to oblige a guest or host.

"Then I shall ring for Traubin to fetch it up there," said Honoria, in order to say something. The stillness that had reigned during the greater part of dinner had been quite awful to her, and she was most eager to have done with it. In the sitting-room, at least, there was the fire to look at and listen to, for though there was, naturally, a hearth in the dining-parlour, the apartment was so large as to render it insignificant.

"You were most entertaining last night," said poor Honoria, as she passed a dish of coffee to her husband. "What you said about town-hours, I mean."

"I am glad you think so." Alexander scrutinised the parallel gilt bands that were painted round the rim of his cup, and relapsed into silence.

"We are certain to be late at the Throstles' tonight. You will not be over-tired?"

"I hope not."

Honoria sighed and resolved upon one more attempt. "How does your monograph progress? You must find all our visiting and so forth most frustrating. I am afraid you are interrupted here twenty times more frequently each day than you were at home."

"My monograph? I am nearing completion, I think," said Alex, and retired again into revery.

It was their first night at Stonebur all over again, thought Honoria; her disappointment at the realisation was great. One would have imagined, said she to herself, that nearly four months of marriage must alter the relations between them—make them somewhat familiar with one another, if nothing else! But it did not do so; she was obliged to own everything just as strained and uneasy as ever, and saw Alexander finish his coffee with relief.

Still, there was the ball to be thought of. Preparations for that event amply filled the next few hours: when her own gown had been donned, and her hair becomingly coiffed, Emily must be roused and dressed as well. Alexander repeated the miracle he had first performed on the previous evening, and was waiting for them in the drawing-room at precisely half-past ten.

"It wouldn't have answered to depart any earlier," said he, as they entered the carriage. "One does not care to arrive on time in London." Evidently he was preparing to assume that other, most disarming, rôle that he reserved for London society. Honoria determined to observe him closely tonight, to see if she might learn what animated him so in *ton* circles, and perhaps benefit by the knowledge.

The ball-room at the Throstles' answered all Mrs. Blackwood's expectation in regard to grandeur and festivity. It was half-full of people when they arrived, and quite thronged shortly afterwards; flowers decked the walls, the faces of the guests were made brilliant by candlelight and high spirits, and the music of the orchestra was heard everywhere. Miss Charlotte Throstle, whose uncertain marital prospects had inspired her parents to entertain so lavishly, welcomed the Blackwoods with civility and then turned her attention (as was her duty) to the next arrivals. The three new-comers then stood for a time together, politely ignoring the unfamiliar faces round them and straining to see those farther away. "There is Sir Malcolm Rowley, I think," said Honoria in a low voice.

"Yes, and Lady Margaret. Look, she is wearing purple again; I wondered last night if it were a momentary lapse in taste on her part, or a permanent fault of judgement." This, of course, came from Emily, whose eye for colour never failed her.

"I wonder if we ought to say hello to them; does one make one's way over to people, or wait until they are nearby?"

"I shouldn't think it signifies," said the sensible Miss Blackwood.

"If only Lady Jane were here," sighed Honor.

"Lady Jane *is* here," her husband broke in suddenly; "and she's with—can it possibly be?" He leaned forward in the direction of the entrance-way to the ball-room, evidently endeavouring to make out the identity of Lady Jane's companion. "It is!" he cried suddenly, and with no more explanation than that was off like a shot, his graceful figure passing swiftly and easily through the crowd. Honoria watched in horror as her husband, pausing only to fling an indifferent bow towards Lady Jane, seized an unknown lady's hand and bent deeply over it.

"See how long he holds her hand!" gasped Honor, too surprised and curious to govern her tongue.

Miss Blackwood gazed with her and beheld her brother, still in possession of the stranger's hand, interrogating her with a most ardent and delighted countenance. The lady replied to him with animated smiles, evidently joining fully in his pleasure at their meeting. Lady Jane looked on silently in mild astonishment.

"O, she is awfully beautiful!" said poor Honor, with a sinking sensation that travelled quickly from her throat into her stomach.

"Not so very," Emily scoffed, but she was lying and knew it. The unknown, whoever she was, was very lovely, indeed. She was of middle height and perfectly proportioned, possessed of a pair of sloping shoulders and bosom dazzlingly white. The extreme *décolletage* of her gown did nothing to detract from this last feature, nor did the diaphanous white stuff conceal her form. A feather boa dripped luxuriantly round her arms, and a diadem set in her rich golden curls admirably complemented the length and suppleness of her neck. The diadem was set with pearls, as were the rings on her hands; no colour disturbed the snowy purity of the lady's costume, save a single blood-red rose at the centre of her bodice. As for the traits of her countenance, these were in perfect conformity with the notion of beauty in that day: large blue eyes, a fair unblemished complexion, plump pink lips, and a straight, chiselled nose. No woman in the room could hope to compete with her in appearance—at least, no woman of that type—and both Honor and Emily were sensible of this at once.

Alexander still spoke with her (though he had, at length, relinquished her hand) but Lady Jane Sperling, apparently finding their discourse less than compelling, had excused herself and now appeared before the female Blackwoods. "Your husband has a past, I think," said she, but rather more sympathetically than archly. "You did not tell me."

"I did not know," said Honor. Her voice was small, but quite even and controlled.

"Indeed?" returned her ladyship and at this her eyebrows did rise wryly. "Then tonight must prove very intriguing to you. Good evening, Emily," she added. "You look dreadful."

"I am fatigued," said Miss Blackwood, not at all stung.

"Do you know her name?" Honoria asked still in the same small voice.

"The name of your husband's past? The same name attached to any number of gentlemen's pasts," replied Lady Jane, with a significant cough. "Lady Annabella Willoughby, Countess Dredstone. The term *lady* is, I assure you, a mere accident of nomenclature in her case; if she has any attribute of a gentlewoman, I am a Siberian bear."

"How came you to be entering with her then?" enquired Emily.

"Everyone is obliged to enter with her sometime, or to chat with her or leave with her. One may meet her any place in London; she is among our foremost hostesses. *That* is nothing to do with her moral character, you know; the patronesses of Almack's dare to slight her, perhaps, but no one else. The count is of too much consequence, you see."

"And does he not distress himself for his wife's reputation?"

Lady Jane shrugged prettily, and smiled. "I believe he may have fought a duel or two, in the beginning; he is twice her age, however, and leaves her pretty much to Providence now."

"Providence has dealt generously with her," observed Emily dryly.

"It has not forgot her," the other agreed, but her expression indicated clearly that she for her part entertained no wish of being Lady Willoughby, or anyone like her for that matter.

"How do you suppose Alexander knows her?" asked Honoria, who had been gazing in growing dismay at her husband and the charmer, both still rapt in conversation.

"Your husband is a very handsome man, and the countess is partial to handsome men. I suppose he knows her as any other man might know her—and not a few have," she finished uncharitably.

"I am certain she cannot be as bad as all that, if Alexander likes her," said Mrs. Blackwood.

"I do not say she is bad," Lady Jane clarified, taking Honor's hand in her own. "I say she is fast. Actually, she is very clever, and as a rule confines her interests to unwed gentlemen, or confirmed philanderers. I do not remember her ever interfering in a marriage that was healthy to begin with: the women of the *ton* envy her her looks, and pretend at least to deplore her morals, but I do not think anyone condemns her. But here comes my father," she interrupted herself suddenly; "Emily, you must be prepared to stand up with him: he told me he thinks you very attractive, indeed."

Lord Sperling did in fact appear, and solicited Miss Blackwood's company for the first two sets, which were now forming. A little time later, the scion of the Throstle house, Master Quinlan Throstle, came to claim Honor's hand for the same dances, and Mrs. Blackwood thenceforth was sufficiently distracted by the necessity of making conversation with a rather backward fifteen-year-old boy, and dancing with him at the same time, to think of her husband with only half a mind. She saw him standing up with Lady Willoughby, but the figures of the dance precluded her staring at them as much as she might have liked to.

Master Throstle was not to blame for his own gawkiness; it was a part of growing up, and Honoria courteously attempted to ignore the break in his changing voice when he escorted her to a chair and thanked her for her company. Miss Blackwood soon joined them, her partner declaring himself more than satisfied with the lightness of her feet; but shortly afterwards his lordship excused himself, and Quinlan did likewise, and the two ladies were left alone near the wall.

Honoria searched the room anxiously for Alex, but could not find him. Her idea of attending a ball had never included being left alone at the side of the room, and she found the situation excessively uncomfortable.

"I daresay someone will rescue us," said Emily placidly. "No one has even taken to the floor, as yet."

"That is because it is a waltz, I think," Honor whispered. "There are no sets, but you can see all the couples just waiting for the music to begin."

"Then we must sit through it," said Emily. "Waltzing is of questionable propriety, anyway."

"Emmy! I never thought to hear *you* talk of propriety so missishly."

"Well, there is some comfort in the thought, at least," shrugged the other. "Anyway, I can think of a dozen things worse than having to sit through a dance at a ball," she continued stoutly.

"Name one," Mrs. Blackwood challenged, without spirit.

"Claude Kemp," came the unexpected answer, so unexpected that Honoria forgot about Alex and turned with a puzzled inquiry to her sister-in-law.

"Claude Kemp?" she echoed.

"Yes—Claude Kemp," Emily hissed through teeth clamped shut, and Honor now perceived that her eyes were fixed upon someone in the crowd before them. Anxiously, she followed the direction of Miss Blackwood's gaze; scanned the faces there; hoped against hope, and discovered Claude Kemp coming towards them, and none other.

"My very dear friends, my Pittering friends, how I have hoped to meet you somewhere," cried he as he drew near. "Miss"—he bowed—"and Mrs. Blackwood"—he took her hand and kissed it—"you are prettier than ever I have seen you."

The ladies replied with the sparsest civility possible, but Mr. Kemp did not seem to notice it. He inclined his gleaming blond head towards Honoria, and begged the honour of the next dance.

"Thank you, no. I do not care to dance just now," she said stiffly.

"But you must—listen, the music is starting. A waltz at a London ball! You must not let this opportunity pass. We will have abundant time later for exchange of news—come, I implore you." Throughout this speech he had been holding firmly to her hand; try as she would, she could not extricate it from his grasp.

"I beg you will excuse me, sir; I do not wish to dance," she said fiercely, but to no avail. Encouraged by the lilt of the music, and never lacking in arrogance, Mr. Kemp quite literally pulled her from her chair and swept her off to the dance-floor, his arm embracing her firmly round her waist. Honoria had no choice, finally, but to comply with his wishes: it was either that or create a scene inevitably embarrassing to everyone. She waltzed with him, therefore, but did not speak a word until they had quite done.

They returned to the chairs where they had left Emily, and found her there in company of her brother. "Mr. Kemp," said Alexander, bowing slightly, and with no tone of any sort in his voice.

"Mr. Blackwood," the other gentleman returned, with his mechanical smile.

"Alex—" Honoria began on a gasp, and stopped.

"My dear?"

But she found she could not say anything, and only regarded him with soft, imploring eyes.

"I should like to present to you the Countess Dredstone," said Alexander, when it became evident Honoria had nothing to say. Honor had been too confused to notice her before, but Lady Willoughby was indeed standing near her husband, apparently inspecting her feathered fan, and wearing her habitual air of serene contentment. "Lady Willoughby, my wife," Alex continued.

The two ladies curtsied to one another, though Honoria had rather have fallen at the countess's knees and begged her to forget her husband.

"Alexander, I do not feel at all well," Honor burst out suddenly. "Might we go home?"

Alex looked in surprise from his wife to Mr. Kemp, and then to the countess. "It would seem terribly rude to the Throstles," he said quietly. "Perhaps Mr. Kemp would be kind enough to escort you home; that way, Emily and I may stay until it is more gracious to leave."

This, of course, was worse than anything: not only to be alone with Claude, but to leave Alexander behind with Lady Willoughby! "O no, you are right, of course. It would be dreadfully rude—I had not thought of it. It is only a slight headache, after all," she hedged. "I am certain some fresh air will mend it at once."

"I should be delighted to take you onto the terrace," offered Claude promptly.

"O no, please! I mean, I pray you will not be at such pains. Emily looks quite pale herself . . . it is awfully warm in here, don't you think, Emily? Come with me to the terrace, won't you, and let us permit Mr. Kemp to pursue more amiable pastimes."

Miss Blackwood naturally obliged her at once, and Honoria employed the brief respite afforded by her desperate attempt to quit the ball most usefully; that is, by enjoying a thorough cry on her best friend's shoulder.

Miss Blackwood was sympathetic, but begged Honoria to take hold of herself. "It is not the end of the world, you know," said she, patting her hand. "And the next time we see Claude, we may give him the cut direct and have done with him."

"He will never leave me alone," cried the other wretchedly. "He is all conceit, and will pretend he did not see it."

"In that case, I shall slit his throat," Miss Blackwood suggested practically.

"O, Emily, would you?" sobbed Honor, between laughter and tears. "I should be so obliged."

"It would be a rare pleasure, I assure you."

"But that is not the greatest trouble," Honor resumed, her spirits somewhat restored by her sister's macabre jest. "It is Alex, after all; you see his demeanour with me . . . and with Her."

"Well, as for Her . . . you heard what Lady Jane said about her morals. She will not toy with a marriage that is intact."

"But mine is not intact!" cried the distraught young lady. "O, Emily, what shall I do?"

But Emily, unhappily, had no easy answer to this. It was all she could do to rally Honoria to some semblance of calm, and to persuade her they had best return to the ball-room presently.

"You will not leave me, will you?" Mrs. Blackwood pleaded.

"Not if I can possibly avoid it," the other promised, and turned to lead the way indoors again.

Her progress was impeded, however, by the sudden appearance in the door-way of a tall, masculine figure, a figure whose voice (for it was too shadowy on the terrace to be sure by other means) soon identified the interloper as Mr. Ambrose Tayt, the gentleman who on the night previous had seemed so familiar to Honor.

"Miss Blackwood, I think?" said he, inclining his head. "And Mrs. Blackwood?"

"You are Mr. Tayt," said Honoria, finding this meeting with a known person unexpectedly bracing. She smiled, and went on, "It is insufferably warm inside, don't you think? Although quite, quite beautiful," she added. "The Throstles are perfectly hospitable."

Mr. Tayt agreed. "I am delighted to meet with you again, Miss Blackwood," said he. "With both of you, indeed—but particularly with Miss Blackwood. I am sure you understand, ma'am," he excused himself to Honor.

"O, yes, absolutely. We married ladies cannot expect to be so fascinating as those with less definite futures." She found her spirits lifting amazingly at this encounter with another human being, and one so kindly disposed towards herself and Emily. Really, she refined too much upon her own difficulties.

"The last set before supper is forming, Miss Blackwood," Ambrose went on smoothly. "May I hope you are not yet engaged for it?"

"Well—I do not know," Emily temporised, looking anxiously at Honor.

"O, do go ahead, please. You need not bother about me," she said cheerfully, and meant it. "I shall do very well."

"But—Claude," Emily murmured to her.

"If Mrs. Blackwood is unengaged also—though I know not how such a happy chance develops!—I know a gentleman who has begged to meet her all night. Might I present him to you? He really is a capital fellow, though a bit eager."

"I—I should be glad to stand up with him," Honor replied.

"You will make him a very happy man," said Mr. Tayt, leading both ladies back into the ball-room. "I told him you were married, and he was quite glum, but this will improve his spirits." And with similar easy, inconsequential remarks, Mr. Tayt brought the ladies to where his friend stood (a Mr. Munroe, if Honoria heard his name right) and contrived for all of them to take their places in a set.

Mr. Tayt said little to Emily while the music continued, but when it had ceased he begged the pleasure of accompanying her in to supper. This honour was accorded him (for Miss Blackwood had no desire to stand alone until, perhaps, Mr. Kemp might discover and descend upon her) and the two of them walked from the ball-room together. Honoria, attended by her husband—who had at last deserted the countess—preceded them by a little, and so could not hear their conversation. This was well for Emily, for it was a curious conversation, if closely observed.

"I think you paint," said Mr. Tayt lightly, and delighted in the palpable twitch of Miss Blackwood's hand upon his sleeve.

"I paint," said she.

"So do I; I was most interested, therefore, when Lord Sperling told me you are something of an adept."

Mr. Tayt was smiling down upon her, but Emily kept her regard fixed rigidly before them. "Might we sit near my brother?" she asked as they entered the brightly-lit supper room. "He is the tall gentleman, just there."

"I remember your brother," he replied, leading the way toward Alex and Honor. "I suppose he shares your interest in art? I should adore to hear his views on the artists of the Royal Academy. The annual exhibition opens any day now, I believe."

But Miss Blackwood, rather than encouraging this seemingly acceptable topic by a rational reply, instead showed a lively alarm of a sudden, and seemed by her answer to be a most flighty young lady. "Do not let us sit by Alexander, after all," said she at once, pulling away from the direction they had taken. Mr. Tayt observed her with evident amusement. "Pray, I see sufficient of my brother at home. Might we not join the Rowleys?"

Mr. Tayt obliged her with a smile indicative of something deeper than mere civility, and Emily took care thereafter to steer their discourse away from the topic of art. Her relief was manifest when the light repast was finished, and she hastened from Ambrose's company with all due speed.

"Mr. Tayt seems a kind young fellow," Honoria said to her, when they had left the Throstles and regained their own home. "Do not you think so?"

"He is—quite adequate in kindness," Emily conceded.

"My dear!" Honor said reproachfully, reaching at the same time for her slippers and removing them thankfully. The three young people sat now in their own snug sitting-room, exchanging impressions of the evening before they should go to sleep. "His manner is such as must please, I am sure, and he struck me as being most intelligent. You are excessively severe with him, really."

"I may be severe with him if I like, I suppose," said Emily crossly, and instantly turned the topic. "Alexander, would you do us the kindness of stabbing Claude Kemp, please? In the back, if you can manage it."

Alexander, who had more or less resumed his habitual distraction, begged his sister to repeat herself; he had not heard.

"I say, will you be good enough to kill Claude Kemp? He is here in London, as you must recall, and I do not think I shall enjoy this city until he is gone out of it again."

Alexander regarded her with an air of mild bemusement, and said he did not see why.

"Because he is a boor, dear brother, and a great beast as well. Why he very nearly tore Honoria limb from limb tonight, when she would not waltz with him. I am grateful we contrived to avoid him after that, but I doubt it will be possible henceforth, now he has discovered us."

"Did you wish not to waltz with him, Honoria?" he enquired dispassionately. "Then you ought not to have."

"But he *forced* her to do so; I tell you, he is a brute!"

"Emily, you might not wish to meddle in matters that do not concern you," Alexander said evenly. "Whatever Kemp is, we have known him all our lives, and I think it most unlikely he should tear anybody limb from limb."

"But he *did*, Alexander," cried his sister in exasperation. "Honoria, did not he?"

"He did—he was rather—forceful," said she, her old timidity regaining possession of her, and making it impossible for her to join wholly in Emily's energetic censure.

"Well, then, you see, Emily," Alexander resumed, in the tone of one who has been vindicated, "there is a great difference between being forceful and brutal. You refine too much upon the matter. Besides, if Honoria has any quarrel with Claude, I am certain they are well-acquainted enough to settle it between them."

"Alexander, sometimes you make me ill," Emily declared, and sprang rather violently from the sofa. "I am going to bed," she snapped, and immediately made good her words.

Alexander, utterly untouched (it seemed) by the tone of his sister's pronouncement, rose lazily and yawned behind his hand. "A very good notion," he said to his wife. "I believe I shall retire myself. Good night, my dear."

"Good night," she returned, helpless to do otherwise, and so matters were left for a few days: Emily's absences entirely mysterious, Alexander's friendship with the countess unmentioned and unexplained, and Honoria positive that her husband persisted in believing a guilty connection linked her to Claude Kemp. At least Emily was home on Sunday, and they all went together to church; Honoria employed the ample time left to her husband's occupation with his monograph to do a great deal of letter-writing, and even received a few letters herself. Among these was a note from her aunts, dated Bench Street, April 21. The closely scrawled sheets proclaimed the hand of Miss Mercy Deverell, and indeed her signature was to be found at the bottom, with "& Prudence" pencilled in afterwards.

"My Dear Niece," it read, "I am told every girl in London for the first time forgets everything but what is under her nose; and so, if that is true, perhaps I must remind you that I am your aunt, and so is my sister—which is why I address you 'Dear Niece.' My sister Prudence has just asked me to read what I have written so far, and now I have done so she informs me we received a letter from you not three days ago; this being the case, I am reassured that the business mentioned above (about every girl forgetting her past in London) is fustian merely, and will no longer regard it. If you will excuse me one moment longer, I will read that letter to which my sister refers . . . if she can only find it . . . she is looking for it now . . . Ah yes! She has found it and hands it to me.

"*Now* I am in a far better case! Before I had no notion what to tell you, and only wrote because Prudence desired it—but here comes your letter to us, and provides me with any number of queries and remarks. The Post Office is a very great institution, my dear, and we ought to value it highly."

Honoria had to break here, and steal a moment to laugh in. It was so like Aunt Mercy to begin a letter with no object, and to make the letter itself her subject. She continued to savour this eccentricity as she read on.

"You say you have got a great many new gowns; well, I have got a new shawl myself, which I think is very pretty. It *is* very pretty, is it not? Squire Kemp gave it me, you know—he is the magistrate here in Pittering, in case you had forgot—for being so kind as to play chess with him each Wednesday. Truthfully, I do not find it much of a task, and had far rather play chess than lace my boots, for example, but I do not tell Squire Kemp so, and I beg you will not either, for he would feel mighty silly about giving me a shawl for playing if he knew. Prudence reads over my shoulder and interrupts me to say all men are silly, and would I like some tea?—but no doubt you know all men are silly, for I believe you brought one with you to London.

"As always, the blessing of our existence here continues to be our small friends, who mew and bark their regards to you constantly. A very secret project, about which Prudence now reminds me you must be told nothing, is going forward in their behalf—and I do not think Sir Proctor will be sorry when he learns what he is to do, or at least when he has done it . . . or at least, that is what Prudence says. Prudence is always right, my dear; or did you know?

"You say you have taken a house in Albemarle Street.

"We live in Bench Street as we have for years. I would not mention it except for the fact that *your* mentioning *your* direction has proved very convenient indeed—as otherwise we should not know how to send this letter. Perhaps my including this intelligence as to our location will prove equally valuable to you.

"Perhaps not.

"In any case, the bottom of the page advances more rapidly than anyone could have dreamt it would when I started, and Prudence says if I close now she will scribble her name in below, and Mary may take this letter to be posted immediately, when she goes to visit Mr. Morley. Mr. Morley is a butcher.

"Your very obdt., etc."

This missive, extraordinary though it was, did more to improve Honoria's spirits than any reasonable thing could possibly have done. She thrust it into Emily's hand, for that lady was just returning from her daily errand of mystery, and could not otherwise greet her for laughing. Emily laughed, too, when she had read it, and relations between the two young ladies were easier than they had been in days.

"Your Aunt Mercy is truly the oddest little sprite! What can she mean about a secret project? And Sir Proctor's not being sorry for it?"

Honor blushed a little and said, "I will explain it to you some day, but you remind me of something: Emily, if I were to guess the truth of your life away from here, would you tell me?"

"I do not think you could guess it," said the other.

"Then let me attempt it, at least. Is it possible you have taken a studio of your own, and paint there all day?"

"No," said Emily, smiling tightly. "Would to Heaven it were."

"Then you have found an artist to instruct you—is that it? And you go to him all day?"

"No again," Miss Blackwood replied. "I feel as if we were playing a parlour game, don't you?"

"A little," Honoria sighed. "Emily, why won't you tell me?"

"Because you would say it is impossible, and it is not impossible, for I am doing it."

"But you do not paint here! And I know you too well to believe you have given it up altogether."

"Do you? Then you know me rather too well, indeed," said Emily mischievously. "Or, perhaps, not well enough. One more question now, and the game is at an end."

"Only one more?"

"Only one—and that was it," cried Miss Blackwood, and she jumped abruptly from her seat and fled the room, laughing at her outraged sister, who pursued her to no avail.

"Lady Jane invites us to drive in the park with her tomorrow," said Honoria that evening at tea. "Will you come, Alexander?"

"I think not," he answered, idly turning over in his hands a number of notes that had arrived for him in the morning's post, and that he had been too much engaged with study that day to examine till now. "Perhaps Emily will accompany you."

"Perhaps," said his sister, with a significant glance at Honor—which was meant, as its recipient knew, to remind her she was lying. Naturally she would not be able to go; but Alex need not learn that.

"Here is an odd invitation," said he, having opened a letter and perused it. "It is from a Mr. Ambrose Tayt, Esquire. Do we know a Mr. Tayt?"

"Know him?" muttered Emily, almost inaudibly. "I shall wring his noble neck."

"I beg your pardon, Emily?"

"Nothing, Alex. What does Mr. Tayt suggest we do?"

"He desires us to accompany him to the exhibition at Somerset Place, the artists selected by the Royal Academy, apparently. I wonder he did not send the invitation to you, my dear. I am sure I do not recall him."

"Perhaps he felt it too forward to address me a letter," Honoria guessed. "You remember him, don't you? He was at Emily's come-out, the gentleman who wore his cravat *à la Byron.*"

"Who *affected* to wear his cravat *à la Byron*, you mean," Emily corrected darkly.

"I can't think what makes you so ill-disposed towards him," said Honor mildly.

"Anyway, he wishes we will go with him on Saturday next," Alex resumed. "Shall we?"

"I wonder why he chooses Saturday," Honor mused.

Miss Blackwood's mouth worked angrily, but she said nothing.

"I think we ought to accept," Mr. Blackwood said finally. "It will be pleasant for Emmy."

"O, very pleasant," said she sarcastically, but prudence restrained her from saying more, and the matter was thus decided. In the interim, however, there were also a soirée at Lady Frane's to be attended, two invitations to the opera, and a masked ball.

"I am not certain we ought to go to that," said Honoria. "It was very good of the Rowleys to include us in their party, but I believe it may not be proper."

"Perhaps not," said Alex, "but it is sure to be diverting. I suggest you ask Lady Jane, tomorrow, when she takes you on your drive."

"I will do that," Honoria agreed, and did in fact.

Lady Jane, upon learning that her only companion was to be Honoria, had persuaded the coachman to let her take the phaeton out herself, and arrived in Albemarle Street holding the ribbons in fine style.

"You won't be distracted from your driving, if I talk to you?" Honoria asked, for she mistrusted such a high, light vehicle in the first place, and was equally uncertain of Jane's command of the horses.

"Not at all, dear lamb," said she soothingly, and increased the pace of the horses somewhat as if to ridicule the idea. They turned into the gates of the park and entered the press of carriages there.

"Such a lot of people!" exclaimed Honor, who had not driven in the park before. "I dareswear everyone of our acquaintance is here."

"Not at all unlikely," said Lady Jane. "Did you have a question for me?"

Honoria told her of their doubts regarding the *bal masqué,* and was informed that she might go, though it would be wiser not to. "Such quantities of scandals seem to begin at masked balls," said Lady Jane. "It is almost as if people could not wait for them, to behave outlandishly."

"Then I think we shall stop at home," Honor decided. "Alexander has—O dear," she interrupted herself suddenly. "Can we possibly turn round?"

"Turn round?" smiled Jane; "I hardly think so. We have scarcely sufficient space to crawl forward, let alone reverse ourselves. Why?"

Honoria's consternation was now plainly legible on her face, and her voice trembled as she replied, "Someone I do not care to meet— coming the other way—Lady Jane, do you care if I hide? Might I, please? I shan't mind the floor of the carriage."

"Well, whoever can it be, to throw you into such a fright? You must certainly not hide," the older lady said. "It would give a most awkward appearance."

"O, but you do not know—" Honor began, but she was prevented from saying more by the immediate arrival of Claude Kemp's curricle, which stopped opposite them no more than a foot away.

"Hallo!" cried he heartily to the ladies. "Good morning!"

"I pray you, Jane, save me," whispered Honor, visibly shaken.

Such conduct was too particular to fail to arouse Lady Jane's curiosity. Her interest piqued quite exhilaratingly, she begged of her companion an introduction to the gentleman and, observing him most shrewdly, proceeded to engage him in a lengthy conversation. Throughout the whole of it, Honoria continued to quake and quail beside her.

Chapter XIII

"Mr. Kemp," began Lady Jane, "I must own I noticed you at the Throstles' ball the other night, and even sought to learn your name. It is not often we see a cravat tied *Primo Tempo;* I am always on the watch for clever cravats."

"I am gratified to hear it was remarked," said he, "particularly by a lady so obviously conversant with the current vogues." Mr. Kemp raised his quizzing-glass and surveyed Jane's smart fawn pelisse with unmistakable approval.

"Surely a gentleman as sophisticated as yourself has learned by now to associate with fashionable women only. Ladies whose attire is out of date are fatally liable to be antiquated in other areas as well: in their ideas, for example, or their morality."

"Or their ideas of morality," he replied, smiling carefully, as if this were a witty rejoinder.

Lady Jane humoured him with a laugh. "Precisely. Now don't you think so, my dear Honoria?"

"I suppose," said she, though barely audibly. She was too much discomposed by this unlooked-for meeting to follow the conversation; however, she knew enough to be extremely sensible of Lady Jane's kindness in drawing Kemp off.

"You see? Dear Honoria supposes so, too. Now we have a unanimous opinion, and the vote carries."

"My lady interests herself in politics, I think?"

"In government, which is to say, behaviour; and politics, which is to say, the manipulation of behaviour—yes, I do. Who cannot, who lives among society?" She smiled that brilliant smile that had been observed upon her lips before, and looked with disarming candour into Claude Kemp's icy eyes.

"And what, then, of affairs of state? Of—war, for example?"

"O, a battle always intrigues me," she answered lightly. "As much its strategy as its action, in fact."

"We must discuss strategy sometime, ma'am."

"Discuss it! But all the diversion would go out of it, then."

"We might discuss diversionary tactics, if you like."

Lady Jane again indulged him, this time by smiling at the pointless pun, and resumed, "But I think we are wearying poor Honor with our chatter. She does not care much for military matters, I suspect."

"Not even when she witnesses a flank attack?" asked he in a low tone, leaning towards Lady Jane's ear.

"But this is not a flank attack," she parried. "It is a frontal attack. Mr. Kemp, will you join my party tonight at the theatre? You will oblige me more than you know."

"I am promised to attend a supper at White's, alas!"

"Then you must disappoint your friends. It *is* sad; you are right." And she joined him in crying alas.

"You are not very kind to my friends," said he.

"Nor have you been very kind to mine, I think," she pointed out, with a sidelong glance at Honoria.

"I have endeavoured to be kind," he retorted, his colour rising a little at this accusation.

"Too much like Master Petruchio in *The Taming of the Shrew,* I fear: you seem to kill her with kindness."

"That's as may be," he muttered stubbornly.

"Not at all," she contradicted promptly. "That's *As You Like It*—or rather, as *I* like it. I will see you in Berkeley Square tonight at nine, sir. Good day." And so saying, she started her horses before he could reply, and was soon lost to him among the jostling throng of coaches.

"How you did manage him!" exclaimed Honoria, once they were out of earshot. Her eyes went wide with admiration, and she fairly stared at Jane.

"It was not very difficult," she said, with her pretty shrug. "I had hoped for a greater challenge, in fact, but I suppose he will do. You *are* indifferent to him, are you not?" she queried suddenly. "I mean, I do not intrude where I am not wanted, do I?"

Honoria assured her she was most welcome to Claude Kemp—indeed, more than merely welcome. "But I must caution you," she continued, feeling it only fair. "As delighted as I am to see him cease his pursuit of me, and pursue you instead, he is a thoroughly disagreeable man. I may even say—though I hate to cast suspicion where it may not be due—I have sometimes thought him dangerous."

"I appreciate your warning, my dear; truly I do. However, you make one crucial error. You say that Kemp pursues me," Lady Jane responded, as she turned the horses out of the gate and into the street again. "He does not pursue me; I pursue him. And so long as that is the case, the peril is all on his side. No hunter fears his hare, and I do not fear Mr. Kemp."

"He thinks he pursues you," Honoria objected. "I saw it in his eyes. He regarded you—so greedily—rather, I fancy, as a wolf regards its prey."

"I am glad you observed that, my dear. It is precisely in that circumstance that all my security lies. Mr. Kemp believes he tracks me down; I *know* he is my quarry."

Honoria drank this in in silence, fascinated by so bold a speech. "What will you do with him once you have caught him?" she enquired at length.

"Do with him?" Lady Jane repeated almost dreamily. "I had not thought of it. Throw him back into the sea, I suppose, as an angler who hooks an uneatable fish. He does not look very palatable to me," she added, "nor even very wholesome."

"Then why do you bother with him at all?" asked Mrs. Blackwood, overawed at such confidence.

"For sport, I daresay. To amuse myself. And naturally, to protect my poor dear lamb," she added, with a comforting pat to Honor's hand. "Has he given you many bad moments? The way you trembled at his approach might lead one to suppose he had sullied your virtue."

"Well, he has not done that, quite," Honoria hedged, "but he has indeed proved excessively troublesome." She thought for a moment and went on, "May I tell you something in confidence?"

"If you wish," Lady Jane replied, at the same time neatly avoiding a collision with a stately carriage. "I will not betray you."

"Alexander believes—that is, my husband believes . . ." her voice trailed off. "Mr. Blackwood believes I am in love with Mr. Kemp."

"Does he, indeed?" the other exclaimed. "He must find that most disconcerting!"

"Not nearly as—as disconcerting as I would hope," Honoria confessed. "In point of fact, I think he rather likes it. It permits him to —to behave similarly with other ladies."

"With the Countess Dredstone, you mean," Lady Jane said thoughtfully.

"Particularly with her. And that is what I wished to ask you: Lady Jane, do you think I might call upon the countess, and beg her not to— to renew her acquaintance with Alex? Do you think she might listen?

You said she does not intrude where a wife might be injured," Mrs. Blackwood pleaded earnestly, "and I have no notion what else to do."

Lady Jane pondered this a moment, but soon shook her head decisively. "No, poor dear; if you succeed in your petition, your husband will only find himself driven elsewhere . . . and perhaps to less acceptable quarters. Lady Willoughby at least will not embarrass you in public; she is not a spiteful woman, nor a vulgar."

Honor was obviously crest-fallen. "I could die when I think of them together," was all she said—and that in a very small voice.

"Hmmmm," Lady Jane mused. "You cannot feign an interest in another man, for that only encourages him. This is very puzzling indeed, Honoria; I am glad you told me. I will think of it," she promised, and since they had arrived again in Albemarle Street, the interview closed there.

A quantity of rain drenched the next few days, painting them so thoroughly in grey from dawn to dusk that one could not, as Emily said, "tell Wednesday from Thursday. They all look alike, don't they? It is most dispiriting."

"Well, if it interests you, today chances to be Friday," her sister-in-law told her. "And we are engaged for whist at the Huffles', and to-morrow we see Mr. Tayt."

"And the exhibition in Somerset Place," said Emily, a smile of pure pleasure lighting on her lips at the thought of it. So great was her anticipation of the excursion, in fact, that she forgot to be nettled at the mention of Mr. Tayt.

They had just done with dinner, and Honor was about to suggest they all remove to the sitting-room upstairs, when Alexander spoke up suddenly, and interrupted her.

"I am afraid I cannot go with you to the Huffles' tonight," said he. "I am terribly sorry."

Honoria was so frightened at what might be the significance of this that she dared not even ask for an explanation.

Emily was not so timid. "Your monograph, Alexander?" she inquired.

"My—monograph, yes. I am anxious to finish it, now it is so near completion. I hope you will excuse me, dear ma'ams; I am certain John Coachman will see you there and back safely."

"I might write to the Huffles and suggest another evening," Honor burst out, in a voice scarcely under control. "I might say you were ill—or I was ill—"

"I beg you will not," Alexander said, with a sort of languid air unusual in him. "I do not truly care for whist in any case, and am just as glad to miss it."

Honoria could not speak—due to a sudden lump in her throat—and only nodded assent.

Miss Blackwood thought her brother was despicable, and said so to his wife as they drove to Lady Huffle's, but Honoria beseeched her not to talk of it; it only made her more wretched. She succeeded in putting on a brave front at the whist table—though it was evident to all that her mind wandered sadly—and restrained herself from pleading a headache and fleeing the inspection of society. When supper was at last laid out, however, she thought she had never been so happy to see a meal in her life (in spite of the fact that she could not swallow a mouthful) and when Emily finally suggested their departure, she agreed most whole-heartedly.

"And do go directly to bed," Lady Agatha Huffle advised her officiously. "You look dreadfully worn down, and have not been at all yourself tonight."

Honoria promised that she would follow this counsel, but though she went to bed at once, she could not go to sleep. Alexander, it was learned when they reached Albemarle Street, was not at home, and had given Traubin instructions not to wait up for him.

"And he didn't say where he was going, ma'am," said Traubin, anticipating his mistress's next question.

"You know you might have done better with Kemp," Emily muttered in a fury. "Alexander is practically invisible when he is present, and all too conspicuous when he is gone. I must ask him how he does it sometime," she continued, adding, "Let me read to you while you lie in bed, at least. It will distract you."

But Honoria declined this kindness, for Emily seemed dangerously fatigued herself, and she feared for her sister's nerves as much as for her own.

"Happily I have the constitution of a horse," said Emily, with a notable lack of gentility. "The shoemaker's children go barefoot, they say, and I do not remember when my father or mother ever paid the least attention to my health, which was well, for it taught me to mend on my own." This discourse, however, was the most bracing she could manage. She was presently obliged to admit to exhaustion, which left Honor alone and at the mercy of her own imagination.

That imagination proved more vivid, suddenly, than it had ever done before. Alexander's whereabouts, and the company he was in, recurred in her mind with never-ceasing variations, each one crueler than the last. When she finally fell asleep it was not because she had succeeded in governing her thoughts, but because she had heard (at four or five of the morning, she guessed) her husband enter the house at last, and steal quietly into his room. Her first thought was to throw open the door that stood closed between their chambers and fling herself tearfully at his feet. Her next—and perhaps, better advised—was that now he was home safe, she could quit her fretting for the night, and lose herself in sleep. This she did, and rose rather late in the morning.

Alexander did not show himself until noon, and since Mr. Tayt arrived at one Honoria had not much opportunity of conversation with her husband, had she chosen to initiate one at all. He did not refer to his unexpected absence of the previous night, and their situation was not private enough to encourage questions. They all drove to Somerset Place in Ambrose's capacious equipage, and descended together to see what might be seen.

Confronted with such a quantity of works of art, it was to be expected that discourse might lapse somewhat among the small party. It did so, yet everyone continued to say something now and then, except for Emily. She, whose dream it had long been to be precisely where she now was, wandered through the galleries in a blissful revery as impenetrable as any that had ever descended on her brother. The others allowed her to take the lead, and followed her meanderings murmuring sporadically of colour and composition, and sometimes of beauty. At length, however, Mr. Tayt detached himself from Mr. and Mrs. Blackwood and drifted forward to the side of the rapt admirer. Until he offered her his arm she still did not notice him, but then even she was obliged to.

"All this walking makes you tired, perhaps," said he, with that peculiar smile he reserved for Emily, half-way between courtesy and the keenest amusement. "Pray, lean upon my arm; I shall not regard your small weight."

"Mr. Tayt, I beg you will quit teasing me," she hissed, so that her brother and sister might not hear. "I am aware you are aware; we are both aware of our awarenesses; there is no need of your alluding to it every five minutes."

"But I do not understand," said he, dropping his mocking accent and speaking most sincerely. "Why on earth do you do it? I am sure it is most uncomfortable for you."

"You may be certain of that," said she.

"And your reason—?"

"Because I have no choice," she answered flatly. "Now, unless you mean to inform upon me, I implore you to let the subject drop for ever."

"Aha!" cried he, while she shushed him, glancing anxiously back towards the Blackwoods, "Then your family does not know; I thought as much!"

"No, of course they do not," she whispered fiercely. "Do you think they would allow it?"

"Miss Blackwood, this is all excessively intriguing. I will engage to stop teasing you about it, if you in turn will promise to acquaint me with all the particulars of the matter as soon as may be. Will you?"

"I do not see why it is any of your concern," she said crossly, pretending to be absorbed in a painting though she was too distracted to look at it.

"What a warrior you are!" he exclaimed. "I only thought I might prove helpful to you. Can you not take me into your confidence, as a friend?"

"I don't know how you can be helpful," she began; "but I suppose if you are so incapable of forgetting the affair, I must tell you its cause and circumstances. But not here, I pray you; I simply must look at these paintings or I will die."

"No, not here," he agreed, remarking at the same time that the Blackwoods had quickened their pace and were nearly upon them. "It is unsuitable, clearly. However, if I were to call upon you tomorrow, could you contrive to be alone?"

Many a young lady would have baulked instantly at such a proposition as this, but it did not even occur to Miss Blackwood to be niffy-naffy. "Yes," she said, eager to be done with the business, "I shall stop at home while the others go to church, and receive you by myself."

"Such secret scheming," cried he, smiling again. "I have never encountered another young lady half so enigmatical as you, Miss Blackwood."

Miss Blackwood frowned at this observation, for she prided herself upon her candour, and it did not please her to be thought devious. "My brother and sister come," was all she said, and turned to greet them in the same breath, and to point out to them the brush-strokes in a certain work by Turner.

In the morning Miss Blackwood reported herself afflicted with the headache, not so serious, she assured her sister, as to prevent the others' going to church, yet severe enough to oblige her to keep her bed. She was alone, then, when Mr. Tayt arrived, and at liberty to speak. The visible result of their interview was that an hour after Ambrose's arrival, both he and Miss Blackwood were driving together down Albemarle Street through the light mist, Miss Blackwood smartly dressed in a frogged and ruched pelisse. An animated conversation was going forward within the equipage, though most of the animation was on Miss Blackwood's side.

"But it is Sunday," she kept repeating. "Surely this is no occasion—"

"I tell you he is my uncle," said Ambrose with a smile. "Not only will he receive us, he will be most delighted to see me."

"And me?" she inquired sceptically.

"*And* you," he countered. "Miss Blackwood, he is a very jolly old gentleman, not the least disposed to make difficulties. I promise you he can never have heard of your case. If he had, you should not have been obliged to go to such extraordinary lengths."

"But Sir Geoffrey said all the directors discussed it—"

"The devil fly away with Sir Geoffrey," cried he. "He's a weak old fool who never got anything done for anybody. Besides, my uncle is not a director—he is the founder. Doubtless he is not consulted in such matters."

"I really don't think—" she began with a frown.

"No, of course you don't," he interrupted. "If you had, none of this would have been necessary. Cedric Blackwood, indeed! I never heard the like." He was silent for a moment, then added, "It shows a deal of spirit, however. My uncle will like that."

Emily took issue with him on this point, naturally, and the lively speculation continued right up to the moment when Lord Greystone Howard, founder of the London Academy of Art and uncle to Ambrose Tayt, Esquire, discovered his nephew and Miss Blackwood in his drawing-room in Grosvenor Square.

"And what brings you here, you young rapscallion?" asked he jovially, extending a slightly palsied hand to Mr. Tayt. "Mischief, no doubt; I hope the young lady knows you too well to get mixed up in your affairs."

"Uncle, this is Miss Emily Blackwood," said Ambrose. Lord Howard took Emily's hand and gallantly bent his silvered head over it.

"Miss Blackwood," said he. Emily looked up to find a pair of bright blue eyes twinkling into her own, accompanied by a warmly inquisitive smile. "My nephew rarely has the good sense to bring attractive young ladies to meet me. You ought to do it more often, Ambrose."

"I will take pains to do so more frequently, if you like it, sir," said the young man.

"Every week, if possible," his lordship replied, seating himself on a velvet settee and laying his gold-headed cane across his knees. "Do you know, ma'am, you seem just the slightest bit familiar to me. Is it possible I've met you before?"

Miss Blackwood coloured to the roots of her hair, and murmured, "I think not."

"No, eh? Well, I'm very glad to do so now. Is this call merely to cheer an old man along," he asked, "or am I right in suspecting something deeper?"

"You are perfectly right, sir," Ambrose began, while Emily attempted to hush him. "Miss Blackwood here has a tale to tell, which I think may be of some interest to you. And you *have* met her before, I think—in a manner of speaking at least."

"Mr. Tayt, please—" Emily commenced.

"Miss Blackwood moves under an alias," Ambrose continued undisturbed. "Two, in fact. Mr. Cedric Blackwood—"

"I thought the name was familiar!"

"—And Margaret Hamble. Better known as Maggie. Better known as 'girl!'"

"Damme, I was sure of it!" cried Lord Howard. "The new girl at the academy. But—"

"Miss Blackwood wanted an education," said Ambrose. "She is a painter."

"Well, you'd do better to apply through the usual channels," Lord Howard told her, "than to hire yourself out as a serving wench."

"I had no choice," Emily burst out at last. "It was either that or learn nothing at all. You must understand, sir," she said, and went on to explain how she had entered the competition, and won, and persuaded her father to let her come to London, and applied to Sir Geoffrey, and been told it was impossible. "So you see, my lord, all I could think of then was the girl we saw up in the studio, and what Sir Geoffrey had said about its being so difficult to find proper servants. I got up a disguise as quickly as I could, ran directly to the academy, and presented myself for the vacant position. Sir Geoffrey never recognized me—indeed, I am amazed you should, sir, for I think my own mother would hardly know me in such rags as those I wear in the studio—and was glad enough to find a girl so easily. And it's turned out rather well," she added, a little proudly. "I pay all my wages to a lady who keeps a shop in Bond Street near the school, and change my clothes there every day. No one has guessed my identity but your nephew, and I have learned a very great deal merely from eavesdropping and so forth. Of course, it has been a trifle tiring, for I could not tell my family, and have been obliged to live in society as well as working all day."

"The strongest woman in England, I dareswear," said Ambrose. "Why, I have seen her carry out endless errands, submit to sharp rebukes and insolent orders, run up and down stairs two score of times a day; and danced a quadrille with her in the evening—the same evening, that is. And a very neat dancer she was, too."

"Miss Blackwood," said his lordship, "this is a most extraordinary history. I hardly know whether to laugh or to cry. How could you bear up under such a strain?"

"You know the common adage, no doubt, about wills and ways," said Emily modestly. "Though, naturally, it tells on my hands." She pulled off a glove, then, to reveal a very chapped, raw hand, indeed.

"Dear, dear, this can't go on," cried the good old gentleman. "I am sure you have demonstrated enough talent and determination to warrant the admission of fifty applicants into the academy, let alone one lady. There is no question but that you have shown more aptitude than my nephew here, at least—*he* never goes to the studio unless it pleases him, and then fiddles about with his brushes only to pass the time."

"I have attended every day, sir, since Miss Blackwood and I met at her come-out," Ambrose defended himself. "It was all too intriguing not to."

"Yes, intrigue—that's all you're after. An education is what this young lady wants, and an education she shall have," he declared with energy. "Yes, damme," he went on, striking his cane against the floor, "she shall have it if I have to found another academy—this one for females."

"O, sir!" was all Emily could say.

"Goodness, gracious," Lord Howard exploded suddenly. "Damned if I won't throttle Geoffrey Penningdon myself! It's all his doing—no doubt of it. Probably put the case to the directors so damned apologetically, no one would think twice about accepting her."

"You must excuse my uncle's tongue," Mr. Tayt murmured to Emily. "He is not accustomed to the society of ladies."

"Fustian," his lordship objected immediately. "Miss Blackwood don't mind a damme or two; now, do you, my dear? She's made of finer stuff than that."

"You needn't trouble over me," she agreed. "A servant girl is spoke to none too civilly. I've learned that at the academy, too."

"There, you see?" his lordship flung at his nephew. "Silly, frippery fellow," he explained in an aside to Emily. "Though he did well to bring you here."

"I really don't see, Uncle," Mr. Tayt took up, not the least bit offended, "why Miss Blackwood should not be permitted to take her lessons in the studio, with the rest of us. After all, she's been there all along."

His uncle only replied with a pensive "Hmmmm."

"And as for the exhibit, I think her painting ought to be hung with her right name on it. She deserves a better reward than to win her fame incognito."

"Yes, yes . . . All these are details to be settled as they can be. The main thing is, Miss Blackwood, you may resign from your post as serving-wench immediately; and I hope Sir Geoffrey works up a good headache finding a replacement."

"A headache!" cried Emily suddenly, jumping from her chair. "Dear Heavens, I had completely forgot. Mr. Tayt, my sister must be mad with anxiety by now; I left no message as to my whereabouts, and she thought I had the headache. O dear, I despise to be uncivil, but might we leave right away? Begging your pardon, sir," she added to Lord Howard, "but you see how I am fixed."

"See it very clearly, very clearly, my dear," said he. "No matter, off you go," and he rose and packed the two visitors out of his house with the most hospitable haste. "You'll be hearing from me in the morning," he promised, "or the next day at the latest. No need to resign your post in person; just send Sir Geoffrey a note."

The exultation rampant in Miss Blackwood's breast in consequence of this interview may easily be imagined. She arrived home alone, having wished Mr. Tayt a breathless and grateful good-by at the doorstep, and discovered Honoria in a considerable pucker—so much so, in fact, that it was some time before Emily could tell her her news.

"But you mustn't run off this way!" young Mrs. Blackwood kept saying, "and on a Sunday, too. What was I to tell Alexander? Did you not think of that? He made sure you had been abducted, and was speaking of the Bow Street runners not two minutes ago. Emily, pray, promise you will never disappear again on a Sunday!"

"But I shan't disappear at all," Emily broke in. "That's what I keep telling you. It's all been set right, it's all perfectly heavenly," she insisted, and at last succeeded in telling her sister where she had been the last weeks, and what had passed that morning.

"Then that is why Mr. Tayt seemed so familiar to me at your come-out—I must have noticed him when we visited the academy. I *told* you he was an amiable man; now, how could he have been kinder?" said Honor, when a certain amount of exclaiming and rejoicing had been shared.

"Of course, he is an amiable man," Emily fairly sang. "The world is

amiable, everyone is amiable, Sir Geoffrey is amiable!" and she
danced off in a sort of slow waltz to acquaint Alexander with the glad
tidings. She did not feel it quite necessary, however, to tell him exactly what she had been about the past few weeks: her brother had
never missed her, after all, and it was just as well to leave him in the
dark.

That darkness that had previously shrouded Emily's days—at least
where Honoria was concerned—had been lifted to reveal secrets much
more innocent than any she had feared. Of course, it was dreadful to
think of Emily employed as a common serving-girl—and in Bond
Street, of all places—but Emily promised Ambrose Tayt and his uncle
could be relied upon to say nothing, and no one else knew. The mystery surrounding her husband's life, however, could not be removed
with as pleasant results—or so Honoria had reason to suppose. She was
excessively relieved for Emily, naturally; but her own difficulties continued, and she did not know how to approach them. Alexander evidently had no use for her; she could not bring herself to ask him for a
confirmation of this, and so she never alluded to his unexplained absence from home the other night, but only prayed it would not be
repeated. It was repeated, however, that very Sunday night, and on
the Tuesday following.

That Wednesday evening they were engaged to join Lady Jane
Sperling's party at Vauxhall. Poor Honor found that no amount of
coiffing and primping and fussing could erase from her countenance
the pallor her anxiety had left there. Emily had been radiant ever
since Sunday, and was especially so now that word had arrived from
Lord Howard of her present acceptance into the academy. It had
been arranged with the masters to instruct her privately, three hours
each day, in whichever of the two studios was not then in use.
Moreover, consent had been obtained from the judges to hang her picture with her true name below it. Her exhaustion had ceased as soon
as she was released from her double life, and her toilette Wednesday
evening was as simple and as effective as could be. It was Honoria—by
rights the lovelier of the two—who required extraordinary attention,
and even that (though freely given by her sister and her abigail) was
to no avail.

"I look pale," she said finally, with a little sigh. "I *am* pale. I shall
be obliged to go looking pale; there is nothing else for it."

"I think Alexander is simply unspeakable," said Emily.

"Then don't speak of him," Honor answered sadly, and turned from
her mirror with another sigh. She did not know how things could go
on in this way much longer. She dared not confront Alexander as yet,

but all the joy of London was lost to her, and she thought of going home more fondly and more frequently each day. Now that Emily's affairs were so well settled, it seemed possible to her that she might in fact leave Albemarle Street and go back to Pittering. Lord Sperling would take Emmy in, and Alexander might do as he wished. No doubt Stonebur Cottage would be open to her; though it might be more cheerful to return to her aunts. To return to one's childhood home after marrying was a lowering prospect, indeed, but Honoria had lost a good deal of her pride, and she did not think she would mind it too very much. At least she would be out of Alexander's way.

Lady Jane contrived and managed in her most skillful way, meeting her guests in Berkeley Square, rallying them to good spirits for the journey across the river to Vauxhall, and arranging them, once they had arrived, round the table in their box. Besides the Blackwood party there were Lord Sperling, the Rowleys, Mr. Ambrose Tayt—but here the list grew somewhat disastrous. Lady Jane, for reasons Honoria could not possibly guess, had invited not only Mr. Claude Kemp, but the Countess Dredstone as well. Honoria fairly blanched when she saw her acquaintance from Pittering, but the sight of the countess came near sending her into a faint.

"Jane—" she had whispered, leaning heavily on her hostess's arm as she crossed the threshold of the drawing-room. "Jane, how—"

"I know what I am doing," Lady Jane had murmured firmly. "Now brace yourself for some unpleasantness, and I promise you will thank me before a se'ennight has gone by."

"Lady Jane, please, I cannot do it," Honor had returned in a failing voice. She retreated back into the entrance hall, bringing her ladyship with her. "Let me go home to Albemarle Street, I beg you. No one will think it odd—you may say I have the headache—you may say anything, only—"

"My dear girl, it is absolutely imperative that you come!" the other replied. "Forgive me for surprising you, but I knew you would never agree to it. Now it is as good as done, and you *will* brace yourself," she added fiercely, "if you love your husband at all, I tell you you will."

Mrs. Blackwood was about to protest again, but she found herself suddenly propelled forward into the drawing-room so forcefully that she could not resist. "If you love your husband, my lamb," Lady Jane had repeated once more in a whisper, and then cast her (as Honoria felt) into the thick of the wolves.

She had borne it as well as she could, and managed to arrive at the box, and to take her seat between Alex and Mr. Tayt, without disgracing herself utterly. The countess seemed not the least perturbed by her presence; on the contrary, she appeared quite enchanted to meet Mrs. Blackwood again, and was simply bursting with curiosity.

"You won't think it rude in me to ask you, my dear," she said to Honor—for she was seated directly opposite the Blackwoods, and at no great distance from them—"but I positively must know if this is your first visit to Vauxhall. For if it is, I should feel perfectly wretched if I did not show you round a bit. I have been here dozens of times, and I must admit it has palled somewhat upon me, but with a novice to introduce, I believe I must enjoy myself very well."

Honoria confessed, with the greatest reluctance, that she had never been to the Gardens before.

"O, she is absolutely charming, Alexander," cried the countess, and she reached across the table (to Honoria's horror) and patted her hand warmly. The very touch of the countess's elegantly gloved hand upon her own mittened one was strange. She endeavoured to smile, but failed miserably.

"There is no fresher bloom in London," Alexander assented, demonstrating by this remark that he had not looked at his wife recently, if nothing else.

"Truly, the most absolutely charming," the countess echoed herself. "And you will permit me to show you about, later, won't you? There is the most lovely little garden, just brimming with statuary and all sorts of fountains. You must see it."

Honoria cast a despairing glance at Lady Jane—who did not catch it, since she was engaged in some animated banter with Claude—and finally answered, "Certainly. I should be most grateful."

"Because Alexander will never show you anything, you know," the countess rattled on—and Honoria made sure she had never met a woman so intent on talking—"for he never shows anybody anything; do you now, Alexander? You never see at all, I think; you have not even remarked my cameo bracelet, and I wore it specially for you. Your husband is an old bear, don't you think, my dear?" she added pettishly. "Of all the gentlemen in the world, I believe he is the most difficult to coquet with properly. He simply does not notice!"

Honoria had long since given up feeling faint; in fact, she had more or less given up feeling at all. The countess's bombardment continued without a stop until the oysters and lobster patties arrived, at which time the countess turned her attention to Lord Sperling (who sat on one side of her), and Claude Kemp turned his upon Honoria. "You can't think what the incendiary exhibition will be like," he assured her. "Of all things in London, I protest the brilliance of Vauxhall impressed me most, my first time down." He glanced sidewards at

Alexander and Lady Jane, now chatting across the table, and seemed suddenly to regret having begun his conversation with Mrs. Blackwood. "Alexander looks very fit," he commented, before Honoria had thought of any reply to his first statement.

"Yes," she said. "I believe London agrees with him."

"And does it with you, Mrs. Blackwood?" he enquired. The cold gleam that always haunted his eyes now sparkled with particular iciness.

"Whatever agrees with Alex agrees with me," she said, astonishing herself by having thought of so long a sentence.

"Does it?" the countess broke in, looking up as if startled. "Forgive my eavesdropping; I always do; in fact, I make quite an art of it. Well, that is very sweet in you, Mrs. Blackwood."

"Not at all," Honor contradicted. "It is only natural to love what sustains one's belov—one's dearest friends. I am sure you feel the same about your husband."

The countess looked in amazement from Honor to Claude. "Well you have got a most peculiar style," she murmured almost inaudibly. "Alexander, your dear wife proves herself far deeper than one ever expected."

Mr. Blackwood looked up from his tête-à-tête with Lady Jane, and regarded the countess interrogatively.

"She says whatever agrees with you, agrees with her," the countess explained.

Alexander appeared displeased for a moment, but only said mildly, "She is kind to say it."

"Honoria has always been distinguished for her kindness," Claude injected. "Animals love her."

Honoria knew this was meant to sting, but the oddest feeling had come over her. It was a kind of recklessness, and it had begun to supply her with all manner of surprising things to say. "Mr. Kemp has no great fondness for animals, I fear," she answered calmly, without the faintest blush. "And one I know in particular does not care overmuch for him either."

No one but Claude and Honoria knew the full meaning of these references; even Lady Jane was obliged to turn the topic in order to maintain control of the general conversation. She led the party on to a discussion of the past year's elections; then to speculation as to the quality of the singer who would entertain them later on; then to some rumours regarding Miss Charlotte Throstle—who, it was said, would soon become the Baroness Duval. She contrived to keep the conversation running along such lines—at her end of the table, at least, for at the other Emily was maintaining a lively discussion of the arts—until the creams and jellies arrived. At that juncture it got away from her again, and it was some time before she regained government of it, or of anything else that evening.

"Lady Jane," Mr. Kemp said to her suddenly, "I do not believe you have ever visited your cousin in Pittering; is that not so?"

"I have not had the pleasure of visiting Honoria, if that is who you mean."

"Yes, Honoria, of course. It is a shame you have never been there; it is a very quaint old village. Honoria is excessively attached to it, I think."

"Most people love their home," Honoria said quietly.

"You must make a point of calling upon the Blackwoods there sometime," Claude went on. "Honoria's aunts, the Misses Deverell, are a most picturesque pair."

"Indeed?" was all Lady Jane could say.

"O, very picturesque," he assured her. "They collect cats about them, and dogs. I think they have it in mind to found a hospital for them; I suppose you are very fond of cats and dogs, Countess?" he added, turning.

"Any lively creature interests me," said that lady, gazing curiously—as Claude had meant her to do—on Mrs. Blackwood. "How very charitable in your aunts," she observed.

Honoria knew she was meant to be embarrassed by these allusions to her humble origins. She knew, too, what other information Claude was intending to convey, so she anticipated him by saying, "They are known for their charity, yes—and their eccentricity. I trust no one could find two more gentle, or peculiar, old ladies."

"They brought her up," Claude hastened to note.

"And very generously." Honoria positively refused to be cowed by his behaviour. "I am an orphan," she informed Lady Willoughby.

"An orphan—how very sad," the countess murmured, with a quizzical glance at Alex.

"But the Deverell sisters are not the only eccentrics in Pittering," Mr. Kemp went on. "Quite the contrary. Pittering abounds with eccentrics. Dear dear, Honoria! That reminds me of something I have been meaning to ask you for weeks: whatever came of Miss Blackwood's scholarship?"

She had understood by now that Claude had abandoned his ridiculous *tendre* for her, and was determined to avenge himself for every pang she had ever caused him, but this was unexpected. So far as Honor had known, no one but the immediate family—and Lady Jane, Mr. Tayt, and the academy, of course—knew anything of Emily's education. It was hardly the sort of thing one liked to bring up in public, even now that her case had been settled so satisfactorily. They had agreed among them to keep it a secret, though anyone might see her prize painting, and make enquiries if they cared to. But the exhibition had not opened yet. In a flash Honoria realized how Kemp got his information. That dreadful interview in her sitting-room at Stonebur, and then the day his arm had been bitten, at Sweet's Folly; she would never forgive him for this, never—she made sure of that. Her own embarrassment was one thing, but what touched on Emily's reputation was another.

Her only advantage was a suspicion that Claude's knowledge must be imperfect. Gambling on this, she said lightly, "Scholarship? Whatever can you mean?"

"Miss Blackwood's education—the competition she won," he prompted. "Surely you must recall it?"

Honor feigned contemplation for a moment, then called down the table to her sister. "Emily, dear, do you remember anything of a scholarship? Something to do with the competition, perhaps?"

Emily had not been attending to the others' conversation, but she knew very well what to answer. "I don't think so, my dear," she replied tentatively. "No, I am certain I do not. Why?"

"O, nothing," Honor said, fixing Kemp with a look. "Do forgive me for intruding upon your discourse with Sir Malcolm. Mr. Kemp, I am very sorry, but I cannot think what you wish to refer to. Do you remember where you heard of it?"

But it would be too much for him to say he had come by the intelligence while eavesdropping on a family dispute. "Now that I think of it . . . no," he answered, extremely annoyed at this set-back. "Perhaps it was some other young lady."

"Perhaps," she agreed, tilting her head to one side and smiling as innocently and as condescendingly as she could.

It was very effective. In no time at all, Mr. Kemp discovered the table to be much too confining. He invited the countess to walk a bit with him before the singing began, but she refused, casting a brilliant look at Alex. Lady Jane saw the look and approved it. "I will walk with you, Mr. Kemp," she offered, adding with an arch smile, "if you do not mind the substitution. I freely admit it to be inadequate."

Mr. Kemp was only too glad to accept her companionship—anything to be from that table—and he rose, bowing to the company, and strolled away with her. Honoria was not sorry to see him go, but she did regret being left alone by Lady Jane, especially as the countess chose this moment to become excruciatingly interested in her once more.

Chapter XIV

"Your . . . aunts," the countess began, resting her splendid head on one gloved hand and gazing sweetly into Honor's eyes, "did they—did they arrange your marriage with Alex? You won't mind my asking; I do so long to know you."

Lady Willoughby's celestial regard made Honoria just a trifle uncomfortable, but she answered evenly, "No, not at all. In fact, my aunts did not seem to care very much about the match, one way or another."

"How perfectly fascinating," the countess answered. "And your new family, the Blackwoods; I suppose they cared?"

"I believe they were pleased by our betrothal," Honoria replied. "Emily and I have been bosom bows most of our lives, you know, and the Blackwoods have never been otherwise than kind to me."

"Alexander, do tell me how it all came about," the countess implored, turning her bewitching eyes upon him. "Your marriage to your wife, I mean; I am sure it was terribly romantic."

Alexander appeared irritated—and was in fact irritated—by Lady Willoughby's request. "I trust Honoria will answer you as well as I might," he said repressively.

"Oh, but she cannot understand quite *exactly* how it happened," the countess exclaimed with exaggerated dismay. "No lady understands precisely how she came to be chosen. You know that, Alex."

"If I know that, I have forgot it," he informed her.

"Alex, I shall be most disappointed if you won't tell me," Lady Willoughby coaxed. "I do not think it the least bit kind in you to refuse me over a trifle."

"Annabella, *this* is a trifle too much," Alexander hissed at last. He had grown visibly angry in the past few minutes: his complexion showed white above his cravat, and his lips were tightly controlled.

"Dear me, crueler and crueler!" the lady exclaimed.

Alexander rose abruptly and stood glaring across the table at the countess. "Madam," he spat out, "I wish you will do me the honour of walking a bit with me."

The countess looked carefully at Honor, apparently unfrightened by Mr. Blackwood's threatening tone.

"Lady Willoughby," he repeated grimly.

"Mrs. Blackwood, I know you will excuse me," she said finally, in the mildest accents, and yet the careful look accompanying her words seemed to attach additional significance to them. She stood at last, and accepted Alexander's support; then they passed out of the box together.

"Why, Mrs. Blackwood," said Mr. Tayt at once, for he perceived the discomfort of her circumstances, "you are left alone. Now is my opportunity to tell you how enamoured my friend Munroe is of you. He never ceases to sing your praises, and attributes to you every known virtue—and a few he invented, I think."

Now that her adversaries had gone, and her protector and her husband with them, that feeling of limitless assurance that had supported Honor throughout the repast subsided somewhat. She replied to Mr. Tayt in vague murmurs, and gratefully permitted him to carry the burden of their conversation. This (being a most obliging young man) he did very willingly, and adroitly; however, when the singer began her performance both he and Honoria were relieved at the diversion. Mrs. Blackwood could not enjoy the singing much though, in spite of the performer's being a very passable soprano, for neither Claude and Lady Jane, nor Alex and the countess had returned to the box as yet. In the event, both couples stopped away throughout the recital, and seemed thoroughly lost to their party. No one at the table said anything of their absence, of course, but after a time no one thought of anything else. It was too remarkable, in each case.

Lady Jane Sperling was sensible of her unseemly failure as a hostess, but she was too enmeshed in her own schemes to persuade herself to give them up merely for the sake of form. Mr. Kemp was coming along famously, just famously, and she had high hopes of winning a battle with him before their walk was done. Naturally, it had taken her a little while to mollify him when they first started off, but now she felt she had begun to succeed in turning his mind to more useful thoughts, and she could not bear to quit early.

"Mr. Kemp, you have disappointed me tonight," she was saying teasingly, as they strolled down one of the many lighted paths. Other couples passed them, chatting and laughing, and occasionally a solitary gentleman.

"I am all apology, if I have."

"Then you are all apology, most certainly, for you have forgot to tie your cravat *Primo Tempo*, and affect a style quite sadly simple, I think."

"Dear me, and I had thought to please you with the innovation," he answered. "At least I can assure you its simplicity is deceptive; I was an hour and a half tying this knot."

"Indeed! In that case I must retract my admonishment, and congratulate you instead." She tilted her handsome head to look into his eyes, and added prettily, "I expect deception is second nature to you now, if not instinct. How odd that the knot should take you so long."

"Your ladyship is too harsh with me," he objected. "I never deceive where I have not been deceived."

"And Mrs. Blackwood?" she sniffed sceptically.

"I trust Mrs. Blackwood has no reason to complain of me."

"But you have used her most ungently, I am sure! It is legible on her countenance whenever you appear."

"Mrs. Blackwood," said he, flushing deeply under cover of the night's shadows, "deceived me long before I ill-used her."

"Honoria?" she asked incredulously. "Impossible!"

"Mrs. Blackwood led me to hope—well, since she had doubtless confided as much in you already, I need not stand on discretion. Mrs. Blackwood allowed me to believe she might someday be Mrs. Kemp. And very pretty she was at it, too."

"As it happens, Honoria never mentioned such a matter to me," Lady Jane returned, "but it is extremely interesting. And how, exactly, did she foster these hopes of yours?"

"By—by modest refusals, and looks that belied her words, and—well, I needn't tell you how ladies may say no and yes at once."

"My dear sir!" cried she. "What you mean to say, then, is that Honor never encouraged you at all; you only imagined it."

"I did not—" he began indignantly, then remembered his pride. "I see no use of discussing this further," he amended.

"No more do I," said Lady Jane, who had in truth discovered just what she needed to confirm her suspicions, and to fuel her disgust with Claude. "We ought to talk of pleasanter things, after all. The moon is nearly full, and the stars beckon us, altogether a most suitable evening for accord and amiability."

"I think you tease me with this talk of the moon, my lady. You are no star-gazer, certainly."

"Ah no, alas. I am altogether too cosmopolitan to be spiritual much —except on Sundays, of course. I must own the stars do not beckon quite to me; that was an exaggeration. They merely twinkle—and very monotonously, too."

"I rather thought so," said he.

"But you are no astronomer yourself, if I may judge of such matters," she took up. She was leading him purposely farther and farther from the crowds, and they had come to a place where they must either turn back or enter a dark, tree-lined alley. "What care we for lights?" she enquired dryly, when he hesitated at the turning-point. She clasped his arm more firmly with her long, gloved fingers, and propelled him into the dark path.

He did not need much persuasion, naturally. If a lady were willing to walk in the dimness, it was not in his nature to demur. They advanced more slowly between the great, leafy trees, pretending now and then not to notice a pair of entwined lovers; Lady Jane increased her pressure on Claude's arm at every moment, and she spoke in a husky voice unusual in her.

"I am so ashamed of having reproached you for your cravat," she murmured. "I did not tell you how well the new one becomes you, but I think I must, to make amends."

"Nor did I say how beautifully the velvet of your gown sets off your neck and shoulders," offered he. "I ought to mention it, in all fairness."

"I beg you will not," she whispered, and slipped her hand down a little farther towards his wrist.

"But it is beautiful," he insisted.

She stopped walking all at once, and stood wordless near the trunk of a great oak, looking up through the shadows to his face.

"Lady Jane—" he said.

She did not answer.

"Lady Jane—" He turned a little to face her squarely, and lightly laid a hand upon her waist.

"O, dear sir, please do not—" she began, and halted, gazing breathlessly into his eyes.

"My beautiful Lady Jane," he murmured, and swept her at once into a crushing embrace.

In an instant she had boxed his ear, and fetched him a kick on the shin as well. These were no mere lover's taps, for Lady Jane Sperling was as righteously wrathful as woman could be. Astonished, he jumped back from her, involuntarily raising a hand to his smarting ear. "The box on the ear," she informed him coldly—no hint of huskiness remained—"was from Mrs. Blackwood. And I have taught her how to administer them, too, so you needn't ever trouble her again. And the kick," she added, pausing with satisfaction, "was from me. You have just witnessed a lady encouraging you falsely. I hope it will teach you to distinguish between that phenomenon and an honest refusal. Good night, sir."

She turned on her heel and was off in a moment, not deigning to hear how he might reply. The darkness under the trees soon concealed her from pursuit, and she returned to her box by the most direct route, not the meandering one she and Kemp had followed. She trusted even he would not be such an idiot as to return there himself, and so he arrived making his excuses, saying he had chanced upon a dear friend of his just home from an extended visit abroad, and hoped their party would forgive his rushing off.

Nobody particularly cared what had happened to Kemp; they were only glad to see Lady Jane back safe and sound, and evidently in excellent spirits. Alexander and the countess had preceded her somewhat in their return to the table, the former looking out of patience, the latter a little subdued. The company waited to see the incendiary exhibition, though no one had much of a taste for it. The Rowleys thought their hostess amazingly harum-scarum; Miss Blackwood and Mr. Tayt had long since run through all possible topics of conversation; Lord Sperling, though disinclined to censure his daughter, could not quite like her conduct. Honoria, of course, was just barely alive, having again survived the terrible hurt of being publicly abandoned by her husband, and for much longer than was proper, while he flirted with his paramour. The countess and Alexander pretended to marvel at the fire-works, but it was quite clear they meant nothing by it. Both were preoccupied, and at their parting regarded one another long and strangely. The significance of this look was soon revealed to Mrs. Blackwood: her husband departed alone from Albemarle Street the moment they arrived there, and did not return till four.

Lady Jane had had no opportunity of informing Honor of the victory she had won for them both, so there was not even that to comfort her. Alex's absence now made two nights in a row. Without even saying as much to herself, Honoria decided she did not care to witness the third, and began packing to leave long before Alexander's return.

"But you can't just run away," Emily pleaded with her. "I know my brother is abominable—and I can't think what Lady Jane meant by inviting the countess to Vauxhall—but you mustn't run off, really you mustn't."

"I am writing to Lady Jane just now," Honoria told her, sitting down to a rosewood escritoire in one corner of her bed-chamber. "I will beg her to take you into her home, and to look after you as I would. I am certain she will."

"But that's not the point," Emily argued. "I don't want to be with Alex, or with her. I want to be with you. Please, Honor—if I promise to speak with Alex? I can make him stop this outrageous behaviour, I am sure of it. He has run quite mad of late; a sound lecture will bring him to his senses."

"It makes no difference," Honoria answered, dipping her pen into the crystal standish. "His behaviour only reflects his feelings, and you cannot alter those no matter what you do. I am not interested in a husband who carries on discreet affairs; I had much rather be alone than force him to such measures."

"But, Honor, it is your right as his wife! He has no business shaming you as he does. You mustn't allow him to run you out of town: if anyone leaves, it ought to be he."

"I do not care to wait for that event," Honor replied. She signed her name to the note before her, and folded the letter carefully. Then she took another paper, and began to write again.

"What are you writing now?" Emily asked sullenly.

"A note to Alex. I suppose I could as well entrust my message to you, but this seems more civil." She was silent for a time, and only the sound of her pen scratching the paper was audible. Emily sat brooding on one corner of the bed until her sister rose and whisked her aside. "I must pack, if you'll excuse me. You may sit there," she added, indicating a chair.

"Honoria, I have never known you so stubborn."

"And I have never known you so unrealistic. It is clear that either Alexander or I must leave London, and since I have nothing to keep me here, it may as well be me." She had begun this speech with a certain amount of spirit, but by the end of it a tell-tale tear had escaped her, and her voice shook.

"Honor, really," Miss Blackwood said gently, crossing the room at once to embrace her sister. "Delay this at least until the morning. You are fatigued, and ought to sleep on it."

"I wish to leave tomorrow," the other answered quietly, though she leaned a little into her sister's embrace.

"You will leave soon enough," Emily soothed her, "only do not

hurry yourself so. At least Alexander ought to be warned of your intentions—"

"No," Honor interrupted suddenly. "Do not tell him, please. When
the matter is brought to his attention, he will undoubtedly offer to accompany me, out of duty, or to quit London himself. I do not wish to
inspire such courtesies in him."

Emily released her friend and reseated herself on the small chair
that stood near the door communicating to Alexander's chamber. She
felt rather defeated, and sighed.

"Traubin tells me I may be on a post-chaise heading towards Pittering at noon tomorrow. I shall travel first to Sweet's Folly, and stop
there until servants can be found to help me at Stonebur. You will
kindly see to it that Alexander receives this note, and Lady Jane this
one. Your parents will be surprised to see me, naturally, but I shall
think of something to tell them."

"Honoria, you are being very silly," Emily said listlessly, while her
sister pulled the bell-rope that summoned her abigail.

"Maria will be here in a moment to help me with my valises. I will
ask Mrs. Traubin to send my trunks after me when there is time.
Maria will come with me to Pittering, of course. You may as well go to
bed now; you have said all you can to dissuade me, I think, and you
see its futility."

Emily stood reluctantly and went to the door. She wanted to talk
longer with Honor, but Maria arrived too soon for her to say anything
more than that she would speak with her again in the morning. "You
will see things differently then, I know," she added.

"Good night," said Honor, and resolutely went to work with her
abigail, laying out and packing what she would need. Her valises
stood ready for her departure at the end of an hour, and still Alexander had not come home. Knowing nothing else to do, she dismissed
Maria and went to bed, though she felt very certain she would not
sleep. She could not help but picture to herself where Alex was, and
what he said to the countess, and what she said to him. She would
have been astonished indeed to learn how far her imaginings strayed
from the truth.

For at that moment Alexander was excessively annoyed with the
countess, and though he was indeed within her boudoir, he was stalk-
ing up and down its length, and glancing at the lady now and then
without the least tenderness. "I agree it is a very pretty story, Annabella, but that does not make it accurate. How could you learn in
one evening what I have been hoping to know for years?"

Lady Willoughby's head drooped with fatigue; she was simply

aching with boredom and annoyance, but she felt she must persuade Alex of her argument or fall asleep in the endeavour. "For the hundredth time, my dear boy, I learn it through instinct. I know it as absolutely as I know my own name; any idiot can see it at once."

"Any idiot—" he snorted. "Then apparently I am not an idiot, for I do not see it at all. And I have been looking for it all the time. I tell you, you are misled by her."

"Alex, how much longer can we tread this weary circle? You do not see it precisely *because* you look for it too hard. Trust a scholar to overlook what is directly beneath his nose," she added disgustedly.

"Well then, why does she say nothing of you to me?" he demanded. "I have been absent three nights out of seven—four now—and she has never breathed a word in question of it."

"I don't know why she is so quiet!" the countess exploded in return. "Perhaps she is frightened of you; perhaps she thinks a wife is meant to suffer in silence. How could I know why that is? I only know that it is *not* because she is indifferent to you. Will you do me the kindness of believing that finally?"

"And what of Kemp?" he challenged.

"What *of* Kemp?" she repeated. "Anybody can see he is nothing to her."

"You are trying to rid yourself of me," Alexander accused her after a pause, still pacing the room furiously. "You are tired of me, and do not know how to send me away but by telling me my wife loves me."

"Why on earth should I go to such lengths? Don't you think I have sent dozens of gentleman away? And I promise you, never once have I bothered myself about where they would go afterwards. When I met you again at the Throstles', and heard your account of your marriage, I believed you. I was foolish to do so; this is the first time I have made such an error. I ought to have looked closely at Honoria that very evening—and now I have done so, I see my mistake."

"But our marriage came about exactly as I told you," he persisted, striking the mantelpiece with his fist. "Exactly! Honoria needed to be married; my sister informed me of it; they both believed me to be utterly indifferent to her, and on those terms she accepted me and took me for a husband. Now you chat with her for a quarter of an hour, and come to me insisting she is mad for me, and dying of lovesickness. It is doing it a bit too brown, Annabella; surely I, who have observed her manner towards me for years, am in a better position to judge."

"And here we are back again at the start," Annabella yawned. "You refuse to believe what is crystal clear to everybody else, and what she herself—by your own admission—has told you. If you will not credit

my appraisal of the situation, you will at least be obliged to allow *me*
to believe it. Your wife is in love with you; and that being the case,
our connection is broke and behind us. It is against my principles to
proceed in such circumstances, and you very well know it. Think as
you like; that is my decision and you must abide with it."

"If I am to believe you," Alexander began carefully, "at this moment Honoria is off her head with worry about me, and certainly incapable of sleep. But every time I leave you, I go home to find her retired; she never acknowledges my entrance, or even my exits. It is
contrary to every known fact," he concluded abruptly.

"Do you ever look to see if she is truly asleep?" Lady Willoughby
inquired. Her own beautifully lashed eye-lids drooped heavily, but
she forced herself to maintain an erect posture, and to put her question energetically. "I will lay you a hundred pounds she is not asleep,
but only feigning."

"I never looked," Alex muttered incomprehensibly.

"I beg your pardon?"

"I say, I never looked!" he shouted at her, and the circular dispute
was off again in a fresh round. It lasted till well past three, and even
then Alexander did not go directly home, but wandered the streets of
London, gazing at lamp-posts as if they might speak, and knocking
into not a few late pedestrians. Some time near four he reached Albemarle Street and let himself into his own house. He flung his cape
and hat onto a convenient chair and mounted the stairs slowly. If
Honoria were awake . . . he might knock at her door, quietly, and see
. . . but it would be painful if there were no reply. He arrived at his
own bed-chamber still undecided, and discovered there a note that his
sister had penned, directly in contradiction to Honoria's request.

> "Alex—" it said. "Honoria means to return to Sweet's Folly
> alone, tomorrow morning. It is all on account of your revolting
> unkindness to her, I know, and your flagrant neglect. If you do
> not dissuade her from this project I may never forgive you.
> "Emily.
> "P.S. She begged me to say nothing of this to you, so pray destroy
> this letter."

Alexander's first impulse was to go to his wife, whether asleep or
awake, and insist on an explanation. To drive her away from London
was most certainly not what he desired. He stood poised at the door-
way between their apartments, ready to knock, when he decided on
second thoughts to re-read Emily's letter. This time he noticed her

phrase, "I know," and inspected the postscript more closely. It might be as Emily said, but more likely she went only on guess-work, just as Lady Willoughby did. If Honoria was in love with Kemp—as Alexander was still persuaded she was, in spite of everything—she was not likely to take her husband's sister into her confidence, friends though they might be. He sat down with the note in his lap to deliberate further. At once the image of Lady Jane Sperling departing from the box on Claude's arm that evening came to his mind. *That was it!* he told himself, triumphant and bitter in the same moment. Lady Jane had stolen Claude from Honoria, and Claude had complied; now she wished to remove herself from her faithless lover, and that was the explanation of this precipitous departure. There was no more question now of his interrupting either her sleep or her plans. She was at liberty as always to pursue what course she chose: at such a juncture as this, Alexander was a meddler and nothing else.

These surmises pained him, but at least they justified what he had always believed. His sister would simply be obliged to learn to forgive him; Honoria's sentiments and decisions remained, as ever, beyond his sway. Emily would see that in time. For now there was nothing to be done but go to sleep as well he might, and hope to rejoin her in Pittering when the sting of Claude's rejection had dulled somewhat. With a dejected sigh he climbed under the coverlet, and with another extinguished his candle. For some while silence reigned in Albemarle Street, and Mr. Blackwood fell into an uneasy sleep.

His repose, such as it was, was disturbed most startlingly by the sudden eruption of a piercing shriek from his wife's room. It was followed by another, and another; before the third Alexander had leapt from his bed and—not stopping to wonder how or why—had burst through the door that separated them. Flinging back the curtains that sheltered her bed, he discovered Honoria sitting upright there, her face contorted with effort (for she felt a scream rising again, and could scarcely control it), and on the point of relapsing again into her pillows. The sight of her husband helped her to check the scream—supplanting it with a gasp instead—but it did not stop the tears that had begun to course down her cheeks. Still without thinking, he threw his arms round her and clasped her as best he might, presently sinking to the bed himself, and rocking and consoling her with inarticulate compassion. She was far too distraught to do otherwise than yield to his embrace, and no more asked herself what she was doing than he did. He held her for a full minute, nothing of significance being said between them—but everything communicated—before Maria arrived at her mistress's door. She bore a candle, and was too much alarmed by what she had heard to knock before she entered. She checked at the door-way, however, and Alexander rose to meet her, pausing before he did so, though, to place a kiss on Honoria's neck, and embrace her once more.

"Mrs. Blackwood is well," he told the distressed abigail. "If anything is wanted I shall ring for it. You may go back to bed."

Maria nodded, begged the master's pardon for intruding, and departed. She met Emily as she started down the corridor—for Honoria's ear-shattering cry had awakened the whole house—and repeated what Mr. Blackwood had told her: Mrs. Blackwood was well, and required no attention.

"Then they are together," Emily thought sleepily, with satisfaction. "I knew that note would bring him round; really, I have never seen such a baby." She stayed in the corridor long enough to encounter Mrs. Traubin, who was hastening to her mistress on the same errand as Maria, and to instruct her not to enter the bed-chamber.

"But that wail, miss," Mrs. Traubin objected. "I never heard the like, I am sure. Are you certain I mustn't enter?"

Emily looked into the fishy eyes, made fishier by sleep, and issued her order more clearly. "Mr. Blackwood will ring if anything is needed," she said. "Go back to bed."

Mrs. Traubin looked suspicious. "I don't know," she said disapprovingly. "A body could lose her post over a thing like this. A housekeeper has responsibilities, you know, and—"

"To bed," Emily hissed furiously, for they stood directly outside Honoria's door. She saw Mrs. Traubin draw away reluctantly, and watched until she had disappeared up the staircase. Then she retired again herself, hoping Honor's screams had not been occasioned by anything Alexander had done, or said.

Quite the reverse was true, of course. At that moment Alexander was enfolding his wife's hands in his own, and it would have been difficult to determine who was the more relieved. "I had a dream," Honoria told him, when she felt she could speak coherently. "In the dream you and Emily and I had gone to a ball, or something—only it wasn't really a ball, it was a sort of examination, where people came to be tried in what they knew. And there was an inspector—at first I thought he was Lord Sperling, or maybe your father—I know they are not much alike, but in the dream . . ." She looked at him and was obliged to pause for a moment, so deeply concentrated was the regard with which he had fixed her. It was precisely the gaze she had seen him bend on his studies, and which she had wished he might turn upon her that night—ages ago, it seemed—at Sweet's Folly. He kissed her temple and encouraged her to go on.

"You'll feel better once you've told your nightmare," he assured her. "That's always how it is."

"Well," she recommenced, "we were all doing well in our examinations—or whatever they were—except for Emily. I felt so dreadful for her: there she was among everyone we knew, and she could not remember anything. So I drifted over to where she stood, as surreptitiously as I could, and tried to gain her attention. Only she would not look at me, nor hear me, and I realised all at once that it was not she who was failing the examination, but I myself. Emily was gone—I don't think she returned during the rest of the dream—and there was no one I could turn to but you. It sounds silly when I say this—" she broke off suddenly.

"Not silly, not at all," he murmured. He brushed a strand of dark hair from her eyes, and took her hands in his again.

"For some reason it was terribly important that I do well in the inspection," she resumed. "It was crucial, the most important thing in my life. You were the only person left to turn to, and as I began to look about for you, all at once I realised the examiner was not Lord Sperling, or your father, but Claude—Mr. Kemp. Alex, it was awful, just awful! I knew he would disgrace me, and there was nothing I could do to stop him. I had had all the answers, I was sure of it—but now I seemed to know nothing; and as soon as he put the first question everyone would see that, and despise me. I began to cry, and Mr. Kemp observed me. Alexander, he took such delight in my tears—he started to laugh, and to point at me, and all the time he kept shouting 'Your husband! Your husband!' You see, he knew I was looking for you, and he was so glad I would not find you. So I shouted at him, too; I knew I would be ridiculed forever after for it, but I had to do so. I screamed at him, 'I will find him, I will—' and that was when you heard me, I guess, for I do not remember anything more. I must have awakened myself, but I couldn't stop screaming for a while—O, Alex, I am so ashamed," she ended suddenly, and buried her head on his chest.

He received her gladly. "For what? It is I who ought to be ashamed."

"For waking the house—for waking you—I should never have cried out, if I could have helped it. You know that, don't you?"

Alexander nodded mutely.

"Why do you say you should be ashamed?" she asked after a pause. "You have not raised the house."

"But I have very nearly destroyed it," said he. "Honoria—from your dream—in the dream you turned to me. Do you—mind my holding you?"

It was the first time what had happened between them had been referred to openly. "I do not mind—never, never at all."

"But you are—you are indifferent to me, are not you? Now you are frightened, of course, and it is good to have someone to sit with you— but does it matter to you"—he stumbled over his words—"does it make a difference that I am the one with you?"

"But, Alex," she whispered, "I have told you I love you. Do you still not believe me?"

"Then how abominable I have been!"

"But how?"

"By carrying on with—by my behaviour towards you, here and at Stonebur. I left you to Claude, and I—Honoria, can you forgive me if I make a confession?"

This was so absurd as to cause her almost to laugh. "Anything," she said, smiling expectantly.

"Well, then, these evenings I've been out so late, alone. I don't know where you thought I went, but—" he hesitated, bracing himself, "I have been with another woman. Honoria, I will understand if you never speak—"

"I know that," she said mildly. "Did you think I could help but know?"

"Yet, if you love me—"

"If I love you that intelligence must hurt me, but it does not remove my love. It is only if you love me that your behaviour becomes inconsistent," she went on quietly, a little gratified to reflect that whatever else she had done, she had never interfered with his freedom. "As things stand, it is your prerogative to . . . to visit whom you will, when you will. Our marriage was made on terms of convenience; you have pointed it out to me yourself."

"But that was because I thought you did not care for me," he broke in. "Honoria, I think I must tell you a story, though it is so full of folly you will scarcely credit it. My dear wife, picture to yourself a young gentleman, who grows up in the country in his father's house. He is thoughtful, and studious, and his distracted air is the joke of the neighbourhood."

"Alex," she interrupted, "no one laughs at your—"

"Everyone laughs about it, and they might well. In London I take pains to be presentable, or at least courteous, but in the country it never seemed to matter much. Anyway, this young man grows older, and goes away to school, and sees London, and meets the ladies there; he returns home, and takes up his studies again—and in all this time no woman has ever seemed of value to him, no woman has ever appeared in his fancy or his dreams, but one. That woman is his sister's friend—"

Honoria gulped.

"And visits his father's house only to see her. Now, years are going by. The young woman comes of marriageable age, but there is nothing in her manner to suggest to him she thinks of him at all; he considers endeavouring to procure her regard, but he feels certain he is such a familiar object of contempt to her, no means could answer his end."

"Alex, no one laughs at—"

"Then one day," he continued determinedly, "the young man's sister comes to him and begs him to marry that particular lady. You may imagine his sentiments: at first he is overjoyed, for nothing on earth could suit him better; then he thinks a bit, and comes to understand that this marriage will change nothing. She is obliged to marry him by her lack of fortune; he soon grasps that only a beast would attempt to take advantage of her unhappy circumstances. So he resolves to marry her, yet to remain as reserved or open, as cordial or removed, as he was with her before. The wedding vows are said; throughout the ceremony the young man repeats to himself what must be his perpetual resolve; on the night of the wedding they are left alone, and he fairly faints with effort while he says a quiet good night to her, and sends her to her chamber alone. But he manages, and from that time forward he knows he can continue to manage, for as long as need be—probably forever."

"Alex, why did you say nothing?"

"What could I say? As the weeks go by, he notices his new wife more and more markedly the object of attention from another country gentleman, a former suitor of hers. He stumbles upon a scene that appears to confirm their connexion. He is obliged to conclude she regrets her marriage—which took place in haste while the rival was from home—and loves, or still loves, the other man. It is not his place to interfere—"

"That is precisely how I felt about you!"

"So he says nothing for a time. Gradually the situation becomes more painful, however, and he feels he must at least sequester himself where he cannot observe what goes forward—"

"Alex," she confessed all at once; "I was leaving London tomorrow."

He merely nodded, and resumed, "But when he offers to remove himself, she informs him that she does not wish it. This is worst of all, for now she pities him, and makes false and corrupt what was only painful before—"

"Yes, yes; I hated your duty to me, your courtesies—"

"And so he is more dispirited than ever. The scene changes to London now. The young man happens upon a lady—whom he knew in his youth. His wife's lover is also in London; the young man anticipates no further harm in consoling himself where he may, and so—"

"O, my dear Alexander, you have said enough," she cried suddenly, embracing him so he nearly choked. "You have said enough," she repeated.

A quarter of an hour more was passed privately between them; then they decided to have a mid-night nuncheon in celebration. Mrs. Traubin was rung for, and arrived smug as always, and a trifle grumpy; she was instructed to have a collation prepared, and sent to the mistress's apartment.

"For one?" she enquired, for she was as good a spy as any who served under Wellington, and knew very well the state of affairs between her employer and his wife.

"For both," Honoria informed her, dismissing her directly. The nuncheon arrived a little time later; they discovered they were starved, and ate and laughed and drank famously till they both fell back exhausted. Then they drew the curtains round Honoria's bed—a place where no nightmare would dare to go now—and began the life together they had promised so many months before. Maria attempted to warn her mistress the post-chaise would leave without them, but she found her concern unappreciated. She was obliged to return to the kitchen alone, and confess herself mystified. Neither master nor mistress were seen until well after two that day.

Chapter XV

"I don't know when I have felt so confused about a thing," said Lady Jane Sperling, looking indeed mid-way between tears and laughter. She stood in the entrance hall of her father's house, her arm round Emily Blackwood's waist, watching Mr. and Mrs. Alexander Blackwood draw on their travelling cloaks and hats, and gather together a variety of other objects necessary for a journey. "It will be splendid to have Emily with me, naturally," she continued, "but I simply abhor parting with you."

Honoria laughed, adjusted her bonnet, and assured her bracingly, "You will come to us just as soon as Emily has her holiday; remember, you have promised."

"O, I know, but that is months, and I have grown so fond of you, dear lamb—" She left Emily for a moment and went to embrace Honor. "You will watch over her carefully, now, won't you Alexander? You know she oughtn't to take much exercise, or to worry in any way. And she must be nice in her diet: no exotic tid-bits, or strange sauces—"

"How you do fret, my dear," Honoria exclaimed. "Anybody would think it was the first time a woman was ever—in my condition," she finished, flushing faintly.

Nearly three months had passed since the excursion to Vauxhall; in that time a number of things had begun and ended, the most interesting of these—at least just now—being little Charles Blackwood ("Or Corinna," Honoria was in the habit of reminding her husband). The elder Blackwoods had been so pleased on hearing of this heir's present arrival, they had forgot to be agitated about Emily's lack of marital prospects, and were anxious only that the young couple should return to Pittering for Honor's confinement. Such a project agreed entirely with the couple's own inclinations, for much as they both were devoted to Emily, it was clearly time for them to establish a household all their own, and to begin to enjoy it. Lady Jane Sperling had become something dearer to them, too, especially when they learned she had purposely invited the countess to Vauxhall in hopes she would see precisely what she had indeed seen, and it was a wrench for Honoria to take leave of her; but Emily would stop at Berkeley Square until her term at the academy was completed, and Honoria did not believe she knew three people more likely to deal well together than Jane, Emily, and Lord Sperling.

The latter had taken an especial interest in Miss Blackwood, and had learned to admire her when her prize portrait had been revealed at the academy's exhibition. It had been a proud day for Emily, and for her sister and brother: much general curiosity was stimulated among the *ton*, and for as long as a day and a half Emily's inordinate ability and ambition were the *on dit* of London. No one but Lord Sperling was allowed to discover, however, that she had actually availed herself of the education offered to her, and so the excited gossip soon grew faint and died a natural death. Miss Blackwood's ardour only increased with training, and though Mr. Tayt hung about her when she appeared in society, she did not encourage him.

"You tell your father-in-law I've an eye on Ambrose, and will not allow Emily to shrug him off for ever," Lady Jane whispered to Honoria while Miss Blackwood said her adieux to her brother.

Evidently Miss Blackwood heard her, in spite of the hushed tone employed, for she said immediately to Alex, "Now, I depend upon you to stop this conspiracy for good and all, my dear. You may remind my father I never sought to interrupt *his* rise to prominence, and dwell a little on how you might have felt if Honor had prevented your writing your monograph"—this last had been completed finally, and was in the hands of a London editor—"and then give him my best love. And my mother, too, of course," she added.

"The sun rises and Emily is resolute," Alexander commented to the company in general, his crooked grin breaking out delightfully. "Certain things never change."

Lord Sperling laughed at this, for he had grown extremely fond of the young woman, and was particularly drawn by her determined spirit. "We will keep her from running quite rampant," he assured Mr. Blackwood, "if you will engage to prevent my god-daughter's fretting over everyone and everything except herself."

At this Lady Jane laughed, and Honoria, too. "I think even Honor may be easy in the country," Lady Jane said, "particularly since—O but, my dear, I utterly forgot it! Did you see this morning's *Gazette?*"

Mrs. Blackwood had been too much occupied with vacating Albemarle Street.

"Then stay right here; do not move," Jane instructed her, and ran off to fetch the newspaper. The coachman respectfully looked in during her absence to remind his master the horses were lively and eager to get started; Honoria found a hundred things to tell her sister before her ladyship's return for they had never been parted since early childhood; at last Jane reappeared, slightly breathless and clutching the *Gazette*. "It is Mr. Kemp," she said, pointing triumphantly to a certain column; "he has bought himself a pair of colours, and departs for the Continent next week. There now! You *shall* be at peace in the country, or I misjudge things very widely."

"And there is one thing you may be sure of about Jane," her father interrupted. "She never misjudges at all."

Privately, Honoria no longer cared where Claude was—he had lost the power to distress her—but she appreciated Jane's concern. She suggested to Alex that they'd best heed the coachman's warning, and be off before the horses went mad with impatience. Another round of embracements were in order, and were duly performed. Regards and love were sent from everyone to everyone else, and then Mr. and Mrs. Blackwood entered their carriage and settled themselves on its cushions, the perfect picture of snug, almost smug, conjugal accord. The last words they heard came from Lord Sperling, who had suddenly appeared on the steps of his town-house to bid them carry his greetings to the Deverell sisters. "And tell them when we arrive in Pittering, we shall all have a long cose about your mother and that madcap, Newcombe . . . And kiss their hands for me!" he shouted above the orders of the coachman to his underlings, and waved his arm at the travellers.

The Misses Deverell, though they might have enjoyed a chat about their departed sister one time or another, were at that particular moment by far too engaged with their own schemes to be much intrigued by reminiscences. They had not been idle; while the season unrolled its familiar program of delights to less provincial ladies, these enterprising would-be benefactors had devised plan after plan to attract the patronage of their unsuspecting friend, Squire Kemp. Some of these schemes had perished untried; a few had been launched, and gone awry; certainly none had succeeded. Sir Proctor continued to visit them weekly, tolerating their meagre fare with great civility, and their small friends with the same; he played chess with Mercy with enormous zeal, especially since he had begun to win sometimes; but at no time did he mention the animal hospital, or seem to understand

Miss Prudence when she alluded to it herself. Thrice he had invited
the ladies to Colworth, but as a general rule they met in Bench Street,
it being more convenient for him to ride to them than for them to
drive to him. At the time of the young Blackwoods' departure from
the metropolis, Squire Kemp was giving orders for his horse to be
prepared, and reluctantly allowing his valet to help him into his riding
habit.

"Shall I have them saddle Brownie for you, sir?" Mr. Boothby
asked, while bowing to his master's instructions.

"Brownie? Hah! Why should I ride such a paltry nag as that, I'd
like to know?" snorted Sir Proctor.

"I merely thought, sir," said the diplomatic Boothby, "that with the
sudden heat you might prefer Brownie's slow and steady pace to that
of your more spirited mounts."

The "sudden heat" to which the butler referred had come upon Pittering two days before, at the start of July. Everyone had noticed it; it
was most marked. No one cared to take tea any more, and the resi-
dents of those homes erected proudly atop hills wished themselves
heartily below in an obscure hollow. Mr. Boothby's suggestion had
been prompted by a most sensible concern for his employer's health,
for he feared the old gentleman might be tempted to a gallop if he
rode a lively horse, and the exertion would be salutary for neither man
nor beast.

"Brownie!" the squire ejaculated again, with evident disgust. "Have
them saddle Thunder, my good man, and no more fustian about it.
Brownie, indeed . . ." he muttered towards the valet, while Boothby
bowed again and disappeared. "Heat, indeed. Think I'm an old
woman, that's what it is. A nice impression I'd make on the Deverells',
eh? Plodding down Bench Street on a child's mount!"

He continued to grumble on this theme awhile, overlooking the fact
that the Misses Deverell, not being fanciers of horse-flesh but only of
dogs and cats, were unlikely to notice what horse he rode, or if he
rode at all. At present, a vigorous debate—carried on chiefly by Prudence—absorbed all their attention. Squire Kemp was due in an hour
or less; and what were they to do with the opportunity?

"I do not see why we can't just play chess, as we always do," Mercy
suggested, in her customary mild accents. "I know I find it pleasant, if
you do not."

"But that is not the point," Prudence snapped, in the manner just as
habitual with her as mildness was with her sister. "Really, I think you
would lose your feet if they were not attached to your ankles."

"O now, I think that is a little severe," Mercy remonstrated.

"But you never seem to recall our aims!" said the elder sister. "Remember, we are engaging in all this sociable nonsense for a purpose—a purpose, Mercy. We are providing for our small friends . . . and doing a tolerably miserable job of it, too."

"I don't think any of them are hungry," Mercy ventured. "Indeed, they were all just fed. I saw Mary feeding them."

"Now, you see? There is a perfect example," Prudence pounced on her. "I was referring to their eventual provision—perpetual provision for them. *You* assume I mean their dinner, tonight's dinner. I truly believe you cannot see beyond the end of your nose."

"I can see your cap is askew," Mercy countered, a trifle plaintively.

Miss Deverell righted the cap, but muttered, "I was speaking figuratively."

"Then you oughtn't to have mentioned my nose," Mercy defended herself. "It isn't the least bit figurative, but very real, indeed. In fact, I should be grateful for a handkerchief just now."

Prudence took one from her pocket and handed it to her; then she sat down to think. For a while Mercy amused herself by teasing Divinity with the lace borders, and reproaching him when he came close to tearing it. At length she grew restive, and inquired of her sister what might be expected for dinner.

"Strategy," said Prudence.

"That will make a very dry repast."

"Strategy. That is where we have gone wrong," Prudence resumed, her thoughtful air making it clear she had not heard her sister's question.

"I do not think we have gone wrong, exactly," Mercy remarked. "It is true, we have not achieved great things; we have not even begun families of our own. But we did bring Honoria up, and we do go to church every Sunday, and I don't think anyone would say—"

"Squire Kemp!" Prudence explained in exasperation. "Our notion of gaining his support by stratagems, and plots, and so forth. It was wrong, wrong from the start. He must be won by reason—that is the key. Reason and . . . persuasion."

"You will recall, my dear," said Mercy, "I never did like that business about turning my ankle, and so forth. I always said that was a foolish idea; I did, you know," she insisted pettishly.

"O yes, very well . . . whatever you say," Prudence agreed, making a gesture as if brushing something aside to illustrate her words. "The significant thing is, he is coming here tonight, and we will have an opportunity to sway him. We must be forthright; that is how battles are won. We must point out to him how lovely our small friends are; how they enhance his pleasure here, as they do ours; and how easily he might arrange for funds to keep them—and their heirs, assigns, et cetera—healthy and happy *in saecula saeculorum.*"

"I thought they were to stay in Pittering!" Mercy objected at once. "Prudence, I would never have lifted a finger to assist you if I had known you meant to send them to—to Secula-Secula, or whatever you said. Where is it? In the East Indies?"

"No, my dear, I said, '*in saecula saeculorum.*' It means for ages and ages—forever, that is. We want perpetual care for our friends, you see. In Pittering," she stipulated.

"Yes, quite," said Mercy. She was sorry she had said so much, and retreated again into silence.

"Now, when the squire arrives, let us be chatting with one of the doggies—"

"Ragamuffin?" Mercy interrupted hopefully.

"Ragamuffin, if you like. We will fetch him in here, among all the cats, and illustrate to Sir Proctor what a peaceable kingdom is here, and how worthy of preservation." Miss Deverell went on to give a number of directives, regarding how Mercy must address the cats, and what to emphasize when speaking of their characters, and so forth and so forth until Mercy was fairly yawning. When a yelp and a persistent scuffle became distinct in the next room, she was glad for the opportunity to break in upon her sister.

"One of the doggies is distressed," she said, pointing a fragile finger towards the corridor. "Do you hear him? Excuse me, dear Prue, but I really must investigate this." She stood and hurried to the door, stepping unerringly over and around the purring cats, and returned a moment later with Fido in tow—or rather, Mercy was in tow, and Fido leading her.

"Well, what on earth—?" Prudence exclaimed, for Fido appeared quite overwrought.

"I don't know. He won't say."

"Let him come to me; I'll ask him," Prudence replied. Mercy released the excited mongrel, but instead of trotting obediently to Prudence (his favourite), he leapt from the parlour in a mighty bound and scrambled towards the kitchen. Mary informed her mistresses, some moments later, that he had come tearing through the kitchen and had run pell-mell out the open door, for with the heat, she explained, she could not possibly sit by the fire to cook without opening that portal.

It was the most extraordinary behaviour. In general, the dogs were aired twice a day; if they had any complaints with that schedule, Prudence observed, she was certain they had never mentioned it to *her*. Mercy agreed that it was curious, but she was sure Fido would return as soon as could be; after all, where else had he to go? Besides, the squire was due at any moment now, and they really ought to put on their best caps, at least.

The ladies departed on this mission, and rejoined one another in the parlour presently, where they waited for their guest. The latter, however, did not come at the appointed hour, yet he was always punctual, Mercy reflected aloud; truly it was the most curious day. She was in the middle of observing this for the fourth time when a noise was heard in the corridor and Fido returned, panting with exertion, and still yelping for all he was worth.

"Fido, hush," Prudence enjoined him.

The anxious barks continued.

"Fido, my *dear*," Mercy attempted.

Nothing silenced him.

"I think this doggie must go back to the dining-parlour," Prudence declared. "A certain doggie in Bench Street is behaving very badly." She took him firmly by the collar and began to drag him to the door, but when they had reached the corridor Fido took the lead and pulled the frail old lady towards the entrance-way.

"Fido, NO!" Prudence shouted, but to no avail. The beast continued to scramble towards the street-door, whining and yelping, and scratching the carpet a good deal with his paws. "O, for Heaven's sake," Miss Deverell exclaimed. "What will Sir Proctor think of such a scene as this?"

But hardly were her words got out before the dog erupted into such a yowl as had never been heard in Bench Street before; and a fair quantity of yowling had been heard there.

"Fido, what is it? Is it Sir Proctor?"

Thunderous barking answered this suggestion.

"Sir Proctor is here?"

A terrific growl issued from Fido; he ducked his head down low to the floor, and swung it back and forth.

"Sir Proctor is *not* here?" Prudence offered. The mongrel barked.

"Yes, but we knew that already," said Mercy, who had been observing this conversation from the parlour door-way. "Prue, do you think he's forgot today is Wednesday? It hardly seems likely, but—"

She was interrupted by Fido, who seemed to have gone quite mad, and snarled at her menacingly.

"Fido!" cried Prudence. "Do you know where Sir Proctor is? Sir Proctor—where is he? Is he coming? Take us to him!" Fido's excite-

ment had increased with each phrase; at the last, she opened the door
and allowed him to spring outside. He did so, but looked back at her
as if waiting for her to follow.

"Excuse me, Mercy. Fido and I must go somewhere."

"You haven't got a bonnet—" Mercy began, but Prudence was already out the door, and in an instant Mercy followed, too. The dog
turned down Bench Street and headed away from the village, check-
ing and turning ever and anon to see if his mistresses pursued him.
They did, though not at the pace he recommended; clutching their
skirts with one hand, and their caps with the other, both good ladies
skipped along as swiftly as they could, calling to each other sporadically.

"I hope he is not taking us to Colworth Park," Mercy said breathlessly as she caught up to her sister.

"I cannot imagine it," the elder replied, and ran a little farther after
Fido. They were out of the village by now, and had attained the road
that led to Sweet's Folly, and beyond that to Colworth. Here Fido
trotted briskly, yelping encouragements and running back and forth
impatiently while he awaited the Misses Deverell. They would run a
hundred feet to where he pranced about and stop there to regain their
breath while the animal covered another hundred feet; in this manner
they proceeded for a quarter of an hour along the dusty road, when
all at once Fido veered off and bounded into a field.

"Fido, if this is some nonsense—" Prudence said threateningly as she
reached the place where he had quitted the road. But she saw, as she
stopped there gasping for air, that it was no nonsense at all, for there,
by a small bridge spanning a rather desiccated stream, lay the squire
himself, and his horse beside him.

It would have been a fine spot for a pic-nic, but it was evident this
was not what kept the horse and rider there. An accident, brought on
by the imprudent racing of an over-heated horse, had obviously sent
horse and rider tumbling. Sir Proctor lay sprawled in an awkward attitude, his right leg at what appeared to be a most inconvenient angle
to his body. Thunder looked uncomfortable as well, for a horse does
not lie down on his side in the middle of a field as a general rule. Fido
ran immediately to Sir Proctor, nuzzling his hand and licking him, and
looked up expectantly at his mistresses.

"Fido!" was all Prudence could say.

"Sir Proctor!" was all Mercy could say.

"My good ladies," the squire interrupted, "if it would not be too
much trouble to you, I am in need of some assistance. I am afraid I
may have broken my leg—not to mention my horse's. I desired your

H

friend here to fetch Dr. Blackwood, but he appears not to have understood me." He spoke with obvious effort, but seemed determined to be courteous to the last. It would have been difficult to decide which was more painful to him: his leg, or the necessity of asking for aid. "I will trouble you, therefore, my dear ma'ams, to despatch someone on that errand."

"Sir Proctor!" cried Mercy again, and knelt by his side to comfort him, while Prudence set off in search of a messenger to notify the good doctor of the crisis.

Epilogue

Sir Proctor Kemp had indeed broke his leg, and though the Misses Deverell could not keep the invalid in their home, as he had kept Mercy at Colworth Park, they did all they could to nurse him while he remained abed, and fussed over him till he swore he would die of their steadfast solicitude. The accident, he told them, had occurred towards the close of a gallop along the high-road: all would have been well had it not been for the sudden appearance of a heavily-burdened gig crawling at snail's pace in the opposite direction. Thunder, probably a little dazed by the heat, had panicked at the sight of it and careered off towards the little bridge where the Deverells found them. The horse had missed the bridge, however, and endeavoured too late to jump across the stream. His hoof had struck a rock near the bank, and down he had come, Sir Proctor with him. The squire had not had time to see the driver of the gig; if he had, he promised he would have murdered him, for he never stopped to see what the fate of the galloping rider had been. No, it was Fido who had discovered him, and Fido who had saved him. Sir Proctor freely admitted it, and admitted too (rather handsomely) that his own folly had been the cause of the accident.

The kindly sentiments towards animals that the Deverell sisters had for so long been trying to instill in him, were now fixed there by happenstance more powerfully than they ever could have hoped. Fido was a hero, and dogs in general a most estimable breed. It was not long before the squire agreed—after discreet intimations from Prudence—that the animal hospital was an institution badly in need of founding; a little more coaxing convinced him that he was the very man to do it. There was grumbling on his part, of course, but it subsided in time, and Mercy and he presently resumed their habit of playing chess each Wednesday with the greatest mutual pleasure. Prudence's conscience was at peace now that their small friends had been provided for, though she continued every day to discover some cause or other for complaint and brisk directives. Fido and his colleagues, and their heirs, assigns, et cetera, naturally lived happily ever after.

The squire's son, when he finally came to assume his father's responsibilities and privileges, arrived at that position with a far better character than might have been expected. His temper was never quite even; but he did learn, while in the army, to distinguish assistance from intrusion, and government from tyranny. He never married, though he did indulge for all his days in an abrasive flirtation with Lady Jane Sperling whenever she stopped in Pittering for a visit with the Blackwoods (which was frequently). Her ladyship never married either, but grew to be a formidable *doyenne* of the *ton,* and enjoyed herself always very well.

Miss Emily Blackwood eventually completed her education in London, and returned to Sweet's Folly, where she never ceased to paint. Her name may be found in foot-notes here and there, wherever English artists of that period are extensively discussed. Her name was not always Miss Blackwood, of course; it altered when she took a husband —but that is another story altogether.

As for Mr. and Mrs. Alexander Blackwood, they set up very comfortably in Stonebur Cottage. The arrival of little Corinna did nothing but increase their content, though little Charles's advent forced their removal into more spacious quarters—Sweet's Folly, to be precise, for Dr. Blackwood passed away about that time, and his wife did not long survive him. The state and duties of motherhood enlarged Honoria's self-confidence remarkably, even to the point where she was commonly known (in her middle years) for her fierceness regarding the protection of her family. Alexander continued to study, and occasionally to publish, till well into old age. In all, their home became a very placid one, the scene now and then of domestic disputes and domestic joys, and a bastion (if truth be told) of the most flagrant self-satisfaction.

And since that is, after all, a chief purpose of marriage, who will begrudge it them?